Between You and Me

"So many threads that weave together beautifully and a twist I didn't see coming! Thoroughly enjoyable read with characters I could connect with and feel for, bringing out a rollercoaster of emotions. Definitely recommend."

—*Sarah Ross*

"I love love loved this book by Emer Rohan. I couldn't put it down! I particularly loved the little 'lightbulb' moments when the reader is delivered a perfectly written sentence of clarity at exactly the right moment that sends the story in a certain direction. Tension builds so well that you don't notice time slipping by as you read on! And I loved the thrilling finale. Already looking forward to the next Saltreach book! A fantastic read, highly recommend!"

—*Deirdre Harris*

"This is a gripping, emotionally charged family drama—easy to read yet impossible to put down—with dialogue to die for and a writing style reminiscent of JoJo Moyes and the fear of a Tami Hoag. The pacing throughout is spot on, with chilling moments that every girl has felt … that make this story both intimate and unforgettable."

—*Angela Cort*

"*Between You and Me* is that rare book – a debut novel that reads as though it's an integral part of an existing literary canon rather than the beginning of one. Tightly plotted with fully-developed characters and a distinct sense of place, it seamlessly blends several threads … into a deeply satisfying read. Thought-provoking and intelligent, *Between You and Me* deftly manages to combine the warmth and safety of decency and family life with the precarious and sometimes sinister forces beyond the individual's control. This reader is looking forward to seeing what happens in Saltreach next."

—*Mary O'Donnell*

"I picked this book … and before I knew it I was finishing it later that evening. It was that addictive, honestly I found this so hard to put down. As each chapter progressed, I was hooked and dreading what was coming next especially for the character Lauren and I could never have predicted the outcome. The suspense was unbelievable oh my god! This book was incredible and I would definitely say this has got to be one of my favourite books ever!"

—*arcreviews_by_m_*

"Emer's book is an absolute gem – captivating, heartfelt and impossible to put down. With vivid honesty, it feels incredibly true to life, filled with moments that any parent will instantly recognise. Emer's writing is warm, authentic, and deeply engaging, making this a standout read that lingers long after the final page."

—*Catherine Whelan*

"A warm yet gripping portrait of modern life, with richly drawn dynamics, intertwining secrets, and a resilient woman holding everything together. Easy to read, engaging, and well paced, this novel offers a compelling exploration of what it means to be a family today, and explores issues that will resonate with many readers."

—*Sharon Prendeville*

"*Between You and Me* is a page-turning contemporary tale of two families whose worlds, already intertwined, crash into each other revealing secrets, lies and the modern-day dangers of lives lived online. Deftly told across multiple POVs, Rohan does a beautiful job of showing how we can all get wrapped up in our own worlds, underestimating our impact on others over weeks and even lifetimes. A richly woven family saga, set in the imaginary UK coastal town of Saltreach, it pulls you in and doesn't put you down until you reach the satisfying end. A great read that will leave you thinking it about it for a long time after."

—*Susannah Rigg*

Between You and Me

EMER ROHAN

Published in 2026 by
Misneach Press

ISBN (paperback) 978-1-9193484-0-7
ISBN (ebook) 978-1-9193484-1-4

Map: © Darren Bennett at DKB Creative Ltd (www.dkbcreative.com)
Author photo: © John Knight at John Knight Photography (www.johnknightphotography.co.uk)

Cover Design and Interior Layout by authorelevator.com

For Mum and Dad

SALTREACH

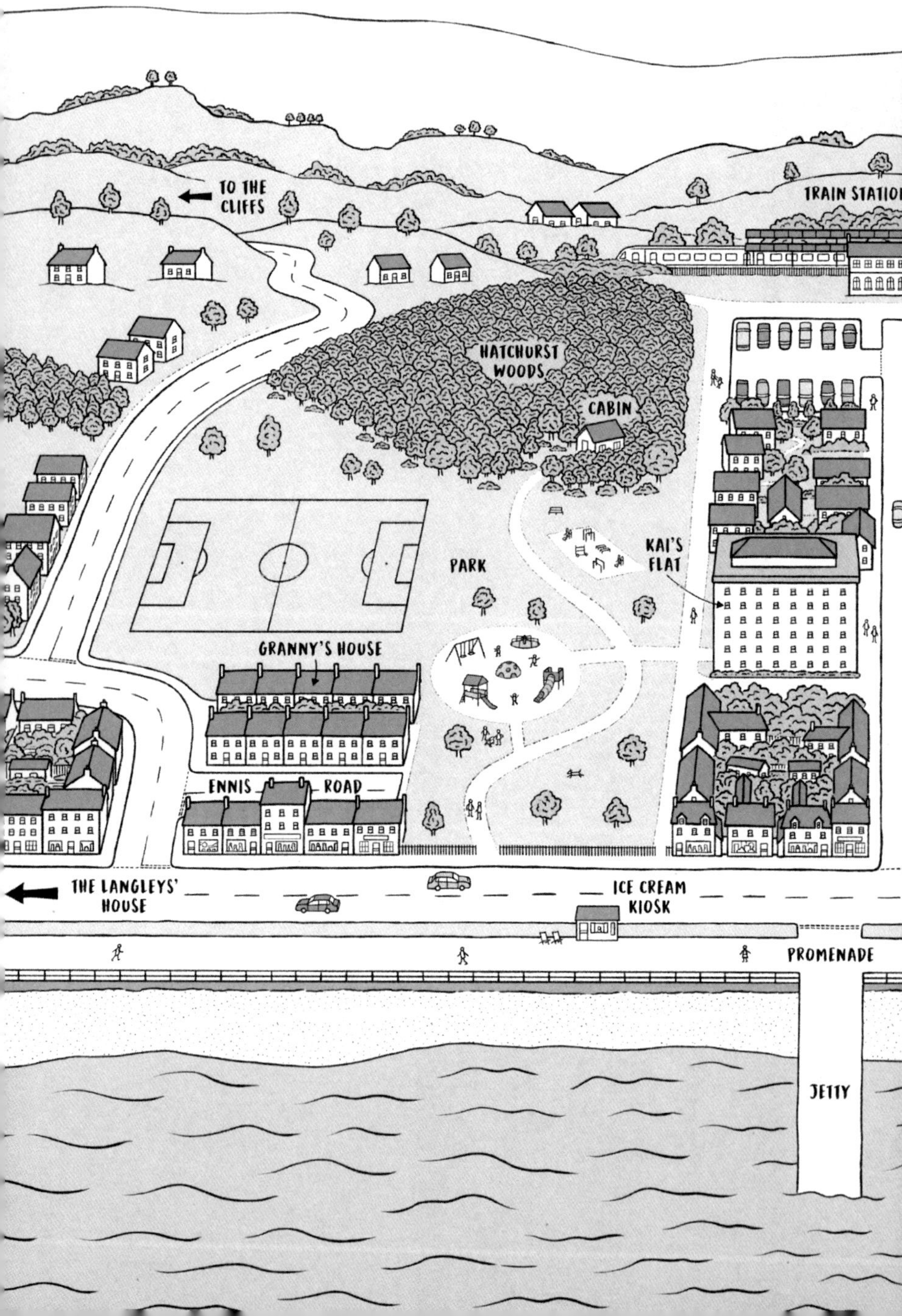
TO THE CLIFFS
TRAIN STATION
HATCHURST WOODS
CABIN
KAI'S FLAT
PARK
GRANNY'S HOUSE
ENNIS ROAD
THE LANGLEYS' HOUSE
ICE CREAM KIOSK
PROMENADE
JETTY

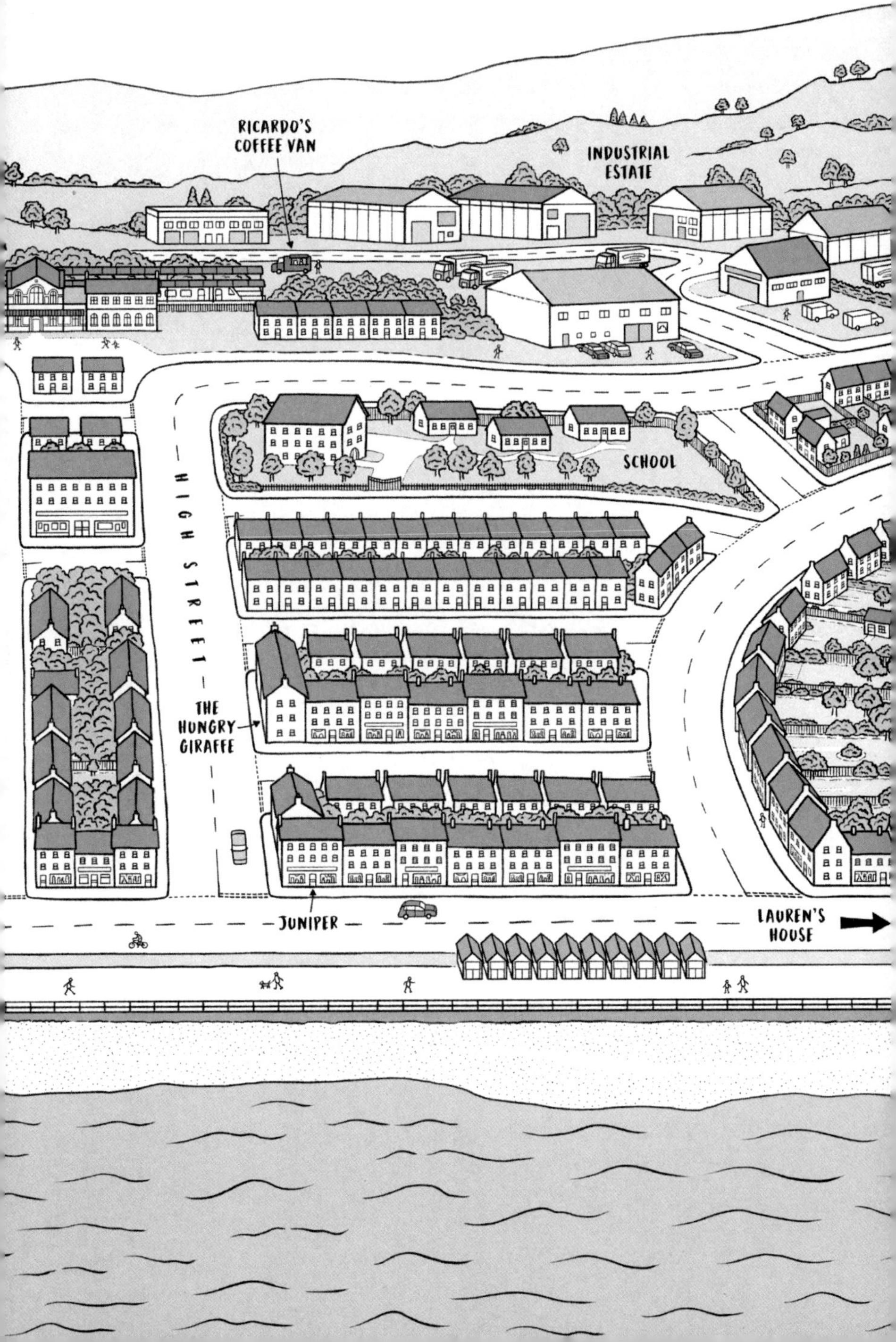
RICARDO'S
COFFEE VAN
INDUSTRIAL
ESTATE
SCHOOL
HIGH STREET
THE
HUNGRY
GIRAFFE
JUNIPER
LAUREN'S
HOUSE

Kerry

Kerry stood in the driveway, keys biting into her palm, as her family spun in opposite directions. Andrew strapped the twins into the back seat. Ella, already mid-FaceTime, blew her a kiss goodbye, and Theo, fighting with the straps of his backpack, trailed behind his sister with a scowl that could scare away the seagulls. Day one back to routine after the Easter holidays, yet Kerry already felt the first crack of the day split open before she'd even left for work.

Let them. Wasn't that what Mel Robbins said? She repeated it through clenched teeth on the drive to work, air-con on full blast. Let Theo be grumpy. That's what fourteen-year-olds were like.

But that one was hard. It was like a switch had been flicked off inside her son, taking away all his sunshine. She was left with a snappy, miserable so-and-so who'd skulked around the house all Easter, not a civil word to say, not a single friend to meet. It worried her.

She needed to find something more manageable to focus on. Let her house be chaos, breakfast dishes still in the sink. They could tidy later. Let the twins go another day without a shower. Seven-year-olds don't sweat. Let Andrew do the school run without her feeling guilty.

And now let me *have a productive day at work*. Wasn't that the key to this whole concept? *Let* me *discover why Henry's been AWOL since Wednesday.*

Let me finalise the new apprenticeship scheme with Pete. Let me remember to book parent-teacher meetings. Let me not drink too much coffee. Let me not stress-eat the leftover Easter eggs. Let me not swear out loud. Let me find time to swim tonight. The list was still going when she pulled into the Bullfinch Glazing car park fifteen minutes later and opened a text from Pete.

Coffee?

Hmm. That was out of the ordinary. *Please let him not want to retire.* She could *not* do this job without Pete. She grabbed two lattes from Ricardo's van, slipped into Pete's messy office and put one on his desk. Beyond the grubby glass partition, aluminium frames rested in neat piles along the walls; Kent FM cut through the whine of machinery and the slice of the lathe; and the ops team moved like synchronised swimmers. Pete's team always ran like clockwork.

"Lovely." He removed the plastic lid and poured the latte into his favourite mug.

The coffee was delicious. Two today so far. "So, what's up?"

Pete reached inside the V-neck of his bobbled navy jumper and fumbled in the breast pocket of his shirt for his glasses, pulling them out for an unnecessary polish. Shit. It must be bad. Pete's direct gaze hadn't wavered in the thirty-odd years they'd known each other, since her father had hired him.

"Henry took me for a pint last night," he said, putting on his glasses and finally meeting her eye. He looked every one of his sixty-two years, and she resisted the urge to hurry him along. But a Sunday night business meeting? They certainly weren't planning the summer party.

"And?" She sucked in her breath.

Pete put his hands out, palms up, a gesture of surrender. "He's sold the business."

Henry had sold Bullfinch. And he didn't even have the nerve to tell her – or the staff – himself. What a bastard. She let out the breath she'd been holding, feeling the buoyancy she'd tried to create in the car dissipate. It was a joke, trying to get on top of things. There was always another wave to knock you over.

"Who's the buyer?"

"Oh God, Kerry. It's Stonebridge."

"Jesus. They'll crucify us."

Stonebridge Holdings had decimated every company they'd bought in the last ten years. Super slick, they already had HR in-house; that was Kerry gone. They'd take the ops abroad: that would be Pete gone – they'd ship it in for nothing and flog it over here for half the price. No quality, no service. No good.

"Yeah." Pete folded his arms, resigned.

"You know what that means?" Kerry said. "We're screwed."

The telephone on the wall began to ring. Neither of them moved, hearts sinking with each trill. Eventually, one of the men on the floor picked up an extension, and their conversation un-paused.

"We may as well join the dole queue now," Pete said. "They manufacture in Poland. I hear the commute is a nightmare." He gave her a shaky smile.

"Oh, Pete." She touched his shoulder.

"Your father would be so disappointed." He shook his head. "Four hundred staff. How many do you think they'll keep?"

"No!" Kerry said, snapping into action. "We can't let that happen." She paced the tiny office, rattling off points, counting them on her fingers. "We'll fight this. Get the unions involved, get legal advice. Talk to Henry." But Henry had held, tight-fisted, onto his control of the company ever since her father's death. He wouldn't help now. "We'll fight this," she said again.

Pete didn't reply. Kerry knew he didn't have faith. They were all on the wrong side of forty-five, and Saltreach was hardly thriving. Pete's children were grown, but Kerry had her four. Christ, *four*.

"You can talk about it with Izzy, ah … somebody," Pete said, unfolding a sheet of paper from his breast pocket and running a finger up and down, scanning for the correct name. "She's asked to see us at three. She's briefing the entire company at four."

"Wow. That's a bit fast." Irrationally, she thought of *her* Izzy, the Izzy she'd seen every day of her life until she'd finished uni, and not once since. She was being ridiculous. That Izzy, according to her last LinkedIn stalk, was in New York. "Izzy who?"

"Don't know. She's in charge of the takeover."

A car door slammed outside. Pete leaned over stacks of paperwork on his desk to peer out the window. Only visitors were allowed to park out front.

"Look at this," he said, beckoning Kerry over.

A white Audi, not unlike Kerry's own but a far newer model, was parked at an angle, occupying two spaces. Slamming the boot with unnecessary force was a tall woman with expensive caramel highlights, wearing an immaculately tailored royal-blue suit, complete with pussybow blouse. Very Kate Middleton. She swung a cream leather bag – Mulberry, Kerry guessed – onto her arm and strode towards the front entrance. At the last minute, she turned to point her key fob at the car and a familiar silver scar glinted on the back of her hand. Kerry drew in a sharp breath, remembering with shocking clarity the day ten-year-old Izzy had knocked it against the hot oven door while pulling out a tray of fish fingers. Now she rubbed her own hand reflexively. Izzy's dream had been to get out of Saltreach. Exactly like Kerry. What the hell was she doing back?

Kerry

At three o'clock on the dot, jittery with caffeine and adrenaline, Kerry and Pete entered the boardroom. There, centre stage at the long table, was Izzy Holt, paperwork fanned around her in neat piles. She rose elegantly as Kerry entered and calmly appraised her with cool eyes. She'd known Kerry would be there. Of course she had. A tidal wave of hot rage spread through Kerry's chest. She gritted her teeth and visualised herself plunging into a freezing winter sea, a trick that hadn't let her down yet.

"Hello, Izzy." She didn't offer a handshake. She clasped her fingers together on the tabletop, praying they wouldn't shake. "It's been a long time."

Izzy's expression was neutral as she took her seat. If she harboured any nerves – or guilt – about showing up like this, Kerry couldn't tell. "It certainly has. You haven't changed a bit." But she stopped short of a full smile and pulled out her first folder.

*

"A quarter?" Kerry scanned the paperwork furiously. "That's a hundred jobs!"

"It's the quickest way out of debt," Izzy said, steepling her long, slim fingers, as though in prayer. "Without it, we'll be forced to consider closing the entire business."

"But cutting 25% of the workforce," Kerry said, "means putting a hundred families into the dole queue." She showed the numbers to Pete, who mumbled something about Bullfinch having never been in debt. Izzy bulldozed onwards.

"We've outlined a competitive redundancy package." There was iron in her voice, but she hadn't the guts to read the offer aloud.

Pete snorted. "Competitive, my arse," he muttered. His face turned scarlet, and he kept fiddling with the end of a tie he'd put on especially for the meeting. Kerry knew he was just as upset as she was.

Izzy didn't flinch. "I understand this is a shock."

Pete expelled a mirthless laugh. Some of his people had been there for over thirty years, ten years off retirement and too old and expensive for newer firms to hire. Some were only starting out with mortgages and babies – this would cripple them.

"What do you expect *me* to do?" Kerry said.

"I'd like you to start with the Operations team and canvass for voluntary redundancy. Report back in two weeks."

"Christ," said Pete under his breath.

Kerry leaned forward. "I'm not taking this bullshit offer to a single member of staff," she said slowly, drumming her middle finger on the centre of the boardroom table to hammer home her point. "It is an insult to our people. Take your paperwork back to Stonebridge and let them come back with something more competitive. In the meantime, I'll be setting up a meeting with legal."

Izzy simply nodded and closed her binder as if Kerry had suggested no more than a coffee break. The meeting was over.

Kerry

"Christ, Andy," Kerry said. "It's everything I've worked for my whole life!"

"I only said there might be a silver lining." He shook the pan, coating the asparagus in garlic. His voice was mild, but his eyes didn't meet hers. Either he didn't get it, or he was doing a good job of pretending he didn't.

"Well, there isn't."

"I'm sorry." Always the first to apologise. Thank God one of them could do it. Kerry leaned against his shoulder and felt the cool Italian cotton against her cheek. He was as pristine as when he left the house that morning. Beneath his spotless navy apron, pale pink sleeves were rolled up to reveal tanned forearms, soft hands, and neatly squared-off fingernails. She'd had to have a cool shower the moment she'd come in and was now braless in shorts and a camisole. This heatwave was ridiculous.

She hunted at the back of the fridge and found a bottle of Pinot Grigio. She sent Poppy and Alby upstairs with an iPad and Easter eggs, bugger their bedtime, and poured two large glasses. Her phone flickered from the worktop – already a hundred and forty-one messages on the WhatsApp group she'd set up today. Maybe that had been a mistake. Her swim bag hung from the peg by the back door, but she'd never get to the beach tonight with that lot to go through. But before she could read even one, Andrew lifted the salmon out of the air fryer and plated up, twisting rock salt onto the potatoes and adding a dollop of butter. It wouldn't do her cholesterol any good, but she couldn't be bothered to protest. She'd stayed after hours to address the staff, and now it was too late to eat. Either way, her appetite had vanished.

"I have to fight this. Bullfinch is the biggest employer in Saltreach, and the town is already on its knees."

"I don't want to speak out of turn," Andrew said, spearing a piece of asparagus, "but are you sure this is all about work?"

"What does that mean?"

"Well, if this Izzy person wasn't running the show, would you feel quite the same?"

Surely he didn't just say that. Surely he got it. He was a smart man.

"You're kidding, right?" she said. "These are my colleagues. I've hired most of them. I know their financial situation, their health problems, their kids. They're my friends, for God's sake! How could you think I wouldn't be upset?"

"That's not what I meant," he said, taking a sip of wine. "I understand the shock and disappointment." He finally met her gaze. "But you seem even angrier with this woman, Izzy, than with Henry. It's confusing."

He reached out and patted her hand. Andrew liked the path of least resistance. He never fell out with people. But with something this enormous, she wanted him to get angry with her, to feel the injustice of it. She needed him in her corner.

"I don't trust her." It was the shortest, most honest answer she had.

"I get that you two had some kind of falling out, love. But that's all water under the bridge now, surely? Ancient history?"

It *could* have been ancient history if Izzy hadn't shown up today, if she hadn't taken this particular job, if she hadn't laid down the gauntlet with a 25% redundancy target. Within two fucking weeks! No, Izzy had proven twenty-four years ago that whatever she wanted was more important than loyalty and it seemed her priorities hadn't changed.

"She was my best friend," she said. "Since we were five years old. We went to Manchester together, worked in bars, and rarely came back. It was brilliant."

"And then what?"

"Then Dad died."

It was that simple. She'd been coming out of her last exam, the bright June sunshine making her squint after three hours in the hall, hands aching after writing for so long. Izzy was there, still fizzing from adrenaline and Red Bull. Kerry had flipped open her Nokia and seen eight missed calls: six from her mother, and two from another local Saltreach number. The hospital, it had turned out.

Andrew reached over the table and took Kerry's hand. "Of course he did," he said. "And Izzy?"

"She didn't even come to the funeral."

"Why not?"

"I don't know. She never returned my calls. She blocked my number, defriended me on social media. She literally disappeared."

There was an extended silence, and Kerry felt bad for ruining the meal. Andrew was a good cook. Better than her. She couldn't face washing up tonight. There was a pile of laundry waiting to be ironed, spellings to be checked. Those texts to be read. No, she couldn't think about work any more today. Let them wait. Let her find something positive to take her mind off it.

"How was your day?" she asked, reaching for his hand. "Any news?"

"Actually." He grinned, clearly chuffed about something. "I do have news. Ready?"

"Go for it."

"I got the promotion!"

"No way! That's bloody brilliant!" Her pique with her kind, understated husband dissolved in a heartbeat. "You deserve it. I thought you wouldn't hear till Friday. I'm so happy for you. Why didn't you call?"

"I wanted to tell you in person," he said, accepting her kiss. "And then there was … well, your thing. And Theo – don't you think something's up with Theo?"

So Andrew had noticed, too. It wasn't just her imagination. Worry etched a familiar path in her heart.

"I do," she said. "Is this what we can expect, now that he's fourteen? Or do you think there's something more serious going on?"

"I'll chat to him tomorrow," Andrew said. "Man to man." He pretended to beat his chest and Kerry was grateful that he hadn't allowed them to be sucked back into the black hole of worry and stress.

"Thank you, Mr Financial Director," she said. "Wow. I didn't think anything could turn this day around."

"It comes with a decent pay rise," Andrew said, stroking the inside of her wrist. He gave a tiny preparatory cough, much like he had when he'd proposed. Something else was coming. An announcement. She felt an irrational stab of panic. She'd had enough surprises for one day. She hoped he wouldn't say he wanted to move house or do anything crazy. She hadn't the mental capacity for something big.

"So," he said, pulling out his phone, "I think we should do something fun!" He showed her a picture of a herd of giraffes nibbling from the treetops.

Phew. That was *fine*. "The zoo? That's a good idea. The twins . . ."

"Botswana," Andrew interrupted. "On safari. I've been doing some research. We could go next Easter; it wouldn't be too hot, and the kids would love it."

"Oh," Kerry said, taking the phone. She swiped through the photographs. Families in camouflage jeeps peered through binoculars at elephants and rhinos grazing within stampeding distance. She tried to be generous. "It looks incredible." She handed the phone back. "Expensive, though. No?"

"Yes," Andrew said. "After fifteen years of driving to French campsites, I'm about ready for expensive. Aren't you?"

Kerry felt foolish. It wasn't that she was afraid of the animals, or the heat, or the flight. Fine, she'd never flown long-haul or needed vaccinations. They'd honeymooned in Vienna. Had a few city breaks before the twins were born, leaving Mum to babysit Ella and Theo. And she liked France. This felt too big for right now. For today.

"Think about it," Andrew said, patting her hand. "Do your research."

"You know me well," she said, relieved. Andrew was the ideas person; she did the details. She'd scour the reviews, find the discount codes, get the best deal.

"But I want to buy myself a little celebratory present first."

"Oh?" Kerry could be more positive about this.

"Check this out." This time, it was a photo of a bicycle on his phone. Clearly, it was more than *just* a bicycle, but for someone who refused to go on her own exercise bike, that was all it looked like to Kerry.

"Theo can have my old one and Alby can have Theo's," Andrew said, obviously thrilled with himself for thinking the whole thing through. "Wolf just bought the same model. We've earmarked

Tuesday and Thursday evenings for cycling." His forehead crinkled. "That works, doesn't it?"

Kerry felt ashamed of the tinge of envy that crept over her. She'd never had a best friend after Izzy. Wolf Bauer, the geeky German boy with the thick black eyebrows and sauerkraut in his lunchbox, had been both her schoolfriend and Andrew's squash partner, something they hadn't pieced together until Wolf moved back to Saltreach a few years back with his prickly wife and daughter. Andrew had been thrilled.

"How does Nicole feel about that?"

Andrew grimaced and tried to hide it. "Maybe you and she could hang out too?"

"You must be joking," Kerry said. "Nicole made it pretty clear she was not interested in making friends. I think I dodged a bullet, to be honest. You guys do your thing. But seriously, *two* nights a week?" Two nights she would have to do dinner, homework, and sports clubs by herself. Two night she couldn't swim or work late.

His face fell, and she softened. As if she ever said no to Andrew. The bike wasn't even that expensive. And she was sure there was a government grant for that sort of thing. She'd look into it. "Of course you can do it, you wally."

She leaned over the table for a kiss.

"I love you," he said.

"I love you, too."

Theo

Theo turned into St Leonard's Crescent and passed the empty Airbnbs with their colourful front doors and a view of the beach. Anyone visiting Saltreach this summer would be disappointed. The beach was a mess of seaweed that the council had suddenly stopped clearing. Dad said it had something to do with protecting the chalk reef, but Mum said everything came down to money. At least the stench from the water was mild this early in the morning. Yesterday afternoon, it had been so powerful he'd actually checked to see if he'd left an egg sandwich at the bottom of his schoolbag.

He hated walking into school alone. But he couldn't text Kai, not after last week. And now there was drama at home too.

Mum had cried in the kitchen last night. Theo had heard her telling Dad about something being a disaster. A total fucking nightmare, to be precise. He and Ella had taken the twins upstairs and played Top Trumps with them, Ella disappearing every few minutes to listen from the stairs. She'd reported back that someone was losing their job and they needed to start saving money. Dad was going to sell his car and cycle to work. This was bad. Mum already obsessed about money. And even though Mum never drank during the week, there'd been an empty bottle of wine sitting on the side this morning. Dad had been checking up on him, all *champ* this and shoulder-clap that, as if Theo were the one with problems. As if he was going to tell Dad about Kai. God. He'd had to fob him off with a story about upcoming exams and got landed with an offer to help revise.

He came to the regular houses, with movement and chatter behind the open windows, the sound of Heart Radio, and the delicious smell of bacon and eggs. He'd only had cornflakes for breakfast. A girl in uniform left a house a few doors ahead, rolled her skirt up a couple of inches, and walked ahead of him, texting as she went.

"Theo?"

He took out an earbud and looked around, one eye on the school gate. It would close soon.

"Theo? Hang on a sec."

He shielded his eyes and spotted a tall, thin man hurrying over the road towards him. He wore a black shirt, black jeans. Probably a substitute teacher.

The man raised his hands in a peace gesture. "Can I have a word?" He had a chirpy London accent. "I don't mean to make you late for school."

His smile was crooked, and Theo could only see teeth on one side. Probably not a teacher after all.

"You're Andrew Langley's son, yeah?"

Theo nodded.

"Only your dad ..." the guy scratched his neck, where the skin was already pink and raw, "well, I think he's my dad, too."

What the hell was he talking about? Was this some kind of prank? Theo didn't want to end up on YouTube. He went to replace the earbud, but the man touched his elbow and he jerked backwards out of reach. This was weird. If only Kai was here. Kai would know what to say.

"I'm late for school," he said, which was true. The gate was closed now. Shit. He'd have to walk all the way round to the front entrance and sign in at the office.

"My mum was your dad's girlfriend," the man said, talking faster now. "When he was training to be an accountant. In Stevenage, right? Burke's, it was called."

Theo turned slowly. Dad often talked about Burke's. The guy was staring at him, his hands in his pockets, just rolling back and forwards on his feet, as if waiting for the penny to drop. This was stupid. Dad couldn't have another son.

"I have to go to class," he said, walking onwards. The guy jogged to keep up with him.

"I know," he said. "It's a lot to take in, I get it. Look, let's grab coffee after school. I'll tell you what I know."

"I don't drink coffee," Theo said, speeding up. He wanted to run. He wanted to say, *Why are you following me? Talk to Dad.* But he pictured Dad's face as he tidied away the wine bottle after breakfast, felt the longer-than-usual pat on Theo's shoulder. Mum crying last night. "I'll meet you later," he said. "A quarter to seven at the park."

Thankfully the man stopped chasing him. "Perfect," he said. "Before your football training. See you then."

Bloody hell. How did this guy know about football?

Theo

Ten minutes till training and the guy was a no-show. It must have been a prank; but the thought didn't comfort Theo like it should have. He took a seat on the bench at the top of the park and adjusted his shin pads, the breeze raising goosebumps on his arms. Behind him was the small woodland with the deserted cabin where teenagers smoked weed and had sex. His teammates already gathered on the football field to his right, and there were at least eight other people within shouting distance. Enough to feel safe. Technically.

If he didn't show in two minutes, then Theo would forget about him, pretend he'd never existed. He didn't even know his name. Ahead, the park ran downhill, past the playground and the outdoor gym equipment. No sign of him there. Over the road was the promenade with its red ice cream kiosk, the seaweed-clogged beach, and the English Channel. Seagulls swooped and screeched. The people were smaller there, but nobody moved with the jerky, nervous energy of this guy.

Then there he was. Walking, practically bouncing, along the path from the woods. The guy who claimed Dad was … Theo didn't want to think about it. He was wearing the same black clothes – no shorts, despite the heat – and he fiddled as he walked, hands in and out of his pockets, twisting the buttons of his shirt, scratching that pink stain on his neck. A light coat of stubble covered his jaw.

Maybe this was a mistake. Shit, it was too late to leave. The man nodded and sat next to him, a few inches too close, crossed his ankles and said, almost shyly, "I'm Mitch."

"Theo," Theo said. But Mitch already knew his name. Knew a lot – too much. Where Theo played football, what school he went to. And, apparently, all about Dad.

"Liverpool, eh?" Mitch nodded at Theo's jersey. "One big win and they never let you forget it."

It was true, but Theo wasn't going to admit it. He had six minutes.

"It's not true, what you said about my dad."

"Theo, I'm sorry." He was apologetic, like he'd no choice except to come and announce himself and blow Theo's family apart. "But it's true. I've known it my whole life."

"How old are you?"

"Twenty-two."

Ella was sixteen. Mum and Dad had been married for eighteen years. "Who's your mum?"

"Your dad's last girlfriend, I suppose." Mitch grinned, but something literally sparked up beneath the surface of his smile. Anger? Resentment? Theo couldn't tell.

He examined Mitch's face. Dad had fair hair. Mitch's was brown. Dad's eyes were green-grey. Mitch had dark eyes, with long, thick black eyelashes. Theo had inherited *his* brown eyes from Mum. And even then, they were far lighter. Dad was solid, calm and steady with a low, gravelly voice that used to put Theo to sleep in seconds when he was a little kid. Mitch talked fast, and he was skinny. He wriggled and scratched and rubbed, like a child with a serious case of nits. Even now, as he turned to face Theo, serious for the first time, he plucked at the smattering of uneven stubble with his fingernails, examining each hair he pulled before tossing it into the air.

"Sorry," he said. "My mum is called Diana. She was your dad's girlfriend when he was training to be an accountant. They broke up before she knew she was pregnant. He doesn't know about me."

"Why don't you speak to him, then?" Theo said, angry now. He hadn't a clue if any of this was true. "Instead of stalking me. It's weird, man."

"I never had a dad," Mitch said, plucking more stubble from his cheek. He blew the hairs from his fingers, and they caught in the wind. "I wouldn't know what to say. Don't want to scare him off."

Theo checked the time on his phone. "What do you want from me?" If Mitch wouldn't talk to Dad, why should Theo talk to him?

"Just, you know, to get to know you," Mitch said. "Surely that's okay, isn't it?" He leaned forward and touched Theo's shoulder. "After all, we're brothers."

"Fuck you!" Theo jumped up and put a hand where Mitch had touched him. He stumbled, tears blurring his way, towards the football team, now grouped on the far side of the pitch, ready to start. Mitch didn't move.

"Fuck you," Theo said again under his breath, feeling Mitch's eyes watching him as he jogged away.

Kerry

"Excuse *me*," Kerry said, as Theo barged past her on his way in from training, in a mood as black as his football boots. He flung his phone on the side table as though it were on fire and charged straight upstairs. "Don't hurry back down," she said under her breath.

"Mum!" Ella appeared at her shoulder in a waft of Kerry's Chanel perfume.

"Oh!" Kerry put a hand over her mouth. "Sorry, love. I didn't hear you. I didn't mean it, of course. It's just ..."

"I get it," Ella said. "He's *unbearable*." She inched past Kerry and grabbed a denim jacket off the hook. Kerry's denim jacket. She didn't need it this evening. It was still at least twenty-five degrees. But there was no point saying anything – Ella knew her own mind.

Kerry touched her daughter's arm to slow her down.

"Do you think he's being bullied?"

Ella laughed gently. "Don't get all extra over this, Mum. He's fourteen. He's supposed to be unbearable, isn't he?"

"Not now, Ella. Be serious, okay? I'm worried about him."

Ella rolled her eyes, a replica of her father. "I'm sure he's fine, Mum. The kids he hangs out with are so lame. They're never going to get into any real trouble."

"Which kids?"

"You know, the usual ones. Oliver, Dan. Ché."

"Not Kai?"

"I think Theo was, like, Kai's *only* friend." Ella shrugged. "He's a loner. Not like the usual lot."

Kerry knew what she meant. While the others dressed in joggers and sports tops, Kai wore workmen's boots, old, faded jeans, and an eclectic set of t-shirts featuring eighties' rock bands that looked original. He even shaved. He could easily pass for a university student. "Kai *was* his friend? Have they had a row?"

"Mum." Ella tried to slither past her out the front door. "Nobody actually *rows*. I've got to go. I'm meeting Jen."

Kerry tugged on the hem of the jacket. Ella always had somewhere to go. "Promise me, if you hear anything, you'll let me know."

Ella kissed her on the cheek. "Course. And hey, you want answers?"

Kerry followed her finger. Theo's phone lay face down where he'd thrown it on the hall table. In full view, an open book. Sure, it was locked, but it wasn't hidden. From upstairs, she heard the hiss of the shower.

"Gotta go," Ella said and slid out the door.

*

Yes, yes, it was an invasion of privacy and all that, and, as HR Director, Kerry was more than up to date with all the moral and legal complications of broaching other people's boundaries. But, and it was a big but, she was worried. Andrew had promised to talk to him, but Andrew was looking after the twins right now. *Let them*, she thought. She could let them handle it together, man to man. Like she said she would.

But, for crying out loud, she was Theo's mother. This would always be her domain. She took the phone into her study and shut the door. She guessed his password on the second try, relieved he didn't feel the need to use anything more cryptic than his date of birth. She went straight to the usual suspects: Snapchat, TikTok, Instagram. But Theo wasn't a social media guy. He used his phone to follow the football, play music, and in any five-minute period when he had to actually wait for something, he watched YouTube shorts. She flicked into messages. There was very little activity. Should she be worried about a lack of friends? But no, Theo made plans and stuck to them, old-school style.

Her thumb hovered, mid-scroll. Seventeen unread texts and missed calls from Kai. This must be it, whatever *it* was.

Sorry, Theo. Literally can't believe I did that.

Don't know what I was thinking.

Please say we can move on from this.

Can we talk?

I got it wrong, okay? Won't happen again.

Seriously dude, can't we just hang out like we did before?

Why won't you answer?

And on it went. Apology after apology. Kerry hadn't seen Kai in days. He'd stopped calling for Theo in the mornings to walk to school together, but he certainly sounded like he wanted to make up. Kerry felt sorry for him. How could her own son block such genuine messages? But it was an explanation of sorts for Theo's mood. A rift with a pal. Not the end of the world. Phew. She needn't be – what was it Ella had said? – *extra,* after all. Whatever that actually meant. She would talk to Theo tomorrow and help him fix this thing with Kai.

She replaced the phone and went through to the kitchen, where Andrew and the twins were tucking into homemade chocolate brownies, straight from the oven.

"I'll get you one," Poppy yelled, and proudly put a brownie on a plate in front of her. "Tada!"

"This looks amazing," Kerry said. "I am a very lucky mummy." She took a bite. "OMG. To die for."

Poppy beamed and Andrew stood. "Okay, you two," he said, "teeth and pjs."

Hang on, Kerry wanted to say, *stay another minute so I can join in the fun.* But it was already past their bedtime and Andrew was right.

They left her sitting alone at the table, weary, and surrounded by baking detritus to wash up.

Theo

THEO HURRIED TO SCHOOL the following morning, keeping his head down and earbuds in, but there was no sign of Mitch. He went straight to first period. Geography was his favourite subject, but today it was impossible to concentrate. He'd barely been able to look at Dad at breakfast time and had spotted the flicker of hurt in Dad's eyes as he'd slunk away from the table, rejecting the offer of a lift. What the hell was he going to do about Mitch?

"Theo?"

He looked up from doodling in the margin of his workbook. Lauren Bauer whispered his name again and looped one tanned finger over his wrist. It was slim, decorated with a stack of neat gold rings and metallic silver nail polish. A tiny love heart tattoo nestled in the space between her index and middle fingers. Theo forgot about Dad. He wanted to touch it.

The teacher pointed at a multi-layered image detailing the effects of erosion on the Kent coast. "The English Channel …" he said.

"Stinks!" shouted someone in the back.

Theo stared at the heart.

"Technically, the seaweed stinks," Mr Gregors said. "It's a rare occurrence in April, but so is this heatwave. When it decomposes, hydrogen sulphide …"

Theo let his gaze run along the smooth skin of Lauren's hand, across the narrow wrist, up her slender arm. Just beyond her elbow was a mole. A cute, sexy mole. He followed her long, curly hair past her shoulders, wanting, yet not wanting, to be caught looking.

But Lauren wasn't watching him. She leaned towards the window, her chair on two legs, craning her neck to see something a little out of view. She pulled on his arm.

"When the bell rings, come with me, okay?"

"Why?"

Theo didn't hear her answer. The bell rang as if on command and thirty pupils rose in unison, drowning out Mr Gregors. He nodded. Lauren Bauer was the prettiest girl in Year Ten and he'd had a crush on her since she moved to Saltreach two years ago. Okay, she was also Dad's best friend's daughter, but surely that didn't make it weird. He would do whatever she asked him to.

*

She ditched her friends at the classroom door with a story about collecting a new science book. Theo felt their scepticism as he followed her along the corridor, through a side exit, where she pulled him into the shade of an ash tree – a place every couple in the school knew wasn't overseen by security cameras. Was she going to kiss him? Of course she wasn't. Girls like Lauren Bauer didn't kiss guys like Theo.

"See that guy?" she whispered, pointing out onto the road.

Theo couldn't see anyone. He shielded his eyes, squinted. Was it Mitch? Had he told Lauren to get him?

Then he saw a guy, no – a man, approaching. Theo guessed he was in his twenties; short, stocky, light on his feet like a boxer, wearing a baggy grey tracksuit, unlaced high-tops, and a pristine white t-shirt. Definitely not Mitch.

"Him," Lauren said, more insistent this time, her fingers grasping the sleeve of his blazer. "Can you tell him I'm not coming?"

The man was close now. He didn't look particularly threatening. He was texting, grinning to himself, announcing *I'm here*. A stud earring caught the sun.

"Who is he?" Theo asked.

Lauren's gaze slid away from his eyes and settled somewhere near his ear.

"An ex," she said. It sounded like a question.

"Why don't you tell him yourself?"

"I have! He won't go away. Go on, please." She checked her phone again. Theo could see incoming text messages filling the screen. "He'll listen to you. You're bigger than him."

Theo wasn't sure about that. He was tall and fit, but he didn't lift weights. This guy was easily ten years older and was stacked in a steroids-and-protein-shakes kind of way. He had a *beard*, for God's sake. Theo wouldn't be fifteen till August, the youngest in the entire school year.

"I'll get help if he does anything," Lauren said, giving him a nudge in the small of his back. Then she wriggled backwards into the shadows and Theo was left exposed and alone in the harsh sunlight.

What was he supposed to do? Did Lauren really go out with men like this? She was fifteen. Everyone knew girls liked older guys, but this was insane.

He put his hands in his pockets, ignored the sweat trickling between his shoulder blades, and jogged down two steps to the edge of the pavement.

"Mate," he said. "Lauren can't come out."

The guy had pulled out his phone again and was checking for a reply to his message. He hadn't heard.

Theo cleared his throat, gave a redundant wave in the guy's direction, hoping to distract him. "Lauren's in class. She asked me to let you know she can't make it."

Beardface stroked his barrel chest, squinted at Theo with cold blue-grey eyes, as if seeing him for the first time.

"Sorry," Theo added.

"Who the hell are you?"

Theo puffed out his own chest. "I'm a friend."

"Yeah? What sort of friend?"

In his peripheral vision Theo sensed hands being curled into fists. He took a tiny step backwards. "A classmate," he corrected. "Geography. Lauren had some homework to finish." He squared his shoulders, held his breath.

A powerful fist connected with his cheekbone with the precision of a lizard catching prey. The guy – in fact, the entire street – disappeared as his world turned black. Unable to get his hands out of his pockets on time, Theo stumbled, tripping on the step and collapsing on his side, winded.

Theo

Theo groaned when he heard Mum's key in the front door. She ran into the lounge, still wearing her coat.

"I'm fine," he said from the sofa. He scowled at Dad, who hovered by the kitchen door, tea towel over his shoulder like he was on bloody *Bake Off*. "Dad didn't need to call you." He sat up straighter and pushed his crumpled school blazer under a cushion before she could tell him off for not hanging it up.

Mum dumped her bag on the coffee table and brushed his fringe to one side. He leaned away, but she put her other hand on his cheek and manoeuvred his head in a semi-circle to get a better look, as though he were a desk lamp pointing the wrong way. He tried not to wince.

"Oh my God," she said, finally letting go of him. She shimmied out of her coat and dropped it on the floor. "Oh my good God. What happened?"

"He's feeling better already," Dad said in his *I've got everything covered* sort of way.

Mum gave him the side eye.

"Aren't you?" Dad said with a chummy grin. "Thanks to a bag of peas and a homemade brownie." He picked up Mum's coat and took it to the hall. Dad had actually been cool.

"Yeah. Thanks, Mary Berry," he said. Dad came back and threw the tea towel at him.

"What happened, sweetheart?" Mum said. Their jokey act hadn't worked. She sat next to him, squeezing him hard round the shoulder, the pain telling him of another bruise.

"Did school call you?" he asked. Surely they hadn't noticed anything. He'd made it to the rest of his classes, managing to avoid too much eye contact. Told his friends he wasn't feeling well. A dodgy sausage roll from the canteen.

"Nope. Just Dad. Doesn't mean I don't need to know what happened," she said, tipping his chin up again. Theo knew there was already a purple bruise spreading across his temple and under his eye socket, a ridge of skin torn from the outer edge of his eyebrow.

Mum picked up the bag of peas Theo had left on Dad's *Guardian*. It left a damp patch. She held it between finger and thumb for a minute before setting it back down in the same place. "Are you being bullied, love?"

"No!" he said, louder than he intended. "I tripped on some steps." That much was true.

Mum sat back, her eyebrows pointing downwards in the middle. "Were *you* fighting?" she asked, putting both hands over her mouth as if to stop the accusation in its tracks.

Dad said "Kerry!" sternly, but Theo guessed he deserved that. He might have, he supposed, if he hadn't fallen over. So embarrassing. He shook his head.

"I'm sorry, love," Mum said. "Can you tell me what happened?"

He shrugged. What was he supposed to say? Lauren was adamant nobody should know. She'd grabbed his hand so tight he'd feared those metallic nails would draw blood. So, he'd promised.

Mum was staring at him. Literally inches from his face. Dad leaned against the door frame and folded his arms as if he were merely waiting for a bus. Fake casual. Theo felt the weight of their expectations on him like a laser. Where were the others? Nobody ever got Mum *and* Dad to themselves. Ella must have been bribed to take the twins upstairs.

Mum sighed. She pulled his blazer out from under the cushion, laid it across her lap, smoothing down the creases. "Theo …"

"Leave it, will you!" He jumped off the sofa and pushed past her, slamming the lounge door. The sound echoed through the house, as sharp and violent as if he'd slapped her. As he stormed along the landing to his bedroom, Alby and Poppy came out of their room, each holding a pack of chocolate buttons.

"Are you in trouble?" Poppy said, wide-eyed.

"What happened to your face?" Alby asked.

Behind them, Ella sat on the bottom bunk. She had the same brown eyes as Theo, the same head-on-one-side way of sizing him up as Dad, and the same shorthand in her speech as Mum. She knew Theo even better than he knew himself.

"I heard," she said. "You okay?"

Theo ignored them all, shut his bedroom door, and sat on the edge of his bed. His eye hurt. He felt stupid. And he desperately wanted to go back downstairs to Mum for a hug and some paracetamol.

But he couldn't say anything. Mum would want to go to the police. And Lauren had said if her mother found out, she'd be grounded for life.

Kerry

"Hi, Mum."

Mum didn't turn around. Maybe she'd forgotten to switch on the hearing aid again. Or maybe it was finally time to talk to the doctor about memory tests. Kerry picked up the remote and muted the TV. Mum jumped and twisted in her chair. Kerry put the Tesco bag down on the Formica worktop and came round in front of her mother. The confused look vanished, and she was wreathed in smiles. Her lovely mum. They held hands for a moment, and Kerry kissed her cheek, inhaling the familiar scents of lavender and tea.

"You were in a world of your own."

"Best place to be, if you ask me." Mum inclined a head towards the TV, which showed an elderly woman in a hospital bed, her face black and blue from a fall, or worse. Kerry shuddered. Mum was one of the lucky ones. It was normal to be forgetful at seventy-seven. A bit confused sometimes. Kerry made a mental note to try to limit how much TV her mother watched. It wasn't good for her.

"Good day?" she asked.

Mum nodded and heaved herself out of the armchair. "I'll put the kettle on. What's on the menu tonight?"

Kerry switched the oven on to heat and unpacked tonight's dinner. "Fish pie, broccoli. Some of those nice honey yoghurts for after." Better than risking her swigging too much Gaviscon later.

The kettle hissed and Mum made tea. Kerry checked the pill pods were up to date.

"Heard from Clare?" she asked, keeping her voice neutral.

"Not this week," Mum said. "But she'll call soon. Clare's a good girl."

Yes, they were both good, Catholic girls. Named after the home counties of their Irish parents, dutiful and respectful. Just one a little more than the other. Kerry sighed.

Mum's smile faded and Kerry felt bad. "Course she will," she said. "I bet she's up to her eyes at work." That was usually the excuse. Still, Kerry would ring her as soon as the time difference allowed.

They settled at the round, pine kitchen table, taking their age-old places. It was as if the routine brought Mum back to herself. She sat tall and graceful, her eyes clear and soft.

"I'm afraid I've got bad news, Mum. The factory's been sold."

To her amazement, Mum didn't flinch. "I know. Audrey told me."

"What? When?"

"She came round last night for a cup of tea. She said Pete's devastated."

Kerry felt a surge of teenage angst. This was *her* news to share, *her* mother's feelings to consider.

"Don't fret, *alanna*. She wanted to save you a difficult conversation."

There they were again, protecting her, paving her way for her. It drove Kerry mad. They'd always been like that: Mum, Dad when he was alive, Pete, and Audrey. The fab four.

"How's Izzy?"

Kerry sighed. "Always in meetings. Everything's hush-hush. She wants to cut a hundred jobs and our lawyer doesn't think we can stop it."

"She's always been trouble," Mum said, nodding as if to back up her own point and, despite everything, Kerry wanted to object.

Mum had been holding onto this particular grudge a long time. It all boiled down to the fish finger incident, when Izzy's mother hadn't come to the hospital. And of course, Mum remembered exactly who had and hadn't come to Dad's funeral. Those who hadn't remained blacklisted for life.

"You think I should find another job?"

Mum reeled backwards in her chair, horrified. Loyalty to the plant was like a religion in their family. "You'll sort it out." She patted Kerry's hand, her bony fingers far stronger than they looked. "You'll take care of them all. *Cailín maith.*" *Good girl.* Kerry always was the good girl.

"Enough about me. What about you, Mum? Are the new meds better?"

She snorted and waved a hand. "Too many pills, if you ask me."

"Are you sleeping better?"

"There's a man. He's always out on the street. A young lad."

Kerry tried to contain her eyeroll. The neighbours must be tired of her peering out under the net curtains, watching their every move.

"Mrs King's son? You said he was coming to visit."

Mum tutted. "You think I'm imagining things. Go and put the pie in the oven."

Kerry loved these evenings, really. Sure, they reminded her she was still in Saltreach, minding Mum, working at Dad's old company in a job her mother had proudly negotiated for her when Henry persuaded her to let him buy Dad's shares for a song. A job that had felt like a noose around her neck – ambitious graduate turned carer overnight. It was a small life, in many ways. But she had a family. Four wonderful children. A husband who let her be herself, one hundred percent. That was what it was all about. Wasn't it?

Andrew didn't expect her home on a Wednesday. He fed the kids and put the little ones to bed, and then used the free hours to watch nature documentaries or finish scouring the papers, deep-diving into the politics *du jour*. When she got home, he'd be ready to share some new fact or statistic with her, try to engage her in a discussion. But the state of the NHS and the various crises in the Middle East would have to take a backseat for the foreseeable. The mental load was just too heavy. Especially now that the sea, her one and only happy place, had been ruled unsafe for swimming.

Kerry ached to swim long, powerful strokes, feel her blood pump and her adrenalin surge, to freeze all the thoughts that made her head pound. What the bloody hell she was going to do about the takeover. Why Izzy Holt was back in Saltreach. What would happen when Mum needed full-time care. Whether she had remembered to defrost some chicken for tomorrow's dinner. And who the hell had punched Theo. Sometimes she sat at her desk thinking that her body was seizing up from concentration, from worry; that she was heading straight for a heart attack like her father. But in the water, her body felt fresh, alive.

That was life, wasn't it? Never smooth sailing, but rather a series of choppy waves to navigate, much like the fishing trawlers she watched leave before dawn on those mornings when she woke early and couldn't go back to sleep. She'd slip on a pair of joggers and sit on the end of the jetty with a coffee, feeling the water rocking beneath her, as though she might lose her balance on life at any moment. But here, in her childhood home, round the old pine table, she felt like she was moving neither backwards nor forwards. She just felt like herself.

*

On her way home, she called Clare. WhatsApp showed Clare was offline – of course she was – and Kerry imagined her sunning herself on Bondi Beach. Which was ridiculous. Clare was probably still asleep, and anyway, she lived nowhere near Bondi. She left a voice note instead. "Hi Clare, hope you're still alive. Any chance you could find time in your hectic schedule to give me a call back? Need to discuss Mum." She cursed herself for being passive aggressive, deleted the message and rerecorded. "Hi Clare, hope you're having a good week. I'd love a catch-up. Give me a buzz when you're free."

Lauren

LAUREN WAS UNPEELING HER false eyelashes when she spied the delivery driver from her bedroom window. She set them on the dresser and flew downstairs to open the door before he could knock.

"Just Kai returning my French dictionary," she called out, heading back upstairs to her room. She hadn't seen Kai lately, come to think of it. It hardly mattered. Kai was odd.

Lauren always had packages arriving. Samira and Elise believed she had an older, generous boyfriend who took her out on the weekends. Mum thought Saturday nights were spent babysitting for Mrs O'Brien, a fictitious maths teacher with two fictitious little boys. In reality, Lauren took the train to London and wandered around South Bank or Covent Garden. She'd eavesdrop on other people's conversations and then order street food, smoothing out her vowels and clipping her words in an approximation of how they spoke. Sit in a smart bar with a gin and tonic – *Tanqueray please* – and let handsome, well-dressed men flirt with her for a bit. Sometimes a kiss, or a little more, if they were really hot. Or generous. No phone numbers exchanged. These guys were purely for practice. Then she'd get a late train home and creep into her house and lie in bed and wonder how long it would actually take her to get out of this shithole.

In the first parcel was a hot pink phone cover with her name in glitter across the back. She snapped it on, admired it, and took a selfie in her mirror. The second parcel contained a sumptuous new Longchamp purse in raspberry, which she desperately hoped her mother would assume was a fake. User Steve71 was generous. The gift had been his idea. Lauren worried he'd be able to access her home address for delivery, but PeekaBoo's badly spelt privacy policy almost completely assured her all gifts would be routed through the company for complete confidentiality.

She picked up the phone and, still admiring the case, flicked into her bank account. £40 more than yesterday. Good. Then she texted Theo.

Is your eye better?

She added a black eye emoji and a pink heart.

Thanks SO much for sorting that loser for me x

A second later, her screen lit up.

Still sore

U OK?

IDK wot 2 tell Mum

Lauren sighed. She hated text-speak. She had to remember Theo was one of the youngest kids in the year, nearly a full year younger than her. She felt bad for using him, but she'd been properly scared, too. If Theo hadn't been there, who knew what might have happened? She'd been so stupid, wearing her school uniform in that one picture. She'd thought it was cute. Obviously, she'd hiked the skirt right up, opened the buttons on the shirt. She'd even plaited her hair and licked her lips, Britney Spears style. But she hadn't realised the school logo was visible. Then that pervert, User W45, saw it. Messaged her, saying he'd come visit, and bet she was even prettier in real life. She hadn't believed him. Until he'd literally shown up and hit Theo. She'd probably been even more relieved than Theo when he'd jogged off, hood yanked up like it could erase what he'd done. She'd stood there, frozen, no photo, no proof, nothing. Stupid, stupid girl.

And now Theo wanted her to go to the police. He didn't believe her when she said she had it under control, that she could handle it. Because she actually hadn't handled it, had she? She'd needed him. She needed to make sure it didn't happen again.

She logged onto the website, scanned the list of profiles, found W45. What the hell was his real name? Walter? William? Lauren shuddered. Wolf? Wolf was her dad's name. Was this guy someone's dad? She clicked *Block*. For good measure, she pressed *Report*. The link was broken.

She opened administrator settings, clicked on the *Help* section, but it just brought up an error message. She looked up *Contact Us*, but it directed her to a list of *FAQs*. The last item on the list said *Help* and linked her back to the same error message. Shit.

Money. Money fixed everything. Lauren navigated back through her account settings, clicked *Upgrade*. That kind of request always got a response. A chat window opened. How should she explain what happened? She could hardly mention school. Not that anyone seemed to give a shit, but PeekaBoo models were supposed to be over eighteen.

> User W45 ambushed me at college today. I have video evidence of him approaching the building and launching a physical assault. Please delete him from the system or I will be forced to go to the police.

She copied and pasted all his weird messages to the chatbot and hit send. A text window appeared on the screen, confirming her request had been received and her account upgrade would be dealt with within forty-eight hours. Phew.

She opened the last parcel and drew out something pink. There was a lot of lace and some fur. Shit. Steve71 wanted payback for the purse. Jesus, there was even a pair of handcuffs. What the actual fuck? How the hell did he expect her to take a selfie wearing handcuffs? She threw the outfit on the bed, repulsed. She hadn't signed up for this.

By the time she finished her GCSEs next summer, she'd have an agent and live in London, supporting herself as a model. School was so boring, Saltreach so backwards. In her new life, she'd never do shit like this. But for now, maybe she could – just once.

Mum couldn't find out. Mum was always watching. Her head swivelled like an owl every time Lauren went past. She inspected what she ate, checked her homework, snooped on her phone and in her bedroom when Lauren was at school. It was Mum's fault she'd become so secretive, so good at hiding stuff.

But Mum had secrets too. She'd been a teen model and wouldn't tell Lauren anything about it except that being dropped was the best thing that had ever happened to her. Lauren had begged to see some of her old photographs, but Mum refused. So, she'd gone searching and found a box underneath the spare bed. Her mother had been stunning. She must have lied about being dropped.

Well, Lauren wouldn't be stupid enough to get dropped. She was prepared to do whatever it took to go all the way.

Her laptop pinged. A message from W45. What the hell? The *Block* function mustn't be activated yet. Lauren leaned away from the laptop, as though he might jump out of the screen at her, and opened the message.

It was a photograph of her, lifted from the school website, in which she was receiving a certificate of achievement from the head for exemplary behaviour. Dad had sent her the same photo a few weeks earlier with a message.

> Just came across this. So proud of you. I've put some ££ in your bank account for being such a good girl.

Lauren wanted to cry. This time, alongside the school photograph, was a selfie she'd posted of herself on PeekaBoo in a thong and crop top. This time, the message read,

> Wouldn't your headmaster like to see you now, L?

Nicole

Downstairs, Nicole Bauer's phone pinged. She looked up from her laptop, irritated, took a sip of black coffee and unlocked the screen. There was a text from Kerry on the Year Ten group chat, a group Nicole tolerated as a necessary evil.

> Theo got a black eye in school but won't tell us what happened. Could any of the other kids shed light on this? Please? X

Nicole put the cup down with a bang. Coffee slopped over the sides and spilled onto the granite worktop. Who the hell did Kerry think she was, making accusations like this? So presumptuous. But that was Kerry all over. Theo probably had a football injury.

"Wolf!" she yelled in the general direction of the stairs.

No response. Was he having a wank? He probably needed it – she was keeping him at bay over the whole landscaping debacle. He'd agree eventually. But in the meantime, she didn't need to make it easy for him. "Wolf!"

After a few minutes, he appeared, pink-cheeked. "No need to shout. What's up?"

"Check this out," she said, holding out her phone. "Can you believe she has the nerve to point the finger like this?"

Wolf brought the phone closer, squinted, then extended his arm, tilting his head back at the same time. For God's sake. Nicole snatched up his glasses and handed them to him.

"Thanks," he muttered. "What is this? Who's got a nerve?"

"Kerry, obviously."

He looked at her quizzically. He would, of course. He was fond of Kerry. Fonder of her than he should be of someone who wasn't his wife. His best friend's wife, in fact. Wolf thought she had great tits. Nicole had caught him leering more than once after a few beers. That was back when they'd first moved to Saltreach, and Wolf was under the mistaken impression Kerry and Nicole would become besties like he and Andrew. But Nicole had no intention of making up a nice little foursome at the local quiz night. She'd put a stop to all that early on, after a handful of excruciating barbecues and dinner parties.

Kerry had taken it personally, obviously. But it couldn't be helped. What on earth would they have in common anyway? Kerry had no interest in fashion. Everything about Kerry – her clothes, house, even her car – screamed boring and sensible. A day out in London involved a matinee followed by tea at Pizza Express. Nicole hadn't eaten pizza in decades.

"A black eye? What happened?"

"She's accused Lauren of getting into a spat with Theo, that's what's happened!"

"No, she's asking everyone. Oliver's mum, Kai's mum, they're all on here."

"Oh, don't be naive, Wolf. She's always had an issue with Lauren. Probably because of how Theo ogles her every time he sees her. I mean, it's embarrassing."

Wolf began to tap out a reply and she could see him bite back a retort. Probably something about it being Nicole, not Lauren, that Kerry didn't like.

"For God's sake, stop," she snapped.

"You're being silly," he said eventually, but he exited the app and locked his screen. He looked owlish tonight, with his Harry Potter glasses and earnest expression. He was a good dresser and it irked her that even now she could see what had first attracted her to him. He wore a gleaming white, slim-fitting t-shirt that showed off a hint of dark chest hair. Black skinny jeans and high-tops. Thick black hair swept back off a high, unlined forehead. Stubble just long enough to be soft against her cheek if she were to kiss him. Which she wouldn't.

He'd definitely been on the bed; she could tell by the way his hair was flat at the back. No point in him pretending he was working. But she didn't want to get into a debate about Kerry.

"Fine," she said. "Maybe you're right and Kerry's overreacting. I'll have a chat with her."

"Let me know, okay? We can always see if Lauren saw anything."

"I'm telling you, she had no part in this." Nicole mopped up her spilt coffee.

"Fine," he said. "Fine. I'm going back to work."

"You do that," Nicole muttered under her breath. She put her phone on charge and made a fresh coffee. She had zero intention of contacting Kerry Langley. Nicole's daughter had absolutely nothing to do with Theo's juvenile behaviour.

Wolf

Wolf hovered on the landing outside Lauren's bedroom, knuckles raised to knock. Christ, another headache at school. Could she not just do her lessons and leave it at that? If there was ever a time he needed her to work hard, this was it. Nicole didn't get how far out of their budget a private sixth-form college was. He'd even given up his gym membership and taken up cycling with Andrew.

Lauren's door was ajar. She was chatting on the phone. Indistinct words, but even he could tell she was flirting. Giggling. No boyfriends until she was sixteen – she'd laughed at him when he said that. So had Nicole.

His phone blinked. He needed to look at the new tender request in his inbox. Needed to win it, whatever it was. He was about to turn away from Lauren's door when a lamp inside was switched on and he saw her, framed in her dressing table mirror in a yellow vest top. Christ, she was only wearing a thong on her bottom half! Thank God he hadn't gone in. He jerked away and hurried up to his office in the attic.

Had Nicole bought her that? Surely that wasn't normal for a girl her age? There were brightly coloured knickers in the wash all the time, ones with stars and love hearts. He'd just got his head around the crop tops, the bras, the tiny shorts. He'd ask Nicole about it, whenever she stopped giving him the cold shoulder.

His office was cramped. Coffee mugs littered the bedside table, the only surface that was off-screen during his Zoom meetings. A neat pile of clean clothes teetered on the end of the spare bed. He hadn't seen the point of putting them back in his own wardrobe – he could barely remember the last time he'd slept in his own bed. Too long, judging by the three Richard Osman novels on the floor.

He opened his laptop and brought up the tender request from Stonebridge, the UK's second-largest manufacturer of windows and doors. Not some pissy little start-up asking for discounted advice. Not some local company that wasn't really prepared to bring their IT system into the twenty-first century. But a huge, sophisticated, household name, coming to him, Wolf Bauer of Bauer Consulting, who worked with a bunch of freelancers he couldn't afford to put on the books and a nine-foot square office that doubled as a guest bedroom. This; this was what he needed. This could pay for private school, if he had to. He could buy his high-maintenance wife into a good mood, maybe even take her to New York – she'd been asking long enough. Or get the damn landscaping done.

He would win this tender. He had to. But he needed more information before he gave them a quote. He read on. Stonebridge was taking over Bullfinch. Kerry would be furious. They wanted all the IT systems aligned, merged, protected. Training for all the staff, those remaining as well as new hires. That was a sobering thought. Wolf knew a lot of people who worked at Bullfinch. Stonebridge was not known for keeping on loyal, trusted, expensive staff. Nor were they renowned for their safety record. There would possibly be redundancies, but hopefully no accidents. At least health and safety were not Wolf's domain. He should have no qualms about taking this on, there would be months of work in it for him. Much-needed work.

He squinted at the name at the bottom of the email. Izzy Holt. It rang a bell. Kerry had had a friend called Izzy in school, a skinny girl with Doc Martin boots and fuck-off vibes. Still, there were lots of Izzys, he supposed.

He worked on his proposal all the next day, rang two freelancers and got them on board in case of a good outcome. Then he called Pete. He'd agreed to support Pete's campaign challenging the council to clear the seaweed. Pete would help him with this.

Pete was subdued. "We're devastated," he said. "Especially Kerry. She's determined to save every single job. You know how she feels about protecting her father's legacy."

"Actually, Pete," Wolf said, "I was ringing to see if you knew anything that could help me win this contract? Nicole's got my balls in a vice-grip at home, and I really need a steady income for the next few months. What's this Izzy person like?"

A silence stretched between them. Wolf held his breath. He'd put Pete in a bind. But he had to trust that Pete would see the practical side to his request.

Eventually, Pete spoke. "Some old enemy of Kerry's from school, I believe, so you might have known her back then too. Between you and me, she's a real piece of work. But she's obsessed with going local on this, so you could use that to your advantage. I overheard her say she was using an old school friend for the IT, so if that's you, you're in."

Wolf grinned and punched the air. He thanked Pete and rang off, finished his proposal, whacked another five grand on the price, and emailed it back.

His phone blinked again. The Visa bill was in.

Kai

KAI LAID THREE SETS of cutlery on the table, swore under his breath, and put one back in the drawer. He fetched two glasses of water and took his usual seat.

"Everything okay at school, darling?" Mum asked, handing him a giant plate of chicken tikka masala.

She set a dish of homemade naan breads and raita between them and sat opposite. Her portion was half the size of his. He nodded and tore a naan in half. He wasn't giving anything away.

"I hear Theo was in some kind of accident."

That was one way of putting it. Kai dipped the naan in the raita and took a large bite to excuse himself from answering. He pointed at his mouth and made a *can't talk right now* face at her.

"Did he have a tumble in PE?"

God, he wished she'd just say it. She obviously wondered if Kai had anything to do with Theo's accident. His phone vibrated in his pocket. Again. The gossip was ridiculous. Oliver said Theo must have tried it on with Lauren – they'd been seen sneaking off after class – and she was having none of it. Lauren, unusually low-key for her, said it was an accident and everyone should leave Theo alone. Obviously, that fired up a whole new conversation on Snapchat. One that excluded Lauren.

Theo wasn't responding to anyone's messages. But then again,

Theo hadn't responded to any of Kai's texts for nearly two weeks now. Even the apologies.

"I don't think so," he said.

"What happened, sweetheart?"

Kai swallowed. "He didn't say. I didn't see." The first part was true. But Kai had seen something. He'd seen Theo slip out the side entrance at break time and face off with that guy. He'd seen Theo keep his hands in his pockets the whole time. Last term, when Saltreach Comp's reputation had taken a nosedive after a year nine put a year eight in hospital, parents had randomly started handing out self-defence advice. The hands in the pockets thing was what Theo's dad had told both Theo and Kai to do. That way, he'd explained, you'll never be goaded into throwing the first punch. Andrew Langley's hand on his shoulder had been reassuring and protective, and Kai had felt chilly and bare after he took it away.

Mum looked relieved. Did she really think he'd punch Theo in the face? If anything, Theo probably felt like punching Kai, after what had happened. She patted his hand.

"Everything okay between you two?"

No. Everything was not okay. Not since he'd kissed Theo.

"Course," he said. What on earth had he been thinking? Theo had hugged him and it had felt … well, he'd just misunderstood. He'd tried to fix it but Theo wouldn't even meet his eye. The shame and sadness and loneliness were overwhelming.

"Theo loves his football, doesn't he?"

Mum studied her food, tearing a naan, avoiding his gaze. Instantly, Kai knew where this conversation was going. The curry began to repeat on him, curdling and souring in his stomach. He turned away to put his plate by the sink.

"And I bumped into Oliver's mum earlier. Did you know he swims every morning at six? He's preparing for a national competition."

Of course he knew. Everyone knew Oliver Nowell was a bloody superstar in the pool. Kai didn't turn around. His fists balled in his pockets. "Yeah, his mum is a proper slavedriver."

"Oh," Mum said. He'd let her down. "I thought he liked it."

"Yeah. Maybe." Kai shrugged. Hopefully, she would leave it there.

"Would you like to try a sport?" Mum's voice was light, as though she were offering him a choice of puddings. "The athletics club is looking for new joiners on Saturdays, and I see kids playing basketball at the park all the time. Oliver's mum says there's even a new martial arts centre in town."

So, she'd actually discussed him with Oliver's mum. Freya Nowell was one of those annoying women who talked loudly about Waitrose and Pilates. A bit like Lauren's mother. Mum shopped exclusively at Tesco and, since Dad left, went late at night so she wouldn't have to run into anyone she knew. She must have sought Freya out specifically. Looking for advice. Kai cringed. Had she talked about him with Oliver, too? That would be beyond humiliating but she'd never know about local sports clubs otherwise. Kai imagined himself doing laps round the running track, his fat rolls spot lit under the tall lamps, bouncing and jiggling with every step, his thighs red and chafing. He reached for the door handle, scooped up his camera from the side.

"I'll think about it," he said, without meeting her eye, and left.

Andrew

Andrew checked the mileometer and sped up. The crest of the hill was in sight. Two more minutes and they'd be freewheeling down the other side. The new bike was light, responsive. Worth every penny.

"How's the new job?" Wolf asked, panting at his shoulder.

"Good," Andrew said. "Great. It's literally as far as I can go in the company. Glass ceiling officially reached. Unless they expand or do something crazy."

"That must feel good."

Andrew heard the envy in Wolf's voice. "Mate," he said, "I've been there thirty years. I could do it in my sleep. It's just a formality, to be honest."

It was more than that; he knew. He had a secure place on the board of directors, he was already getting more input into strategy, recruitment, new products. He just didn't care very much. That was the problem. They topped the hill and Saltreach opened up in front of them, right down to the water. The sea was Kerry's happy place, but he loved all of it. He stopped pedalling and let gravity do its job.

"Kerry must be delighted for you."

"Course." She *was* happy for him. She'd booked a table for tomorrow night at Juniper, where they did a mean rib-eye and an earthy

Rioja. But no doubt, after the glasses were raised, they'd be right back to discussing Bullfinch. Or rather, Izzy.

It was fine. Andrew got it. Kerry was as much a mother at work as she was at home. It was in her DNA. He'd mentioned Botswana again and, knowing she didn't like to feel railroaded, had also suggested Egypt and India. She'd liked the sound of India, and he'd stored that nugget away.

"Did you win that tender you were after?" he asked Wolf. "Has Nicole managed to spend it yet?" He chuckled to show he was only joking, but Wolf didn't laugh. "Sorry, mate," he said. "Only teasing."

Wolf still didn't reply. They pushed on, pedalling hard, Andrew's speedo telling him they were doing nineteen miles an hour, better than usual on these roads. They were back on the flat, and the evening commuters were already out in full force, forming a queue behind them, no doubt frustrated with so little opportunity to overtake on the windy road.

"It's not that," Wolf said at last. "I got the work." He made a show of pedalling faster and Andrew did the same. "But the client, well, it's Stonebridge. Mate, I'm sorry."

Wolf pulled in front and they kept tight to the ditch while the stream of traffic overtook them. It was Andrew's turn to be quiet. Stonebridge was a big operation with multiple sites. Wolf would finally have the financial security he'd craved for years. But in Kerry's eyes, he'd simply be working for the enemy. She'd be blindsided. Andrew had never fully grasped his wife's intense views on loyalty, but he instantly understood this would be a problem.

Suddenly tired, Andrew looked down to grab his water bottle. With his eyes off the road, he felt, rather than saw, the shadow of the last car come over him. There was a thunk, and the smashing sound of metal on metal, and the ground hit him hard in the shoulder.

Between You and Me

The car accelerated with a roar and a spray of gravel. Andrew lay face down in the ditch and already he knew it was bad. The pain was concentrated around his temple, his neck, his shoulder, his right arm. He knew the skin on his face was shredded, pimpled with stones, and he couldn't quite grasp what angle his body lay at.

"Lie still, mate," Wolf said. "Shit. Don't move. Ambulance, please," and he was giving their location. It must be bad, then. He'd had tumbles before, on his old bike, but he was usually up already, feeling sorry for himself, catching his breath and cursing the drivers.

Kerry

KERRY AND ELLA LOCKED eyes as Theo shoved his plate in the dishwasher, seemingly determined to chip every piece of crockery he could, before stomping out of the kitchen.

"Day three in the *Big Brother* house," Kerry murmured, "and the tension is getting to everyone." Freya Nowell had replied to her text saying Oliver thought that Lauren Bauer may have rejected Theo's advances and he'd had some kind of accident fleeing in embarrassment. If that were true, she could cut him some slack. Secretly, she was glad. Lauren Bauer would eat Theo up and spit him out. If it wasn't true, well . . . there were no other suggestions forthcoming.

Ella laughed. "What are you on about? What big brother?"

"Never mind," Kerry said. She was starving. She would have been happy to eat sausages with the kids, but Andrew had insisted he'd cook something delicious after his bike ride. She hoped he wouldn't push the safari idea again. She'd felt guilty when he'd given her a massive hug this morning and told her he was sorry she was under so much pressure at work. He only wanted to help make things easier for her. She checked the time. He'd be home any minute.

"Alby, tell me about school today," she said. "Did you learn anything interesting?"

"Yes." Alby pretended to be very serious. He picked peas off his plate with his fingers and positioned one on the end of each tine on his fork. Then he put the fork in his mouth. "I learned that I don't like chicken pie!"

"I like chicken pie," Poppy said. "I ate mine *and* Alby's."

"Wonderful," Kerry said. "How was your day, Ella?" Her phone vibrated in her pocket. She checked the screen. Unknown number.

It could be the lawyer. Morgan had warned Kerry that Stonebridge were known to play dirty. She was delving into Stonebridge's previous takeovers, uncovering what action had been taken against them in the past. She'd said that, beyond Izzy, there would be multiple layers of intimidation, paperwork, and lawyers. Izzy was only the talking head, caught in the middle without any real decision-making power. Kerry wasn't so sure.

But this was family time. She put her mobile face down on the worktop and took out the cordless vacuum cleaner, just as it rang a second time.

Ella touched her arm. "You get that if you need to," she said. "I'll run the bath for the twins."

"It's okay, love. Tell me about your day."

Theo barged back into the room and tripped over a stray schoolbag, almost knocking Poppy over as he struggled to right himself.

"For God's sake," he groaned, as Poppy began to whimper. He turned to leave.

"I beg your pardon," Kerry said. "How dare you walk off like that? Apologise to your sister. Now."

Poppy's eyes filled with tears and she held her elbow dramatically. Kerry knew it wasn't hurt, but that wasn't the point.

"Mu-um, she's *fine*!"

Poppy wailed louder and Ella led her away.

"Please, Theo! Talk to me." The landline started to ring. For God's *sake*.

"Ella! Get that, will you?" Kerry shouted over her shoulder. "Theo – is this about Lauren?"

"Mum, it's Wolf," Ella said, coming back into the room, the twins at her side.

"Take a message, will you, love? Theo …"

Ella interrupted. "Dad's in hospital."

Theo

Dad's collarbone was broken. The doctors had reset it, and said he'd have to wear a sling for a few weeks. He also had two cracked ribs. That was all they'd been told when they got to the hospital, so when they were finally allowed into the room and saw the skin torn off his face and the bandage over his eye and forehead, the twins started crying.

Mum said, "Oh my God, you could have been killed!" which made Theo want to cry too, but Ella gave him a look warning him to keep it together. She picked up Alby and held him where he wouldn't knock against Dad, so Theo did the same with Poppy. She clung to him, crying into his school jumper. He'd felt awful for barging into her earlier. He hadn't even apologised, but he could make it up to her now. He hugged her back until her crying steadied, and his own tears stopped before they could fully start.

When he dared look at Dad again, his chest tightened. Scratches ran the length of Dad's arms, red and angry against the white sheets. A small machine, like a mini stapler, was clamped around the end of one mangled finger. But there were no machines around his face or head, which must be a good sign. His eyes were closed, but hopefully he was only asleep and not unconscious or anything.

Mum said they should find a doctor and dragged them all back out to the corridor, where Wolf waited for them on a steel bench, under a sign warning patients and visitors that abuse towards staff members would not be tolerated. He was still in his bright orange cycling gear, which looked a bit silly in these surroundings. He hugged Mum. He didn't seem hurt at all.

"Hey, kiddos," Wolf said in that fake-cheery voice grownups always used with little kids. He fist-bumped the twins and grasped Theo hard on the shoulder. Theo turned away, mortified to feel tears resurfacing behind his eyes. "Your dad's going to be fine," Wolf said. "Just fine."

"What the hell happened?" Mum asked, her voice high and stringy. "Was it the new bike? Was it faulty?"

"Christ, Kerry," Wolf muttered. "For a minute there, I thought he was a goner. The car was right up our backsides."

"Was anyone else hurt?" Mum said, looking Wolf up and down, as though she could see through his clothes. "Are you all right? And the driver?"

Wolf grunted. "The car didn't even stop. I could kick myself, Kerry. I didn't even get the number plate."

"Don't worry," she said, her hands frantically smoothing Alby's hair as if to soothe herself. Alby wriggled out of reach and he and Poppy ran to the water cooler to play with the taps.

Theo felt ill. Had someone done this on purpose? "What kind of car?" he asked. Maybe he could help if he knew the car. But Wolf was disappointingly vague.

"Oh. Something dark. Black or navy," he said, his hands upturned. "Hatchback, I think. Nissan, maybe?" He turned back to Mum and Theo deflated. Wolf wasn't into cars. He drove a little electric Fiat 500. Nicole owned the BMW. "But seriously, Kerry. Who in God's name wouldn't stop? He must be a right bastard." Then he noticed the twins. "Christ, sorry about the language. I'm not myself."

"Don't worry," Mum said grimly. "They've heard worse."

The doctor arrived then and said Dad would have to stay in overnight for observation because he'd had a knock on the head and the doctor knocked on his own head and made the twins laugh. Tomorrow, Dad would come home, and they'd all have to cut up his food for him and put on his socks and pants for him and that made the twins laugh again and Theo couldn't understand why they were all laughing when Dad was covered in bandages and had a broken collarbone. He left them to talk and joke around and crept back into Dad's room again and held his good hand. It was very unfair to end up hurt when you'd done nothing wrong.

Theo silently apologised for shrugging him off the other day, for being so grumpy at home, when all Dad had actually wanted was to make sure he was okay. God, he felt so bad. He'd make it up to them all once Dad got home.

But now he couldn't tell Dad about Mitch. He'd googled Mitch a hundred different ways. Mitch, Mitch and Diana, Mitch and Andrew, Diana and Andrew. He'd put in the name of the accountancy firm, the name of the town, and the years Dad and Diana had worked there. All that had come up was Dad's LinkedIn page, newly updated to reflect his promotion. Every single thing Mitch knew about Dad was on that page. Everything. Mitch was definitely lying.

Everyone came back into the white hospital room with its gross, anti-bacterial smell and bleeping machines, and suddenly, there was no room around the bed anymore, so he went out into the corridor to see if Wolf could remember anything else about the car.

*

Wolf was sipping coffee on a bench, but Lauren and her mother had arrived, and Nicole was acting all upset, like Wolf was the one who'd been hit. Lauren gave Theo a big hug, and for a second he forgot about Dad and felt embarrassed, and a bit delighted because normally she'd never do that. Her hair smelled like apples and strawberries, and she had on a crop top. He didn't know where to put his hands because when he hugged her, they were right on her skin and she felt warm and soft, and he wasn't sure he was supposed to do that, so he pulled away even though he didn't actually want to at all.

"Is your dad all right?" she asked.

"He's got a broken collarbone and he's got all these bandages and cuts on his face and arms."

"Oh. Shit."

"Yeah. We'll have to help him eat and get dressed and all that, but he's coming home tomorrow. If his head's okay."

"Oh, that's good then," Lauren said. She checked over her shoulder where her mum was making a fuss over Wolf. "Hey," she said, touching Theo's bruised eyebrow with her pinkie. "I'm sorry about the other day."

Her breath was sweet on his cheek. "It's fine," he said, trying not to flinch. "Seriously. Forget about it. As long as he's gone."

Lauren bit her lip.

"He's gone, isn't he?"

She pulled him further away from her parents. "I'm sure he won't come back to the school again. You really scared him."

That was hardly true. He'd barely spoken to the guy. Lauren might be older, but for once, he thought *he* might be more mature.

"Seriously, Lauren," he said. "You need to go out with normal guys. Guys *our* age."

"Oh, relax. It had its benefits. See?" She took a small pink purse out of her handbag and waved it at him. He'd taken a punch in the face for a purse. Kept her secret and worried Mum and Dad for nothing.

"What did you have to do to get that?" It came out sharply, but he didn't care.

"Just look pretty," she said, pouting. But she shifted uncomfortably and he knew she wanted to change the conversation. "Hey, there's a Costa. I'll get you a frappé." She put her handbag back on her shoulder and took Theo's hand in hers. "Seriously, you don't need to worry about me."

But Theo did worry. He'd overheard a couple of sixth formers talking about photographs of Lauren and they'd been pretty into it. Lauren might think she was using these guys for gifts. But what if it was the other way round?

He waited for her to turn the corner before opening her socials. There she was on TikTok, doing a funny dance with Elise and Samira, wearing baggy jeans and a black t-shirt that said "MEOW" on it, underscored by a pair of whiskers. She was on Snapchat in an oversized Gymshark hoodie, applying mascara. On Insta, wearing Nike Pros and a yellow crop top in some kind of graffiti tunnel with the hashtag #banksyiscool. Her photos were basically normal. Maybe the sixth-formers had been discussing a different Lauren. Or were there other photos?

Mitch24652 requested to follow you.

Shit. Mitch was actually going to pursue this thing. He was serious. Damn. Theo clicked on his avatar – a photo of the Saltreach promenade, a silver path trailing across the water, the ice cream kiosk silhouetted to one side in the moonlight, beach huts in the distance behind him. There was no actual photo of Mitch. He followed nobody, posted no videos, had zero followers, and was tagged by nobody. This was a totally brand-new, set-up-for-purpose account, to contact Theo without revealing *anything* about himself.

It was weird. Nothing about it said, *Hey, I'm your friendly older brother. See, I have a life and a job and friends and hobbies, and you have nothing to be afraid of. I am completely normal.*

Theo's thumb hovered over the delete button. Mitch was clearly a weirdo. A stalker. He could even be a paedophile.

Or else he was desperate. Protecting himself. What had he said – *I've never had a dad.* No; if, just *if*, Mitch was telling the truth, then Theo was the lucky one. He had a dad. Not just any old dad, but the very best dad there was. He could afford to be the bigger person here. To find out more. To give Mitch a chance. And if things got out of control, then he'd get help.

He tapped the blue button to accept the friend request.

Instantly, as though Mitch was staring at his own phone at precisely the same time, a message popped up.

> Hey man. Thanks for meeting me. I know this is a lot to take in. I really want to see you again. Here's my number. Stay in touch, little bro.

Kai

Kai punched out a text.

Want to meet at the park? I'll bring a football?

Kai didn't even want to play football. Doing PE at school had become a nightmare. Getting changed in front of everyone was the worst. He put his hand inside his t-shirt and felt his belly. He could grab a handful and squish it. Disgusting. A layer of fat was building on his side, where the skin sagged back on itself. He could fit a finger inside the overhang.

He would do anything to hang out with Theo again. But Theo was impossible to get close to now. Lauren Bauer was always hanging out with him, draped over him like a scarf, touching him proprietarily. Lauren and her gaggle of silly friends: stuck-up Samira, who still chewed the ends of her long hair like a little kid, and Elise, who clearly felt her prettiness outweighed her stupidity. Kai had actually heard her ask the science teacher whether the periodic table could be used to figure out when her period was due. Kai couldn't see how Theo even tolerated them for Lauren's sake. At least Lauren was clever. If only she wasn't such a bitch.

Maybe he should try a different approach. He sent a second text.

Or GTA? You online?

The two ticks stayed stubbornly grey. Theo mustn't even open his texts anymore.

Kai turned on the PlayStation. He could check if Theo was online and try to join the game anyway. He opened a packet of chocolate Hobnobs from his bedside table.

An hour later, there was still no reply.

Fed up and disappointed, Kai sent a new text. Something he would have preferred to discuss in person. But Theo wouldn't answer his calls and Kai didn't think this should wait.

Oliver says there are pictures of Lauren online.

Like, X-rated ones.

Kerry

KERRY TURNED LEFT INTO the industrial estate and immediately met red construction lights. Damn. She should be working from home today in case Andrew needed her. She'd left him on the sofa surrounded by papers, the remote, his phone, painkillers, and a full cafetière, promising she'd be an hour; two, tops. There was just so much to do. Too much. She closed her eyes, counted to ten, breathing from her abdomen, feeling no calmer when she reopened them. She picked up her phone. It wasn't as if she was actually driving.

"Hi, stranger." She deleted the voicenote and tried again. "Hi, Clare. I know you're up to your eyes, but I need a bit of a dig-out. Work's intense and minding Mum is taking its toll. Even the kids are having to pitch in. Any chance you could come home for a bit?"

A young man leaned against a low wall next to her car. Not one of the construction workers. A thatch of brown hair fell awkwardly over one eye as though reminding him to go to the barbers. She'd seen him somewhere before, she was sure of it. His hands were stuffed in his pockets, shoulders hunched, and he was scuffing the pavement with the toe of his shoe. As Kerry watched, he pulled out a phone, squinted at the screen and shoved it back in his pocket without texting or making a call. Kerry laughed softly. *We've all been there, mate. Getting stood up sucks.*

It was a weird place for a date. Andrew's building was right behind him, its shiny glass-and-chrome exterior exuding the transparency modern businesses pretended to strive for. On either side were similar buildings: a software company, a medical device supplier, a couple of car dealerships.

The young man was striding away from her now, clearly having given up on his meeting. The way he bounced on the balls of his feet was oddly familiar. Theo walked like that. She shrugged. Lots of boys did.

The lights turned green, and Kerry glanced up at Andrew's floor before accelerating past the roadworks. Sometimes she could see him up there, sitting on the main floor with his team, even though he had his own office. He said they had a laugh together, shared the coffee run, took turns bringing in biscuits. He'd earned himself the nickname Mary Berry because his were homemade. But he wouldn't be able to bake for a while. She would bring him home something from Gail's. A Danish, maybe. He'd like that.

*

Wolf was waiting for her in the lobby. "How's the patient?" he asked.

"Did you come all the way down here to ask me that? You are good."

"Actually, I wanted a word," Wolf said. "With you. Any chance we could go to your office?"

"Sounds serious," she said. "Did they make you wear a lanyard just to see me? God. They've already replaced our nice blue ones with their awful orange ones."

Wolf fidgeted with the ribbon hanging from his neck with one hand, the other on the white plastic laminated square at the base. If she wasn't mistaken, he was hiding something. She tugged it free and watched his face fall in the same way Alby's did whenever she discovered his iPad hidden under his pillow. "This says *Contractor*." The words jumbled in her head but the panic in Wolf's eyes told her all she needed to know. "You're working for Stonebridge?"

"I wanted to tell you at the weekend," Wolf said, taking the lanyard back, as though she'd tightened it around his neck like a noose. "But after the accident, it didn't seem fair to dump it on you like that. I told Andrew, though, on our bike ride."

It was funny, she thought, that this last bit stung the most.

"Andrew knows?"

"He probably doesn't even remember. It happened right before he was hit."

Had Andrew lost concentration on his cycling and veered into the path of a car because of this? He would have known that this would matter to her. It should matter to him too.

"You're working for Stonebridge?" she said again, trying to stay on point.

"Izzy offered me a contract," he said. "I needed the work."

It felt like a personal move. Izzy rubbing salt in the wound. Izzy, who had barely tolerated Wolf at school just because Kerry was fond of him, had now put him firmly on *her* team.

"Right." What else was there to say? Andrew would tell her to rise above it. And she had a meeting to get to. "I've got to go. Congratulations."

*

Two hours later, she watched relief inch over Keith Dwyer's face as he stood to leave her office. When he opened the door, she peered through the crack and saw that she'd finally made it through all the people who'd queued outside her office. They'd huddled in the corridor, talking in hushed voices like they were in church. They all had the same questions and Kerry wished she could address them together and have it over and done with in five minutes. *Yes, Stonebridge were a shower of bastards; yes, she was fighting tooth and nail for them; no, she didn't know exactly what would happen next, but she would not let them down.*

But they each deserved the privacy of a quiet chat, a little reassurance, as much as she could give right now. She popped two paracetamol from the pack in her desk drawer and swallowed them with a gulp of cold tea. This headache was worse than usual. Hardly surprising.

With ironic timing, a reminder beeped on her phone – to book a doctor's appointment. She'd been putting it off for months. The headaches were only part of it. The tightness in her chest was another. There wasn't time. For goodness sake, it was Monday again already. Where had the weekend even gone? It had been a low-key affair, everyone tripping over themselves to help Andrew to his armchair or to bring him tea. Theo had watched football next to Andrew, the volume high enough to limit any of her attempts to ask more questions about his eye. She'd watched his match on Saturday, walked him home, bought him an ice cream. Good cop had always worked for Andrew, but Theo merely deflected any of Kerry's probing questions with a series of grunts.

Let him have his privacy, she'd told herself. He was a smart kid. He could handle a falling out with his friend, a brush off from a girl. *Let her figure out how to cope with work* and *this accident. Let her focus on staying strong, on keeping it together.* At least she'd managed a swim early yesterday morning before anyone else was awake, the pool a poor substitute for the sea.

She deleted the reminder from her phone. She needed more coffee. Actually, she needed a litre of water or, at the very least, a herbal tea. But no. Coffee. Because screw logic. Because tension coiled under her skin, and at least coffee knew how to fight back. As she walked, she tuned out the noises beyond the walls of the corridor, the hurried footsteps as people scampered past, the low urgent voices, the tension seeping through the air, infesting the workplace. In the lobby, a crowd huddled around the reception desk. In normal times, the sight of her would have sent them scurrying back to their desks. But these weren't normal times. Kerry wanted to pretend she hadn't seen them, to just slide on past and make her coffee. But she couldn't. Paula, the receptionist, was crying.

"What's going on?"

"Izzy fired me."

Fucking fucks. Izzy had really crossed a line now. Kerry seethed inwardly. Hiring and firing was *her* territory. Disciplinary meetings, wages, bonuses, probation, promotion, pensions – Kerry did *all* of it. Not even Henry would have fired a staff member without her say so. And never, ever, in front of her colleagues.

"Don't go anywhere," she said.

*

Izzy was hosting a meeting in Henry's office. It was Izzy's office now, Kerry supposed. She'd already installed several plants around the room and some headache-inducing spot art on the wall behind the desk. Had Izzy actually coughed up for an original Damien Hirst? It looked more like something you'd have to analyse at the opticians.

It was also cleaner than Kerry had ever seen it, giving it the impression of having doubled in size. By now, it was clear that Henry had taken a payoff big enough to simply vanish from the business, no questions asked, and was probably sunning himself in Marbella already.

Seated opposite the giant desk were two men Kerry didn't recognise – and Wolf. She could have it out with Izzy in front of them, let them all see what Izzy was really like behind the immaculate façade, but for the sake of her own credibility, she wouldn't. Besides, Wolf would be mortified. She settled for opening the door fully and standing in the frame until Izzy lost her train of thought and trailed off. It took an impressively long time.

"Izzy. A word?"

Izzy looked annoyed. Today she was dressed in navy wide-legged trousers and a silk shirt that must have cost a fortune. Not a centimetre of skin showed between wrist and neck. Izzy knew how to keep their eyes on hers.

"I'm in a meeting," she said, indicating the men, as if Kerry were stupid.

"It's urgent." Kerry resisted the urge to put her hands on her hips. Instead, she slid one hand into a pocket and leaned, ever so casually, against the door frame, hoping it was crystal clear she wouldn't be fobbed off. One of the men coughed quietly. Wolf turned away, no doubt embarrassed on her behalf.

Izzy apologised to the men and followed as Kerry marched to her own office. For the first time in her career, she wished she'd taken more care over it. It was functional, painted magnolia with a chevron-patterned carpet in various shades of brown. The walls were lined with locked metal filing cabinets, and in the centre stood a desk her father had chosen surely thirty years ago. Kerry leaned against it, giving Izzy no choice but to stand too. "You fired Paula."

"Who?" Izzy closed the door.

"Christ, Izzy, how many people did you fire?"

Izzy stood tall, one hand resting on the door handle. "I fired one exceptionally obtuse receptionist who has been late every day for the past fortnight. Really, Kerry. How do you let them get away with it? It's ridiculous. I needed to set the tone for the other staff. They're sloppy."

"You fired a twenty-four-year-old single mum with a sick baby!" Kerry yelled, no longer caring about her credibility. "Paula's been struggling to settle her at crèche, a place *no* sick child should have to be, while she gets over a chest infection. She asked me for leniency, and she's been making up the time with a shorter lunch break – even though I didn't ask her to. Not only that, but Paula is a very clever marketing graduate who is in line for promotion. Or at least she was, until Stonebridge sent you here to fuck everything up."

Izzy faltered. She looked around the office, clearly buying time, seeking ammunition. Her eyes landed on a photograph of Kerry's family. All four children sat astride bikes, eating ice creams, bookended by Andrew and Kerry on either side. It was a happy photograph, from their last camping holiday in France. Kerry wanted to turn it over, to stop Izzy getting this sneak preview into her family, her private life.

Izzy opened her mouth to speak, but Kerry beat her to it.

"I am the HR director here and I make those decisions. Despite what Stonebridge seems to think, this is a very successful company. You don't get to come in here and pretend it's a failing business that needs you to turn it around. We progress our young people through the ranks and give them every opportunity to succeed. At work *and* at home. You can piss around with the IT systems, but the people are *my* responsibility. Is that understood?"

A tangible silence formed in the air, stretching beyond her office, hinting at tilted heads and finger-shushing along the corridor. Kerry's blood pulsed in her veins. She felt as clear and sharp as she did pushing through the waves of the English Channel on a crisp February morning.

Izzy didn't reply. Maybe she didn't even care about the receptionist. She picked up the photograph and ran a finger over the children's faces.

"They all look like you," she said, pausing on Ella. "Remember us at that age?"

"I'm reinstating Paula's job," Kerry said, itching to snatch the photograph away.

"Fine." Izzy put the picture down and turned to face her. "More significant, however, is your lack of progress. It's been a week. How many redundancies have you secured?"

The unyielding wood of the desk bit into the flesh of Kerry's thighs. "None."

Izzy smoothed the front of her blouse and folded her hands, the epitome of calm. But Kerry saw her jaw clench, the vein at her temple throb. Just like when she was a teenager and her mother had left the fridge empty.

"I instructed you to …"

"I'm not sure what your actual remit is here, Izzy. But I do know what mine is. It's to protect the people who work here. That's never going to change."

"I must say," Izzy said, the vein pulsing faster, her fingers rubbing against each other as if willing herself not to form fists, "it's the perfect job for you."

Adrenalin powered through Kerry's chest. Here it was, finally. The crux of it all. She could feel it.

"HR?" she asked.

"Martyrdom." Izzy spat out the word as though it were poisonous. "The high road. Your favourite place. It must be *wonderful* to be perfect. Saint Kerry."

Kerry reeled, unbalanced, gripped her desk tighter, uncrossed and recrossed her legs. Where on earth was this coming from? Saint Kerry? Never, not even in the midst of a teenage spat, had Izzy ever shown this kind of poison. She'd have been entitled to have a chip on her shoulder back then. Kerry was the adored eldest daughter of a loving couple, her photographs and certificates in pride of place on the mantelpiece. She always had a new winter coat, took swimming and piano lessons, and was taken to the pantomime every Christmas. Izzy's coat came from the Salvation Army shop, and even though she was the fastest kid Kerry had ever seen run, she'd never had the right trainers to make the cross-country team.

Was this her comeuppance? Izzy coming home to pull the rug from beneath her, to even the score, taking a hundred families with her? Hadn't Kerry already paid the price for her coddled upbringing by remaining chained to her childhood by the umbilical cord which moored her in Saltreach?

"I beg your pardon?"

"I need numbers," Izzy said, reaching for the door. "Stonebridge want an update."

"I told you," Kerry said, her voice rising now, shrill and girlish. *Wait,* she wanted to say, *tell me more. Tell me everything*. But it was the wrong time, the wrong place. She needed to be professional. "I'm not taking that offer to anyone. I'm working with legal."

Izzy's shoulders sagged and rounded, exhausted by their stalemate. She sighed. "I'm caught between a rock and a hard place here, Kerry. Stonebridge know what they want and, unless we can give them a very definite reason otherwise, they're going to get it."

She closed the door quietly behind her and Kerry dropped into her chair. Had she heard right? Had Izzy said *we*?

Kerry

Kerry sat at her desk, gazing through the window, listening to the lawyer's tinny voice on the other end of the line and replaying her conversation with Izzy. *Martyr.*

"Play the game, Kerry," Morgan said. "We've a mountain of paperwork to get through. We're researching every takeover Stonebridge has ever made. I've spoken to four ex-MDs who have alluded to, but not specifically accused them of, intimidation. We know others, like Paula, have been fired for no reason except to save on redundancy payments. Question marks over bank accounts and taxes, but that's not what we need right now. All you can do is slow things down. Go back to Izzy with a better redundancy package. She'll have to take it to Head Office – it'll buy us more time."

"She said *we*, Morgan. She said Stonebridge would get what they wanted unless *we* stopped them."

"I thought you didn't trust this woman?" Morgan sounded irritated. "Kerry, this is a pretty hostile takeover, and Stonebridge are nasty. You need to let us handle it."

Kerry thanked her and put down the phone. She felt flat now, tired, the adrenaline from earlier having seeped away after her confrontation with Izzy. The certificates on her office wall seemed to come from another era and she could barely remember the ambitious young woman who had earned them. She needed to get back to Andrew; she'd been gone far too long. As she left the building, sunlight blinded her, and she grasped at a pillar until the world steadied around her.

The industrial park hummed with activity – the builders' providers, tilers, the carpet company, the fireplace shop. People just wanted a comfortable home. Doors, floors, bathrooms. It wasn't rocket science. Saltreach mightn't be thriving, but there was still a sizeable population, and Bullfinch had never been short of business. Why on earth would Stonebridge want to destroy that?

In the centre of the car park was Ricardo's coffee van. Ricardo was as busy as ever, since most of the buildings around here only had instant coffee, no doubt on purpose in case the staff spent too long sipping lattes in the canteen and gossiping.

Back at the beginning, Kerry had regularly been sent out to the van for cappuccinos and croissants for the directors' morning meetings, the queue already snaking around the corner if she'd missed the early bus. Andrew had often been there – not that she knew his name then – lost in a world of his own. Tall, lanky really, a bit bony, as if he still had some filling out to do, even though he must have been nearly thirty, which had seemed ancient to twenty-three-year-old Kerry at the time.

He'd frown if a colleague came along, wanting to discuss year-end accounts or some such. Kerry used to watch him in fascination when he was alone – he'd direct his face towards whatever meagre sliver of sunshine reached down between the factories and warehouses. Occasionally, he'd hum, and she'd lean in to listen.

But it was his aura of calm that had pulled her in. She yearned for it. Peace radiated from him like sunbeams; she wanted to be caught in the rays. She'd never seen someone so entirely comfortable in their own skin. Her skin had felt wrong since her father died, as though it had been put through the washing machine at sixty and no longer quite fit.

One day, he said *hi*, made a comment about the weather, his voice a rich and velvety baritone. A week later, she was rushing, red-faced and awkward in her cheap, ill-fitting suit and uncomfortable heels, and he let her join the queue in front of him, right near the top, ignoring the groans from behind.

One morning, she'd asked him what he was humming.

"Hmm? Oh, Elton John, I think."

That was right. She could hear the lyrics then. 'The way you look tonight'. She'd found herself wondering if he danced to that with his wife, and the thought had caught her off guard.

"You know what?" he'd said, head tilted to one side.

"What?"

"Every Sunday morning, I have coffee at this place in town. The Hungry Giraffe. They serve the very best coffee. And pancakes, with bacon, drizzled with syrup."

She'd nodded, unsure if a reply was required.

"Why don't you meet me there this Sunday? At eleven."

Then Ricardo had given him his order, and he'd left with a wink. Dazed, Kerry had waited for the four cappuccinos. She didn't even know his name.

But she knew she would go, because when she spoke to him, the world faded out, and she was no longer aware of the ugly buildings, the impatient executives in their suits, the lingering grief that pinched her heart, and the cold wind that blew her skirt. She felt bathed in that one stream of sunlight and wanted to feel it again.

She'd heard Elton John's voice in her head for the rest of the day.

Kerry

"Are you all right by yourself for another hour?" Guilt bit at her. It was half three already. The twins were at a friend's for tea. "Ella and Theo will be in shortly."

"I'm absolutely fine," Andrew said. "There's a fascinating documentary on farming. When I get back to cooking, fancy going veggie for a while?"

"Sure," she said. "Whatever you like." Phew. She reassured herself that he never had the house to himself. That she'd cancelled her last meeting. "I need to ask Mum something."

*

She let herself in, calling out so as not to startle her. Mum was sitting in her usual chair. The TV and radio were off, and there were no books or magazines around. Marta would have left over an hour ago. Had she just been … sitting, all this time?

"Were you asleep?" she asked. Hopefully she hadn't forgotten how to work the TV or make herself a cup of tea.

"Of course not," Mum said. "I was on the phone to Clare." She pulled the iPad from under a cushion, and Kerry let out a breath. Clare hadn't returned *her* calls, but at least she was in touch with Mum. She needed to stop worrying. About everything.

She opened Mum's fridge and slid a lamb tagine onto the middle shelf. The fridge was spotless, well-stocked, the bins emptied, and the worktops shining. Marta was the best carer ever.

Uncharacteristically, she'd bought a bottle of Pinot Grigio and a tub of Pringles at the Asda by the roundabout. She was probably at the wrong stage of life to begin day-drinking, but she felt shaky after her altercation with Izzy. One drink wouldn't do any harm. It might help her relax. She poured her mother a small glass and herself a larger one.

"What's all this for?" Mum raised her glass in cheers and took a sip.

Kerry opened the Pringles and crammed a handful into her mouth until she felt that satisfying, salty dopamine hit. Then she took a long glug of her cool, crisp wine.

"Feel better, *alanna*?" Mum grinned at her. *Sweetheart*. Like she was still a little kid, but she didn't mind. Today, she was glad to be mothered.

Early-stage dementia, assuming that was what it must be, stung every day. But for now, it was manageable. Mum was still living at home, after all. But the day would come when she'd need round-the-clock care, and Kerry would do everything in her power not to put Mum in a home and watch her fade away a little more each day, muted by a cocktail of sedatives, beige surroundings, and incontinence pads.

"I do," she said, putting the lid back on the tub and the bottle in the fridge. "It's been a crazy few days."

"I can't find the remote control. *Coronation Street* is on later."

It could be fixed in a moment. She dug about under the sofa seat and found it in seconds. Mum laughed and clapped her hands.

"What's going on with you?" Mum asked, taking another sip of wine. Kerry made a mental note not to leave the bottle behind when she left.

"Someone knocked Andrew off his bike with their car and drove off." She'd already told Mum this on Saturday when she'd made a speedier visit than usual. She counted off the problems on her fingers. "Theo has a black eye. I need to save a hundred jobs at work."

"That man," her mother said. "He's been back again. I don't know what he wants." She pointed at the net curtains.

"Mrs King's son?"

"Was it him?"

"Who hit Andrew with his car?" Kerry laughed. "I don't think so, Mum."

"Andrew spoke to him." Mum was suddenly intensely serious.

"What?" Moments like this always threw her. Andrew called in twice a week, and Ella and Theo popped in for an afternoon each. She came on Wednesdays and, when she could, Mondays. On Sundays, Mum came to them. Nobody had mentioned a man. "Why would Andrew be talking to Mrs King's son?"

Her mother banged her fist on the table, and her wine jumped in the glass. "*Not* Mrs King's son. Andrew knows. Ask him." She fluttered her hands, ending the conversation.

This was peculiar. Mum often got confused, but never angry. She changed the subject. "How's Clare?"

"On a new documentary." Mum nibbled on the Pringles. "In the Northern Territory. Says she won't be in touch for a while."

"That's convenient," she muttered.

"Don't be like that, *alanna*," she tutted. "Clare isn't as lucky as you. Her job is all she has. And the documentary is about *cockroaches*!" She made a horrified face, and Kerry felt guilty for laughing.

"Her job is all she *wants*," Kerry corrected. "Not everyone is cut out for family life."

"If only she'd married that chap from the bank," Mum said wistfully. "She could have had a house full of children like you."

Kerry mopped up broken Pringles with her thumb and tipped them into her empty wine glass. "Mum," she said, giving the table a final wipe. "Do you think I'm a martyr?"

Mum grasped her hand with bony fingers. "Why?"

Unexpected tears burned behind Kerry's eyes. She couldn't be upset about this. It was ridiculous. She was being stupid. A good night's sleep would sort her out. But deep inside, the fourteen-year-old schoolgirl, the twenty-two-year-old daughter at her father's funeral, and the forty-six-year-old HR director she was now, just needed … something. Reassurance, or honesty; she wasn't sure.

"I just wondered." It sounded pathetic.

"Sounds like someone's upset you, love."

"But is it true?"

"Sweetheart, are you going to let someone call you silly names because you try your best to do the right thing? Because you take care of your family and your colleagues and stand up for what you believe in?"

A sense of déjà vu crept over Kerry. Wasn't this the lecture her mother had always given her as a child? *Hold your head up and be proud,* alanna. *You're a good girl. Never let anyone tell you otherwise.*

"It was Izzy, wasn't it?"

"How on earth did you know that?"

"Barbara Holt never forgave me for taking Izzy to the hospital that day. *She* called *me* a martyr for taking care of that poor little girl while she was down the pub, drinking. Like she always was."

Kerry

Kerry punched two tablets from the foil wrapper and handed them to Andrew with a glass of water. She smoothed the duvet cover and drew the curtains. Ella's bedroom was spotless, as always. Since Ella had refused point-blank to share a bed with Kerry, she was reluctantly in the bottom bunk below Alby, and Poppy was in Kerry's room. Just until Dad was better and back in his own bed, Kerry had warned Poppy, who'd gleefully filled the king-sized bed with teddies and stacked a pile of *Mr Men* books on the bedside table. Secretly, Kerry loved it. Poppy might be a hot water bottle that she didn't need, but she didn't wriggle or snore, and spending the night curled up together went some way to assuage Kerry's guilt that she never managed to spend enough time with her littlest daughter during the day. In fact, she was sleeping better than ever, though that was more likely something to do with crawling into bed with exhaustion after midnight each night.

Andrew probably wasn't sleeping nearly as well. He was propped up awkwardly on at least four pillows, the sling still on, his fingers obediently higher than his elbow, as per the doctor's advice.

"Have you seen a strange man hanging round Mum's?" she asked.

Andrew could hardly keep his eyes open. Kerry felt bad she'd been so late home. The rest of the evening had disappeared in the general chaos of making dinner, driving Ella to hockey practice, picking up the twins, doing laundry, and trying to answer a hundred unexpected questions from Theo about when she and Andrew had met and gotten married, which he said was for a personal development project at school. At least he was talking to her and being civil. She would take the wins where she could. She'd asked him about Lauren and got the less-than-satisfactory answer, "Relax, Mum, she's just a friend."

"Mum says you were speaking to a man hanging around her house. She's worried about him."

"Yeah. A young guy." Andrew yawned. "He said he was thinking of buying number twenty-four."

"And?"

"And what? He wanted to know about the area, the neighbours, the local pub, the bus service. You know, normal things."

Kerry chewed a hangnail. Who was this guy? And why was he hanging around?

"The police called while you were out," Andrew said. Clearly, there was nothing more to say about the lurker. She would keep an eye out for him herself.

"Any news?"

Silly question. If there was news, he'd have told her as soon as she came home. "They've managed to get hold of four CCTV videos, mostly from the big houses on the hill, the ones with the electric gates. No sign of a dark Nissan anywhere. They've set up boards around the area requesting information and put it on all the socials. Theo and Ella have already shared the hell out of it."

"They'll get him," Kerry said, patting his hand.

"Unless someone comes forward with information, they'll shut the case soon enough," Andrew said with a one-shoulder shrug. "Oh, and the bike shop rang to say my bike is a write-off. Alby thought it was a ride-off."

"Aw, I'm sorry." She kissed his cheek. "Your brand-new bike."

"These things happen, love," he said, pragmatic as always. "What sort of person would lose their licence over a minor accident? They probably didn't even realise. At least it was insured, thanks to you." He blew her a kiss.

Kerry bit her tongue. What sort of person didn't realise they'd knocked a grown man off his bike? She had plenty of words to describe that particular kind of prick. But Andrew was being predictably brilliant. Hadn't complained once. Signed off on full pay, thank God, although he'd already asked where his laptop was. She'd hidden it in the airing cupboard next to her secret stash of Green & Black's chocolate.

"Okay," she said, kissing him on the forehead. "Have a good sleep. Yell if you need anything. I'll leave the door open."

"You're the best," he said, switching off the bedside lamp. "An absolute saint."

Theo

"Take off your football boots," Mum called from the lounge, as she did every single time Theo returned from training.

Theo held up the boots as proof and tiptoed past them in his socks. Mum and Dad were watching the news. The twins would be in bed already, and Ella was nowhere to be seen. Good. He could ask Dad about Diana. Mum hadn't told him anything he didn't know already, and the internet had thrown up no information on Mitch. Obediently, he put his boots in the box outside the back door, too smelly to be allowed inside, stripped to his pants in the kitchen, fed his training kit into the washing machine, popped in a tablet, and put on the quick cycle. Mum refused to wash his kit anymore, ever since he'd left it a full week on his bedroom floor and complained that it wasn't ready for his match the following Saturday. He'd had to start the match covered in mud. The coach had not been pleased.

As he passed back through the lounge to head up for a shower, Mum opened a packet of Hobnobs. That was good. For once, they weren't talking about Stonebridge. They sipped their tea and dunked their biscuits and shook their heads at the atrocities on the news, just like they used to before everything started going wrong. Except Dad was pale, the shadows from the lamp warping his bruises, disfiguring him further.

He speed-showered and was back downstairs in less than six minutes, his questions ready, casual, curious. Mum's space was empty. She must have gone to bed early. Even better. He planned to say his career coach at school had suggested he ask his parents for inspiration about how they'd chosen their careers, what steps they'd taken. That should get Dad talking.

"Can I ask you something?" he asked, taking a biscuit from the plate on the coffee table, perching on the edge of the sofa. Dad folded his newspaper. There was a huge bandage by his neck, sticking out from under the collar of his shirt, and Theo tried not to look at it. He took a deep breath.

"Fucking fucks," he heard from the kitchen.

They stared at each other for a moment. Dad jerked a thumb towards the kitchen, indicating Theo should go and see what was going on.

Theo peered through the glass double doors into the kitchen. Mum was kneeling on the floor, surrounded by foam and large, soaked towels. She was crying. Shit. Mum never cried. Well, not until recently.

"What happened?" he asked. Mum jumped up and pressed a wet towel to her face.

"Has the washing machine leaked?" He panicked. Had he not shut the door properly? Put it on the wrong setting?

"Get more towels," Mum said. "For God's sake, Theo, what did you do?"

Theo grabbed a couple of tea towels from the oven door and spread them on the foam, damping it down a bit. There wasn't much water, just suds oozing from the door like a bubble bath. Mum stood, the front of her blue jeans stained navy, and opened the bin. She lifted the empty Hobnobs packet and then a silver foil pouch. "Theo!"

He'd put in a dishwasher tablet.

"The boxes are next to each other," he said. He sounded stupid. "I was rushing …"

"Get the mop," she said. She jabbed a finger at the dials of the machine. "Stop, for God's sake, STOP."

Theo grabbed the mop from the utility and tiptoed back into the kitchen, suds foaming between his bare toes. Mum leaned on the worktop, her head hanging down and her hair covering her face. Her shoulders shook. The washing machine was finally silent. Theo leaned the mop against the counter and gently wrapped his arms around her. He was taller than her now, only by an inch or so, and today she seemed even smaller than usual and, for some reason, older. She shrugged him off and wiped her face with her sleeve.

"Sorry, love," she said, taking a deep breath. "It's all a bit much at the moment."

"I'll clean it up," he promised, his face hot. He'd made Mum cry. Apart from at the hospital, Mum hadn't ever cried in front of him. He kicked himself for being so stupid.

"I'm just tired, love," she said, patting his arm. "You tidy up here and I'll go to bed."

"Okay," he said. "I'll bring Dad up."

She nodded and he heard her tell Dad she was off to bed.

Theo wiped the floor with the towels and mopped up as best he could. Dad hobbled in and started poking around in the cupboard for his pills.

"Rinse and spin," he said, pointing at the machine. "No more detergent."

Theo spun the dial to the right place and turned the machine back on, crossing his fingers. "Thanks."

But Dad didn't smile the way he usually would, if Theo spilled a cup of tea or dragged in mud on his shoes; the kind of *I won't tell your mother* conspiratorial grin, the good cop vibes. Theo felt even worse than he had before. "I'll help you upstairs," he said. Dad nodded and pushed a glass of water across the counter for Theo to carry. They took the stairs slowly, and when they got to Ella's room, he helped Dad unbutton his shirt.

"Did you always want to be an accountant?" he blurted out, hanging the shirt on the back of Ella's desk chair. But Dad grasped his elbow hard. Theo winced and tried not to pull away.

"Don't pick something so utterly *boring* to do with your life," Dad said. "You're a smart kid. You can do *whatever* you want. There's a whole world out there."

Wow. He hadn't expected that. Did Dad actually hate his job? That was a depressing thought. And now, it didn't seem right to get the conversation back on track. *When you were training for the career you hate, did you get someone called Diana pregnant?* No, that would be a bit thoughtless. He'd have to try another way.

Dad patted him on the shoulder and said he didn't need any more help. "Run down and hang your kit up to dry," he said, and there was that conspiratorial wink that made Theo feel both better and worse at the same time. "And put in the right powder next time."

Theo

"Would you recognise him if you saw him again?" Lauren asked Theo, as they joined the back of the queue in the school dinner hall.

She was chewing the end of a pen, a very un-Lauren thing to do. Everything Lauren had was stylish, new, pretty. Lauren used coloured gel pens, not chewed Bic biros. That was more Theo's style.

"Maybe."

"What did he look like? Tracksuit, we know that. You said he had an earring? A beard?" She leaned a tiny notebook against his shoulder and scribbled in it.

"Why?" Theo asked. "I thought it was over."

"It is. I was just curious. If I *did* report him, and the police asked you to ID him, would you be able?"

"The police?" Theo said too loudly. Some of the kids in the cafeteria sniggered.

"Ssh!" She pulled him out of the lunch queue and marched him to an empty classroom. He wasn't buying lunch anyway. He had a soggy cheese sandwich in his bag that he'd made last night. And Lauren barely ever ate. She smelled gorgeous, her hair draped over her shoulder in a sexy side plait. "Just in case."

"Maybe," he said again. "He was short and had a beard. Shaved head, I think. He looked strong, you know, stacked." He wasn't really sure. He'd avoided eye contact as much as he could. But Lauren was clearly worried. He didn't want to be responsible for that. "I think we should tell your mum."

She pushed her hair out of her eyes and looked up at him through ridiculously long eyelashes. A constellation of stars and moons decorated her left ear, a tiny sun shone from her right. He wanted to kiss her.

"No," she said casually, putting away her notebook. "I'm being dramatic. I've blocked him on my phone. It's over."

Her fingertips dug a little harder into his arm and he knew she wanted him to drop it, to stop asking questions. Only he couldn't. He hadn't replied to Kai's text about the online photographs of Lauren, but his phone had burned a hole in his pocket ever since. It had taken all his self-control not to search online for them. It wouldn't be right, especially if someone was taking advantage of her. Then again, if Lauren was posting them herself … no. Kai had said they were like, proper X-rated. She wouldn't do that.

"Where do you even meet guys like that?" he asked her. "Online?"

It certainly wasn't at school. And Lauren didn't seem to have many hobbies, apart from posting selfies on social media.

"You're so sweet to worry about me," she said. "You'd be a great boyfriend."

Theo forced himself not to be distracted. She couldn't mean it. She was avoiding his question. But her fingers stroked the skin on his lower arm and gave him goosebumps. If she *did* want him to be her boyfriend, well, that would be … awesome, actually.

Maybe Kai was exaggerating. He could be jealous. Jealous that Theo was spending so much time with Lauren. And *not* hanging out with Kai any more. Was he stirring up shit to get Theo's attention? Theo hadn't even known Kai all that long, he'd only moved here a few months ago. Maybe this was a side to him that Theo hadn't yet seen.

Deep down, Theo knew that wasn't the problem. He knew he was fairly popular at school, hung around with a good crowd and, of course, he had the football team. But he hadn't really ever had a proper best friend before. He and Kai talked about normal things, music, girls, school, but they also talked about things that mattered. About climate change and electric cars and whether Elon Musk was actually dangerous or just plain brilliant, about uni and growing up, and the world's expectations of them. Theo didn't feel stupid discussing stuff like that with Kai. He felt cool and mature.

Was that why Kai had kissed him? Had he recognised that this friendship was new and exciting for Theo, a little like having a crush on a girl? Had *Theo*, subconsciously, put those vibes out there? Thinking about it now made him feel overexposed, raw. Like he didn't know what kind of energy he was giving off. Even now, he couldn't tell if Lauren was serious or not, couldn't trust himself to answer in case he got it wrong again.

But Kai had apologised, wanted to forget it and go back to being friends. He seemed genuine. Theo had to assume that his text was sent in good faith.

"Kai says ..." God, this was awkward. He leaned in to whisper into her ear, a curl tickling his nose. She smelled like strawberries. "Kai says there are photos of you on the internet. Like, ones of you in your underwear?"

"Oh." Lauren leaned away from him and flicked her hair over her shoulder, shrugging off his concern. "Right." The air was cool on his arm where she'd removed her hand. There was something manic in her voice and she stared out the window for a second before turning back to him and taking his hand between both of hers. "You have to keep it a secret, okay?"

God. It was true then. Theo nodded. He wasn't entirely sure he wanted to know any more.

"I sent some photos to a modelling agency and they paid me for them," Lauren was confident, her fingers twining between his. Her nails were black today, a single silver star painted on each pinkie. "*Not* in my underwear." She tutted. "They're very tasteful, actually. And they're only on the agency website."

"Oh." He exhaled loudly. "That's cool, I suppose. Can I see them?"

"Sure," she said. "I'll send you some later. For your eyes only, okay?"

"Yeah. Of course," he said. It gave him a thrill that she was going to confide in him. "It's nothing to do with that creep though, is it? You know, I still think we should tell someone about him. What if he does this to other girls too? He could hurt someone."

"Never mind that guy. It's nothing to do with him. I meant what I said, by the way. You'd be a lovely boyfriend."

"Yeah?" How was he supposed to respond to that? She'd said it twice now. Maybe she meant it. "Do you *want* me to be your boyfriend?" He looked over her shoulder, at the whiteboard, out the window, anywhere he wouldn't see the pity in her eyes if he'd got that wrong.

"Course I do," she said, standing on her tiptoes and giving him a kiss on the cheek.

He forgot about the guy with the beard.

Lauren

LAUREN SAID GOODBYE TO Samira and Elise at the corner and wandered along the promenade to the high street. A group of guys in white socks and Crocs hanging by the beach huts tried to get her to talk to them and she felt disgusted with herself for being pleased at the attention. They had mullets, for God's sake. Mullets. Ugh.

She browsed the aisles in Zara and Wardrobe without really seeing the clothes, pocketed an eyeliner in Boots when the cashier wasn't looking. She stopped at The Hungry Giraffe for an iced coffee and sat at the back where nobody from school would see her.

There was a lot to mull over. It had gone well with Theo today, considering she hadn't expected him to have heard *that*. Theo was sweet. Naive, but sweet. Didn't he watch porn? All the guys she'd been with did. Then again, she didn't usually date boys younger than her.

Shit, though. The photos were actually out there. In the real world. In *Saltreach*. Not just in the cyberverse, that in her head she'd limited to sexual deviants, incels, and pathetic losers who couldn't get laid. Or, maybe, hot guys who actually appreciated her figure. She should have known this would happen eventually. You needed an actual credit card to get onto the website, which she'd stupidly assumed would preclude her schoolmates because you had to be eighteen to qualify for one of those. But she was right about Kai being trouble. Clearly *he* was no stranger to paying for it. Kai was weird, always staring, always on the edge of a group. She hoped he and Theo wouldn't make up. Theo told her they'd had a falling out but wouldn't say why. She'd have to make sure Kai kept his distance from both of them.

Glancing over her shoulder to make sure she was alone, she checked her bank account, satisfied. Another £70. She logged into PeekaBoo and scanned her messages. The blocking hadn't really worked. Sure, User W45 was gone, but it was definitely him who'd liked all her pictures. The way he paid her was a dead giveaway. £15.15, every time. He knew exactly how old she was and he wanted her to know he knew. He used different profiles, different accounts. No pictures of himself of course, none of the men did. But she knew it was him because of the way he messaged her, the names he called her. W45 didn't call her a sick bitch like some of the others. He called her Baby Girl and Sweet Lauren. But mostly he called her L.

She pinged off a couple of replies to various men and two women who'd complimented her latest set of pictures. She wrote a little teaser on her profile about wanting a new bikini. What colour should she get? Would anyone like to send her one? Size six, please. That would gain her some new followers.

She actually did need a new bikini. Especially if this weather was going to continue. Her cheap Shein ones had earned her a fortune, but now she wanted something a little more sophisticated.

Mum had an amazing collection of bikinis. Mum also had a bank account she didn't even know about, with over two grand in it, increasing daily. It had been so easy: a brand new email address, a gas bill, and a photograph of her mother's passport.

A message pinged up from a new viewer.

Hi L,

I'll buy you a red bikini.

And hand deliver it myself.

Can't wait to see you again.

Oh God, oh God, it was him! It *had* to be. Hand-fucking-deliver? Would he actually show up at the house? And what did he mean, "again"? She'd stayed hidden behind the tree that time at school so he couldn't see her. Was he *stalking* her?

The website had promised her private information would be kept secret; gifts would all be routed through the company for a small charge. He *must* be bluffing.

But he'd found her school, hadn't he?

He knew she lived in Saltreach.

He even knew her name.

Kerry

"These are our terms," Kerry told Izzy, holding a bunch of papers over the boardroom table. But as Izzy reached out a hand, Kerry's fingers refused to relinquish the file.

Electricity crackled inside her. It was Friday, exactly one week since Andrew's accident. She still had to cut up his food. He'd already ordered a new bicycle. She hadn't managed to swim all week. Andrew hadn't missed a UEFA League match yet. She'd worked until midnight every evening on the new redundancy deal and had had a migraine since Tuesday. He'd kept up with his physio and had a good prognosis from the doctor. She'd managed to make a chocolate cake with the twins, and take Ella clothes shopping, guilt-splurging in Zara. She'd even managed a little FIFA on the PlayStation with Theo. Andrew had told his company he could do some light work from home, and from next Monday, he would do meetings and phone work exclusively, no typing. Since he was planning on using her study, Kerry had decided to throw him in the deep end and spend a full day at Bullfinch for the first time in a week. This was a conversation she needed to have in person.

"What are you doing here, Izzy? I mean, really."

Izzy's crease-free brow struggled to frown. "Let's not make this personal, Kerry."

It was too late for that. The phrase *Saint Kerry* had swum in her dreams all week. It had fired her up, kept her awake, pushed her to work harder. She was no martyr. She was simply good at her job. And she would do as good a job during this takeover as she possibly could. "Why come back if it's not personal?"

"You think I came back for you?" Izzy snorted, an ungainly sound that didn't match the five-foot-ten blonde in the Whistles pencil skirt. Who even wore pencil skirts anymore? Bitches who wanted to tower over you in four-inch stilettos, that was who.

"Why, then?" Kerry said crisply. "What could bring back the woman who couldn't even come to her best friend's father's funeral for fear of being trapped here? Who hasn't been back in over twenty years? Who was so obsessed with her career that she turned her back on someone who needed her more than ever."

Izzy folded her arms and leaned back in her executive chair. "I've been back."

"You have *not*."

"Oh, I don't come home to hang out in the dive bars we went to as teenagers. To call up old friends and ask them out for dinner." She was too professional to spit the words out the way Kerry knew she wanted to.

"What did you come back for, then? If not to stab me in the back? There's no point pretending you wouldn't have known I'd be here. I'm on the website, for God's sake."

Izzy's haughty façade faded and there she was, the Izzy who'd held teenage Kerry's hand when boys had teased her for her puppy fat and her freckles. Who'd punched Toby Fletching in the nose because he told everyone she'd kissed him behind the bike shed. Who'd pinkie-sworn that they'd get the hell out of Saltreach together and never come back.

"My mother has motor neurone disease."

Kerry's hold on the file wavered. She knew the statistics on MND. Barbara Holt was a small wiry woman who never sat still, who would clip Izzy round the ear sooner than give her a hug, yet worked two jobs Izzy's entire childhood, cleaning by day, bartending by night. Mum's words about Barbara not making it to hospital rang in her ears. Was Mum simply tone deaf to the situation? She hadn't worked outside the home after Kerry was born. She'd never needed to. Kerry felt a prickly heat spread across her chest and had the sudden urge to remove her blazer.

"I've been visiting for years. This was the first local job that means I can afford the mortgage on my flat in London. I don't want to be here anymore than you want me here."

"I'm very sorry to hear that," Kerry said. "How is she?"

"Still complaining." Izzy gave her a watery smile. "Remember the time she complained to the supermarket that the vodka was watered down? Little did she know …" She touched Kerry's hand.

The touch was like an electric shock. The past receded and the present came sharply into view. This was business. Kerry snatched back her hand and flung the folder on the desk.

"Send her my best," she said and left the room.

Kerry

Kerry arrived home from the leisure centre, two swim bags under her arm, and ushered the twins inside the house. Poppy wore a towel turban around her hair and a Lilo and Stitch onesie. Alby stood behind her in a Liverpool onesie, damp hair carefully formed into a mohawk. Whoever scheduled swimming lessons on a Friday evening hated parents.

"Thank God it's the weekend," Kerry said to nobody in particular. She assumed Andrew was in his regular spot on the sofa behind the lounge door, newspaper on his lap, remote on the armrest. "Fancy a takeaway?" she called out.

He hobbled out from the kitchen, Thai menu already in hand. "Hey, kiddos," he said. "Good class?"

He handed Kerry the menu with a kiss on the cheek. "Great minds think alike. In fact, we have company tonight."

"You're joking." Kerry's body sagged. "I was hoping for a bath and an early night. You must be shattered, too. It's been a hectic week."

Andrew shrugged. "Actually, I'd love a bit of company."

Shit. Of course he would. He'd only had the kids and her to talk to all week. "Who is it?"

"Wolf and Nicole. And Lauren."

Kerry knew he wanted her to be happy about it. She wasn't, but she would try. On the bright side, she didn't have to cook. The twins were already fed. And maybe this would finally be the beginning of the beautiful friendship that Andrew had secretly hoped for. The doorbell chimed. "Already?" she mouthed at Andrew. She hadn't even got her coat off.

*

"We got a mix of everything to share," Wolf said cheerily, loading steaming bags onto the kitchen table. Enough to feed five families. "Our treat."

"Right, grab plates and find a seat" Andrew said, pulling out cutlery and napkins with his good arm and dumping them on the table in a heap. "Kids! Dinner! Wolf, Nicole, this is so generous. You didn't have to pay for all of this."

"No trouble," Nicole said tightly. Clearly, there *had* been trouble. She hung a fabulous leather jacket over the back of her chair and perched on the edge, one slim leg wrapped around the other like a coiled spring. A bad start to the evening. Kerry would have been happy to split the bill. She grabbed her purse and pulled out cash. Thank God she'd been to the ATM today. It was meant to be a bonus for Marta for everything she did for Mum, but it could wait. She peeled off four twenties and handed them to Nicole.

"Let's split it," she said. "I feel bad."

Nicole looked at the cash as though Kerry had handed her a load of dirty underwear to wash.

"No need," she said. "Like Wolf said, it's our treat."

"Thank you for the offer," Wolf said, reaching over and kissing Kerry on the cheek. "But put your money away. It's the least we can do. It's so nice to enjoy a meal together. It's been too long."

Kerry's cheek burned under Nicole's white-hot gaze. It was a *hello* kiss, for God's sake. They had *all* kissed hello, although

Nicole's had landed a few centimetres out from Kerry's cheek. Maybe that was how you were supposed to do it. But Kerry grew up in a house full of real affection, top-to-toe hugs, endearments, hair-ruffling and hand-holding. She couldn't do it any other way. Embarrassed, she turned away to find some wine.

"Makes me feel German again," Wolf continued. "Even though I didn't cook. My mother used to produce the most enormous spreads. As if she expected the entire apartment block to show up. Which they often did."

"Are you German?" Alby asked. "Did you know Hitler?"

Kerry nearly dropped the wine. "Alby!"

But Wolf chuckled. "Luckily, I didn't. I never actually lived in Germany myself. I'm not quite as old as I may look."

"You're pretty old," Lauren said, slinking into the kitchen behind Kerry. Were she and Theo holding hands? Theo's face was bright red, but whether he was chuffed or embarrassed, Kerry couldn't tell. It certainly looked like they'd patched up whatever had happened between them. Good. Ella appeared, also watching the hands, a wicked glint in her eye.

"Are there wolves in Germany?" Poppy asked. "Is that why you have a funny name?"

"Poppy!"

But the kids were laughing. Wolf and Andrew were laughing. Nicole was not, but Kerry decided that that was not her problem tonight. She poured the wine. Generously.

"My full name is Wolfgang," Wolf explained, pronouncing his name with the v-sound and a hard German accent. "Wolfgang Harald Ernst Bauer." The twins copied him diligently. "It sounds like my mother didn't love me, but she called me Wolfie. That's a secret." He winked at the twins and handed them each a chicken satay skewer and they skipped into the lounge, delighted to get a free pass on bedtime.

Everyone else sat, Theo pulling up a stool on the end next to Lauren, whispering self-consciously as they filled their plates. Ella sat next to Nicole, who looked very glamorous for a Friday night in, in a belted gunmetal-grey jumpsuit, her hair in a boho French plait over one shoulder. Her bare arms were tanned and muscular. Kerry's work outfit of Boden blouse and trousers felt out of place, and she wished she'd had time to change into something lighter. She watched, fascinated, as Nicole and Lauren each put miniscule portions of food on their plates, carefully counting out four prawns apiece.

"How's the body?" Wolf asked, indicating up and down Andrew with his fork. "Recovering?"

Everyone stopped eating and stared at Andrew. The scratches on his face were healing, but there were scabs from his right temple down to his jaw, and the bruising was still purple with yellow undertones. He looked like an unfinished jigsaw puzzle.

Andrew twirled a fork gracefully with his good arm and laughed. "You should see the other guy."

Kerry felt a rush of love for him. Even his breathing had been impacted by the broken ribs. But he wouldn't want them all staring at him like that.

"So, Wolf," she said lightly, changing the conversation. "What's it like working for the enemy?"

It landed like an accusation, which hadn't been her intention, but there it was all the same, and she couldn't take it back. The atmosphere in the room chilled a couple of degrees. Now all eyes were on her, and heat flooded her chest. Andrew looked even more wounded, if that was possible. And then Ella, lovely, wonderful Ella, asked Nicole where she bought her jumpsuit and the awkward moment passed.

"I needed the work," Wolf said quietly across the table.

"Don't you remember her?"

"Izzy? Yeah, I'm pretty sure she was the one who snitched on me about the weed. I got suspended over that." He laughed, as if to say, *see, this childhood stuff doesn't matter anymore. We're all adults now.*

He hadn't a clue. And yet the thought bloomed unbidden: *Izzy would never have snitched.*

"You know she doesn't care about Bullfinch!" she said and felt disappointment leach from Andrew. She wasn't being fair. Tonight was supposed to be about him. He was probably sick of hearing about Izzy and Bullfinch. Yet hot tears stung her eyes. This was ridiculous. Even discussing Izzy Holt reduced her to a spotty, hormonal teenager. "Stonebridge are making a mockery of everything we've built. You should see the redundancy offer they've put together. I'm supposed to be canvassing for voluntary redundancy while you're in there acting like everything's normal!"

"Kerry ..." There was a warning in Andrew's voice and silence from the rest of the table, but she couldn't stop.

"What are you even doing for them?"

"Syncing the IT systems," Wolf said. He sighed. "I have to make a living too."

"Of course," Andrew said, leaning across the table, interrupting the flow of tension radiating from every pore in Kerry's skin, breaking the spell. She was ashamed of herself.

"Sorry, Wolf," she muttered. "It's been a stressful week. If you need any help, just ask."

"I get it," he said. "Andrew filled me in on your history with Izzy." He punched Andrew lightly on his good shoulder and Kerry felt a pang of discomfort. Had they laughed behind her back about women being bitchy and holding grudges? She desperately hoped not.

The men lapsed into conversation about bikes. Kerry searched for something to say to Nicole. "How's the house?" she asked politely. "Andrew mentioned you're thinking of an extension?"

"Mum thinks we need an *orangery*." Lauren's voice dripped with disdain from the other end of the table. She looked around the table, garnering support. "Yeah. For real." A loaded comment that told of eavesdropping and, for whatever reason, wanting to drop her mother in it. Nicole bristled and looked to Wolf for support. Wolf merely rolled his eyes back at her, as if to say *what can we do?*

If any of her children spoke to her like that in public, Kerry would suspend pocket money for a month. *And* double their chores. Wow. She was actually empathising with Nicole over a singular comment uttered by a teenager in a particular tone of voice. She must have overdone it on the wine already. She topped up her glass. At least this was not her drama.

"Dad suggested she start with a herb garden." Lauren sniggered behind her hand like a toddler. All eyes were on her. Whether or not she was aware of the vitriol emanating from her mother, Kerry couldn't tell, but she was certainly enjoying the attention. Maybe *she'd* sneaked some wine.

"An orangery?" Andrew scratched his head at the opposite end of the table and all heads swivelled away from Lauren. "Isn't that like a conservatory?"

"It would look fantastic off the dining room," Nicole said. She turned her attention to Wolf. "We'd catch the evening light. Think how lovely it'd be to watch the sunset together over a glass of wine."

Wolf waggled thick black eyebrows at Kerry. "My wife clearly thinks Stonebridge is a generous company."

Kerry felt another sting of disloyalty on Nicole's behalf. Andrew would never make a comment like that. She was annoyed that he'd brought the conversation back to Stonebridge, too. Clearly, tonight was not the night for it. She tried to visualise Wolf and Nicole's dining room but it had been so long since they'd been invited round, she couldn't remember what it looked like.

"I'm sure it will be lovely. Kids," she said, giving Ella a nod of the head towards the lounge, "why don't you guys grab an ice cream and turn on a movie? I'll put the twins to bed."

*

When she came back, the dishwasher had been stacked and a fresh bottle of wine opened. The kitchen was spotless and Kerry had the distinct impression that it was Nicole, repaying a little kindness, who was responsible. Andrew was mid-monologue about the state of the beach, his pet peeve, so she gave Nicole's shoulder a little squeeze and took a seat next to her.

"There's a new Facebook page," Andrew said. "Local businesses getting together to lobby the council about the state of the beach. The council maintain they can't afford to start clearing the seaweed till June, which is when they normally start. Pete is leading it."

"They want us to put up with that awful smell till then?" Nicole said, horrified.

"I've offered to help," Wolf said. "Who knew a heatwave could cause havoc like this?"

"We've never had this problem in April before," Andrew said, "but if tourists get wind of it, they'll cancel their bookings. We're due a scorching hot summer and Saltreach needs every penny it can get from visitors. So, I hope you don't mind," he gave that little cough Kerry knew so well and her heart sank, "but I've agreed to co-chair the committee with Pete."

What a sales pitch. She should have known there'd be something at the end of it. But he'd be brilliant on the committee. Fair, sensible, a good listener.

"You're due back to work soon," she said. "And you still can't drive. Don't you think that you've enough on your plate?"

That we've *enough on* our *plates,* she wanted to say. *That* I *have.* When Andrew committed to a project, he committed all the way. It was something they had in common. There would be research, weekly meetings, focus groups, interviews. Great for the community, but for Kerry that meant solo parenting in the evenings, more cooking, doing all the hockey lifts. All the while trying to stop Stonebridge bulldoze her beloved company.

"Tell me about it," Andrew said. "But don't you want to be able to swim in the sea this summer?"

He had her there.

Wolf coughed. "Speaking of Facebook, now that the kids are out of earshot, there's another matter we need to discuss . . ."

This was directed at Kerry. Uh oh. Another work thing. This was the danger of working together. The evening had regained its equilibrium, was fun, almost. The four of them were actually hanging out together, something Andrew had wanted for such a long time. Even Nicole was relaxed, as far as Kerry could tell.

"Can it wait till Monday?" she asked.

"It's a Facebook group," he said, as if she hadn't spoken. "Some local people, including employees at Bullfinch, have gathered online to complain about the takeover."

Kerry heard the scrape of chair legs on tile as he pulled his chair in tighter under the table, as if readying himself for a Q&A. She didn't really want to know. She didn't care about Facebook. All anybody ever did on Facebook was complain.

"How did I miss this?" Andrew muttered, pulling out his phone. Nicole did the same.

"I've scanned through it and followed a couple of links," Wolf continued. "Found some other chatrooms where the talk is a little more …" He drained his glass. "Lively."

"You mean threatening?" Kerry pulled the door to. It wouldn't do for the kids to hear this.

"I'm just telling you as an FYI. I'll keep an eye on it, mitigate the chat. Keep it calm. If I spot anyone getting out of hand, I'll flag it to you, and we can take it to the police. Okay?"

Nicole and Andrew put down their phones and everyone stared at Wolf.

"The police?" Andrew said. "Is it that bad? Really?"

"Not yet. But it might go that way. I'll handle it, okay? You don't worry about it."

Nicole

NICOLE ASSESSED HER SPREADSHEET over a glass of red wine. Forty-seven job applications in the last three months alone. More than half hadn't bothered to respond. She couldn't understand it. Her CV was painstakingly curated, and professionally edited by a career counsellor so expensive, she had started home-dying her hair to afford him. In return, she had glowing – albeit dated – references, a highly polished cover letter, and the answers to virtually any potential interview question perfectly rehearsed. She missed her immaculate highlights, but she'd sell her soul to have her career back.

She moved onto the next column. Seven companies had rejected her, citing over-qualification. It was true, but she didn't care. She'd make coffee and photocopy if they'd let her. They'd soon see how capable she was. The career counsellor had warned her against coming across too needy; any scent of desperation would be a disaster.

And so, after twelve interviews, she'd learned not to overplay her experience. She removed some of the instantly recognisable brand names from her client lists and credited her teams and her managers for business she'd won and delivered single-handedly. She played up the online training courses in social media marketing that she'd attended, the seminars and talks she logged into late at night when Wolf was asleep, to prove that she was as current, as fresh, as the twenty-somethings who now owned the marketing and events sector.

At five final-round interviews, she bit her lip when they asked about salary expectations, deferring politely to their declaration of competitive rates. She confirmed that she had taken a career break to raise her daughter and was now excited to bring a new layer of maturity to the role.

Old, old, old. She'd seen it in their eyes. She'd been met with platitudes and limp handshakes as she rose to leave in her tailored midi dresses, passing people in the waiting room in their boldly chaotic ensembles, knowing she wouldn't be getting a phone call that evening. She was only forty-four, for goodness sake. She tipped back the end of the wine.

Wolf was on the stairs, thudding heavily onto each step, noisy for someone so slight. She pictured him ineffectually pushing his glasses up higher on his nose. Any second now he'd come in and tell her how tired he was. It was always the same. She closed the spreadsheet, replaced the job-board website with the one about the orangeries.

"Have we any paracetamol?" Wolf said, bringing a welcome draught of cool air into the room with him. "I've an awful headache."

"In the cupboard, darling. No, the other one, where you found them yesterday. Yes, there." She poured the dregs of the wine bottle into her glass.

"Oh," he said, pointing at the empty bottle as he popped the last two tablets from the foil. "Wine all gone?"

Nicole felt a tiny bit bad. He'd treated himself to a pricey case of Châteauneuf-du-Pape for winning the Stonebridge contract, and they were drinking it like it was on two-for-one at Tesco.

"Relax," she said. "Still two left."

Wolf peered into the box and grimaced. "One of those is for Pete, for helping me get the contract."

This was tedious. "Darling, surely you won't be wanting a glass if you've a headache."

"And I should give one to Kerry. I do feel bad about the whole 'working for the enemy' thing, especially as I kind of need her cooperation. Do you think she meant it when she said she'd help?"

Nicole would bet on it. Women were always delighted to help Wolf. He was so polite, so attentive, and he still had that skinny, techie vibe with his serious, black-framed glasses and intense brown eyes. He'd made a change from the drama queens she'd worked with at the events company, who traded on gossip and backstabbing. No, Wolf listened when she talked and asked insightful questions and took the same studied, keen-to-impress attitude into the bedroom. But he'd always been a bit *too* keen to impress Kerry.

"Didn't you buy her whole family dinner yesterday evening?"

"Oh, yes." Wolf grinned, headache clearly forgotten. "Then let's open the last one, shall we?" He kissed her cheek as he reached behind her for the corkscrew. "What have you been up to down here by yourself? Catching up on Instagram stories? Buying shoes?"

Nicole's eye strayed to the laptop. There was no point.

"Exactly," she said. "What about you? Did you get those links I sent?" She couldn't give a fig about an orangery if she was being honest, but if he insisted on carrying on like Jeff bloody Bezos every hour of the day, she could play the spoiled housewife.

"God, no, sorry, I've been slammed. But it'll be much simpler now if Kerry will give me a hand. She's right about Izzy being a taskmaster."

As long as Kerry wasn't giving him anything else. Dear God, what had gotten into her? Maybe she'd drunk too much. Still, she pushed her glass towards him for a refill.

"You know, Henry might have been the actual boss, but it seems like Kerry's the one everyone relies on down there. I guess because her dad started the business … anyway, they all worship her."

"Do they now?" Nicole would bet that not everybody was so taken in by Kerry's square, sensible mummy persona. It took a hard woman to sit on the board of directors. Kerry will have pissed plenty of people off in her rise to fame and celebrity. Nicole might even have another peek at this Facebook page Wolf had mentioned. No harm to have a little ammunition. Just in case.

"Yeah. She's so *normal*, you know? No airs or graces."

For fuck's sake. She might as well get drunk. It wasn't as if she needed to be up early for work.

Wolf opened a large bag of crisps and pushed them towards her. Ugh. Salt and vinegar. He shovelled a handful into his mouth and Nicole recoiled. "She was like that in school, too," he said.

What the fuck? He had an actual *crush* on her. "Did you ever go out with her in school?"

Wolf squinted at her. "Kerry or Izzy?"

"Kerry. Either of them!" Nicole snapped. Surely she'd have known before now if his best friend's wife used to be his girlfriend. Bloody hell, this conversation wasn't going the way she'd planned. She'd imagined discussing paint colours and lighting by now.

"God, no." He grinned again. "Maybe a bit of snogging round the back of the bike shed, but only when we were like fourteen or fifteen, I suppose. More wine?"

Nicole bit back tears. What the hell was wrong with her, feeling jealous over a childhood kiss? She shook her head angrily and pushed the wine away. This was ridiculous. She must be getting her period.

"I'm going to bed," she announced. "I've got a headache myself. Why don't you sleep in your office?"

She avoided Wolf's eye as she passed him on her way to the door.

Theo

THEO TYPED MITCH LANGLEY into Google. There were lots of results.

Mitch Langley, Watersports Instructor, São Rafael Beach, Portugal

Mitch Langley, Chocolatier, available for private tuition in Edinburgh

Mitch Langley, nudist, artist, sculptor, seeks company at his private retreat in the Dordogne Valley

Right. Definitely not them.

He typed again: Mitch Langley, London. There were more than twenty results on LinkedIn alone. He started scrolling. This would take forever. But he had to do it, and he had to do it alone. There was no way he could go to Dad right now, after his accident. And he definitely couldn't take this to Mum. Her work problem had dominated the house for weeks, and she was being super annoying, snapping and then apologising, and then snapping again. This would push her over the edge.

After rummaging through a hundred profiles, he gave up. What a joke. He didn't know *anything* about Mitch. How was that even possible? He would have to meet him again. Ask questions. Demand answers. He felt sweaty at the thought of it. Ella would be better at this … but Ella was revising for GCSEs. He needed someone who didn't care. Someone without a strong moral compass.

Lauren. Her name snuck up on him in the same surprising way she'd inserted herself into his life, sliding her hands under his t-shirt in public, borrowing and never returning his hoodies, kissing him hard down by the beach huts when no one was around, snapping her hair band onto his wrist like a dog collar, marking her territory.

Lauren was streetwise, sophisticated even. More than he was. But there was one snag. He wasn't sure he could trust her. She refused to tell him where she'd met Beardface. She hadn't shown him any photos like she'd promised. She was sometimes just … unavailable, like on Saturday night. Her phone was switched off for hours, she stopped sharing her location on Snapchat, and this morning at school she said she'd gone to bed early with period cramps. Theo wasn't convinced. Lauren was not simply the pretty, confident, selfie-obsessed person she pretended to be. She might be his girlfriend, but she made him nervous, and he couldn't trust her with a secret this big. He just couldn't.

He'd have to meet Mitch again. Alone.

*

Ella put her head around Theo's bedroom door and he locked the screen on his phone.

"How's Lauren?"

He gave her the middle finger.

Ella laughed. "You ever seen some dodgy guy hanging around Gran's house?"

"Like who?"

She shrugged. "Early twenties, brown hair."

Theo's stomach clenched. Mitch? Beardface? Was one of them following him? The thought of Beardface wanting a rematch was terrifying.

"That could be anyone." He rubbed the palms of his hands on his jeans. "Why's he hanging around Gran's?"

Ella sighed like he was dumb. "How would I know? Mum said to ask you."

"I don't know, okay!" He got off the bed and looked out the window. The street below was empty.

"Jeez, relax." Ella left and then put her head back around the door. She was grinning inanely now. "Does Mum know about Lauren?"

"What about her?" His hands were really sweaty now.

"That she's your girlfriend, moron."

"How do you know that?"

"She posted it on TikTok. Personally, I think you could do better."

Theo snatched up his phone. Ella was right. Lauren had uploaded a selfie of the two of them she'd taken in school, drawing a red heart around them.

"Woo-oo, Theo's got a girlfriend," Ella said in that annoying sing-song voice that girls did. "Theo's got a girlfriend."

"Shut up!"

Ella laughed and started to close the door.

"Hey, don't tell Mum, will you?"

"Seriously?" she said, coming back into the room. She shut the door behind her and Theo braced himself for a lecture of some sort. "After the last time," she circled a finger around her own face to show she meant Punchgate, as she called it, "don't you think it's wiser not to keep secrets?"

Easy for Ella to say. She never seemed to put a foot wrong. She got good, if not brilliant, grades at school. She wanted to be a primary school teacher or a social worker. She was regarded among her friends as some kind of agony aunt, and treated the twins like they were her own children. She'd casually dated a geek from the grammar school called Chris that she'd met at hockey camp last summer but dumped him when school restarted so she could concentrate on her exams. She was the model child.

Theo said nothing.

"All right." Ella shrugged. "Suit yourself. I just didn't like seeing you so upset." She gave him a little push on the shoulder. She was sixteen, more than a year older than him, but only came up to his chin. "You'd watch out for me too, I know you would."

He nudged her back. "As if you'd ever need it."

When she left, he scrolled through his phone, searching for Mitch's number. There were at least ten messages, each growing more insistent. Theo hadn't replied to any of them.

Y RU still hanging round?

The reply came back within seconds.

Told you. I want to get to know my family.

Stay away from my Gran.

Can I meet up with you again?

When?

Now?

Aren't you at work?

Took the afternoon off to come to the seaside. How's Dad?

God. First, he was hanging around school, then Granny's house, now just … *here,* in Saltreach, doing nothing. Watching them.

Meet U on the prom by the ice cream kiosk in 10

*

Mitch was eating an ice cream cone and wearing a parka and those chunky boots. That was weird; it was boiling. Theo was in shorts and t-shirt. And jeez, he could have waited five minutes and bought Theo an ice cream too.

"Stinks down here," Mitch said in greeting, thumbing over his shoulder at the seaweed-strewn beach.

It did stink. But Theo wasn't in the mood to listen to Mitch complain. He led Mitch to a low wall and sat. "How do I know you are who you say you are?"

"Of course I'm who I say I am. What do you mean?"

Mitch twitched, one eyelid blinking rapidly. Was it a sign he was nervous? Theo sighed. Mitch always twitched.

"I mean, you don't exist on social media, I can't find you on Google. You always wear the same clothes. I don't know if you have a job or where you live or anything about you!"

To his surprise, Mitch laughed. He stuffed the end of his cone into his mouth and pulled something out of his pocket. "I'm so stupid," he said. "Of course you think I'm some kind of weirdo. Here. Does this help?"

He pulled out a business card. The name *LinkWell* sat next to a corporate blue and white logo. There were phone numbers, an email address, an actual physical address in Hackney. *Keeping Business Connected,* it promised on the back.

"You work here?"

Mitch nodded.

"I'm keeping this. Okay?"

"Sure," Mitch said, nodding enthusiastically. "Anything to help you feel better about all of this. I just came out of the blue. Right?"

He was like an eager toddler. But he seemed to get it, to understand. He held out the business card like a peace offering.

"Thanks."

"So. How's Dad?"

This guy was relentless. So much for Theo being in control. At least there was nobody close enough to hear. Only a pair of cyclists sipped takeaway coffees at a picnic bench further along the promenade.

"We don't actually know that he's your dad," he said through gritted teeth.

"I can show you," Mitch said, his hands moving wildly in the air. "I have proof."

No. No way. This wasn't supposed to happen. Proof? Theo realised that, deep down, he'd been convinced this was all a mistake. That he would humour Mitch until he could tell Dad, and Dad would say there was no way he'd had a girlfriend called Diana and therefore there couldn't possibly have been a baby. And this, whatever *this* was, would be over, and things could go back to normal.

"I have a photograph," Mitch said, excited now. "Of Mum and Dad together. Before I was born. I'll bring it next time."

Mum and Dad. But not Mum as in Theo's Mum. This was so fucked up. Mitch beamed at him with pure pleasure, as if he'd only just had the brainwave, that he'd fixed the problem, and for a split second his wide, toothy grin and mussed-up hair reminded Theo of Alby.

"Why didn't you bring it before now?"

"I didn't want to rush you, did I?" Mitch said, rubbing the side of his nose.

Alby did that too, sometimes, when he was trying to concentrate. Fuck.

"But I'm just so excited. Look at this place," Mitch said, gesturing at the expanse of sea and sky before them. "This is just nature at its best, you know. And you know what else is natural? Family, man. *Family.*" He took a deep breath and smiled at Theo with those crooked teeth and Theo's heart sank.

"I need to see the photo and I'll show it to Dad when he's better. Okay?"

The second the words left his mouth he knew he'd made a mistake. Mitch's face fell and he put a hand out to touch Theo's arm. Theo shook it off, but not too viciously. "Is he hurt?"

Hurt? That was a weird word to use. Sick would have made more sense. Or ill. Or poorly. He replayed his own words in his head, mentally scrolled through their messaging thread. Had he mentioned Dad's accident? He was sure he hadn't.

"He'll be okay, won't he?" Mitch pulled at the ends of his hair, fistfuls floating away on the breeze.

"He fell off his bike, that's all," Theo said. "He's recovering at home. I've got to go." He needed to get out of here. Mitch was being too weird. Maybe he was just a bit hyper or whatever. Or maybe he was dangerous. But until Theo saw that picture, he wasn't going to see him again. "You let me know when you've got this photo, okay? Then I'll meet you. But not before."

Mitch nodded. "Okay, sure thing." He visibly calmed and they walked back to the road. Home was left. But he needed to know where Mitch was going. Needed to know that at least one thing Mitch said was real. "I'll walk you to the train station."

"Actually," Mitch said, shoving his hands back in his pocket, "I'm hungry. I fancy some proper seaside fish and chips before I head back to London. I don't suppose you could lend me a tenner?"

Lauren

THE SECOND THE BELL rang, Lauren stood. She marched out of the classroom without giving the boys in the back row even the tiniest hint that she'd heard them. Elise and Samira jogged beside her to keep up.

"What are they *on* about?" Samira asked, flicking her long black hair over her shoulder. Lauren knew she was using it as a final chance to decode what Oliver was implying. She sped up.

"How would I know?" she said, ice in her voice.

"They're *so* lame," Samira added. But Lauren saw the way she smirked at Elise. They knew there was gossip and the minute her back was turned they would go right back to Oliver and Dan to find out what it was. She needed to find Theo.

"I need the loo," she said, switching direction, causing Elise to crash into her shoulder. "See you in French." She walked off before they could question her, but not before she saw Elise whisper something into Samira's ear and Samira's sculpted eyebrow arch.

She went to Theo's locker area and waited a few minutes, but there was no sign of him. Shit. She'd be late for class if she waited any longer. She texted him to meet her after school.

Theo wouldn't be able to help. She hadn't shown him any photos and he hadn't asked again. But she felt better when she was with him, when he held her hand and asked shyly if he could kiss her. He didn't expect sex, or anything close to it, even though she was older, even though he assumed she'd been with that guy who'd punched him – a guy who seemed like he'd expect far more than a kiss.

Trainers squeaked behind her and she pivoted. Oliver was jogging towards her, a shit-eating grin spreading across his spotty face. What did he want?

She turned for class and assumed what she knew the boys in her year generally referred to as her bitch face. She stared past him, as if she were searching for the right classroom, as if he didn't even exist. Oliver was the most disgusting one, the one who would boast to the entire class how many fingers he'd jammed into some poor unsuspecting girl on Saturday night, the one who liked to shout the words other boys only dared to use under their breath.

He fell into step beside her. Beneath an overload of Lynx, she could smell his greasy hair and stale sweat.

"Looking sexy today, L," he said.

She ignored him.

"No need to be like that," he wheedled. "I've got something to show you."

"Nobody wants to see your dick, Oliver," she said, staring straight ahead. "I hear it's nothing to be proud of, anyway."

"Don't pretend to be so stuck up," he said, pulling out his phone. "Not when I know what a little slut you really are."

Lauren's armpits prickled. What did he know? She willed her cheeks not to redden, forced herself not to look at his screen. But he backed her up against a row of lockers, the metal hard against her shoulder blades, a lock cutting into her spine.

He held out his phone. She saw a photo of herself wearing black Nike Pro shorts and matching sports bra in the downward dog yoga pose. Simple enough. She'd angled the camera to catch a good shot of her cleavage, but the PeekaBoo comments had all focused on her behind. More specifically, on what the viewers would do to her if *they* were behind her. But, and this was the only reason she hadn't taken it down, it had already netted her over £200.

"I haven't shown it to anyone," Oliver said. "Yet."

He leaned even closer and she smelled his tuna sandwiches, saw the open pores on his nose, felt his sweaty hand on her hip. A skein of fear shivered over her skin.

"I could, you know," he said. "Unless you can think of a way to persuade me not to."

A bell rang, shaking her back to reality.

"Fuck off, Oliver," she said, stepping hard on his toe as she passed him.

Kerry

"MORNING, KERRY," SAID PAULA from the reception desk.

"Hi, Paula. How's the baby?" But she barely heard the answer. Something was different. People were standing, chatting, and actual laughter could be heard. The radio had been switched up a couple of notches. Things felt as they used to. Relaxed. Productive. Enjoyable.

"No Izzy today," Paula said, beaming. "In fact, no Izzy for the rest of the week."

"How come?"

"Personal stuff, apparently." Paula sniffed. "Maybe she's gone for good. Wouldn't that be a treat?"

But something didn't sit quite right about this. It was only Tuesday. Nobody took time off a fortnight into a new job. Besides, Izzy had booked a meeting with her this morning to discuss the two-week deadline for voluntary redundancies. She wouldn't want to miss that. Her mother must have taken a turn for the worse.

Barbara Holt had smoked like a chimney and couldn't have weighed more than eight stone. She'd cleaned houses by day and served drinks at The Crabby Mermaid in the evenings. There were no steady boyfriends, no holidays. Only the occasional trip to London where she and Izzy would watch the Changing of the Guard and stock up at Primark. Izzy had been left alone in the small flat by the park a lot. Other girls might have smoked, had boys over, kept a bottle of vodka under their bed. But Izzy had done her homework, cooked her frozen fish fingers, and earned her place at Manchester with top marks. Better marks than Kerry, whose parents had had to fork out for both a maths *and* French tutor.

Her bio was now up on the Stonebridge website and Kerry had scoured it, searching for clues as to how Izzy might expect this takeover to pan out. Bullfinch appeared to be considerably smaller than what she was used to. She'd been running M&A operations internationally for a decade with boutique management consultancies. Some of her target companies had virtually disappeared, broken down and sold off, never to be heard of again. Others had changed beyond recognition. Only a few remained intact. She needed to make sure that Bullfinch remained one of those.

"In that case," she said to Paula. "Could you please book me a table for two at The Hungry Giraffe for brunch?"

*

"This is a nice surprise," Andrew said, sliding into the booth opposite her. Their first-date booth, with its soft, worn, sea-blue seats and scrubbed wooden table. Andrew's bruises had healed. He'd showered and looked rested in a soft khaki short-sleeved shirt. "I was just pulling out my laptop when I got your text. So I messaged in to say I wasn't feeling up to it today and I'd start back tomorrow." He chuckled like a teenager who'd gotten away with having a sneaky beer.

"Good. I've ordered us both the pancakes," Kerry said, although it was a given. They didn't even read the menu any more. "I know my work has been non-stop and I've been stressed and snappy. But," she clinked her coffee against his, "you're on the mend. Theo's happier now that he's going out with Lauren, even if she does seem a little … mature for him."

"Wolf says she's very fond of him."

"Freya Nowell thought that she'd rejected him and *that's* how he got the black eye. But who knows anymore." She shrugged. "I'm just glad he's feeling better. I'd still like to see him make up with Kai, though."

The waitress arrived with two plates of bacon and syrup pancakes, and as Kerry reached to accept the plate, a pain shot through her left arm. She flinched and set the plate down with a thump.

"Ouch. You okay?"

"Nothing two paracetamol won't fix," she said lightly, and thanked the waitress. God, that had been embarrassing. At least the café was pretty empty this time of morning, apart from a young couple with a small baby in a yellow romper suit sitting by the window. It was a colourful, friendly place, stacks of colouring books and chunky crayons in the corner, water bowls for dogs, newspapers for solo customers.

"I'm worried about you," Andrew said. "You're doing too much."

"I don't have much choice, do I?" She didn't mean for her voice to have an edge to it, to sound bitter. She could try and take it back, but that would complicate things. Anyway, it was true. She would let Andrew make of that what he would and let herself get on with her delicious pancakes. She swore they got better every time they came here.

"You could take the redundancy offer."

He said it nonchalantly, as if it were the most normal thing in the world. Kerry nearly choked on her bacon. What the actual fuck? She hadn't seen that coming. It was as if he'd reached inside her and pulled out all her energy and drive and ambition and integrity and held it up in front of her and said, *this is worthless.*

She'd achieved so much at Bullfinch: overhauling the maternity cover, the pensions, the health and safety. She'd introduced proper apprentice and graduate schemes with better training. It might not have been her first choice of career, but she had created a legacy she was proud of, and she wasn't done yet.

"I'm not quitting," she said, impressed her voice held steady when her hurt threatened to unravel her. "I'm an HR Director. This is my job. The staff at work are relying on me to get them through this takeover and I owe it to them to do it right."

"You owe them nothing!" The couple with the small baby glanced over. Andrew lowered his voice and leaned in. "For twenty-five years, you have put them first, and Henry sold out without even discussing it with you. You should grab that redundancy offer with both hands and get the hell out of there."

Expletives went off in her head like fireworks. "Excuse me. I've put *them* first?"

"That's not …"

"You want me to put *you* first, is that it? You and the kids. Like a good wife and mother. My God. The patriarchy never ends, does it?"

"You are a terrific wife and …"

"You work just as many hours as I do! In a job you don't even enjoy, with a promotion you couldn't care less about. I do the bulk of the housework and am *still* the default parent at home. Yes, you cook, you cut the grass, you help with homework. But up here?" She pointed to her temple. "You have space. You don't go to bed at night worrying if you've bought Poppy's friend Liam the same Lego set for his birthday as you did last year, or why Alby doesn't have a best friend or whether Ella isn't eating enough or if we should …"

"Okay, I get it. I swear I do." The couple with the baby had left and the waitress was politely pretending not to hear their argument.

"Kerry, you are a marvellous woman and I appreciate you with all my heart. It is absolutely not for *my* benefit or *my* stress levels or *my* workload that I suggested it. I want *you* to be happy. Do you believe me?"

"Why don't you quit, then?" She was being provocative now, but she couldn't help it.

"Don't be silly," he said and laughed. He actually bloody well laughed. Swearwords she didn't even know she knew fired off in her brain. "What would I do?"

"You could take care of the kids and the house. I wouldn't be stressed then, would I? Plan that holiday you keep banging on about. There's no need for me to throw away my career on a three-month expedition to the Sahara or whatever the hell you're planning."

"Kerry, it's true I don't love my job. But it pays the bills and I have a good pension."

"My job also pays the bills. I, too, have a good pension."

He ignored her. "I'm fifty-two," he said. "I'm just tired of the endless drama. And I fancy a nice holiday. Okay?"

He pushed the plates of cold, uneaten food to one side and took her two hands in his. Kerry felt the rage inside her subside. Thank God the café was empty. She needed to come at this from a different angle.

"Why did you volunteer to help Pete with the beach protest?" she said.

"He needed the help," he said. "I have more experience with the council …"

"That's not why," Kerry said. "And you know it."

"Because the beach is a mess."

"It's because you *care*, Andrew Langley. You care about the people in this town, even though they are not your responsibility, as you put it. You care about those whose businesses rely on tourists. You care that local families can bring their kids to the beach with their buckets and spades to make sandcastles. You want me to be able to swim. You are *proud* of this town and you want it to be at its best. And that's why you are going above and beyond with this campaign, even though you are recovering from a hit-and-run injury and have extensive demands at home, as well a full time job. Am I right?"

"You are," he conceded. "You are absolutely right. And you're telling me that you feel the same way about Bullfinch. Correct?"

"Correct."

Wow. Izzy calling her a martyr was one thing. But her husband suggesting she quit? That had hurt.

The waitress cleared their plates and handed them dessert menus.

"Well. Since brunch was a bit of a disaster," Andrew said with forced jollity, "how about a giant chocolate pudding to share? And I can apologise for being a total idiot."

Kerry's appetite had vanished, but she desperately wanted to reconcile. She nodded and turned the conversation towards simpler things. The twins' upcoming birthday party. Concert tickets they'd promised Ella. Theo's school report. They were just finding equilibrium again when Andrew's mobile rang.

As he answered, Kerry slid her mobile out of her pocket, still on silent. Three missed calls from Mum's carer.

"Your mum's had a fall," Andrew said, just as Kerry realised it was going to be bad news.

Nicole

Nicole stood in her state-of-the-art white walk-in wardrobe, with its immaculate white shelves and hanging racks, handbags and shoes neatly lined up on the end wall, next to the full-length mirror. She needed to choose an outfit for an interview tomorrow afternoon. In London. Not easily commutable from Saltreach, but she couldn't afford to be picky any longer. It was a young company with a twenty-something female CEO who had specified *maturity* as the key desirable trait. Nicole read the subtext: old. Someone who'd been around the block, who could supply the experience required to reassure potential clients; a figurehead of sorts.

The pre-screening video call had confirmed as much. Gloria, head of Glorious and bankrolled by a wealthy, indulgent father, staged fashion shows for up-and-coming designers. She had the contacts, the media, the technical knowledge, but she had no gravitas and she knew it.

Nicole needed to invent a reason for her trip to London tomorrow. She'd been pretending to call on old friends and visit her old hairdresser for months. Wolf mightn't even notice she was gone. She hadn't told him about job interviews for years, couldn't bear to see the pity in his eyes. When they'd met, she'd been the bigger earner. He'd never questioned her decision to return to work full time after Lauren was born, even though the crèche fees had been astronomical. He'd simply adjusted his schedule so that he did the early shift, and she did the late one. She'd done the night feeds and the cooking, and Wolf had taken care of the endless laundry. They'd been a team. Until she'd lost her job. Because, of course, nobody could host fancy events during a global pandemic.

They'd even managed to have sex at least twice a week back then. Now she had a drawer full of silk and lace underwear she hadn't worn in forever. It was more efficient to do it herself. Not better, just … easier. Now how long had it been? Months? She knew it was mostly her doing, but she needed to feel emotionally connected to want to have sex. That elusive connection.

She couldn't understand it. She kept herself in good shape, better than most of her peers, and she knew he still fancied her, as she did him. And with Lauren more independent than ever, they had plenty of opportunity.

And the biggie. She had *moved* here for him. Yes, of course it had made financial sense for them to sell their flat in London. A flat which had been bought based on two incomes. It had been hard to reason logically with Wolf as to why they *shouldn't* move to the seaside town where there was fresh air, more school places, old friends, parks and playgrounds. Together with the small inheritance from the sale of his mother's bungalow, they could buy a bigger place.

And so they'd moved to Saltreach. And all Wolf did was complain that she spent too much money, that she didn't want to spend every weekend at the fucking Langleys', or eat giant fish and chip takeaways after a boring cliff walk on a Sunday, or go wild swimming in the freezing fucking sea that stunk like fucking seaweed all the time. He had no interest in London's cocktail bars or sushi restaurants any more. And so, the divide between them had grown. She loved him, she really did. She missed him. But she missed her old self even more.

She dug her toes into the thick-pile carpet and brought herself back to the present. Glorious wanted gravitas. At least that meant she could wear something age-appropriate. She pulled out an aquamarine cap-sleeved midi dress from a new designer that matched her eyes and paired it with navy Dior slingbacks and tote. Perfect.

Where would it leave them in the long run, though? A sexless marriage had an expiration date. Her mother always said that. And she wasn't stupid; men got frustrated. Hell, women got frustrated. Maybe tonight she'd make an effort, cook something nice, wear something nicer. Lauren had texted to say she was going to the cinema with Theo. Nicole would pop to the fishmonger for some scallops. She felt lighter than she had in a while as she put a bottle of white wine into the fridge to chill.

Wolf

Wolf tapped on the door to the finance room. A pretty redhead in a crisp white shirt was tapping with one hand on what appeared to be a large calculator plugged into her computer, the index finger of her other hand running down a list of numbers on a sheaf of papers with the other hand. She spotted Wolf but didn't smile. "Time for a fag break, ladies."

"I just need to do one quick check," Wolf said, flattening himself against the door as the women grabbed their purses and filed passed him. "I don't need to interrupt your work."

"Take your time," she said. "No point in killing ourselves, is there? It's not as if Stonebridge care about us."

It was the same across every department. He couldn't blame them; he was a Stonebridge hire, after all. Throughout the building, pockets of people huddled together, shaking their heads, the occasional, "fuck's sake," whispered a little too loudly. It felt like a morgue – except on Kerry's floor, where voices were frequently raised and outcries about the kids, the mortgage, the nursing home seeped out from beneath her office door. How she endured that every day he didn't know.

The thrill of winning the tender was wearing off fast. The technology at Bullfinch was a mess and Izzy had high expectations. A London company would have charged three times as much. Wolf felt foolish for thinking that his reputation had been impressive enough to capture the interest of a company as big as Stonebridge. He and the couple of freelancers he'd cobbled together at the last minute must look to Izzy like a bunch of amateurs. Still. A regular income was nothing to be sneezed at.

*

He worked quickly and left the finance room. At the top of the stairs, he met Kerry, rubbing her shin and swearing softly. It was nearly midday and she still had her coat on. "Everything okay?"

She reddened when she saw him, straightening up and giving her eyes a quick wipe. "I fell up the stairs," she said, trying and failing to laugh it off. "Sorry, I'm late. My mother had a fall yesterday."

"Oh, dear," he said, taking her bag from her. "How bad is it?"

"Fractured pelvis. Sprained wrist. Bruising."

"God, Kerry, I'm really sorry." He was due in a meeting in five. It could wait. He fired off a quick text. "Come on, and we'll get a cup of tea. How's she doing?"

"She's on bed rest at the hospital for the time being. They're hoping it'll all knit itself together, but that's it for living on her own."

"Where'll she go?" Wolf asked, but he already knew the answer.

"The kids'll have to give up their den. Andrew's already contacted a builder to see if we can convert part of the garage into a wet room for her. I just can't put her in a home."

The canteen was quiet, morning break over, lunchtime not started yet. They made their tea, took a couple of KitKats, and walked back to Kerry's office.

"Could you get a carer for her in her house?" They sat facing each other in the two chairs in front of her desk, hunched over their

Bullfinch-branded mugs. He should have run down to Ricardo for a couple of cappuccinos.

"That's how she's been managing until now. And to be honest, she shouldn't really be at home anymore, not by herself. I'm sure she's got dementia. This way, she'll have company and we can keep an eye on her."

"You're a good daughter."

"I haven't much choice, have I?" she said bitterly. "My sister in Australia hasn't even called me back yet. Andrew's being brilliant, of course, but I know how disappointed he is. He thinks we need to shake up our lives before it's too late. Thinks it's all too stressful." She laughed, a dry bark. "He wants me to take redundancy and toddle off to Africa with him on a jolly."

Wolf felt a spike of anger towards his best friend. How the hell did Andrew not know his wife better than that? And to guilt her over this, now, when she'd been minding him without complaint after his accident. That was inexcusable. Then he caught himself. Andrew was letting his mother-in-law move in indefinitely. Wolf thought of his own mother-in-law and shuddered.

"There'll be plenty of time for that down the road," he said gently, rubbing her hand.

"When she's dead, you mean," Kerry said flatly. "God, sorry Wolf, I'm being awful today."

"When the children are a little older," he said. "When you've saved everyone's jobs here and sent Izzy packing. When your sister runs out of money and comes home and you can put her in charge of the lot of them and go skinny dipping in Thailand or whatever you want." Kerry smiled through damp eyelashes. "See, that's better. There's always light at the end of the tunnel."

"Thanks, Wolf." They stood and she gave him a hug. He had a flashback to a school disco. They must have been about fifteen and the DJ was playing 'Take My Breath Away'. She had her arms around his neck and for the four minutes that they'd swayed together, he'd tried and failed to work up the courage to kiss her. In the end, she'd kissed him.

Clumsily, he turned his head and kissed her now, just as she was beginning to pull away from the hug, his lips landing awkwardly on her neck. Kerry tensed and he felt her hold on his shirt tighten for a second, as if she were about to push him away. But she didn't. She stayed, frozen in place, as if daring him to do it again.

Her earring was millimetres from his cheek, her perfume in his nostrils. Her heart beat against his chest. He kissed her again.

*

"What the hell are you doing?" Kerry shoved him backwards, and he caught his leg on the edge of her desk. She rubbed furiously at her neck where he'd kissed her and stared at the palm of her hand as if there was something dirty on it.

"Oh, Christ, Kerry, I didn't mean …" What didn't he mean? He *had* meant to. "I'm sorry," he said, arms spread wide, backing towards the door.

"For Christ's sake," she hissed. "I was upset, and *this* is what you do? What in God's name will I say to Andrew?"

Shit. *Shit.* Andrew was the straightest person Wolf knew. Andrew was the kind of guy who'd remember to send a good luck text when he knew Wolf was pitching for new business, who would volunteer to be the designated driver on a night out and still buy the first round of drinks. And he'd never, ever commented on the fact that Nicole didn't want to hang out with them. He was Wolf's best friend.

"I'm sorry," he said again. He was backed up against her office door now, desperate to escape. "Forget it ever happened. You've done nothing wrong, Kerry. It was my fault. Don't tell Andrew, please. There's no point. Nothing really happened anyway."

"We don't keep secrets in our marriage," Kerry said, smoothing her hair. "Does that mean you're not planning on telling Nicole, either?"

"No," he said quietly and slipped out of Kerry's office. He hurried to the gents, locking the door behind him. He needed to think.

He certainly wasn't planning on telling Nicole. She would hang it round his neck like a noose for the remainder of their marriage, short-lived as that would be. There was a time they had told each other everything as well. But Nicole had secrets too, he knew she did.

There was something on her laptop. He'd resolved not to pry, even though he knew he could easily cover his tracks. He'd prefer if she'd just tell him. Yet he didn't want to ask. He sighed. She was so tricky. Maybe she was seeing a therapist. Someone had definitely put that bloody orangery idea in her head. Nicole would never sit still long enough to watch a sunset.

Since she'd been made redundant, she'd run six half marathons, turned the lagging school PTA into a well-oiled money-making machine, decorated the house top-to-bottom, and kept Lauren in top sets in every subject. She cooked from scratch despite loathing every minute of it, read self-help books until after midnight and took the occasional online class. He knew she still craved the hum of a busy office, the pressure of events.

But somewhere along the road, she'd stopped confiding in him. Once, he'd made the fatal error of suggesting maybe she should try giving off a relaxed vibe, to come off a little more easy-going. *Manageable* was what he'd meant. Nicole would be a tough employee to manage. It had not been a pleasant conversation.

Still, it hurt that she had simply stopped talking to him. He was shut out of more than the bedroom. But lately she'd upped her game. There were two new dresses in the wardrobe, a smart bag beside her bed. She had a game plan and clearly, he wasn't part of it.

Kai

Kai narrowed his eyes and zoomed in, snapping randomly. The new lens was awesome. From his bedroom window he could see the entire park. Being on the fifth floor was the only good thing about this crappy flat.

He panned across the playground, where a couple of young mums chatted, toddlers playing in the sandpit. He snapped a little girl mid-cartwheel, another at full height on the swings, elation and terror sweeping her face in equal measure. He leaned further out of the open window and panned right, higher up the hill, to the adult gym equipment that the old people used and the bench in front of the trees that everybody loved. It was practically a date if you arranged to meet someone at The Bench. You could see beyond the park, the promenade, the red-and-white-striped ice cream kiosk, to the beach. Nobody was swimming today. Nobody sunbathed. Kai had no intention of ever sunbathing. The prospect of stripping off and just lying there, exposed for everyone to gawp at, made him literally nauseous.

If he twisted to the left and leaned out a little further, he could see the English Channel, sunshine bouncing off the water. A tourist boat chugged towards the jetty and a single family climbed out, handing yellow life jackets back to the skipper and pulling on flip flops. Apart from them, the place was deserted. This bloody town was worse than the last one. Dead.

Kai pointed his camera back up the hill. Theo and Lauren had entered the park, hand in hand. Kai put down the camera but stayed in place, hoping Theo might look up and see him, beckon him down. But Theo's attention was on Lauren. Was *she* the real reason Theo was still avoiding him? It had to be more than the kiss. Theo wasn't gay. And he, Kai, wasn't gay, he was almost sure of it now. But there was definitely something up. Ever since Theo's black eye, he'd been … different.

Mum was being weird too. Some days she was all over Kai like a rash, wanting to know how he was coping without Dad, all the ins and outs of his private life. Other days … well, other days, she literally didn't notice if he was in the flat. She might actually be depressed, but he didn't have anyone to ask. At least she hadn't said any more about the swimming club.

Theo and Lauren were kissing. Kai zoomed right up to their faces. Up close, it was kind of gross, messy-looking, and sloppy. Lauren had her arms around Theo's neck and he had her pressed up against the back of the climbing frame, a simple wooden wall with footholds and dangling, knotted ropes on one side. They obviously thought nobody could see them. Theo's hands were inside Lauren's top. Kai lowered his camera. This was disgusting, watching them like some kind of pervert. He stepped away from the window.

When he looked again, they'd stopped. Lauren was walking in the direction of the promenade. Theo obviously wasn't walking her home. Kai couldn't blame him – Lauren's OCD mum didn't like her friends coming over in case they walked on her white carpets. No, Theo had gone the other way, up the hill towards The Bench. If he were going to hang out for a bit, Kai could join him. Pulling on a pair of trainers, he took the lift downstairs and pushed open the gate leading directly onto the park.

Theo was nearly at The Bench. Kai hesitated. Theo was effectively gaslighting him. You were supposed to take the hint and find someone else to hang out with, but Kai didn't really have other friends, apart from Oliver Nowell, who was honestly a bit of a prick.

He was still carrying his camera. Worst case, he could pretend he was out taking photographs. He would seem like less of a loser. Everyone knew he wanted to be a photographer. He was already selling a selection at Elise's mum's gift shop.

Theo stopped at the edge of the woods, shifting his weight from one foot to another. Kai took a photograph, not even knowing why. He felt antsy, nervous, as though he were about to witness a crime. He moved closer.

A tall, thin man appeared from the woods and walked quickly towards Theo. He had on a black windproof jacket even though it was boiling hot, black jeans, and the kind of chunky walking boots that old people wore. But he didn't look like a hiker. Didn't have the steady, sturdy gait, the sense of calm. This guy was twitchy, clicking his fingers and rubbing his palms on the front of his jeans. He offered Theo a handshake, then a fist bump, then let his hand slide back to his jeans. Kai took another picture.

Theo and the man strolled over to The Bench and sat. The man leaned forward, his elbows on his knees, talking earnestly, as much with his hands as his voice. Theo nodded along, not saying much. Kai took another photo, straining to hear, but they were too far away.

Could he be the guy Theo had fought? Theo's body language was taut, uncomfortable. This guy was at least ten years older than them. Maybe they were making up. Kai would step in to help if anything went wrong.

Maybe he was a drug dealer. That theory had been passed around school. Kai didn't know who had started it, but he didn't believe it. Theo was far too clean for that. Took his football too seriously.

But Kai didn't trust Lauren. He heard she'd taken ket at Oliver's party a few months ago. He didn't know who she'd got it from, but Kai wouldn't put it past her to use someone as innocent as Theo to do her dirty work for her. Lauren was too busy keeping up that good-girl image for her parents.

And Theo had had a crush on her for, like, two years. He used to be too shy to even talk to her, but somehow that had all changed. Clearly, Theo was Lauren's lapdog now – and Kai had been side-lined. Maybe Lauren had something to do with that, too. Theo hadn't responded to Kai's text about the photographs of her on the internet. She'd probably spun him a story to get out of it.

Theo and the man chatted for about ten more minutes and stood. Kai watched the guy put something in Theo's hand. He zoomed in as close as he could, took more pictures, but he couldn't work out what it was. Theo was frowning, upset. The man tried to put an arm around him, but Theo wriggled away and practically ran off, leaving the guy to stand and watch for a minute before turning to leave the way he'd arrived, through the trees. Theo stuffed whatever it was the man had given him into his back pocket and started to jog away, back in the direction of his house.

This was Kai's chance. To comfort Theo over whatever it was this guy had given him. To make up. To be friends again. He put his camera away and zipped up his bag.

But Theo was on the far side of the park already and moving fast. Kai started to jog, then to run. Almost immediately, his breath came in gasps and his bag bounced against his hip, making his t-shirt ride up, exposing his skin.

He stopped running, mortified, in case anyone would see, and reached a hand under his top. He put a finger under the layer of fat that hung on his side. He was disgusting. Mum was right. He needed to do something about it.

The park was empty now. The little kids and their mums were gone. There was nobody here to see him. He even had his trainers on.

He approached the gym equipment. It couldn't be *that* hard to use. Old people used them. One machine didn't have any weights. There was a wide bar to hold onto and two things that looked a bit like skateboards to put your feet on. Kai stepped carefully into them and stood still, holding tight onto the safety bar, his knuckles white. Very slowly, he pushed his feet in opposite directions and the machine began a lilting movement. He pushed a little harder until he found a more natural flow and relaxed his hold on the bar. He could do this. He could come here any evening, do a workout. He could wait till it was dark if he wanted. He'd figure out how to use the other machines. He could even work up to jogging round the playing field.

He pushed harder, panting again. He took one hand off the bar, let it swing by his side. There, that felt more comfortable. He pushed harder with his legs, enjoying the unfamiliar thrill of using his body. Adrenalin flowed. He went a little faster. The machine bounced him uncomfortably and wouldn't slow down. He lost his balance.

Reaching to grab the bar with his free hand, he fell sideways, landed on the exercise bike next to him. The seat passed inches from his nose, but he felt the thud of the pedal against his leg, the scrape of metal along his shin.

He scanned the park furiously. Fortunately, there was nobody there to witness his humiliation. Tears burned behind his eyes. Fuck. He climbed to his feet, kicked the machine. He should get back on, do it again, do it better. He knew he should.

On the way home he bought a packet of salt and vinegar crisps and ate them slowly, loathing himself more and more with every crunch.

Wolf

"I'M HOME!" WOLF SCANNED the jackets and shoes in the hall cupboard and tried to work out if Lauren was there. He could use a diversion right about now, even if it was the lofty scorn of his fifteen-year-old daughter.

"Hi, darling." Nicole came out of the kitchen and offered him a glass of ice-cold wine. She was wearing another new dress, a nice red one, but today was not the day to discuss her spending.

He tried to smile, feeling his transgression written all over his face, as though scrawled with Kerry's lipstick. He took a gulp of wine.

"Good day?" Nicole said, standing on tiptoe to kiss his cheek. Something she hadn't done in forever. God, had she heard already? Where the hell was Lauren?

"Yes. Yes, good, thanks. You?" He checked his phone. Andrew hadn't responded to his invitation for a drink. After skipping his meeting and hiding at his desk all afternoon, he'd decided the best course of action was to bite the bullet and get it over with. Andrew's reaction would be the determiner of whatever came next. He sent another text.

Need to discuss something if possible. Pint?

Nicole was watching him expectantly, a tinge of disappointment in her eyes. He'd missed her reply.

"Sorry, love. I missed that. It's just, I might have to go out again tonight."

"Oh?"

"Andrew wanted to talk to me about something. But hey, tell me again about your day."

"Maybe you could meet Andrew tomorrow instead?" Nicole came closer and slid a hand into the back pocket of his jeans. Her perfume was heavy, cloying, and he felt like he might vomit. "Lauren's gone to the cinema with Theo. I thought we could spend a bit of time together."

How fucking ironic. She hadn't wanted to spend time alone with him in months.

"Lovely," he said, wanting to bolt back out the front door. He'd been stupid to think he could brazen this out. It was *Kerry,* of all people. Nicole wasn't stupid. She'd always known he liked Kerry, fancied her a bit even. He'd almost come to believe that she accepted it. She made no bones about the fact that Oliver's dad was a bit dishy; all the school mums thought so. He hadn't batted an eyelid at that. Though he had made sure to get a good look at him the next time he was on school pick-up duty.

Nicole topped up their glasses, although he'd barely had a sip. He hoped she wasn't going to drink too much, tonight of all nights. Nicole was a messy drunk.

"Kerry still showing you the ropes?"

If there was innuendo, Wolf couldn't tell. He perched on a stool at the island and saw that Nicole was preparing an elaborate-looking meal. He spied scallops and relaxed a little. There was no way she'd make his favourite if she knew he'd kissed someone. Unless she was planning on giving him food poisoning.

"No, I don't see her all that much anymore," he said. "I'm with the IT team, she's HR, remember? Actually, it's all going very well my end. Bit of a disaster her end, though."

"The redundancies?" Nicole zested a lemon, opened a packet of baby spinach. There was a carton of double cream by her elbow. She was going all out. His stomach clenched – he wouldn't be able to eat it.

"That, and her mother fell." Why the hell was he talking about Kerry? He couldn't stop. "She's in hospital with a fractured pelvis. I feel like we should do something to help, after what they've been through with Andrew already."

Nicole clutched a handful of spaghetti so tightly he thought it would snap. "What kind of help?" she said frostily.

He'd said the wrong thing. Obviously. "Doesn't matter," he said, taking a quick peek at his phone. "You look lovely. Been to the hairdresser?"

She rolled her eyes at him and smiled. Phew. Back on track.

*

Andrew still hadn't replied by the time they'd finished eating. Wolf texted Kerry.

Have you told him?

His phone burned in his pocket. He sent Nicole into the lounge with a fresh glass of wine and washed the dishes as slowly as he possibly could. She wanted to have sex. He couldn't possibly do it. Not without knowing how this thing would pan out. He wasn't *that* callous.

Christ, they hadn't slept together in so long, she would take the rejection horribly. Talk about double standards – she had no compunction about shutting him out whenever she wasn't in the mood. He could always pick a fight.

His phone pinged.

I'm in The Anchor

That was a blunt reply. Kerry must have already told him. Fuck. Wolf's stomach twisted. Andrew was reasonable, he reminded himself. And he'd agreed to meet. This could all be dealt with tonight, man to man. All he had to do was apologise, take the hit – hopefully not literally – and keep his distance for a while. He'd work from home for a bit. Make it up to Nicole tomorrow, if all went well tonight. He put his head round the lounge door.

"Sweetheart, I'm so sorry. Andrew's asked me to meet him," he said as contritely as possible. "Why don't you enjoy the peace and quiet here while Lauren is out? Maybe have a bath or read a book?"

"Have a bath?" She sneered, indicated her freshly blow-dried hair, the short dress that showed off the kind of cleavage that spoke of sexy underwear. Wolf cringed. She'd dressed up for him.

"Sorry, darling. I wouldn't do this, only Andrew's got something on his mind. He's probably worried about the mother-in-law coming to live with them. They haven't room to swing a cat in their house."

"Just go, Wolf."

Kerry

"Have you had enough breakfast?" Kerry hovered, smoothing the throw on the back of the armchair, straightening the already-straight cushions. "Can I get you anything else? Another coffee?"

"I'm fine." But Andrew wouldn't meet her eye from his position on the sofa. "Just go, Kerry. I'm tired. I've had a bad night."

"Do you want more painkillers?" But it wasn't his broken collarbone or his cracked rib that had kept him awake. It was her. Wolf. The kiss.

Andrew sighed. "No, thank you."

God, this was unbearable. He hadn't spoken since dinnertime yesterday, when Kerry had handed the twins their iPads, stacked the dishwasher, made him a cup of tea and told him what had happened. He'd looked as hurt as though she'd admitted to having an affair for the past six months. He'd just grabbed his keys and said he was going to the pub to think.

The guilt was ridiculous. She'd scoured the kitchen, hoovered the lounge, bathed the twins. She'd put fresh sheets on Ella's bed for him, cleared away his old newspapers, put a bottle of fizzy water and a Snickers bar on his bedside table. He'd deliberately stayed out until he knew she'd be asleep.

Kerry kissed Ella and Theo goodbye as they left to walk to school together. Poppy had woken with a temperature and Kerry felt awful packing her off to school too, hoping a dose of Calpol would see her through till later. She ushered the twins to the car, bags in tow, and told them she'd be back in a minute. She went inside and put her head back round the door of the lounge, tears springing to her eyes, ruining the carefully applied make-up she'd hoped would disguise her puffy complexion. Andrew was staring silently into space.

"I haven't done anything wrong," she said quietly.

Andrew's face crumpled. He climbed awkwardly out of his chair and put his good arm around her. "I know, love. But Wolf has, hasn't he?"

*

She had a meeting at half nine. The four directors of Bullfinch were meeting with their lawyers to discuss their findings and prepare their attack. Monday was D-Day. Izzy was bringing backup from Stonebridge, so they needed to be ready.

Before she entered the building, she pulled out her phone. "Clare. Hope the documentary is going well. I'm sorry to give you this news by voicemail, but Mum's had a fall. Fractured pelvis, sprained wrist, bruising. She'll be fine but I need your help, okay? I really need your help."

Kai

Maths. Final period, thank God. Kai slipped into the classroom, barely ahead of the teacher, and sought an empty space. The tables were arranged in threes, and there was only one empty seat. Next to Theo. Beside him, Lauren curled her lip at Kai and turned to stare out of the window. Theo's school bag sat on the empty chair. The teacher coughed. Kai felt the eyes of the entire class bore into him, felt his face heat up. From somewhere behind him he thought he heard the word *fat*. The waistband of his school trousers dug into his flesh, and he visualised the jagged red line he knew would be there.

"Mate," he said quietly to Theo, who looked up from his workbook, seemingly oblivious to Kai's predicament. "Can you move your bag?"

Theo's eyes swivelled towards Lauren, who let out a noisy sigh and shifted ever-so-slightly away. Bitch.

"Please?" he said, hating the desperation in his voice. The teacher tapped her foot.

"Course," Theo said, lifting the bag and putting it by his feet. He reached out for a fist bump and turned his shoulder the tiniest fraction away from Lauren.

Relief seeped through Kai like a waterfall. He sat and arranged his things, careful not to touch Theo. The last thing he needed was for Theo to think he had a crush on him.

But Theo leaned towards him and whispered, "Sorry I haven't replied to your texts. Are we still friends?"

Kai wanted to punch the air. Instead, he nodded. "I'm still sorry," he said. He wasn't as good at whispering and the teacher gave him a glare. Luckily, he and Theo were both top of the class in maths and she was inclined to overlook a little chatter.

"Doesn't matter," Theo whispered. "I have so much to tell you. My dad was in an accident. And there's … other stuff."

Kai nodded. So it wasn't all about him. Theo genuinely hadn't been ignoring him just because of the kiss. "Walk home?" he said, hardly daring to hope.

Theo gave him a thumbs-up. Kai turned his attention back to the teacher and the trigonometry, feeling lighter than he had in weeks.

*

"Is your dad okay?" Kai asked. They walked along the seafront. Posters were pinned to every second lamppost recruiting protestors for a march against the seaweed next Wednesday. Two women in animal print leggings marched past at electric speed. Kai bought himself and Theo a Coke at the kiosk.

"Two fractured ribs, broken collarbone, bruising," Theo said. "He already looks way better, but he's still in pain. It was a hit-and-run."

"Shut up. Really?" It sounded so dangerous.

"He was on his bike. Dad thinks the driver probably didn't realise it was so serious and didn't want to get in trouble."

"Still, though. That's awful."

"Gran's coming to live with us. Mum's got a crisis at work – everyone's losing their jobs apparently, and she's got to stop it." He bit his lip. "It's awful at home," he said. "Mum and Dad row all the time. Dad walked out last night and didn't come back until after everyone was in bed."

God. No wonder Theo hadn't been in touch. Kai didn't think he'd ever heard him talk so much in one go. It seemed like he'd been holding onto all these thoughts for too long and he needed to pass the burden to somebody else. He might even tell Kai about the man who gave him the black eye.

"Who were you with in the park the other day?"

Theo snapped the ring on his can and took a long drink. "Were you there?"

"Yeah." Kai shifted on his feet. Shit. He hadn't thought this through. Why was he pushing Theo? They'd only just made up, for God's sake.

"Oh." Theo took another drink. "I met Lauren there."

"No, not Lauren." He couldn't help himself now. He'd gone this far. "You were with some old guy."

"Oh, him. That's my football coach."

They crossed the road and headed up the hill towards the park. Kai didn't know Theo's football coach, but he would have bet a tenner that Theo was lying. Shit. He didn't want Theo to lie. And yet, in some perverse way, he'd wanted to catch him out. Wanted Theo to tell him the secret. Include him in it. But Theo had gone quiet.

Kai changed the subject. "And Lauren. You guys are dating now, yeah?"

Theo shifted uncomfortably. Suddenly, Kai felt fully switched on. Given how hard Theo had been crushing on Lauren, he should be thrilled to be going out with her now. Something was wrong. Something clicked in his brain. The thought he'd had earlier. Lauren was keeping Theo from him.

"She doesn't like me, does she?" he said, as nonchalantly as he could.

Theo blushed. "She thinks you watch her," he said and Kai knew he was being honest. Maybe he should be honest, too.

"I'm not the only one," he said, staring across the park. He didn't want to see Theo's reaction. Gulls swooped and called. A woman lifted a baby from a red pushchair and kissed it on the end of its nose. "I think people are looking at Lauren on the internet. I told you about the photographs."

"That's different," Theo said, not sounding sure at all. "She did some modelling and the agency put the photos on their website. To get work for her." He was practically begging Kai to agree.

What should he do? Tell Theo the truth? Assuming that what Oliver had told him *was* actually the truth. He didn't want to jeopardise their friendship again. But he didn't want there to be secrets between them anymore.

"I'll show you," he said. They sat on the swings. The chains bit into the sides of Kai's thighs. He opened his phone, searched for the photo of Lauren that Oliver had sent him. He could *only* show Theo the one from Oliver. The last pictures he'd taken were of Theo in the park, Theo with the guy, Theo kissing Lauren. The photos from his phone and his camera had synced, but he hadn't had a chance to go through them yet. If Theo saw them, he would think Kai was a creep.

He kept the phone tilted towards him as he scrolled, panic rising from his belly. But Theo was impatient and grabbed the phone out of his hands and started scrolling.

"What the hell is this?" Theo hissed. "Are you some kind of pervert?"

Kai peered at the screen and blanched. Bile rose in his throat. Theo had found the photo of him and Lauren kissing. The one Kai had intended to delete. He'd zoomed in, close enough that they could see the skin on Lauren's stomach, where Theo had put his hand under her shirt and the fabric had risen up.

"Are you jealous?" Theo said. "Because nobody will go out with you? Because you're too fat?"

Kai crossed his arms over his stomach and grasped the layer of blubber half way down his side, slicing one deliberately ragged nail into his flesh. He felt the familiar burn and pushed deeper into his skin, despising himself, yet unable to stop, feeling the criss-cross of scabs from the blade he kept in his bedside table opening up. "That's not what …"

"She was right about you watching her," Theo said. "This is seriously creepy." He moved to the next picture. "Why are you spying on me?" He whirled around to face Kai. "Or maybe it's not actually about Lauren, is it? It's because I picked *her* instead of *you*! You *are* gay then, is that it?"

"I'm not gay," Kai said quietly, dropping his Coke can in the bin, clutching the strap of his school bag. He wanted to get out of there. The gate to the flats was thirty feet away. "Go home, Theo, you don't understand."

But Theo was staring at the next picture, another close up. He zoomed in on Lauren's face. Her eyes were closed and she looked beautiful, almost ethereal.

Kai wasn't ready for the full force of Theo's fist on his stomach. He fell on the ground, clutching his middle, winded.

"*You're* the one putting pictures of Lauren on the internet!" There were tears in Theo's eyes. "They're fake, aren't they? You take pictures like this and put them on the bodies of girls in bikinis. It's because you're jealous, isn't it?"

Kai couldn't say anything. He was gasping on the ground. The woman on the far side of the playground put her baby back in its pushchair and hurried away. He wanted to tell Theo that of course he didn't, of course he'd never do that. But his breath wouldn't come.

"You sicko," Theo was crying now. "That's a crime! You can be done by the police for that!" He balled his fists and jammed them into his pockets. "Stay away from me and Lauren, you fucking pervert."

*

The next morning, Kai stayed in bed, replaying his conversation with Theo in his head for the millionth time.

Mum barged into his bedroom without knocking. "Time for school." She opened the blinds and let the sunshine in, bright light searing his eyelids. He scrunched them shut and slid further under the duvet. "I'm not going."

He heard Mum work her way around the room, gathering up dirty clothes and cups, a plate and fork he'd forgotten to return to the kitchen, his overflowing wastepaper basket. He knew it pissed her off. It gave her an excuse to come in when he wasn't there. He just hadn't been able to care enough to do anything about it.

He sensed her still, imagined her standing at the foot of his bed, his dirty socks held aloft, watching him.

"It's double art this afternoon," she said. They both knew that double art was Kai's favourite part of the week. If he refused to go to school today, he couldn't pretend any longer that there was nothing wrong.

"I don't care," he muttered from under his pillow.

There was a tiny pause. Then, with no regard for his privacy, she snatched his duvet back. Kai lay curled in the foetal position wearing only his pants, facing the wall. He knew what she could see. He'd seen it in the mirror before he went to bed last night. Angry, bloody welts crisscrossed his sides like graffiti, raised marks, torn skin, a patchwork quilt of scars from a very small blade.

She put her hand to her mouth to stifle a cry. Kai turned, crossing his arms over his bare stomach, cradling it as though protecting a newborn baby. But it was too late. A purple bruise spread up from his navel and over his ribcage.

"Sweetheart, you're not going to school," she said, stroking his cheek. "We're going to sort this out."

Ella

THERE WAS SOMEONE BEHIND Ella. She couldn't see him, but she knew he was there and she knew he was a he. She'd heard him cough, heard him mutter under his breath when she'd sped up. She'd accidentally walked to Granny's house after school out of habit, forgetting that Granny was in hospital. She rang Theo's phone and when it went to voicemail, she talked out loud as though he'd answered.

"I'll see you in a minute," she said brightly, "I'm nearly there. Can you see me?" She paused, pretending to listen to a reply but instead hearing the laboured breathing of someone struggling to keep up with her. How could she put him off? "Come and meet me!"

She let herself into Granny's house and slammed the door shut behind her. She put the chain on, and pressed her ear against the letterbox, listening for footsteps. Nothing. She peered out from behind the net curtains in Granny's lounge. The street was empty. Who the hell had been following her?

She walked around the house, room by room, checking the back door was locked, pretending to herself that she was just making sure everything was as it should be. But she knew she was really giving him time to leave.

It was as if Granny had been gone for weeks. She'd only been in hospital two days, but already the house was dusty, the air unclean, like dirty laundry. She washed up a plate abandoned by the sink, containing a stale crust of bread, cheese sprouting mould. She retched as she threw it and the rest of the fridge's contents into the bin and then carried it to the wheelie bin, peering over the garden fence into the back lane, checking the key was still in its hiding place under the gnome by the back door, locking it behind her as she came back inside.

She knew about the man who'd been hanging around. A suspicious man Granny hadn't recognised. Mum thought he was Mrs King's son, but Dad said it was some guy thinking of buying a house in the area. The street was empty now; she'd checked from every angle. All the same, she double-locked the windows, afraid to leave, and decided that Granny would hate the thought of her house being dirty so she got out the vacuum cleaner and set to work. When they visited her in hospital later, she would tell Granny that everything was nice and tidy.

An hour later, Ella locked up carefully, then slid the tip of her front door key between the middle and index fingers of her right hand and gripped it tightly. There was no one else on the street now. She would be more visible, but then again, so would he. She video-called a friend, chatted about their upcoming tests, about a party at the weekend, about hockey. She maximised the selfie screen and kept one eye on the space behind her, one eye in front.

Fifteen minutes later, with a trail of sweat down her back, Ella let herself in her own front door. She found Alby and cuddled him until her heartbeat returned to normal.

Theo

THEO'S PHONE PINGED AGAIN. What now? He flipped it over.

Thinking of you. L x

And a photo of her pouting.

What was he supposed to message back? That he was thinking of her too? He wasn't. He was in the middle of a game of *Grand Theft Auto,* and when he finished that, he had to help Mum make tea. Then he'd promised Poppy he'd read her a bit more of *Matilda.* She could probably read it herself, but she was afraid of Miss Trunchbull – at least, she pretended to be. Theo didn't mind. He liked doing the voices.

His phone pinged again.

Are you there?

He ignored it and went downstairs, where Mum handed him a head of lettuce to wash. "Everything okay at school?"

"I got 97% in Maths."

"Course you did, sweetheart. You've got your father's brains."

His phone pinged again.

Show this to your Mum

There was a link. It was a Facebook page, but Theo couldn't see what was on it. He didn't have a Facebook profile. It was only for old people. But Mum had one.

"Have you got your phone? Lauren wants me to show you something."

Mum stuck out one hip and Theo pulled her phone out of her pocket. He texted her the link and opened it.

"Oh, shit," he said.

"Language."

"Sorry. This is bad." Maybe he shouldn't tell her. That would mean keeping another secret. Mum was watching him.

"We've had our fair share of bad luck lately," she said. "So we're pretty much experts at coping now. You can tell me."

Theo took a deep breath and read.

"Bullfinch Takeover: A Total Disaster for Saltreach."

"Well, they're not wrong there," Mum said, tipping chicken into a dish. "Pass me an onion, will you?"

She diced as Theo read on.

"The management at Bullfinch are putting the livelihoods of Saltreach locals at risk by selling out to Stonebridge, a company previously accused of disregarding business ethics in pursuit of expansion. It's a total disaster for our town and must be stopped. Kerry Langley …"

He broke off. Mum sprinkled onion on top of the chicken, added peppers, tomatoes, garlic, olive oil, and balsamic vinegar. The bitter smell got up his nose and he stepped away.

"Show me that," she said, wiping her hands on her apron and taking the phone from him.

"It's just …"

"Maybe I should join. Show the town I'm doing my best."

"You're not upset?"

"Oh, honey," she said, chucking him under the chin like a toddler. "I already know about the group. Wolf told me. He's keeping an eye on it for me."

Phew. Wolf was cool. He would deal with it. Nothing to worry about.

The front door slammed.

"Is that you, Ella?" Mum called. There was no answer. "Oh. Oh, no." Mum said then, her voice different. "Check this one out. Kerry Langley is an incompetent leader and needs to go. She hasn't the balls to …" She made a face at him and didn't finish the sentence. She rolled her eyes. "People are very brave when they're anonymous."

"You could ask Facebook to take it down?"

"No, sweetheart, it's all right. People need to vent. Let them get on with it. They're worried. I'll keep an eye on it." She put the phone back in her pocket and slid the dish into the oven. "Honestly. Don't give it another thought."

She really did seem relaxed about it. Still, it couldn't hurt to check it out himself. Theo went to his bedroom, downloaded the Facebook app and set up an account under the name Jim Bunting. He found the Saltreach Local page and the article and skipped straight to the comments.

Wolf Bauer
Who writes this vitriolic crap? **@Kerry Langley** is doing her best to save jobs. The least you could do is not hide behind an anonymous post.

Anonymous member 564
FFS, what is she, your girlfriend?

Wolf Bauer
Henry Bishop sold the business to Stonebridge, not Kerry. Legal advice has been taken, and all the proper protocols are being followed, but it will take time.

Benj Taylor
This town is going downhill fast. No beach, no holidaymakers, no business for the restaurants and bars and cafés. Now bloody Stonebridge.

Kirsty Avon
I vote we stop paying our council tax.

Pete Murray
Join the march next Wednesday instead. 2.30pm by the kiosk. A PEACEFUL protest. Follow the link to sign the petition.

Jax Wallace
While we're on the subject of the council, has anyone reported the massive pothole under the bridge? My alloys are f**ked!

Verity Sharp
Anyone know why they've stopped providing free dog poo bags at the park?

Joe Poole
@Verity Sharp If you can afford a Labrador, you can afford your own poo bags.

Verity Sharp
No need to get personal, **@JoePoole**, it was a simple question.

And so it went on, on random tangents, one more ridiculous than the next. After all the lectures Theo had to sit through at school about the misuse of social media, he couldn't believe adults behaved like this.

Why had Lauren told him about the page in the first place? She wasn't the type to worry about people. Maybe she was being vindictive, cross with him for not picking up earlier, for not sending her back kisses and love hearts like a five-year-old? He could never tell with Lauren. A notification popped up. Lauren again. Of course.

Can I come round? Please? Xoxo

Theo sighed. After his row with Kai, he didn't really want to see her. He didn't want to tell her his best friend was putting photographs of her on the internet. The police would get involved. His parents would know. They had enough on their plates at the moment. And yet he couldn't *not* tell her. Not unless he got Kai to take them all down. And if they were being shared at school, it was already too late.

Sorry, making dinner. Have football later.

CU at school tomo x

Besides, Theo had his own problem. Mitch.

He pulled out the photograph Mitch had given him. It was definitely Dad. A younger, thinner Dad in a denim shirt, in a pub

Theo didn't recognise. The table was littered with empty glasses and behind him a group of people laughed, a woman's cigarette dangling inches from his head. Dad looked unaware of the crowd. He had one hand around a pint of lager and the other draped over the shoulders of a woman with chocolate eyes and dark, curly hair. She was very thin, with sinewy olive-skinned arms, and wore a gold sleeveless top. She had small, uneven, teeth and dark red lips and she was laughing at something that was happening on the other side of the table.

In the picture, Dad was staring at her. Theo recognised that look. It was the look he had when Poppy made him a Father's Day card or Alby beat him at Top Trumps. He wore it when Theo and Ella brought him cups of tea or offered to help him up the stairs. But mostly he saw it when Dad looked at Mum. It was love. And if Mitch had this photo, he must be telling the truth. Mitch must be his brother.

Lauren

LAUREN GRITTED HER TEETH. Mum was in a bad mood. Like, a really bad mood. It didn't make any sense. She'd spent the day in London seeing old work friends, came home looking amazing in a new blue dress, and ordered pizza, something she never did. Lauren actually wondered if she was having an affair. Only someone special could make her mum light up like that, and it certainly wasn't Dad.

But the pizza came and she started snapping at Dad. It had been pretty repulsive watching him shovel slices of double cheese feast into his mouth like that, but still. Mum didn't even eat any in the end. That made Lauren feel bad about eating it. Did keeping her figure mean she couldn't eat anything delicious?

Then Dad said he was going out. Lauren didn't blame him. It wasn't like him to go out two nights in a row, not to be glued to his desk on the top floor all evening. Lauren knew he slept there, but she didn't really understand why, except that her parents couldn't seem to bear the sight of each other anymore. It was totally screwed up.

When Mum left the table to clear up, she took a selfie and examined her hair. She'd bought the same curling mousse she'd seen in Ella's bathroom and spent ages styling it this morning. It sat perfectly. Graduated waves, not too curly. She'd had highlights put in at the weekend. It was probably even nicer than Ella's now. One more reason not to give up the photos. The money was amazing.

She'd finally worn the handcuffs. She hadn't fully closed them, but she made it seem like she had, and taken a couple of photos. Suggestive, but not too revealing. That was what she usually aimed for. Nothing too incriminating. She'd had a surge in views, compliments, dick pics, insults, and a big influx of cash. Including five separate payments of £15.15. User W45 was still watching. She'd paid for the highlights, put the rest into her secret savings account, and tried to put it out of her mind.

Until Oliver accosted her at school yesterday. She'd thought she'd dealt with him. But he'd sat directly behind her in French today and made moaning noises in her ear. She didn't know if the other boys he sat with knew about the photos too, but they laughed along anyway. Oliver made a joke about his mum virtually *handcuffing* him to his desk to do his homework, said that he'd only *peeked* at his books before finding something much more interesting on his laptop.

She cursed whoever had given him her phone number. She'd had ten texts this afternoon alone.

What picture are you taking today?

Need a hand?

I can hold the camera for you if u wanna be cuffed again

U make me hard

I want a piece of the action

Send me a photo

Better still, show me for real

Meet me at the cabin tomorrow afternoon

Six o'clock

Or I'll show everyone what a slut you are

What the hell was she supposed to do? Even if she stopped posting photos, which she was *not* prepared to do for Oliver fucking Nowell, he'd probably already downloaded everything she'd ever posted. Thank God she'd never made a video, but still. She'd never be able to show her face in Saltreach again.

There was only one thing for it. She'd have to meet him.

*

Mum was perched at the island, staring into her laptop. She was *always* on it lately. She'd probably forgotten Lauren was even in the room. She couldn't tell Mum about her problems, obviously, but really, she couldn't tell Mum *anything*. Mum wasn't one of those warm, cuddly women like Theo's mum, who always offered snacks and wanted to know how your day was and told you how pretty you were. Theo's mum made time for all *four* of her children. Lauren had seen her around Saltreach, cycling along the promenade with little Alby, standing on the sidelines in the freezing cold watching Theo play football, cuddling Poppy on the sofa as they watched animated movies together, and shopping in Zara with Ella.

Naturally, Zara was where Lauren shopped too. Ella didn't know she was the prettiest girl in school. The boys were half-afraid of her, probably because she already had the mildly superior attitude of a primary school teacher. Most likely because she point-blank refused to date boys who were actually *at* their school. But at least she knew what she wanted. In an alternate universe, if Lauren were a mere two weeks older and had been in the year above, they could have been friends.

Lauren's mother did none of those things with her. They didn't even watch *Strictly* together. And she only had one child. Lauren left her mother staring into space and went upstairs, passing Dad silently on the landing. She waited till he reached the kitchen and took the second flight up to his office.

Hopefully Theo hadn't seen any of her pictures yet. She had to make sure he didn't. She looked good in them, she knew she did. But Theo wasn't as into her as she'd expected. She'd be sixteen in September and most of her boyfriends had been older. Theo was still fourteen and was a bit immature. He'd rather play PlayStation and talk football. At least she wasn't fighting to keep her pants on. Older guys expected a lot more. She liked sex – at least, she thought she did – but she didn't like it as much as they seemed to like it. It was too rushed, too uncomfortable, too much about *them*. No, Theo would do just fine for now.

Something smashed in the kitchen. God, Mum was an absolute psycho. She was probably cross with Dad for going out again. Lauren opened his laptop, keyed in his password and changed the broadband safety settings. She'd change them back before he got home. Dad was particular about things like that. It was part of his job, of course. She had the website open when she heard him crashing about in the hallway, grabbing his keys and coat. She deleted the web page from his browsing history, and closed the door silently behind her.

Christ, the house was so claustrophobic. She couldn't wait to get out of there, get herself a flat, and take *control* of her life.

Nicole

THE FRONT DOOR SLAMMED, leaving Nicole alone downstairs. Again. She didn't know where her husband had gone and her daughter was sulking upstairs in her bedroom. As usual. They were both being impossible at the moment.

At least the interview had gone brilliantly. Gloria was a smart girl, smarter than Nicole had originally given her credit for. She wasn't just a pretty face to front fashion show host *Glorious*; she was educated, commercially minded, and knew her limits.

Nicole had remembered to say all the right things. The questions had fallen into her lap like sweets. Her preparation had paid off and she had examples at the tip of her tongue. Gloria had been impressed at her story of prioritising her daughter's education and mental health since the pandemic, how she was circumspect enough not to jump at just any opportunity. It was all about balance. Wellness. Fluidity. Any other Gen Z buzzword Nicole could dig up.

So she'd ordered the damn pizza as a mini celebration, albeit premature and still a secret. She'd also been home too late to cook. But she'd thought they could share it, have a laugh together. Connect. She'd thought they might even watch a movie together. The need to fix things at home was beginning to feel urgent, necessary. There were layers of tension and secrecy she couldn't decipher.

Last night had been a complete disaster, with Wolf rushing off to see Andrew instead of ravishing her on the kitchen island, as she'd secretly hoped. He'd devoured the scallops and pissed off, full of sympathy for Andrew and Kerry and how hard life was for *them*, leaving Nicole alone feeling well and truly rejected, wearing her best lingerie. She still simmered with resentment. But if she'd learned anything during this endless recruitment process, it was that you couldn't give up at the first hurdle.

She hadn't meant to shout tonight. She hadn't intended to drop the plate. Denby crockery was bloody expensive. But Wolf had behaved like an absolute slob, literally shovelling pizza into his mouth like he was actually *trying* to repel her. It was disgusting, not to mention unfair. If Nicole ate like that, her skin would erupt, and she'd have stomach pains. She'd be *fat*.

Thank God he was gone. There was a message in her inbox and she couldn't relax until she'd read it. A plan was forming in her mind. It all depended on the email.

Nicole's hand shook as she clicked the message open. This was *it*. She scanned the top line, holding her breath.

Dear Nicole,

We would be delighted to offer you the position ...

Nicole leaned back and let pleasure and relief sift through her body and land with a satisfying twang right down in her toes. Better than shopping. Better than an orgasm.

This was the end of everything she hated. No more badgering school parents about goddamn cake sales and quiz nights. Pretending she was torn between getting a Miniature Dachshund and a Cavapoo, whatever the hell that was. The end to wearing her activewear like a fucking badge of pride at being a stay-at-home mum. Christ, she could go back to nipping to the gym on her lunch break like a normal person. She could get a cleaner, Lauren could make her own packed lunch, and Nicole could come home at the end of the day to a gin and tonic and a bath instead of the endless rigmarole of preparing the dinner, cleaning biscuit crumbs off the sofa, ironing, the sodding washing up. Wolf could start pulling his weight around the house and they might all stop asking her where their fucking socks were.

She scanned the rest of the email. Everything seemed fine. They wanted a reference and a background check. Easy. The money was decent. She skimmed over the maternity cover and the flexi-working – no need for those, thank God – grimaced at the paltry pension contribution, and typed out her reply.

Dear Gloria,
I would be delighted to accept ...

But she didn't hit send. Not just because she didn't want to appear too keen. The commute was trickier than she'd anticipated, and that wasn't even at peak time. Living in Saltreach might not suit. Two trains and a half-hour walk. They might need to move. She needed to think this through properly. She hit the backspace button.

...to consider your generous offer ... have one more opportunity to consider ... will make a decision soon and be directly back in touch ...

She sent on the reference details and background check information.

Wolf wouldn't be impressed. He loved Saltreach. Loved being in the place where he'd grown up, being by the sea, having Andrew a five-minute walk away. At least, Nicole had always assumed it was Andrew, and not Kerry, he loved seeing.

She'd asked around discreetly and discovered that he and Kerry had, in fact, been teenage boyfriend and girlfriend. How far had it gone? Just snogging and handholding, or sharing those all-important firsts with each other? Was that why he still seemed half in love with her sometimes? Was that why he'd never told her?

She shook the thought away and put a bottle of champagne in the freezer. Who could she invite round to celebrate her good news with?

It took her longer than she'd care to admit to think of someone. The ladies who sometimes joined her on her runs wouldn't understand; they loved being at home. Nobody from the PTA – she never wanted to be reminded of that again. Who did that leave? Nobody. Not even her husband and daughter.

She'd only been here a couple of years, she reminded herself. Saltreach was a strange town, with a clear divide between the locals, like Kerry who'd grown up here, and her. When they'd first arrived, Nicole had refused to get the neighbours round for drinks, as Wolf had wanted. Proximity was no basis for friendship, she'd insisted. They'd wait and find their kind of people. But Nicole's kind of people didn't live in this kind of place, with its small-town mindset and its community centre with the am-dram society and the fish and chip van that parked by the beach on a Wednesday afternoon and always had a queue halfway down the hill.

No, Nicole would wait up and get on Wolf's good side tonight. She would plant some seeds about missing the city. She'd outgrown this place anyway. But the prospect of another house move, being the newcomer *again*, helping Lauren make friends, dealing with a whole new set of logistics, all on top of a new job, was daunting. She'd need to have Wolf on her side. Clearly, she had nobody else. She took the champagne back out of the freezer. If she was going to work in fashion, she couldn't afford to carry so much as a spare ounce.

Wolf

WOLF STARED INTO HIS empty pint glass. What a mess.

Women were so bloody complicated. Most of all his wife. Mainly, she acted as though she couldn't bear to be around him. She tried to hurt him by the way she spoke to him, by demanding he spend a fortune on the house, by exiling him from the bedroom. Last night she'd wanted to have sex and he'd let her down. Tonight, she'd wanted to share pizza and beers as though they were best mates, then bitten his head off for his table manners and refused to eat a thing. She'd practically thrown him out of the house. What was going through her mind? And what the hell would she do if she found out he'd kissed Kerry?

He considered ordering another pint of Guinness. Despite everything, he missed Nicole, *his* Nicole. He wanted her. They'd been tiptoeing around each other like strangers for months and it had nothing to do with the bloody orangery. They were worse than exes – shouting one minute, ignoring each other the next. He should have insisted on coming back to their bed weeks ago, and for once he couldn't blame all that on her. It was too easy to say he was working late and crawl into bed in the attic room. There was no rejection up there. Nobody telling him off for snoring or farting or wanting the window open. But it had gone on long enough. He needed to put things right between them.

He nodded to the barman, zipped up his jacket, and stepped out into pitch darkness. The cool sea breeze was welcome after weeks of blistering sunshine, after an hour wallowing in self-pity. He'd distracted himself by following the online chat rooms, the Facebook group. The talk was ugly. The voices ranged from worried, frustrated, and apathetic, to full-blown malice. But they all had one thing in common: they all held Kerry responsible. She was the person they pinned either their hopes or their blame on. It was completely unfair, of course. Henry was enjoying his retirement in Marbella, and the other directors didn't even feature. He set off at a brisk pace, sidestepping a group of young lads vaping on the corner.

The project at Stonebridge would go on for months yet. That kiss was a disaster. It hadn't been planned, not that Kerry seemed to believe that. But secretly, subconsciously, maybe she was right. He enjoyed hanging out with her at work, even though most of the time she carried the weight of the world on her shoulders. She snapped at him in front of his team and didn't afford him the professional courtesy she should, but she was still the girl he'd been crazy about when he was fifteen. The way she pushed her fringe out of her eyes and it would flop right back into place. The way she rested her chin on her hands and stared at him, listening intently, like his opinions actually mattered. Nicole wasn't interested in what he had to say. But there was still time to put things right.

"Excuse me," he said, sidestepping a young man loitering at the end of their street. The bloke was in a world of his own, staring at the townhouses set four to a block along the road as if he were choosing one to buy. Or to rob. Wolf followed his gaze idly. Most of the curtains were pulled tight and there was nothing to see. Dim light glowed from some. Lauren's room was lit up like a bloody Christmas tree.

*

Nicole was at the kitchen island, tapping on her laptop, as always. Everything was spotless. In seventeen years of marriage, he'd never come home and found her lounging on the sofa watching telly. She never switched off. He went up behind her and put his arms around her waist. He wanted to forget about their row, about Kerry, about everything.

She closed her laptop. She turned around to face him, let him hug her. But her body remained rigid.

"Sorry for snapping," she said into his neck. "I was still upset after last night. But it wasn't fair to get mad at you for not wanting me when I've been the one pushing you away." She kissed him. "I want you to come back to bed."

Wolf drew back and stared at her. Nicole *never* said sorry. It was a thing between them. She'd make it up to him in other ways – buy his favourite beer, book a restaurant she knew he liked, cook a special meal – but she never said sorry.

Yesterday, she'd cooked his favourite, and tonight she'd bought pizza. Nicole didn't even like pizza, yet he'd hardly given her the time of day. And here she was, trying again. Wow. He'd been so stupid. She still wanted him. They could fix things.

"I'm sorry for eating like a – what was it? An overgrown teenager," he said. He kissed her full on the mouth, feeling only slightly like an absolute cad.

"Anyway, I was thinking, it might be time to move on from Saltreach." She pouted. "It's a little dull here."

Dull? Wolf would take dull any day over the chaos that seemed to surround them lately. "But this is home."

"*Your* home," she said. "And it's been great. But Lauren is nearly sixteen. She'll need access to a good sixth form college, not the local comp. Do you really want to be stuck here forever?"

It was a sucker-punch to the gut. "Yes," he said, pulling back from her, taking up position on the far side of the island. "Yes, I want to stay here forever. That was what we agreed. I like cycling the roads I know like the back of my hand, I like knowing the names of all the staff in the local pub. I like having friends here that I grew up with . . ." That thought sobered him up. Was Andrew even his friend anymore? Was Kerry?

Last night had been a disaster. Andrew had been sitting, stiff-backed and uncomfortable in The Anchor when Wolf had arrived, hurt and recrimmination in his eyes. A combination Wolf had never seen before. Andrew hadn't said a word as Wolf apologised. In the end, when Wolf had run out of apologies and explanations, and Andrew still hadn't said a word, Wolf had been forced to slink out of the pub like a kicked puppy. He didn't know what would happen next time they met.

So he wasn't up to a row tonight, and he certainly wasn't getting into this. Had Nicole only apologised so that she could spring this on him? He wouldn't put it past her.

"I'm going to bed," he said, filling himself a glass of water.

Nicole looked disappointed that he wouldn't stay and fight. But they'd done enough of that lately.

"It's not *my* home," she said quietly.

That pissed Wolf off.

"Because it doesn't have a fancy conservatory and a landscaped garden?" he sniped. "If you tried a little harder, maybe it could *feel* like home." He took off his glasses, ostensibly to polish them, but mainly not to feel the heat from her glare. "You could make friends. Not people you boss around at the school to make yourself feel important. *Real* friends."

"Like your friend Kerry?" Her voice carried a warning.

Did she know something? He put his glasses back on. She was baiting him now. She'd always been the jealous type, and in the early days he'd enjoyed it, provoked it, even. But now things felt a little too close to home.

"Goodnight," he said, closing the door gently behind him.

Kerry

Kerry left Andrew in the waiting room of the x-ray department and replayed Clare's message in the lift to Mum's floor. It only made her angrier, but she couldn't help herself. "Hey, sis. *So* sorry to hear about Mum. That's awful. She's so lucky to have you there. I'm shooting in the Northern Territory at the moment, so regarding coming home, no can do, I'm afraid." She had the temerity to sing-song this last part, and Kerry swore profusely in the empty lift, just as she had the first four times she'd played it. "I'll send money. Maybe Marta can do a few more hours to take the pressure off. But darling, thank you *so* much for everything you're doing. You're my absolute *rock*." All in her fake Australian accent. Ugh.

> Thanks for the extra money, but like I said, I need the help. Mum needs to see you. I'm sure the set can cope without you for a fortnight. Book a flight, okay?

She greeted the nurses and entered Mum's room quietly. The room felt cool, soothing, the blinds pulled to keep out the blinding heat. Mum, slack-jawed and hollow-cheeked, slept peacefully under a soft pink blanket. Kerry picked up one of her cool hands and held it between hers. All the chaos and worry of the past few months rose in her like salt water breaking over a shore, flooding her mind until she felt hollowed out and weary.

I'm letting everyone down at work, Mum. If the meeting on Monday doesn't go our way, a hundred people will lose their jobs. They're already blaming me. They've formed a club online and they're saying terrible things. Not just about me – about Andrew and the kids too. I wake in the middle of the night and lurk in the chatrooms. I'm afraid something bad is going to happen if I don't win. And on top of all that, Wolf kissed me and now Andrew won't speak to him. Theo and Ella are running the house. You're here, Andrew's in a sling, and the driver of the car still hasn't shown up. I keep getting these pains in my chest and my arm. What if I have a heart attack like Dad? Who'd take care of you then?

She closed her eyes and imagined Mum's hand stroking her hair, telling her everything would come right in the end. Unbidden, Andrew's suggestion of redundancy came to mind. Take a lump sum and head off on an adventure? It was a laughable prospect. The twins were twelve years away from their A levels; the best redundancy offer in the world wouldn't help them get four children to adulthood without remortgaging. And they might have to do that anyway to allow Mum to move in.

Her chest ached. Her head pounded. Even her lungs burned. She called her doctor and scheduled an appointment. As she hung up, a text came in from Andrew.

X-Ray running late. Grab yourself a coffee. Sorry x

Kerry heaved her weary body out of the plastic visitor's chair and made her way to the Costa downstairs, dismayed at yet another missed school pickup. After-school club was supposed to be twice a week, max. But the twins were nearly always there lately. And she hadn't even brought her laptop.

In the corner, someone blew their nose loudly. Someone tall and thin with well-cut caramel highlights, dressed uncharacteristically in joggers and a faded blue hoodie.

She'd been right, then, about Izzy's mother taking a turn for the worse. She sat at a remove from Izzy's distress, her own thoughts still snagging on work and money worries, until she realised that Izzy's sniffs had become sobs, and she understood that she had lost her mother.

Gratitude and shame flashed through her in equal measure. Her mother was recovering well upstairs. But she knew what it was to lose a parent, and Izzy had nobody else.

She slipped out of her seat and shimmied into the chair next to Izzy and slid an arm round her shoulders. Without a word, Izzy leaned her head on Kerry's shoulder and let herself be comforted.

Kerry

"She's gone," Izzy said, when she finished crying. "Respiratory failure. All those fags ..." Her eyes welled up again.

Kerry pulled a pack of tissues from her purse and handed it to Izzy. "Shall we go back and sit with her?"

"They've already taken her down to the morgue." Izzy's face contorted in pain. "They needed the bed. Oh God, Kerry, I can't believe she's gone. I used to think she'd live through anything."

"She was a strong woman," Kerry said. "Remember that time your flat got robbed? And she heard those bastards downstairs boasting about it through the floor and went down with a baseball bat and made them bring it all back up."

"And fix her door. She was my hero after that. Any time a man gives me shit, puts his hand on my bum, or takes credit for my work, I think about that day."

Kerry shuddered. "Does that really happen?"

"Men don't like ambitious women in London," Izzy said. "And women don't trust the single ones." She shrugged. "Haven't you found the same here?"

And there was the divide, as brittle and sharp-edged as a sheet of glass. London. Here. Kerry stiffened.

"Sorry," Izzy said.

Sorry for what, Kerry wanted to ask. She had lots of questions.

What will you do now? Will you go back to London? Are we still meeting on Monday to fight over jobs? Why should I comfort you now, when you weren't there for me?

But it wasn't the time. Besides, Stonebridge would get their pound of flesh from Bullfinch, with or without Izzy.

*

"There you are!" Andrew entered the café and stopped short at the sight of them. "Everything okay?"

The tension must have been palpable. Kerry chided herself for being petty, today of all days. She put a hand on Izzy's arm and felt how thin she was. "Izzy's mother has passed away."

"I'm very sorry to hear that," Andrew said, hand outstretched. "I'm Andrew. Kerry's better half." He winked at Kerry, a *check you out, burying the hatchet* kind of wink. He looked back to Izzy, sombre again. "Can we do anything to help?"

"Thank you," Izzy said, standing and shaking his hand. "But I'd better leave you two to it."

"Are you still at the flat?"

Izzy nodded. "I wanted to help her find somewhere nicer. I offered a hundred times but she always said the flat was home. God knows why."

She couldn't let Izzy go back there alone. Not tonight. Not to that shithole where the communal door didn't lock and the ground floor flats had bars on the windows. "Have dinner with us."

There was silence while everyone registered this unexpected turn of events. Kerry felt Andrew's eyes bore into the back of her head with shock.

"Thank you for the offer, but I couldn't."

But Kerry couldn't let it go. This would be her some day, discussing the morgue, accepting condolences. The word *soon* swam into view. "We need a drink at least," she said. "Raise a glass to Barbara?"

Izzy nodded and Kerry felt something thaw inside her. She turned to Andrew.

"If I drive as far as The Anchor and collect the twins on the way, can you drive the last bit home?"

"And do dinner and the whole bedtime rigmarole?" he said. "Sure thing. Swimming lessons might be a bit tricky."

"Skip it," Kerry said. "The twins will be delighted."

Kerry was never so relieved that her husband was a peacekeeper. This thing with Wolf would blow over, she was sure of it. They were good friends. As for her and Izzy? Things just weren't that simple.

Lauren

Broken bottles, condoms, beer cans, and general filth littered the path through the woods to The Cabin, and Lauren trod carefully in her thin ballet pumps. When Dad was a kid, it had apparently been a summer camp base. He'd built dens and treehouses in the woods, played cricket and football on the fields, and done water sports on the beach. Dad was the only person who ever said anything good about Saltreach. He made it sound like he'd had an idyllic childhood here. Lauren hadn't swum in the sea for years. She hated the beach for the same reason she hated the rest of the town. Because, unlike when they'd lived in London, everybody knew everybody in Saltreach. Last summer, when there was no seaweed, people shouted to each other over bottles of suncream, kids screamed and kicked up sand, and the seagulls squawked, swooping and diving to steal ice cream and chips. Lauren imagined future holidays on adult-only beaches, with waiters delivering CBD-infused cocktails right to her sun lounger.

She stopped ten paces from The Cabin. A black, beat-up car with a flat tyre sat to one side. From a sunspot on its dented bonnet, a frosty orange cat with one eye missing surveyed Lauren in her walk of shame. Her secret-keeping mission. Her low point.

Oliver Nowell sucked on his disgusting pineapple-scented vape and leaned mock-casually against the wooden door, his phone dangling between finger and thumb. Lauren's nails dug into the faux leather of the knock-off Chanel quilted handbag she'd bought for a tenner in Turkey last year. It sat better on her shoulder for the *real* Longchamp purse inside. Lauren remembered why she was doing this and straightened up, shook back her hair.

"God," she said, injecting as much vitriol into her voice as she could muster. "You're still using an iPhone 12."

Oliver reddened but didn't fall for the bait. "Plenty in here for the wank bank," he said. "Don't need the latest model to see you in your knickers, do I?"

"Piss off, Oliver," she said.

"Don't be like that," he wheedled. "Nobody forced you into it, did they? It's hardly a secret. See!" He brought up the photograph of her handcuffed to the bed, her mouth open, her bare legs askew. "You're literally *begging* men to shag you."

"I'm not," she said quietly, feeling less brave than she had a moment ago, wishing she could have brought someone with her to stand up to him. But nobody knew her dirty little secret, and she had to keep it like that. Shit. What did he actually want from her?

"A blow job," Oliver said, reading her thoughts, his hands thrust deep in his pockets. He held the cabin door open for her in mock chivalry. "Then I'll keep your secret."

"Fuck you!" Who the hell did he think he was? Lauren would bet her entire bank balance that Oliver Nowell had never had a blow job before. He'd aimed too high and she felt braver now. "I'm not touching you, and you're certainly not putting your filthy hands anywhere near me."

"Fine," he said. "Fine. But I want the live show."

Shit. She'd played into his hands. Still, she could do this. She could cope with this. As long as he didn't come anywhere near her. As long as he kept her secret.

Oliver took her silence for agreement and indicated for her to walk ahead of him into the cabin. She made sure not to touch him as she entered the building, no more than an old shed now but surprisingly bright inside, thanks to a slew of missing tiles. A rolled-up sleeping bag, a blanket, and a tatty rucksack lay in one corner. Lauren chose a spot within arm's reach of the door yet out of sight of the windows and pointed towards a spot on the far side of an old, chipped laminate desk, next to a pile of broken tennis rackets and a battered croquet set. Oliver practically ran to it.

"Put your phone on the desk," she said. "I'm not having you recording this."

Oliver did as he was told.

Lauren closed her eyes and pulled up her top. She counted to ten and started to pull it back down, until Oliver's voice stopped her in her tracks.

"*All* the way off," he commanded in a new voice that told Lauren he already had a hard-on, already had his dick in his hand. "Everything off!" he said louder, practically shouting.

Lauren pulled off her top and bra and scrunched them in her fist. She opened her eyes. Immediately, she wanted to cry. Oliver's trousers hovered mid-thigh and the look of concentration, of dirty greed, felt like a poison spreading on her skin. She squeezed her eyes shut and waited for the tell-tale panting, the grunts, the sigh of relief. When it was over, she turned her back on him to dress, kicked open the door, and stumbled into the daylight with tears pouring down her cheeks.

Kerry

When Kerry got home from the pub, Andrew was waiting up, just like Dad used to back in her clubbing days. He closed his paper as she came through the lounge on her way to the kitchen. Andrew still read the newspaper. She loved that about him.

"You okay?" he said.

"Yep." She needed another glass of wine, having sipped carefully tonight, afraid a loose tongue could detonate the new fragile bond between them. To put that on Izzy the day her mother died would have been too cruel.

"Clear the air?"

"Nope." She took a bottle from the fridge. It had been a tightrope walk, to say the least. She'd tried to learn what she could about Izzy's life since they'd gone their separate ways. The generous part of her brain hoped she might be mature enough to forgive and forget, to move on. The rest of her knew she needed ammunition in the boardroom next week and wasn't above getting it any way she could. Izzy might have lost her mother, but a hundred people still faced losing their jobs.

"Don't you think it might have been the perfect opportunity?"

Damn. Andrew was being persistent tonight. The corkscrew hovered mid-air. He didn't often challenge her, but this particular conversation had been brewing for a while. She put the wine glass back in the cupboard.

"Something on your mind, Andy?" She sat next to him and patted his knee.

"She's lost her mum, sweetheart. Can't you cut her some slack?"

Kerry tried not to flinch. She thought she'd been pretty compassionate tonight, all things considered. "Let's see how the meeting goes first."

"It's not good for you to hold onto this kind of resentment. It'll put you in an early grave."

Her left arm throbbed ironically. She shook her head. She was only imagining it. The doctor would tell her so.

"Cup of tea?" she offered.

"Stop changing the subject! You've been waiting on this opportunity for over twenty years. Why don't you take it, so we can all move on?"

"What are you talking about? I haven't thought about Izzy in years."

"But it's not just Izzy, is it? It's this whole life. The one you feel you were forced into. The one you settled for out of duty. But clearly *not* the life you'd ever have chosen for yourself."

"What?" she said stupidly. She couldn't afford to let this get out of hand. There was too much at play. Andrew was too dear to her.

"How do you think that makes me feel, Kerry? We've been married for eighteen years and you still resent not living your other, imaginary life. Will there ever be a time when you'll accept that this life we have is actually pretty great? Or will I always feel like second best?"

Her hand froze on his knee. She gave it a little shake, as if to check he was real, that he'd actually said that. "Is that what you think?"

"Isn't it what *you* think?" He jumped up from the sofa, holding his bad arm with the good one. "You weren't the only one with grand plans, you know. We don't all get the fairy tale."

That stung. She couldn't help it, even though the irony was right there in front of her.

"Where would *you* rather be?" It came out clipped, accusatory.

"There's nowhere on earth I'd rather be than here with you and the children," Andrew said, perching on the coffee table. "But that's not to say I didn't think that one day I might be a professional cyclist, or a stockbroker, or a trader, and make millions and retire at forty-five with a mansion and a fleet of fancy cars."

Kerry hid a smile. Andrew had refused to change his VW Golf for the last decade. But he didn't love his work. "So why didn't you?"

"Why didn't I what?"

"Become a stockbroker or a trader?"

"I didn't get accepted into the program."

"You, the straight-A student, the rule-follower, the slow-and-steady-wins-the-race guy? You didn't study?"

"Of course I studied," he said and she felt bad for teasing him. "They said I wasn't the right profile. Too methodical. Not enough of a risk-taker."

Kerry thought of the safari trip to Botswana and put her hand back on his knee. "I'm sorry, love."

"It's okay. I became an accountant." He rolled his eyes. "Perfect for me."

But something didn't add up. "There must have been more to the dream than a career?" Kerry said.

"I fell in love, okay? With a Brazilian girl. She worked at the accountancy practice with me. We planned to go travelling. Visit her family, do the Inca trail, learn to tango, all that. Sounds silly now, but …"

How had he never told her that before? Had he been worried she'd be jealous? She did feel a little jealous now. She'd never had a big love before Andrew. Never had that swept-off-her-feet moment. Theirs had been a quiet, dependable love, a slow bloom of affection.

"What happened?"

He sighed. "Same as most first loves," he said ruefully. "She broke my heart and went back to Brazil by herself. So I moved too. Home to Saltreach. Took a job I didn't love. Just like you." He shrugged.

"You didn't follow her?"

"I met you," he said, taking her hand. "Why would I ever leave you?"

*

Later, as they brushed their teeth side by side, a thought occurred to her.

"How come you didn't become a professional cyclist?"

"Bugger off," he said, pulling her into his good arm and kissing her.

Theo

Facebook had exploded. Theo sat on The Bench and scrolled. Mitch was late as usual, but today it suited. He needed to read this. The 'Fight Stonebridge' page now had over four thousand followers. This week's front page article from *The Courier* was pinned on top.

Stonebridge Takeover Spells Disaster for Saltreach

Saltreach has been dealt a devastating blow as Bullfinch Glazing – once the pride of our town – has been handed over to corporate vultures Stonebridge in a deal locals fear will strip away workers' rights, destroy local livelihoods, and put the future of our community in peril.

The sale, spearheaded by HR Director Kerry Langley, has left locals reeling. Her late father, Larry O'Reilly, co-founded Bullfinch in 1984 with the promise of steady jobs and fair wages for Saltreach's hardworking tradespeople. But now, his daughter has sold that legacy down the river, leaving workers at the mercy of a company notorious for zero-hours contracts, no pension contributions, maternity benefits or quality training.

Stonebridge doesn't even employ its own installers — instead, they outsource to subcontractors, meaning unregulated, unqualified workers may soon be fitting windows and doors across town. Additionally, Stonebridge do not belong to the National Glazing Federation, raising serious concerns about safety and quality.

For the local workforce, this is a disaster. Bullfinch once provided stable, skilled employment, but now staff fear they'll be cast aside. "This is nothing short of a betrayal," said one furious factory worker. "We've put years into this company, and Kerry Langley has just handed us over to a firm that doesn't care if we can put food on the table."

The timing of this disaster couldn't be worse. Tourism is already plummeting locally, thanks to the council's refusal to clear the beaches until June, despite the record-breaking heatwave and lack of wind, causing the seaweed to produce high levels of hydrogen sulphide much earlier in the year than normal, leaving our beaches foul-smelling and empty, and the sea unsafe to swim in. With local businesses already suffering, our biggest employer has turned its back on us. What future remains for Saltreach?

Locals are demanding answers — but will Kerry Langley dare to face the people she's sold out?

Predictably, Mum had joined in.

Allow me to provide an accurate update to this discussion. 1. Henry Bishop sold the business, not me. After my father

died, Henry retained 100% ownership of Bullfinch, as per their business agreement. The other directors and I were not made aware of the sale of the business to Stonebridge until after the fact.
2. I have retained the services of a top quality solicitor (whose name I'm not prepared to mention on here because of the vitriolic nature of the abuse that I personally have received in the last month and which I wouldn't wish on my worst enemy) who is providing excellent advice to Bullfinch on how to protect jobs and safeguard the future of the business as best we can.
3. I have repeatedly tried to engage with Saltreach Town Council and our local MP @KatelynHarris, both of whom are failing to respond on this matter in a stunning fashion, just as they failed to respond to the community's (and my own) very legitimate concerns over the state of the beach. If anyone has any HELPFUL suggestions in this regard, do call my office.
4. I am, of course, working together with the Trade Unions to provide our valued people here at Bullfinch with every level of information and support available.
I will not make another statement to the general public and would appreciate a general climbdown in terms of public outrage demonstrated on this Facebook page, as it only adds to the already elevated anxiety and concern amongst those directly involved.
Regards, Kerry Langley.

A very Mum response. Clearly she hadn't brought in marketing to smooth this out. Thank God she hadn't made a video. The post only went up ten minutes ago and already the comments were mounting.

A shadow fell over Theo. Mitch had arrived, dressed in a black short-sleeved t-shirt, black jeans despite the heat, and those awful shoes. Theo shoved his phone in his pocket. He'd read the comments later.

"What's up?" Mitch said cheerfully. He sat next to Theo on The Bench. Too close. He smelled of old socks and unwashed clothes. It was Saturday. If he wore the same clothes on the weekends as he did during the week, then he definitely didn't work in an office.

Their arms touched and Theo flinched. He'd decided not to tell Mitch any more private stuff about their family. The photograph wasn't enough to make things better between them. Mitch might actually be his half-brother, but unless he was prepared to meet Dad, Theo didn't have to trust him.

"Nothing, I suppose. Dad's much better. I think I should tell him about you now. You could come and see him."

"I will, mate, I will. I want to get on my feet first, you know?" Mitch said. "When I get enough cash together to put a deposit on a flat, I'll have you all over for a big lunch. A family get-together, you know?"

Mitch was obsessed with money, but he never seemed to have any. He was the most un-adult adult Theo ever met.

"When will that be?"

"Soon, mate, soon." Mitch picked at his fingernails. "It's a big deal. I need to work up the courage, okay? I don't want him to think I'm a loser."

"Dad would never think that," Theo said, indignant.

"Tell me more about him. What does he like to do? What's his favourite food? What's the very best thing about him?"

Mitch always had questions. But Dad should answer them the way *he* wanted to. Theo wanted this whole thing to be over.

"How about meeting Ella, then?" he said. "Ella's cool, you'd like her."

Not many boys could say that about their older sister, and Ella could be really annoying sometimes, obviously, thinking she knew everything because she was sixteen. But they watched out for each other. In some ways, keeping this from Ella was harder than keeping it from Dad.

"Girls blab," Mitch said, grinning. "Can't trust them."

God. He never had a good word to say about anybody. Maybe Theo should stop meeting him altogether. That way, Mitch would either meet Dad or piss off. Theo knew which option he'd prefer.

"Tell me about the little ones," Mitch said. "What are their names again?"

"How do you not remember your own siblings' names?" Theo said. A thought occurred to him. "Do *you* have other brothers and sisters?"

"No." Of course he didn't. Mitch had nothing and no-one. "Mum went back to Brazil when I finished school. I haven't seen her since."

Theo couldn't imagine not speaking to Mum. "Did you have a row?" he asked.

"Not really. She wanted me to go with her. Said she missed her family. But, hey, what do I want to go there for?"

"When was that?"

"Three years ago." Mitch was matter-of-fact.

"What have you been doing since then?"

"This and that. Hey, it's a bit boring at the park. How about we go play pool or something next time?"

"You could come to my house," Theo suggested again. "Everyone's there."

"Stop banging on about it!" Mitch was cross now. This was their worst meeting by far.

"What's the point of meeting like this if you won't do anything about it?" Theo yelled. "If you don't want to come and meet Dad, what *do* you want?"

"Woah," he said, scratching a welt on his neck. "Okay, we'll do it soon." He rubbed his hands together between his thighs. "Maybe you're right about Ella. Bring her next time."

"Good." Thank God. Ella was as good as a grown-up. She would know what to do and Theo wouldn't have to keep this bloody secret any more. "I'll bring her next time. She doesn't look like me, she's small and blonde and has …"

"I know what she looks like."

"You do?" Course he did. Mitch had known exactly who Theo was, the first time he'd approached him outside school.

"She's my sister, isn't she?" Mitch grinned.

"Are you *spying* on us?" Theo stood up from The Bench. This was really bad. Was Mitch actually stalking them?

"Calm down, just bring Ella next time. I've got to go. See you 'round, mate." He gave Theo a sort of fist bump and hurried back along the path that led through the woods. Theo watched his long legs and bouncy stride, hands jammed in his jean pockets as though he were rummaging for change.

He'd never seen Mitch as grumpy as he'd been today. He looked bad too; greasy skin, and hair that needed a wash and a cut, and he'd grown a horrible beard, a patchy thing with gaps where he'd obviously picked at it. He said he was twenty-two. Surely that was old enough to be able to grow a proper beard. He walked home deep in thought.

Lauren

THE HANDCUFFS THING HAD gone insane. She'd cleared seven hundred quid on this photo alone. From her secret bank account, she could buy herself the new iPhone, a laptop, and a designer handbag if she liked, but right now, all she wanted to do was crawl under her duvet.

Had seventy different men paid to see her chained to her bedpost in her bra and knickers? How many of them had messaged her since? Thirty, forty? She'd deleted most of them unopened. They were full of requests for filthier stuff. Asking to see her without her knickers. Sending pictures of other women tied up, one literally *chained* to the floor with, like, a collar around her neck, and the viewer was asking her to do the same.

Dick pics, of course. There were always dick pics. Young, old, hairy, crooked. She was immune to them now. Nearly.

And then the actual messages.

You're so hot

Ur so pretty. Can we video chat? I want to see you cum

Slut. Fucking Slut. Show me more, bitch

> Lose some fucking weight before you post again, you fat cunt

She'd stopped opening them after that.

Except for one. User W45, now posting as W4545. Or Beardface, as Theo called him.

> Dear L.
> I love your new hairstyle.
> You looked so pretty walking home from school the other day.
> Can I come say hi, next time I see you? I don't mean any harm, so no need to send your bodyguard this time. Ha ha.
> I just want to talk.

What in God's name was she supposed to do?

She couldn't call Theo this time. He'd insist on calling the police. Anyway, Theo wouldn't understand, he'd be shocked. He'd break up with her – not that it mattered really, but then he might tell his mates. She didn't want this getting out at school, not after what she'd had to do to keep Oliver fucking Nowell on side. She hadn't heard from him today and could only hope that he would keep his bloody mouth shut in school next week. It was probably too much to expect that he might feel guilty.

No, it was time to get out, once and for all.

The first thing she did was transfer the cash out of the secret bank account, the one she'd had to set up under Mum's name. Once the cash was in her own, normal, account, she closed the other one. The bank was obviously dodgy too, because the minute she hit delete, everything was erased. She should have known it was dodgy, the PeekaBoo website had recommended it.

Then she closed her PeekaBoo account. That had been under

her mother's name too – they didn't accept minors, apparently. What a joke. The fact that her mother's ID gave her age as thirty-nine and, in her selfies, Lauren was clearly *not*, apparently didn't give them any cause for concern.

She had no regrets now. She'd made a packet, bought herself some nice things, but at the end of it all she had nearly three grand saved. That was a good start. But maybe she'd see if one of the local clothes shops wanted help on Saturdays. That would be nice. Maybe Zara. She might even get a discount.

She scrolled through her phone, deleted all the dodgy photos. She'd been proud of them once. Now they made her think of middle-aged men masturbating alone while their wives cooked supper downstairs. It was disgusting.

Kai

THIS WAS WEIRD.

Kai wasn't sure where they were exactly, except that he could see Saltreach today in a way he never had before. He and Mum sat side by side on a picnic blanket among the long scrubby grass up on the cliffs. From here, the town was bigger than he'd realised, spread out below like a semi-circle, framed on one long side by the beach. In the centre, the jetty stuck out into the sea like it was giving him the finger. Amina, all braids and oversized earrings, had actually left her ice cream kiosk for once, and was sipping coffee in one of the two yellow sun chairs she dragged out for customers each morning. Next to her was Mr Mannering, the retired postie, his border collie sprawled between them. It was quiet. No wind. No waves smashing. Kai almost felt he was eavesdropping, like their voices might float through the still air and reach him all the way up here.

The town was split by the railway track, the station bang in the middle. On one side was the park, playground, football fields, their block of flats. On the other was the high street, all neat and proper, shops slotting together like Tetris blocks. Cafes and restaurants near the sea, then charity shops, clothes shops, the big Tesco, the Post Office, and that sad Chinese place further inland. People walked more quickly here, running errands. It was a hive of activity.

Beyond it all, the industrial estate bulged. The Bullfinch sign was visible, with its crisp navy and white branding. Bullfinch sponsored the local football club and the conservation society, bought books for the school library, and sponsored the annual fun run which raised money for the Guy Fawkes fireworks. Its maritime logo was dotted inconspicuously throughout town. There was no Stonebridge branding yet but when it came its crass orange signage would clash horribly with the surroundings.

When he and Mum had first arrived for their "fresh start", Kai was sceptical. Obviously, they'd both wanted to go somewhere nobody would know their story, where they wouldn't be greeted with suspicion, gossip, or pity. Theo had been the first person Kai had met, and his friendly face and easy humour made him feel they might have made the right choice. Now, he wasn't so sure.

If only he'd slept in his T-shirt last night. Mum would never have seen his back – or his stomach. He wouldn't have needed to see the horror in her face, to feel responsible for making life even harder for her. But when she said she'd emailed school, saying he wouldn't be in for a bit, that he might even miss the end of term, he felt sort of … glad, looser, like an invisible belt had been undone.

"Now," Mum said, handing him a tuna sandwich and a bottle of water. "We're going to talk about you and me, and what we've been going through. And we're going to talk about Dad."

He who isn't named, Kai thought. Like Voldemort. Thinking about Dad gave him a pain deeper than anything he could inflict on himself. But *not* thinking about him felt even worse.

"I don't suppose you remember many fun times," she said. "But I want you to know they existed. We were all happy, once upon a time."

"Before Dad became an alcoholic, you mean?" He hadn't said the word out loud before and he stumbled over it.

"Honey, I think Dad was always an alcoholic. He learned young to drink away his bad memories. You remember how he used to get."

Kai remembered. He'd tried to understand. Knew the care system had left his dad damaged. He'd feel a nudge on his sleeping shoulder at stupid o'clock.

"I love ya, son. Just want to make sure you know."

"I know, Dad. I love you too." Three hours till he had to be up for school.

"I'll never let anything bad happen to you. My folks weren't there for me, not after the fire. But I'll be there for you, son."

He hadn't kept his promise. It was hard not to be angry with him for that.

"He wasn't a nasty drunk," Mum said. "So many drunk men are vile. But your dad would cry."

"I thought it was you who was crying," he said quietly.

"Sometimes it was."

They shook off the crumbs, packed away their rubbish and began walking along the path at the top of the hill, each flooded with memories.

"Every single person in his life bailed on him," she said, patting his hand. "I would never have done that. But when you're as far gone as Dad, there are only two places you can end up: the cemetery, or prison. At least he'll get dry in prison."

There was a small, silent moment. Kai knew they were both thinking of the graveyard up in Essex, where a small boy lay buried. All because Dad had driven, steaming drunk, home from the pub.

*

They walked along the cliffs for hours, sometimes talking, sometimes not. The fresh air, the salty wind, the sea pounding in the distance, all slowed Kai's heart rate. He stopped feeling his thighs chafe against one another. He stopped noticing how much more out of breath he was than Mum. He took out his camera.

*

Back home, Mum made dinner, handed him a tiny arnica tablet, and smoothed antiseptic cream on the cuts on his back with cool fingertips. She filled a hot water bottle shaped like a sheep and put him to bed like a little kid.

Alone, he checked his phone. Nothing from Theo, but that was to be expected. There were two messages from Oliver.

Check this out - L's levelled up and gone proper R-rated

And an image. There, in a red vest and knickers, sitting seductively on her bed, was Lauren. One arm was raised over her head, where she was chained to a metal headboard with a pair of handcuffs. Jesus!

Where had Oliver found this? Kai opened the image on his laptop and zoomed in. Could Lauren really have posted this, or was someone else responsible? Surely it wasn't Oliver. He felt nauseous. Theo had accused *him*. He rubbed his stomach. No wonder Theo had punched him. He'd been upset, not angry.

Kai searched the image for signs of editing. Quality, lighting, edges – all legit. No pixelating, good colour. He put it into Photoshop, tried to unpick layers. Nothing. He zoomed back out and tried to think rationally.

He'd never been in Lauren's bedroom, but there was her name spelled out in fairy lights on the wall. A small koala bear on the side that Theo had won for her when they were at the arcades. Her school bag in the corner with her distinctive L keyring. The ankle bracelet that even Kai had to admit was sexy as hell. It *was* Lauren.

Kai searched the picture again. Blended into the pink of the bedspread, in fractionally darker pink, something was written. He adjusted the brightness so that he could see it better. There were three letters: PKB.

He opened a web browser and ran a search, afraid of what he would find. PKB. PeekaBoo. It opened onto an innocuous-looking page, not dissimilar to TikTok or Instagram, inviting him to sign up. Maybe this was some silly girl thing; girls were obsessed with selfies. He checked Lauren's socials. Nothing untoward about her photos there – Lauren and Theo doing a silly dance; Lauren sending love hearts to her friends. Nothing a ten-year-old wouldn't post. Certainly no handcuffs.

He signed up to PeekaBoo using a burner email. Next, it wanted a credit card. It was wrong, on every level, what he was doing. He could get in real trouble for this. But Theo was his friend. And right now, Kai needed a friend more than he needed anything. He typed in the sixteen-digit code from the card Mum let him use for emergencies.

It wasn't porn. But it wasn't *not* porn either. The women were definitely older than Lauren. And wearing less. One picture, *Salty*, showed a gorgeous brunette standing behind a yellow surfboard, one long bare leg poking out each side. In another image, *Spicy*, she was wearing a bikini and lowering a large chilli into her mouth, a wicked glint in her eye. What the hell? The girl's handle was @ deliciousdee.

How would he find Lauren, if she was on here? She probably had some kind of silly handle too, but if she was posting photos in her bedroom with her name on the wall, she wasn't hiding her identity. That was stupid. He ran a search on Lauren, but hundreds of results showed up. He started scrolling.

About fifty profiles in, he found her. Her pictures weren't as explicit as some of the others, not by a long shot. But they were shocking all the same. Shocking enough to turn him on and repulse him at the same time. There she was, in bras and thongs and little shorts, her name on the wall behind her. So stupid. He despised himself for paying to see them, but Theo needed to know what she was doing. He screenshot a couple of them, feeling like a dirty old perv. But he wouldn't share them with anyone. No way.

How much did Theo actually know? There was no way he'd go out with Lauren if he knew she was doing this. Should he tell him? If Theo told anyone Kai was doing this, he'd be in deep shit.

*

After a bad night's sleep, he woke and found Mum in the kitchen, sitting at the tiny table cradling a mug of coffee, staring out the window. Not flicking through a cookbook, not jabbing at her phone, not scribbling things in the diary. Just sitting. He made himself a cup of tea and carried over a bowl of yoghurt and berries she'd left out for him.

"You okay?" she said. "After last night?"

"Yeah," he said, not knowing if it was true or not.

"I'm afraid I've been a bit of a shit mum these past few months. I might be an awesome cook," she grimaced and he knew she was about to say something that hurt, "but I've let you eat enough junk to last you a lifetime."

Automatically, beneath the table, Kai dragged his nails across the bulge of his stomach, felt the sharp sting of pain. He thought of the drawer of snacks in his bedroom, of the biscuits and crisps and bars of chocolate he'd eaten over the last few months. Mum didn't eat like that. Nobody he knew did. He squeezed the bulge around his navel. His fingers itched to burrow inside that flap of flesh on his back. But Mum had put antiseptic on the cuts and covered them with plasters.

"It's not your fault, lovey," Mum said, taking his hand and holding it in hers. "It's your way of coping. I've sat on the sofa in a funk for the past six months and you've tried to fill the void with sugar." She shrugged. "It's time we started to take care of ourselves."

Nicole

Dear Ms Bauer,
It is with regret that we must inform you that, following on from your background check, we are no longer in a position to offer you the role ...

What the hell? Nicole scanned the rest of the email, but it gave nothing away. What in God's name had gone wrong? She knew her references were impeccable. Still, she made a frantic call to each of her referees and put down the phone reassured. Nothing had gone wrong there.

What then? She opened the email back up, examined every last letter, searching for clues as to what they were using to make their final decision. Something that was so urgent they'd emailed on a Saturday. One clause stood out.

We expect the online presence of our team to represent the values of the Glorious brand – honesty, integrity, and transparency.

Was there something in her social media they didn't like? Everything had been so carefully curated. She scrutinised her socials: her at charity events, hosting PTA cake sales, wearing fashion-forward items she couldn't afford and later returned. Championing, but never boasting about, her daughter at various school events. Presenting a loving mother, devoted wife, ambitious, capable woman.

Three hours later, having checked every post she'd ever made, every comment she'd ever liked, every snippet she'd retweeted, she'd found nothing. Nobody she'd ever tagged had turned out to be a rapist. No comment she'd ever liked had incited an argument. She never posted anything political, religious, or remotely contentious. A few diet tips that wouldn't be for everyone, a couple of designers she probably wouldn't wear at her age, but *nothing*. She googled herself, scrolled back fifteen pages, searched the omitted results. Still nothing.

What the hell was she supposed to do about this?

Dear Gloria,

I'm disappointed to hear you've had a change of heart.

Perhaps you could kindly share with me ...

Wolf

It was only half past nine on Saturday night and Wolf was already in bed. In the attic, where it was stuffy and airless. He wasn't even tired. He'd avoided Nicole all day, he'd even gone into the office. But tonight, she was banging around downstairs, in a foul mood yet again, and he couldn't bear it any longer. He wasn't prepared to discuss leaving Saltreach and he didn't want a row about it. He browsed a couple of porn sites but wasn't in the mood. He hadn't heard from Andrew since he'd left the pub the other night. He tried to read but couldn't get past the first page.

Something niggled at him and he put down his book. How come the porn site had opened? It should have been blocked.

He got back out of bed and opened his laptop. Christ, it really felt like he lived in this room lately. He opened the webpage for their internet provider, clicked into the safety settings.

The settings were on, as they should be. He opened the advanced menu, read down through the options: betting, alcohol, violence, drugs – all checked. No access. Last on the list – pornography.

There was no check in the box. It wasn't on the blocked list.

What the hell was going on? This wasn't the way he did it. If he wanted to, he switched off the security altogether. Did his business; switched it back on. Sometimes he ordered wine. Sometimes he placed the occasional bet, if he'd received a tip. But he never went into this menu and only selected one item: pornography.

Surely Lauren didn't watch porn. She was nearly sixteen. Soon it would be legal for her to have sex. She'd had boyfriends – not ones she'd introduced to Wolf, just names she'd mentioned in passing. He'd assumed it was casual. Nicole said it wasn't a big deal. Wolf didn't know if *it* referred to the boyfriends or sex in general, but he'd optimistically assumed his little girl had never actually gone all the way. Was he being naive? Kids didn't hang about these days. Jesus. But she was dating Theo now, and Wolf was happy about that. Theo was a nice kid. Lauren and Theo couldn't be having sex. Shit. He couldn't ask either Andrew *or* Kerry about that right now.

Maybe it was Nicole. Had the tables really turned, come full circle, so that his wife had replaced *him* with porn? He recognised the hypocrisy of what he was thinking, but the hurt at being replaced by what his pride insisted must be a less satisfying orgasm was more than he expected. She'd literally removed him from the bedroom, a process so gradual he'd barely noticed until it was too late. He needed to do something. Fast.

*

In the kitchen, Nicole was holding an empty glass and staring moodily at her laptop.

"Gin and tonic?" he asked, willing her to accept the olive branch.

"Sure." Her eyes didn't leave the screen.

Wolf fetched himself a glass and poured them both a strong one. When he tipped the cans of tonic into the recycling bin, he saw there were already two in there and his heart sank. Things were worse than he'd realised.

"Do you really want to leave Saltreach?" he asked, dreading the answer. But Nicole closed the computer and waved a hand in the air dismissively.

"No, don't worry about that. There's no need now."

"What?" Christ almighty, she flipflopped all over the place. He couldn't keep up. He perched on a bar stool at the island. "What's changed?"

"I was offered a job, okay?" she said, tapping angrily with a finely manicured, pale pink nail. "But it was in London, too far to commute. If we lived nearer …" she tailed off, did that dismissive wave of her hand again.

Bloody hell, his wife never failed to surprise him. At the back of his mind, he remembered this used to be his favourite thing about her. "What job?" he asked gently.

"Just a job, okay!" she snapped. "Events Manager with a fashion company. Perfect for me."

"And you turned it down because it's too far away?" Wolf was incredulous. "Why didn't you talk to me about it?"

"I did! I floated the idea of moving, but you were having none of it!"

"For God's sake, Nicole," he said, "don't put that on me. I didn't know. Maybe we could have made it work. Anyway, since when have you been looking for a job?"

"Oh, you know I have. Don't pretend you didn't see all the new clothes, the high heels that would cripple Kate Moss. And surely you wondered what I was doing on all those days out."

"I see." Her secrets. His career coach guess hadn't been too far off. Better than an affair, at least.

"You don't ask me about it anymore," she said, hurt in her eyes. "I thought you thought I was past it."

"Past it? You're only forty-four!"

"Just because your career has taken off, doesn't mean I've given up on mine. But I'm sure you wouldn't want to accommodate that now."

"Are you saying it's *my* fault you turned down this job? Because it's not. I had nothing to do with it." Christ, they were rowing again, already. Couldn't they have one normal conversation? "And anyway, my career has been a total car crash. Never knowing when the next invoice would go out. You made it bloody clear that I wasn't earning enough."

"I really wanted this one." She swigged the rest of her drink. "They offered it to me and then they retracted the offer. Something about my background check, but they won't say what."

"That's ridiculous," he said. "There must be some mistake. We can fix this."

"What's the point?" She stared at him, defiant now. "I'd be travelling four hours a day, minimum. More for events. It's not practical."

He was backed into a corner now. There was too much at play and he couldn't figure it out fast enough.

"It can't be the only company, surely? Saltreach's a busy town …"

"It's the only company that thought I was good enough," she said, twirling the stem of her glass. "I've applied for hundreds. I'm too old, Wolf. They're all in their twenties."

"But that's not why this company rejected you," he said, cursing himself as she flinched at the word *rejected*. "What I mean is, you deserve an answer. We'll get legal advice, if necessary. If there's something online about you, if some troll has written something unfavourable and it's messing with your career, we'll deal with it." At least this was an area he could help with. The emotional stuff he was crap at, but IT? This was his bag.

"I've searched everywhere," she said morosely. "There's nothing."

"I'll find it," he promised. "I wish you'd told me about all this. I think it's a great idea to go back to work. Let's face it, you're hardly Nigella Lawson, are you?"

"Hey!" But he could tell she didn't mind.

"Promise no more secrets?" But as he said it, Kerry's face swam into view.

"That goes both ways," Nicole said, pointing a finger at him, as if she'd read his mind. "You can't keep secrets either."

Wolf felt wretched. They'd talked more tonight than they had in months. He wasn't about to jeopardise this now.

"No more secrets."

Kerry

On Monday afternoon, sweat trickled under the collar of Kerry's smartest black jacket as she stood next to Andrew at Barbara Holt's graveside, avoiding Wolf's eye. She was desperate for Andrew to move past the kiss, for at least one drama to be resolved. An error in judgement, that's all it had been. But out of loyalty to Andrew, she would wait for him to forgive Wolf first. So she kept her eyes on her hymn sheet, her nails digging moon-shaped creases in the paper.

On her other side, Izzy was pale but composed. Not quite the hard bitch from Stonebridge, yet neither friend nor ally. In different circumstances, they'd be having a face-off in the boardroom right now, deciding the future of the company. Despite the funeral meaning the meeting had to be pushed, Kerry was finally ready for it – and completely exhausted.

She'd spent half the weekend helping Izzy choose a casket, a suitable dress for her mother to be buried in, flowers for the grave. They'd worked from a tatty list of instructions written in scrawled, pained handwriting. Izzy had wanted to hold the funeral somewhere nice, with champagne and canapés, but Barbara had made her promise. So Kerry had called in at The Crabby Mermaid where Barbara had worked and given Trevor, the barman, the details: egg and onion sandwiches and pots of tea, followed by fruitcake and a dram of whiskey. Trevor knew the drill. Turned out, he'd been given his instructions months ago by Barbara herself.

She'd spent the other half of the weekend discharging her mother from hospital and setting her up at home. Marta, disappointingly, had found other work.

When the burial was over, Kerry walked the short distance from the graveyard to the pub next to Pete, afraid to remove her jacket for fear of sweat marks.

"How did she organise a funeral so fast?" Pete whispered, holding open the door, which had a *Closed to the public for a private function* sign on it. Inside, an enormous spread of sandwiches and sausage rolls was laid out. Giant urns of tea and coffee sat up on the bar.

"Catholic," Kerry said, asking the barman for iced water. "We don't hang around. And," she looked at Pete, guilt warming her cheeks, "I helped her." After everything she'd said about Izzy over the past month, she couldn't bear it if Pete thought she was a turncoat. She put her hands up in surrender. "Don't shoot me."

Pete patted her on the shoulder, like her father used to. "It must have cost you to do that."

"She has nobody else."

"No other family?"

"It was just her and Barbara. Her father was never in the picture. Barbara was a cleaner, bartender, did whatever work she could get. Izzy used to pretend she wasn't, not that anyone cared. She wanted so badly to get out of Saltreach, get to London and make her own money, buy an apartment in the city and go for cocktails and fancy dinners whenever she wanted."

"Didn't we all want that once?"

"Did you?" Kerry asked, surprised.

"Of course," he said, as though it was obvious. "Although my dream probably had more to do with a Harley Davidson and Route 66. Still, maybe one day."

Kerry couldn't imagine Pete anywhere besides Saltreach; he was too ingrained. He taught kids squash twice a week and did reiki on the beach every Sunday morning, not to mention leading the seaweed petition. His wife, Audrey, was a retired nurse who led the Saltreach wild swimming group, Undercurrent, which even had its own Instagram page. The town wouldn't be the same without them.

"At least the meeting was postponed," Pete said. "Buys us some time."

Kerry poured them two cups of tea, took an egg sandwich, and almost gagged. It was more onion than egg.

"I kind of want to get it over with now." The ceasefire between her and Izzy was a tricky line to tiptoe.

Pete nodded. "How's your mum?"

"All the better now that Audrey's in charge. I can't thank you enough for asking her to help out."

"She's happy to," Pete chuckled. "Kathleen's a good friend. Seriously though, she sees it all the time, hospitals kicking out patients long before they're ready."

"Tell me about it. The kids weren't happy about giving up their den, but hey ho. At least we managed to rent a proper hospital bed. And Ella's study leave starts today, so she's an extra pair of hands if we need her."

*

When the last glass of whiskey had been drained and the small crowd had drifted back into the sweltering sunshine, Kerry walked Izzy to her flat.

"Do you want me to stay the night?" she asked, praying Izzy would say no.

Izzy embraced her, bending from the waist so that they met at the shoulder, only a delicate whisper of perfume crossing the space between them. "No," she said, stepping back. "But thanks. You've done enough."

Kerry patted her shoulder awkwardly. "When are you back in the office?"

Izzy shrugged. "Tomorrow, I suppose. Why not?"

Because your mother died. Because you're grieving. It was as if the last four days had evaporated and Izzy was once more a ruthless businesswoman without a shred of empathy.

"What about the meeting?"

"We'll do it Wednesday. Ten o'clock."

Theo

"I CAN'T *BELIEVE* DAD has a kid. Like, *another* one. What's he like? Does he look like us?"

Ella scanned the park from their viewpoint on The Bench. There were lots of people around. It was that space between school finishing and teatime and anyone could see them. Theo half-hoped that someone might come over and their secret would be discovered, out of his hands. Mitch obviously wasn't working today, either. Theo had googled the company on the business card – it looked genuine, but it didn't have the employees listed on its website. Maybe he should call and ask. It wasn't as if Mitch's name was even on the card.

"Calm down." Theo had a bad feeling. Ella was too excited. He could tell she'd dressed up especially to see him. Mitch would be pissed off. Theo sweated under the collar of his school shirt. Why was he even worried about Mitch's reaction? Judging by Ella's excitement, she was bound to let something slip at home, one way or another. "You'll see in a minute."

"Don't you think we should tell Dad?" she said, scanning the path from the woods. "What if he knew all along and never wanted it? What if this guy, like, *knows* he was rejected at birth? And now his mother's gone too. I mean, he might be really furious with Dad!"

"Do you think so?" Theo thought about Mitch's questions. Mitch wanted to know everything *about* Dad, about all of them, but he wouldn't *meet* him. Shit. If Ella was right, he'd been really stupid.

"He might not be telling the truth, you know." A strong wind blew over them and she held tight to her denim skirt. "He could be using you."

"For what?" Theo said.

"For money," Ella said triumphantly. "Didn't you say he wanted money from you?"

"Only a tenner," Theo admitted. "But he gave me the photo, remember?"

"Oh! There, is that him? I bet it is. Oh my days! He totally looks like Dad." Ella got her phone out to take a photo. "And like you, a bit."

"Put your phone away," Theo hissed. Mitch didn't look at all like him. But Ella wasn't listening.

*

Mitch paused halfway down the hill from the woodland, squinted at them, and paused. Theo grabbed Ella's phone and put it in his pocket. Mitch resumed his approach, still wary.

"Hi, Mitch," Theo said. "This is my sister, Ella. Our sister."

"*Half*-sister," Ella corrected him. Theo saw hesitation on Mitch's face again.

"Mitch," he said, scrubbing at his chest with both hands. Theo made space for him on The Bench, Ella in the middle. She could do the talking today. She was good at that.

"Do you live in Saltreach too?" Ella asked. "Do you work here? It's Monday, shouldn't you be in work today?" She looked him up and down, taking in the jeans and, today, a blue t-shirt. "Oh, I bet you're a student!"

"I'm not a student," Mitch said. His face was stony. Shit. He didn't like Ella. She was asking too many questions. She always talked too much when she was excited.

"Can I take a selfie of us?" Ella said. "I won't show Dad yet, if that's what you want. I think he'd love to meet you, though. I mean, does he even know you exist?"

Wow. Ella was really putting him on the spot.

"For God's sake," Mitch muttered under his breath. "What are you rushing me for? I thought I was just meeting *you* today. We'll get to your dad. *Our* dad."

"Okay," Ella said. "So, me. Well, I'm in Year Eleven, so, you know, GCSEs coming up soon." She made a face. "I play hockey and I'm going to be a primary school teacher. I love kids. There's nothing else to know, really. What do you do?"

"I'm in accounts," Mitch said. "At a social networking company. And no, I don't work in Saltreach. I drive down from London. I live in Tottenham with two flatmates, and I play five-a-side football."

Theo was impressed. Ella was good. He'd assumed that Mitch didn't have a car. He didn't look like he could afford one. But football? Mitch did *not* look fit enough to play football, didn't look sporty at all, come to that. Was he telling the truth?

"A social media company? Like Snapchat? TikTok?" Ella was impressed too, Theo could tell. She took her phone back from Theo and started showing Mitch her various online profiles, the millions of videos she took of herself and her friends. She came to a goofy one of the whole family, taken shortly before Dad had broken his collarbone. They were at the bowling alley, all grinning at the camera like idiots. It had been a fun afternoon. "That's Poppy and Alby, that's Mum. And that's Dad. But Theo's probably shown you loads of photos already, has he?"

"Not really," Mitch said, taking her phone. "Hey, can I have a copy of this picture?"

"Course, I'll message it to you," Ella said, reaching out to take it back. "What's your number?"

But Mitch held it tight. "Don't worry, I'll AirDrop it," he said casually. Ella looked pissed off as Mitch casually flicked through more of her photos without asking, then selected a bunch and hit the share button. There was a whoosh as they landed in his phone. Clearly, he wasn't about to share his contact details with her.

Theo was getting fed up. "Look," he said assertively, feeling braver now that Ella was there. "Surely the next logical step is to meet Mum and Dad?" He put his hands in his pockets. He wanted to go home.

"You could come for lunch on Saturday," Ella said. "Me and Theo'll make fajitas. It'll be lovely. Dad'll be thrilled. I mean, who *wouldn't* want to discover they have a grown-up son? He works in finance too, you'll have loads to chat ab—"

Mitch stood and cut her off. "For God's sake, stop *rushing* me!"

"Oh," Ella said. "I just don't see the point of all these meetings unless …"

"Nice to meet you," Mitch interrupted, although he clearly didn't mean it at all. He glowered at Theo. "I've got to go, I'll text you, okay?"

"What a weirdo," Ella said after he'd gone, but Theo knew she was trying not to cry. "I bet he's not even our brother anyway. None of us would ever be that rude."

*

"I'm telling Dad," she said as they walked home.

"You can't tell him now," Theo said. God, the whole thing had become so stressful. "You can't tell him he has a son I've been meeting for weeks, and now you've gone and scared him off, and he doesn't want to see him. We can only tell him if Mitch *does* want to meet him. See?"

"Yeah." Ella bit a nail. "Unless he's *not* his son. Then he's some kind of creep and we should definitely tell Dad."

"Mitch says his mum went back to Brazil," Theo said. "We could try to find out if Dad ever had a Brazilian girlfriend."

"Or we could poke around in the woods where he came from? Didn't you say he could be homeless? He looks like he could be." She wrinkled her nose. Mitch had smelled sour again today, like he hadn't had a wash in weeks. "I didn't buy all that stuff about being an accountant."

"Me neither," admitted Theo. "Do you think he was only saying that because Dad works in finance? I think I told him that."

"What else did you tell him?"

"About Dad's cycling and about his accident and how nobody knows who did it. And about how good a dad he is. And where we live." He paused, feeling stupid. "And where he and Mum work."

"Oh, God, Theo. He knows *everything* about us, and we know *nothing* about him! Should we go to the police?"

"And say what? He hasn't actually done anything wrong."

"Yet," Ella said grimly. "I want to find out more about him."

*

By the time they got home, Theo still hadn't managed to persuade Ella to drop it. She wasn't angry or scared, but she was really upset.

"It's such bad timing," she said. "With Mum so stressed and Dad still hurt. I mean, how can we dump this on them?"

"I know," Theo said glumly as they turned into their driveway, devoid of cars. "Surprise, surprise, nobody's home. Again."

He dumped his bag by the front door and went around the side of the house to get the key from the lockbox. Granny wouldn't be able to get out of bed to answer if they knocked. He was fishing it out when he heard a shout from the driveway. Had Mitch followed them home? He ran back to find Mr Cousins from next door standing by the gate post, a great big navy woollen coat over a pair of pale blue striped pyjamas, his hair wild as if he'd just climbed out of bed. He looked like Grandpa Joe in *Charlie and the Chocolate Factory*. A furious Grandpa Joe.

They *never* saw Mr Cousins. Theo hadn't even been sure he was still alive, they hadn't seen him in so long.

"It's not good enough," he shouted at Ella, waving a gnarly walking stick at her. "Not. Good. Enough!"

"I'm sorry?" Ella said, looking dismayed.

"What the hell are we supposed to do now?" roared Mr Cousins. "It's a total disaster. A nightmare."

Ella burst out crying. Theo was shocked. His sister was the third adult in their family. There wasn't a scenario imaginable that she couldn't handle. Mitch must have really upset her.

Theo thought of how Mitch had spoken to them earlier. Of how Lauren's ex had punched him right in the face. Of the man who'd knocked Dad off his bike and driven away. Of Mr Cousins shaking his stick at them as though he wanted to bend Ella over his knee like a naughty child and beat her with it. He was sick to death of people treating them badly. He handed Ella the key and stepped in front of her.

"Mr Cousins, get out of our driveway or I'll call the police," he called in what he hoped was a stern voice. He felt Ella grab his arm.

"Your blasted mother has a lot to answer for," shouted the old man, his face white, two pink stains on his cheeks. He was literally crying. But he shook his stick one more time at them and shuffled back to his own house. Theo and Ella ran inside and slammed the door behind them.

Theo felt dizzy and clammy, like he was going to faint. "Oh God, I shouldn't have done that," he said. "Mum'll be furious!"

"No!" Ella was beaming at him. "You were bloody brilliant. She'll be delighted. She hates Mr Cousins, anyway."

"You think?" Theo wasn't sure. He wished Mum or Dad was home from work.

"Definitely," Ella said. "Now come on, we'd better see what we can make for tea."

Nicole

NICOLE TOOK THREE VENISON steaks out of the fridge and handed Wolf an onion to chop. She was in a pickle. Wolf had spent all of yesterday and today trawling the internet for any sign of whatever it was Glorious was using against her. He'd been brilliant. He'd spent hours talking it through with her. He'd even got one of his guys, the dodgy one, to go on the dark web and see if there was anything there. There wasn't. They'd finally agreed Glorious must have had a better, younger, candidate and were using the reputation thing as a scapegoat. She almost believed she'd find another job and had even sent her CV out again. Wolf had even implied, if not said directly, that if she found another job, he would reconsider a house move. She needed to do something nice for him now. She grabbed a red pepper, set up a chopping board next to his and nudged him with her shoulder.

"I'm sorry I've never made much of an effort with Kerry before now," she said. "I realise how important she and Andrew are to you and I think, now you're working together, we should have them over for dinner."

Wolf backed up as though she'd suggested they all jump into bed together. "Oh, there's no need for all that," he said, his words spilling over each other in their hurry to come out. "I see plenty of Kerry at work. And Andrew will be back on his feet in no time."

He was rambling now, something he only did when he was nervous. But what did Wolf have to be nervous about? And why wouldn't he want to invite his best friend and his wife over for dinner? "But that's very kind. Perhaps you and I should go out for dinner instead, you know, just the two of us. You must be sick to death of cooking."

A shot of adrenalin pierced Nicole's bloodstream. Wolf hadn't taken her for dinner in forever.

"Don't you think it would be good for them to do something fun?" she said. There was definitely something going on. Wolf was scanning the kitchen, searching for a distraction. She saw his gaze land on an open wine bottle and he reached out an arm. Whatever this was, alcohol wouldn't solve it. This was something big. She could feel it. "The takeover meeting's on Wednesday – you'll need to celebrate. Or commiserate. Let's do it then."

"Maybe when Andrew's better," Wolf said, pouring her a glass of wine, pushing it at her, obviously desperate for her to drop it. "In fact, I'll see how he's feeling."

He picked up his phone. As soon as the screen lit up, Nicole snatched it from him.

"Hey," he said. "What was that for?"

Nicole ignored him. She knew immediately where to look. She went into his messages. Flicked to the contact she needed to view. Not Andrew. *Her.*

Have you told him?

The last message he'd sent her. Days ago. Kerry hadn't replied. Nicole hurled the phone across the kitchen.

The two full wine glasses Wolf had just put on the island blew to smithereens, as if she'd put a bullet through them. Glass smashed, splintered and fanned out across the room in every direction. Wolf stood, palms outward in a peace gesture, in the middle of it all.

"What the fuck, Nicole?"

"What the fuck? What the FUCK!" she screamed at him. She picked up her own phone and threw it at him. He was too slow to duck and it caught the side of his glasses. They fell among the shards of glass around his feet. She watched him squint, hold an arm out to pacify her while he ducked down to retrieve them.

"This has nothing to do with Andrew's injuries at all, does it?" she said, venom in her voice. "You don't want to invite your precious Kerry into our home, do you? You've been shagging her all along, haven't you?"

"Nicole, you've got the wrong ..." Wolf was reaching for her, but there was broken glass all around him and he was in his socks. Good. Let him shred his feet to pieces. She didn't want him anywhere near her.

"That smug bitch!" Nicole hissed. "Kerry the bloody martyr, caring for her injured husband and her senile mother like Mother fucking Teresa, saving everyone's jobs, and all the time she's carrying on with you behind my back! Behind Andrew's back!"

"That's not ..."

"How was it, eh? As good as your schoolboy fantasies?" She grabbed an apple from the fruit bowl, hurled it at his head. "How long has it been going on?" A thought swam into view and she grabbed the edge of the island to steady herself. "Oh, dear God. Is that why we live in this godforsaken town? Is this what we left London for?" The second apple caught him on the ear. Good. The anger and frustration she'd so carefully contained for months, maybe for years, was bursting out of her. It was shocking, but she couldn't stop. "Was it so that I could play second fiddle to your fucking teenage crush?" He caught the third apple. Leaning carefully on the worktop, he took one long step away from the debris on the floor.

"I kissed her."

Nicole froze, fourth apple in hand. "You what?"

"A week or so ago. It was a mistake, Nicole, a huge mistake. I was trying to comfort her."

Nicole put the apple down on the worktop. Gave it a squeeze, felt the reassuring solidness of it, the roundness. She dug a nail into it, lifted the flesh with her thumb. Like picking off a scab. She should never have looked at his phone.

"She was upset that her mother was in hospital. I only intended to give her a hug. I don't know how it happened, I really don't."

"Oh, come off it!" Her voice sounded flatter now. Dead.

"It was once, Nicole. One kiss. Nothing more."

"As if I can believe you now," she said quietly, flinging the ruined apple at him. It bounced ineffectually off his arm, left a damp stain on his sleeve. She slumped onto a dining chair, let her head fall into her hands.

"She told Andrew," Wolf said quietly. "He won't speak to me. We couldn't possibly invite them for supper."

"Fuck off, Wolf."

*

Nicole sat in silence as Wolf swept up the broken glass, threw the apples in the compost bin, and slunk back upstairs without another word. Fire raged inside her. What the hell was she thinking, wanting to make friends with Kerry? That snake! She had a good mind to go round there and have it out with her.

But to what end? Wolf was the one who'd cheated. Kiss? Sex? Did it even matter? Nicole would not take responsibility for this, no matter how long he'd been sleeping in the attic. He'd moved up there of his own accord. Took his laundry and everything! Nobody made a fool of Nicole Bauer. But what the hell was she supposed to do now?

There might be one way out. She didn't have to stay here in the middle of this mess, like she was in goddamn *Eastenders*. She grabbed her laptop.

> Dear Gloria,
> You can expect to hear from my solicitor within twenty-four hours unless I receive a thorough and satisfactory explanation regarding your allegation ...

Lauren

LAUREN HEARD GLASS SMASHING. Mum and Dad were at it *again*. She couldn't hear exactly what they were saying, but Mum was clearly blaming Dad for something. She heard Mum screaming *what the fuck?* And *has it been going on all this time?* Dad was pounding up the stairs, right up to the attic. No change there, then.

Lauren pulled on her trainers. She wouldn't sit in this house for another minute. She poked her head into the kitchen where Mum sat at the island, staring into space. All around her were the ingredients for dinner but clearly, nobody was cooking.

"I'll get a takeaway," she said, quietly pulling the front door closed behind her.

As she always did lately, she scanned the road before opening the front gate. She'd ordered herself one of those little rape alarms online and now she worried at the button with her thumb, ready to push at a second's notice. There was nobody about, but still she took out her phone and called Theo. It was safer that way.

"Can I come round, just for a minute?"

*

Theo's house was chaotic. Everyone was squashed into the little den where Theo and Lauren usually hung out. The twins were running around, high on sugar, past their bedtime and it was only Monday night. Kerry was bending over and pointing at her bottom, shaking her t-shirt with her other hand. Ella and Andrew were shouting at her. Charades. A game for five-year-olds. Lauren heard her mother's voice in her head as she thought it, and cringed.

"Backdraft!" Andrew shouted and Kerry finally turned and gave him a thumbs-up, turning pink when she saw Lauren.

A hospital bed had been set up and Theo's granny was propped up in it, looking dazed and frail and nowhere near ready to be let out of hospital, a giant bowl of popcorn between her knees. But she held up a glass of orange juice to Lauren and smiled along as happily as if it were her wedding day. "*Sláinte.*"

"When did she get here?" Lauren whispered.

"Yesterday," Theo said, pulling little Poppy onto his lap, giving her a cuddle. "Mum got all freaked out that the hospital was letting her out early but Dad said we should celebrate that everyone's getting better. So," he shrugged shyly, "this is what a Langley party looks like." He blew a party streamer at her and toasted her with his glass of fizzy orange.

Lauren felt a pain behind her ribs. This mad, jolly home – where there was always some sort of crisis, someone in hospital, someone rushing around – had more love in it than Lauren could ever remember feeling in her house. Everyone in this family played a part, everyone mucked in, helped out, shared the love.

She thought of her own mother, crying in the kitchen. Her father, alone in the attic.

"I'd better go," she said.

"There's no rush," Theo said, putting an arm around her, kissing her hair. He was different here at home. Relaxed. Not trying to impress her. She felt awkward, embarrassed. She wanted to cry. She'd been so stupid.

"No, really, I've got to go."

*

She bought Thai food. It was the most expensive takeaway, more than Indian or Chinese or pizza, but the thought of the money in her bank account, how it came to be there, repulsed her. She wanted to spend it, get rid of it. To be a normal teenager again with no plans for life beyond the weekend. She was smart, she got good grades. She could do anything she wanted.

It was busy out. Smartly dressed people walked home from late commuter trains, heads down. Joggers, headphones in, side-stepped ambling dog walkers. One overly keen runner brushed against her sleeve as he passed, making her jump.

With a bag in each hand, she couldn't hold the rape alarm. For God's sake, it was only eight o'clock. She shouldn't have to worry about being attacked. Theo was right, they should have gone to the police. Something rustled in the hedge and she sprinted the rest of the way home.

"Dinner!" she shouted, slamming the door behind her. Sweat ran down her back.

The kitchen was empty. Lauren started pulling plates and glasses from the cupboards. Maybe her family could sit down together for once and pretend they were normal.

"Dad!" she called in the direction of the stairs. "Dinner!"

"Leave him," Mum said, coming into the kitchen as Lauren unpacked the bags on the dining table, an empty wine glass in her hand. Mum drinking was another new normal she didn't like. She looked old and thin and tired in a way Lauren had never seen before. It made her afraid.

She rummaged in the drawer for napkins, not wanting to see

Mum like this, desperate for Dad to come down and fix things. "He must be hungry, I'll . . ."

"I said leave him!" Mum shouted, throwing forks onto the table with a crash. "Get me a beer, would you? The wine's all gone."

Lauren bit back her surprise. She flipped the lid on a bottle of Peroni and slid it in front of Mum. She watched, shocked, as she forked an enormous helping of food onto her plate. She took a handful of prawn crackers and shoved them into her mouth, wiped her greasy hands on a napkin.

"Not like you." Lauren couldn't help herself.

"Well, turns out starving yourself to keep your figure doesn't always pay off," Mum said, taking a long swig of beer. "Sometimes you've got to do whatever the hell you want." She jabbed the fork in the air at Lauren and let out a tiny burp.

Something inside Lauren tightened. This wasn't the way things were meant to be. She'd watched her mother count calories her whole life. Sometimes she weighed her food. Always had the dressing on the side, the leanest cut of meat, skipped the carbs, chose extra salad. She'd give Lauren a discreet shake of the head if she reached for an extra potato or helping of spaghetti, no matter how much Dad was loading onto his plate.

Watching Mum now, shovelling food into her mouth, was repulsive, as if the massive quantities of food wouldn't fit into her mother's tiny body, that she'd somehow burst apart. Something was very wrong. Maybe everything was wrong. For the second time that evening, Lauren wanted to cry.

Kerry

It was the bloody menopause.

Blood tests confirmed it. The doctor had been concerned about the headaches, the arm pain. Said the hot flushes would only get worse. She'd listened to Kerry's breathing, her heart rate, checked her blood pressure, her breasts, her weight. They'd talked about stress and anxiety. Kerry told the doctor she was not an anxious person. She was a capable woman with a lot on her plate. She would gladly have an ECG. It came back clear.

She was also anaemic. At least she could easily fix that. She left work early, bought two fillet steaks and a carton of orange juice, and then picked the twins up from after school club. She'd even been early, and they stopped at the playground on their way home to play on the swings.

Kerry felt like putting champagne in the orange juice. She would gladly accept a menopause diagnosis. That was normal for a woman of forty-six, if a little depressing. She would even accept a certain degree of stress. All that really mattered was that she wasn't going to have a heart attack.

*

She shut the front door and helped the twins stow their schoolbags.

They ran straight to the den, climbed up on the chairs by Mum's bed, and leaned in for kisses.

"Mind Granny's bad leg," Kerry warned them. "Hi, Mum. Cup of tea?"

Mum nodded, gave her a pat on the cheek.

"I'll get your walker for you in a sec, take you to the loo. Let me check on the others."

She put her head around the door of the lounge. Theo was on the sofa, still in uniform, playing on his phone, an empty Monster Munch packet on the seat next to him. Kerry swallowed her irritation.

"Hi, sweetheart. Where's Ella? Have you done your homework?"

Theo shrugged. "I haven't seen her."

"It's four o'clock, Theo. Text her, will you?"

Kerry helped Mum out of bed, guided her to the bathroom, lowered her to the loo, and took away the big incontinence pants. Thank God Audrey came every morning, although she couldn't rely on her forever. Nursing was not a career Kerry had ever considered.

She left Mum there, went into the kitchen to boil the kettle, opened the fridge for milk. There was a shepherd's pie on the middle shelf.

"Who made dinner?" she asked Theo.

He shrugged again.

"Any reply from Ella?"

"No."

*

"Mum, who made the dinner?" Kerry asked, as she pulled her mother's underwear up and helped her tie her dressing gown. Her mother swiped her away. She was definitely getting better.

"Are we going out for dinner?" Mum beamed.

"There's a shepherd's pie in the fridge," Kerry said patiently.

"Oh." Mum blanked for a moment. Then her face cleared. "Me and Marta."

"You mean you and Audrey? Mum, have you been doing too much?"

"Audrey." Mum sounded out the word like she'd never heard her old friend's name before. "I just supervised," she said, lying back down, grimacing in pain at the effort. "I want to go home."

"Oh, Mum. I don't know if you'll be able to go back to your house."

"I'm nearly better," Mum said, patting the wrong hip.

Kerry hid a smile and pulled up her blankets. "Did Ella come home after lunch?"

"There she is," Mum said, pointing at Poppy.

*

Kerry dialled Ella's number, but it went to voicemail. She texted.

Be home for tea at six, please.

You okay?

Of course Ella would be okay. Her exams were approaching fast, but she was ahead on revision. And it was Ella, for God's sake. It was May and the weather was scorching. She'd probably gone to sunbathe with a friend, maybe done some shopping on the high street. She'd said she needed new trainers and Kerry had put the money for them in her account only yesterday. There was a party tomorrow night and she wanted a new pair of earrings too. Kerry needn't worry. Ella was the most sensible child ever. The kind of sixteen-year-old who always let her mother know where she was. Only today, she hadn't.

Kerry set the oven to pre-heat and called Andrew.

Theo

Mum and Dad were *so* overreacting. And yet Theo's lungs were tight, as though being squeezed by an ice-cold hand. He called Ella for the millionth time. It rang out. Again. He shook his head at Mum.

"Call it again," she said, holding the landline in one hand, reading a text from her mobile in the other. "Audrey says she was still studying when she left at half eleven."

Dad grabbed his keys. "I'll drive around," he said, "see if I can find her."

"Stop stressing out," Theo said. "She probably just took a break."

"She's been gone for hours!" Mum shouted, waving the two phones in the air as if he and Dad were stupid. She took a big breath, pressed the phones against her chest and shut her eyes, but two tears escaped and ran down the side of her nose.

Shit. He should have noticed that Ella was gone. He'd come in from school, made a sandwich, played PlayStation, a little guitar. He'd been totally self-absorbed. Selfish. He checked WhatsApp again. She hadn't been online since two. Not on any platform. He scrolled through his apps, searching for inspiration.

"Look her up on Find My iPhone," he said, relieved to have something practical to suggest, furious with himself that he hadn't thought of it earlier.

Mum started swiping. "How the hell do I do that?"

"You're a genius, Theo," Dad said, fishing his phone from his pocket. "I never thought of that. Look, there. There she is. St Leonard's."

"That's the park!" Mum said. "Okay, phew. She's just hanging out with her friends. She's probably lost track of time. Andrew, run down and get her, will you?"

"Hang on," Theo said, peering over Dad's shoulder. "That was at two-seventeen. And WhatsApp says she hasn't checked her messages since two-ten." Everyone knew Ella couldn't go twenty minutes without checking her phone.

"Well, it's all we have to go on, isn't it?" Mum said. "She's probably out of battery. You know her friends better than we do. Go with your father. If she's not there, chances are one of her mates will be. They'll tell you where she is. I need to feed the twins. You'll have her back in no time. I'm sure you will."

From the manic way Mum was talking, like she was out of breath, and the way she kept pulling the ends of her sleeves over her hands, stretching the fabric, pulling it so tightly Theo could see her knuckles through it, he knew she wasn't sure at all. He went out with Dad, both of them silent, the air still hot, oppressive. It took Dad two tries to start the car.

*

Dad drove slowly. He didn't try to make Theo feel like everything was going to be okay. That was worse than Mum being manic, because Dad was always practical and optimistic and now he was saying absolutely nothing, which Theo knew meant that he was way more worried than he let on.

The streets were quiet. It was almost seven. After they'd driven down three empty streets in a row, Theo quietly opened all his social media and, one by one, posted on them.

Anyone seen Ella? She hasn't come home this afternoon.

God, when she got back, she'd kill him. Being a drama queen, she'd say.

"You're sure she didn't mention a party?" Dad asked.

"On a Tuesday afternoon?" Theo said sarcastically, regretting it instantly when Dad flinched. "Sorry. There might be one later though. She could have gone round someone's house to get ready."

He sent the same message to everyone in his year group and everyone he knew from Ella's. A couple of her friends posted back straight away.

Soz. In France NOT revising for exams

Me and Tilly are shopping in London today, sorry. I'm sure she'll come back soon x

Haven't left the house in days. Totally stressed. Cannot WAIT for these sodding exams to be over

The park was busy. Dad parked on a double yellow line. A totally un-Dad thing to do. But then so was driving at five miles an hour, knuckles white on the steering wheel. There were mostly older kids here, with vapes, the smell of weed, and the sound of laughing, the occasional expletive punctuating the air.

"Right, let's spread out. Do you have a picture of her you can show people?"

"Dad!"

"I'm serious. If we don't find her here, I'll have to call the police."

Theo opened Ella's Insta profile and zoomed in on her latest post. In the photo, she was sitting dreamily by a steaming cup of coffee. The caption read, *Enjoying some me time*. Theo recognised the background as one of the posh cafes on the other side of town. Ella didn't even drink coffee.

"Right, you go that way," Dad said. He was using a photo of Ella from last Christmas. She was wearing a Santa hat and holding up a present wrapped in silver paper. She'd be mortified if she knew he was showing people that one. "Meet you by the gate over there. Be careful."

Be careful. Dad was definitely worried if he was warning Theo to be careful in a park full of kids.

He stopped anyone roughly the same age, but everyone shook their heads. None of her friends were here. Then he started asking random strangers, thrusting his phone right in their faces.

He interrupted a couple kissing on a picnic blanket. They had a plastic bag full of lager cans next to them, a few empties strewn about, and blotchy, sunburned skin that told Theo they'd been here for hours.

"'Scuse me," he said, feeling his face flush as they let go of each other and turned to face him. "Did you happen to see this girl here this afternoon?"

"Lost your girlfriend, have you?" said the guy. "Piss off, mate."

"Shut up," said his girlfriend. She sat up straight and grabbed the phone. Shit. What if she wouldn't give it back? His first fight hadn't ended well and this guy was bigger than the last one. "Yeah, she was here. Like, hours ago. Maybe even this morning."

"Where? Did you talk to her?"

"Nah. She was sat up there. Like she was waiting for someone." The girl jerked her thumb behind her, in the direction of The Bench. Mitch's bench.

"And did she? Meet anyone, I mean?" Theo struggled to keep his voice even.

The girl was flicking through his photos now. He grabbed it back.

"Yeah, it was definitely her. Nice hair. No, nobody came." The girl turned back to her boyfriend. "Give us another can, would you?"

"What did she do then? Which way did she go?" Theo said, feeling desperate.

"Yeah. Up that way," said the girl, pointing to the path that led into the woods.

Shit, shit, shit. What had Ella said? *I want to find out more about him.*

What had she done? Worse, what had Mitch done? God, it would all have to come out now – how stupid he'd been, trusting that Mitch was telling the truth, meeting up with him in secret, bringing Ella. He should never have kept Mitch a secret.

"Dad?"

"Hang on, I'm going to ask these girls over here."

"Dad, I think I know what happened."

"What? What are you talking about?"

"We need to call the police."

Kerry

KERRY RAN TO THE door when she heard Andrew's key in the lock. Surely there would be news by now. Saltreach wasn't that big. Someone must have seen Ella. She'd texted a bunch of parents from Ella's year group to find out if there was any kind of gathering or event she might have forgotten about. A study group, a movie, a sleepover, anything at all. She'd even texted Ella's old hockey camp boyfriend, Chris, just in case they'd rekindled something now that school was over. In case he was a weirdo and kidnapped her. Exes were usually the problem. Everyone knew that. But nobody had seen her.

"Any sign?"

Andrew shook his head.

Poppy and Alby started to cry. "Where's Ella?" Alby said plaintively. They'd finished their shepherd's pie and were now eating crisps in their pjs, becoming more and more whiny as Kerry's ability to remain patient with them dwindled to nothing.

"She's just lost track of time," she said. She'd said it a hundred times already. It was her mantra to herself. "She'll be home soon."

Andrew gripped her elbow. "Turn on a movie for them," he whispered. "Theo says he knows something."

The image of Ella being bundled into a van flashed into Kerry's mind for the millionth time. Ella lying in a ditch. Ella unconscious on the floor of some dodgy flat. Ella being hurt. The list was endless.

She took the twins into the lounge, handed Poppy the remote, and followed Andrew to the kitchen, where Theo was pinching his fingertips against his thumbs in the repetitive, self-soothing way he'd done since he was a toddler. It must be bad news.

"A girl in the park saw Ella earlier," Theo said. "Sitting on a bench."

"Okay. Okay, that's good," said Andrew, rubbing the bridge of his nose. He grabbed Kerry's hand, holding too hard, pinching her fingers together. She pulled her hand away, unable to comfort him, needing the information. She wanted Theo to talk faster, to shake the words out of him, but the poor kid was borderline hysterical. They all were.

"What else, honey?"

"She said Ella looked like she was waiting for someone who didn't show up. After a while, Ella left in the direction of the woods. That's all she knew."

"Oh." Kerry sagged. She sat at the kitchen table, crushed, feeling the chance to rescue her daughter recede faster than it had appeared. "Is that all?"

"No," Theo said miserably. "Yesterday, I brought her to meet someone in the park, someone who always comes from the woods. Ella didn't believe he was who he said he was. She wanted to find out more about him." He was rocking now, pinching his fingers harder. "I think she might have gone looking for him."

"Who?" Kerry said, taking his hand before he made himself bleed. "Theo, who is it?"

"A guy who approached me weeks ago. We've been hanging out. He said …" He bit his lip. There was something he didn't want to admit. Shit.

"Said what, Theo?"

"He said he's Dad's son." Theo started crying. "He said he wanted to get to know his family but he was too nervous to meet Dad yet.

He's been asking me all kinds of questions. I took Ella to meet him yesterday. She thought he might be trying to scam us. For money."

A bubble of laughter nearly escaped Kerry. Andrew's son? It was a joke, surely. A prank.

"How old is this guy, sweetheart?" she said.

"Twenty-two. He thinks Dad doesn't know about him. But now that his mum's gone back to Brazil, he wants to get to know Dad."

Brazil. *Brazil.* Andrew had once had a Brazilian girlfriend.

"Why didn't you tell us about him, Theo?" Andrew's voice was strained.

Theo was hysterical, crying louder now. At once, the situation seemed more far-fetched and ridiculous, and yet more terrifying. Whatever the truth was, there was a man. A real person. Someone who could hurt Ella. Put his hands around her neck. The hairs lifted on Kerry's arms and she put her two hands to her throat. She couldn't afford to become hysterical too. Andrew had turned pale and was holding onto the wall for support. She had to remain rational. The simplest explanation was usually the right one. It must be a misunderstanding between Ella and this … person.

"Do you have his number?" Kerry fished her phone out of her pocket, copied the number from the screen Theo held out to her, her thumbs thick and clunky.

The phone was switched off. No voicemail. "What's his name?"

"Mitch."

Andrew grabbed her hand. "I don't know anything about it."

"Course you don't," she said. "We'll get to that later. Theo, what does he look like?"

Theo was calming down, now that his secret was out in the open. God, he'd been meeting this man for weeks. Kerry thought of all the times she'd convinced herself not to worry about her eldest son. She'd been so stupid. Afraid of overreacting over the black eye. Putting it down to a spat with Kai, or Lauren's rejection. She'd let herself become preoccupied with work. And Andrew's accident, and Izzy, and Mum. Christ, there'd been too much to deal with. Too many spinning plates. And now one had dropped. Splintered and shattered into a million fragments that she might never be able to put back together.

Theo took a breath and sat down. "He's tall and thin. Kind of scruffy. He sort of jiggles and scratches, like he's itchy all the time." It wasn't much to go on. Mitch didn't sound very appealing. Theo looked at her through sad, damp eyelashes. "And he knows where we live."

"What? How?"

"I told him. He wanted to know. I thought I could convince him to come back with me and tell you who he was."

Andrew tilted his phone towards her, showed her he was punching in emergency services. Shit. It had come to this. It was after nine o'clock. Nobody had seen Ella since this morning.

Kerry

It took the police an hour to arrive. They hadn't wanted to come. Young people didn't come home on time every day of the week. But when Kerry told them about the man pretending to be Andrew's son, the operative's tone changed and he promised to dispatch someone immediately.

Now, two young police officers sat at the kitchen table. PC Hathaway had thick chestnut hair tied in a no-nonsense ponytail and a soft West Country accent and was sifting through photographs of Ella on Kerry's phone. Kerry's heart contracted as she zoomed in on Ella's heart-shaped face beaming into the camera, nose crinkled, eyes smiling. In another shot, she stood on the high street, McDonald's in the background, wearing a long black cardigan, white crop top, ripped baggy jeans, and pink Converse, her blonde hair perfectly styled in waves down her back. She was gorgeous. The officer handed her back the phone.

"Can you email the photos I've selected to this email address?" the officer said, writing out a neat address on her notebook and tearing off the page.

Kerry nodded. She, Theo, and Andrew sat in a tight little bunch at the table, holding hands as though drawing hope from one another. Audrey was with Mum in the den. Pete had come with her and was reading the twins a story. By the time they woke up tomorrow, Ella would be home and this nightmare would be over.

There was now a missing person's photo of Ella, which would soon be circulated among the police, the community, their friends, and strangers. Would whoever was responsible see it? Would it frighten them enough to let her go? Kerry fought to stay calm. They could do this, they would find her. They had help on their side now. If Mitch was Andrew's son, they were probably talking. Yes, that would be it, getting to know each other. Maybe he'd taken her to a bar. She'd suggest the police check the bars, too. Ella looked older than sixteen.

But if Mitch wasn't who he said he was … no, she couldn't think like that. She had to be practical. She gathered up all the empty mugs on the table. She would wash them. Make fresh coffee, sandwiches. Would Ella have eaten today? She started to cry and set the mugs back down.

Andrew slid into the seat next to her and put an arm around her shoulder, never breaking off from his conversation with PC Desai, who was scribbling at a ferocious pace. Kerry blew her nose and forced herself to focus. Every detail was crucial.

"Yes, I did have a Brazilian girlfriend – Diana Santiago. Yes, I suppose if she was pregnant when we broke up, he'd be twenty-one or -two now. No, of course, I didn't know. Why wouldn't she tell me? I'd have done the right thing." His fingers sought Kerry's, as though he needed tethering. She understood. The police, the notebooks, even her own kitchen felt surreal, like they'd been plunged into another dimension. He pinched the bridge of his nose and she knew he wanted to cry too. "I … I was besotted with her. *She* dumped *me*."

"How was Mitch with Ella on the day they met?" This was directed at Theo, who'd grown paler with each question. He looked at Kerry now with huge, tear-filled eyes.

"It's okay, honey." Kerry nudged him gently. "Tell them what you told us."

The PC tapped her pen on the table and Theo startled. Kerry felt inexplicably chastised on his behalf.

"Ella was excited to meet him," he said slowly. "She asked him lots of questions. He told us he lives in a flat share in Tottenham and works for a social media company. I have his business card." He pulled the cover off his phone and extracted a blue and white card. Linkwell. Everyone stared at it. There was no picture of Mitch. His name wasn't even on it. Kerry went to pick it up but Hathaway snapped on a pair of gloves and produced a small plastic bag.

"DNA," she said apologetically.

"And I have a photograph of Dad with Diana." He produced the scrunched-up photo from the pocket of his jeans. It was barely possible to see the faces clearly. He gave it to Andrew, who nodded at the police officers and handed them the picture.

"Yes, this is Diana."

"But how was Mitch with Ella?" PC Desai said again, pen still flying across the pages. It was so much, so fast, and Kerry struggled to speak, to ask questions, even to breathe. It was as though she'd been pulled under the waves during a swim and was struggling to regain her equilibrium. She tried desperately to focus on the question, on Theo, on what the police seemed to be saying.

"Was he aggressive?" persisted Desai, pen at the ready, foot jiggling under the table. "Did he touch her? Make her uncomfortable at all?"

"He was awful!" Theo said, jabbing at his eyes with the heels of his hands. "He was snappy with her. He took photographs off her phone without asking and he got angry when she wanted to take a selfie with him." He looked at the floor. "She was really upset."

“Okay,” Hathaway said, in her cool gentle voice. “Okay, thank you, Theo. That’s so helpful. You can take a break now.”

*

“May we see Ella’s bedroom?” Hathaway said.

“Why?” This was surreal. They were here to help find her daughter, not point fingers. Theo was already broken. What did they want in her bedroom? Something to use against her and Andrew?

But Andrew was already leading the way. As they passed the sleeping twins’ bedroom, Pete dozing in the chair next to them, Kerry pulled their bedroom door shut. It wouldn’t do for them to wake up to this.

Ella’s bedroom was as immaculate as always. Andrew had moved back to their bedroom over the weekend and she had wasted no time putting everything back in order. A *Heartstopper* novel on her nightstand. Make-up and perfumes neatly lined up by the three-way light-up mirrors on her dressing table, brushes in a sparkly silver pot. Photographs in silver frames of all shapes and sizes adorned purple walls. Her desk could have belonged to a marketing executive – laptop front and centre, colour-coded timetables on the pinboard, neat binders stacked and labelled, brightly coloured flash cards in tidy piles, covered in Ella’s small, square handwriting. She would be an incredible teacher. The PCs rummaged around a little. One picked up a hairbrush.

“When will you start *looking* for her?” Andrew said. He touched the Sabrina Carpenter concert tickets on the pinboard that they’d bought her to celebrate finishing her exams and Kerry knew he was thinking the same as she was. *Will she get to go?* Of course she would. Ella would absolutely be at that concert.

"Now," Hathaway said. "Now. We have everything we need to get started. We need at least one of you to stay home in case she comes back."

*

While Andrew let them out, Kerry woke Pete and sent him down to the kitchen for coffee. She kissed her babies. Alby had climbed down into the bottom bunk beside Poppy and they were fast asleep, their arms wrapped around each other, Poppy's long hair trailing off the pillow, the covers tangled around their feet. Kerry pulled the duvet up and crept into Theo's room.

He was sitting on the floor, eyes bloodshot, scrolling furiously on his phone, no doubt searching for clues, anything he might have missed. Kerry sat next to him.

"If Mitch is Dad's son, he'll get in touch soon," she said gently, reading his mind. "Even the police said that."

"What if Ella was right and he's faking it?"

"We can't worry about that right now," she said. "The police said the most likely scenario is that she went off to find him and they're talking." She didn't mention they'd also said Mitch might make a ransom demand. They were sending someone round to sit with them overnight in case that happened. Despite what the police said about not paying, she'd seen Andrew totting up how much cash he could get his hands on. It wouldn't be enough.

"Does Ella have his number?" Kerry asked Theo. She was sure the police had asked this, but there were too many details to think straight any more.

"I didn't give it to her." He shrugged. "But she could easily have taken it off my phone."

"Okay, love," she said. "I'll take your phone down and put it on charge in the kitchen. Will you take off the passwords and the facial recognition for me? So I can get into it if I need to."

Theo nodded, thumbs flying again.

"Remind me, honey. What did Mrs Cousins say when you met her yesterday? Ella mentioned some kind of run-in."

Theo flushed deeply and the pain behind Kerry's ribs intensified. "It was Mr Cousins. Not Mrs." He handed her the phone, eyes glittering again.

"*Mr* Cousins?"

Edward Cousins was a recluse, a one-time Bullfinch worker who'd gotten himself signed off on sick pay. Stress. In her mind, Kerry put air-quotes around the word. They'd been glad to see the back of him, but he'd cost Bullfinch a fortune by the time she'd finally managed to get him off the books. He was an arrogant sod, prone to vicious outbursts. But he'd been essentially housebound for the last year. Parkinson's or Fibromyalgia, she couldn't be sure.

"He said it was a fucking disaster," Theo said quietly.

"What do you think he meant?" prodded Kerry. But already, the phrase, *fucking disaster*, sounded alarm bells in her head.

"Well—" He hesitated. "He said you have a lot to answer for. He was shouting at Ella and shaking his walking stick at her."

Blood rushed to Kerry's face. She was glad of the dim light from Theo's bedside table. "Okay." She hugged him. "I want you to get some sleep. I'll worry about Mr Cousins. He's harmless."

The scepticism on Theo's face told her he didn't believe her, but she left him anyway and joined Andrew and Pete in the kitchen. A woman with salt-and-pepper hair, paisley blouse, and no-nonsense navy trousers now sat at the table, taking notes. Andrew introduced her as Detective Sergeant Zoe Gates. Kerry didn't want to go over it all again, she didn't want to talk. She couldn't even cry any more.

She was empty of tears. And she was starting to feel very, very angry. She wanted answers. She wanted action.

"What if it's not Mitch?" she said.

Andrew looked hopeful for a moment and her heart broke for him. To discover a son who'd possibly kidnapped his daughter must be incomprehensible. The detective put down her pen and swivelled round in her chair, alert.

"Theo and Ella had a row with Mr Cousins yesterday," she said and the tiny spark in Andrew's eyes died.

"That grumpy old bastard?" Andrew said. "He can hardly walk, Kerry. What could he have to do with this?"

"Who is Mr Cousins?" asked Gates.

"Our neighbour," Kerry said. "Apparently, he was shaking his stick at Ella and saying it was all a fucking disaster and that *I* have a lot to answer for."

"And?"

"Well, there's an online campaign in Saltreach," Kerry explained, hoping the detective could unscramble Kerry's thoughts for her. She was beyond logic. "Allegedly to muster support for Bullfinch, to save jobs. We're being taken over. Unofficially, it's a smear campaign against me."

"My daughter was fired," Gates said, nodding. "And then rehired. She said you helped her."

"You're Paula's mum?"

"She showed me the forum," Gates said. "It's nasty."

"Exactly," Kerry said, pulling out her phone. "Led by one particularly vicious troll. Look."

She unlocked her phone and showed them a thread. "'It's a disaster,'" she quoted. "'Kerry Langley has a lot to answer for. A fucking disaster.'"

"Sounds like him," Pete said. "That man is a nasty piece of work. But do you really think he's capable of this?"

Kerry turned to Gates. "Edward Cousins has had a grievance with Bullfinch, with *me*, for nearly twenty years. *I* cut off his benefits. Do you think he's taking revenge on me now?" She opened the bifold door and stepped out into the garden, peered over the fence. "I can see him now," she said angrily, coming back inside. "Watching television like a sweet old pensioner. What if he's got Ella locked up in his basement?"

Andrew and DS Gates stared at her as if she'd lost her mind.

Eventually, Andrew spoke. "There are no basements in these houses."

But Gates snapped her notebook shut and stood. "I'd better go and have a chat with him," she said, and Kerry wanted to kiss her. "Although I'm afraid Mitch still lines up as a much more likely prospect. For now."

*

Kerry and Andrew stood in hushed silence, holding hands in the doorway, keeping the front door ajar. The detective had told them to stay out of sight. In fact, she'd warned them to stay inside, but Kerry needed to hear for herself what the Cousinses had to say. She heard Gates knock and the door creak open.

"Oh," Kerry heard Mrs Cousins say breathlessly, and she imagined the old woman flapping the belt of her dressing gown. "Oh. My goodness. You came. You actually came."

"She sounds happy," Andrew whispered. "Why would she be *glad* the police are here?"

Kerry put a warning finger to her lips.

"I'm sorry it's so late." Gates coughed. "Mrs Cousins, is it?"

"Edward? Ed!" Mrs Cousins' voice was reedy and thin. "He'll be so delighted you're here."

"Shall I come inside?"

*

Kerry and Andrew tiptoed back through the house, as though afraid the Cousinses would hear, and stepped into the garden. Theo appeared behind them in his pyjamas, pale-faced and red-eyed. On her tiptoes, Kerry peered over the dividing fence and saw Mr Cousins reach for his walking stick and attempt to heave himself out of the huge, floral armchair, saw the relief in his face as Gates perched on the armchair opposite him. He allowed himself to flop back into his seat. This man hadn't the strength to do anything to Ella. Ella was fit. She was a hockey player. But he'd made it to their driveway and shaken a stick in anger. Fear could freeze a person. And Ella was a good girl. She wouldn't have wanted to antagonise him.

He pulled out a laptop from a side table.

"He's cooperating," Andrew whispered in her ear. "He doesn't look at all nervous."

"He's *glad* the police are there," Theo whispered back. "Jesus, Mrs Cousins is bringing in cups of tea."

Mrs Cousins set down a tray on the tasselled pouffe and lifted a jug of milk. It hovered in the air for a moment and then her smile began to fade. She set down the jug and he closed his laptop, and their faces became hard and impenetrable. They started pointing towards Kerry's house, Mrs Cousins clasping the lapel of her yellow dressing gown tightly around her neck, as though she were feeling violated. The façade of sweetness and light hadn't lasted long.

"You bastards," Kerry whispered under her breath.

Gates stood and showed them something. Ella's photograph. The Cousinses peered at it, and then Mrs Cousins sank onto the arm of her husband's chair and dabbed at her eyes with a hanky.

They were visibly shocked. Dramatic, yes, but genuine. They hadn't known Ella was missing.

Kerry's heart ached as she turned back to the house and hauled her body over the threshold. It was a dead end.

*

"False alarm," Gates said ten minutes later, rejoining them at the kitchen table. The kitchen was beginning to feel claustrophobic, too many bodies, too many dirty mugs, and a half-eaten packet of fig rolls. The remnants of the shepherd's pie Mum and Audrey had made sat on the worktop, crusting along the sides. "They were shocked to hear about Ella's disappearance."

"We saw."

"However, Mr Cousins has been in touch with the local police station, as a concerned community member." Gates rolled her eyes. "Repeatedly. He's behind the online smear campaign. I've instructed him to take it down."

*

Gates left to go back to the station.

"I'm so sorry, Kerry," Andrew said, coming up behind her awkwardly. She'd never seen him so tired. His skin was grey and folds had appeared around his mouth, dragging it down. "About Mitch, I mean. I had no idea Diana was ..."

"You have nothing to be sorry for. You couldn't have predicted this in a million years."

"What if ..."

"Let's not go there." But it was too late. She'd been going there in her own imagination since five o'clock that afternoon. Now it was nearly midnight and the image of her beautiful daughter tied up, or hurt, loomed at her like a nightmare.

She couldn't stay in the kitchen any more. Couldn't pretend to be calm and strong and confident. She wanted to scream and slam doors and rant, and she wanted very badly to punch something. But she couldn't.

She crept into the den and told Pete and Audrey to go home. They protested, of course, but she stayed firm. When they finally left, with promises to return first thing, she took her spot on the chair next to her mother's bed. Mum was sleeping, a rattle in her chest. Kerry took her hand and laid her cheek against it.

"Oh, Mum, what the hell will I do?" she wept. "What'll we all do if Ella doesn't come home?"

Ella

Ella sat on the toilet seat and squeezed her eyes shut as if, through sheer willpower, she could drown out the pounding of fists on the old pine door. How long had it been? Three hours? Four? He hammered now in time with the blood churning between her temples, the drip, drip, drip of the leaky tap, the prayer she silently recited between clenched teeth.

"I just want to talk to you," he said, his voice thin and nasal, wheedling. "I want to get to know you."

He did not just want to talk to her. That much, she knew for sure.

She wouldn't think about *how* he expected to get to know her better. She forced herself to breathe normally, not to retch. Not to make any sound. Not to aggravate him again.

"I bought you dinner," he said. "Fish and chips. It's downstairs, all ready for you. Coke or Fanta? I got both, just in case. Please, El. I . . . I think I *love* you."

Who the fuck was this guy? Did he really think she would open the door and sit at the kitchen table with him? What kind of sick pervert was he? She stuck her fingers in her ears and prayed help was on its way. Mum would know something was wrong when she wasn't back in time for tea. Maybe someone had found her phone. She'd heard it slap the pavement when she'd started to run. Surely, they'd report it.

And then the banging stopped.

*

She opened her eyes. The silence loomed large in front of her, something tangible she wanted to pull to her chest like a shield. She strained to listen to it, shook her head to clear the thunderstorm of fear.

She heard a click. A tiny metallic click.

Had he a gun? A blade? Ella shivered and leaned away from the lock.

Under the door, the shadows of his feet shifted. She heard another tiny click.

*

The key had moved. Only a fraction, but it had definitely moved. He was unlocking the door from the other side.

She clamped one hand across her mouth, pinching her cheeks, tears streaming over the backs of her fingers. Keeping one eye on the door, she reached behind and thumbed the catch for the old sash window again, already knowing there was a twenty-foot drop she'd risk in a heartbeat. But she couldn't undo the bolt.

She pulled her sleeve downward, over her hand, shucked her fingers inside and tried again. It was futile. The window hadn't been opened in years. When she took her hand away, the shape of the bolt was imprinted on her skin.

The door key rattled again.

She needed a weapon. A pink plastic toothbrush holder sat suspended in a ring above the sink. She tipped its contents onto the beige linoleum: a green toothbrush with splayed bristles, which she wielded in one hand, a half-empty tube of Oral B toothpaste, and a hairpin, which she slid into the back pocket of her jeans.

She checked the door.

"El. Let me in, El."

He knew her name. He *knew* her. But with his hoodie up, she hadn't been able to see his face properly.

Oh God. The key was moving again. He was turning it slowly from the outside. She reached out with trembling fingers and twisted it back, held it tight.

"I BOUGHT YOU FUCKING DINNER!"

The scream, inches from her head, sent her reeling onto the floor. She didn't care any longer that he could hear her crying. She couldn't stop.

"Let me *in*!"

Pressing her back against the door, she wedged her feet against the basin pedestal and grabbed the key above her head with sweaty hands. She pushed it into the lock, praying it wouldn't snap.

How much longer could she hold him off?

Nicole

On Tuesday evening, Nicole opened the email from Glorious and went straight to the attachments. She squinted, enlarged the images. There were screenshots, lots of them, from a website called PeekaBoo. Nicole opened up her web browser and typed in the address.

What the hell was this, some lingerie designer? Did they think she was working for the competition?

It wanted her to create an account to log in. She wished she could ask Wolf if it was safe, but, obviously, she wasn't speaking to him. That fucking kiss. She wished he would leave, get out of the house, but he'd sat five paces away at the kitchen table all fucking day. She couldn't think with him there. They hadn't spoken since last night and the tension was excruciating, even when Lauren came in for her tea, vanishing quickly to her bedroom. But Nicole would not leave. She would not let him win.

She created an account using an old hotmail address. *PeekaBoob*, it might as well be called. There were photographs of girls, women. Men too. Some looked very young. All were posing provocatively. Some sort of dating site? *Porn*?

Christ. Did Wolf go on websites like this? Not posing, obviously, but messaging girls, watching them. Men were disgusting. Could that be it? Could she be implicated by association, somehow? She scrolled up and down the page, clicked on a few profiles, but they wanted her credit card details, and she certainly wasn't doing that.

She went back to the email and scanned the other attachments. There was some kind of Excel spreadsheet full of black lines, redacted content. She scrolled up and down furiously, eventually landing on the only line still legible.

Nicole Bauer, 43 The Warren, Saltreach. Model.

There was a postcode and what appeared to be a credit card number, partially redacted. The last four digits didn't match any card that Nicole owned. But the postcode was correct.

She read it again. Model.

She'd done some modelling in her twenties. Even a couple of lingerie shots. A few that would probably make her blush now. Had one of the photographers or agents held onto her pictures, posted them on this website and was charging people to view them?

Nicole sat on a barstool and clutched the edge of the island she had fought so badly for only a few months ago. The laptop screen was blurry. She waited for the tears to pass and her world to stop spinning, for the idea emerging from her subconscious to crystallise.

Her old modelling photos were upstairs. In the attic. Where Wolf had spent the last few months, banished by her from their bed. Surely Wolf hadn't done this? Surely, he wouldn't post semi-naked photographs of his wife online and make money from it? Was that what they meant by revenge porn?

Wolf

Wolf was starving. Nicole hadn't made him dinner and he was reluctant to get in her way, to piss her off even more. She kept shooting him daggers from her seat at the island. She hated him working down here, in the kitchen, in *her* space. But hiding away in the attic hadn't done them any good. So, this morning, he'd set up his computer on the kitchen table. The tension was desperate, the day as long as a month, but he would fix this, once and for all.

He wasn't really working now, anyway. It was late. He needed to find whatever it was that had cost Nicole that job. It was the least he could do for her, and he should have found it by now. Whatever it was, it had either been well hidden – or deleted. But, as Wolf knew, nothing was impossible on the internet.

He went back into the safety settings. The pornography setting was still on. That was the first thing that needed to be corrected. What had he been thinking, leaving that open? He clicked on it.

From the other end of the room, Nicole swore under her breath.

"What's wrong?" he asked.

"Has the internet gone down? It's shut me out." She picked up her phone and peered at it. "My phone's working. God!"

"Mine's okay, too," he said. "Shall I take a look?" He stood, but she slammed the laptop hood down.

"No," she said quickly. "Cup of tea?" She reached behind her and flicked the switch on the kettle.

Cup of tea. Maybe there was a thaw in the iceberg?

"Yes, please," he said, sitting back down.

Oh. It clicked into place in his brain. Oh!

"Nicole, are you on a porn site?" He tried to smile, to take the sting out of it. But as she spun around to glare at him, she dropped the kettle. She screamed and jumped back grabbing her hand.

"Quick, under the tap!" Wolf raced over, pulling her to the sink. "How bad is it?"

"Get off," she said, snatching her hand back. An angry red welt spread over her thumb and index finger.

"It's bad enough," he said, taking her hand, putting it back under the water. He stood behind her, wrapped his arms around her. This time, she didn't shake him off. "Keep it there, I'll get the cream. Do you want a bandage?"

"How do you know about the website?" she said, without turning around.

"It's nothing to be embarrassed about," he said gently.

"It's *everything* to be embarrassed about!" She turned to face him. "Whatever it is, it cost me that job! Whoever put me on there is using me to make money!"

"What are you talking about?" He held her hand under the freezing water.

"Was it you?" she whispered.

"I thought you were having a little … I mean, it's a bit insulting given I'm sitting right there, but I guess I deserve that." He got the first aid kit from the drawer.

"You think I'm sitting here beside you, titillating myself in the kitchen? Oh, grow up, Wolf. I'm talking about someone using my old modelling photographs to make money!"

"What?"

"Was it you, Wolf? Is this your petty revenge for us not having sex anymore? Is this why we have money all of a sudden? Did you go through that box of stuff under the bed and think, I know how to humiliate Nicole and make a few quid at the same time? For God's sake, what if someone I know saw that?"

Wolf backed away from her, his hands up. He felt winded. "I don't know what you're talking about. What box of stuff? I haven't done anything."

"Well, someone has." She turned away from him, patted her hand dry with a towel. She winced. It was a nasty burn.

"What website?" He unscrewed the lid from the cream, smothered her hand with it. "Do you want to go to hospital? It's still very red."

"It's fine," she snapped. "PeekaBoob, Peek at You, something like that. It's on my computer."

He wrapped a bandage around her hand, tucked it in neatly at the wrist, and went to her laptop. "I'll find it," he promised.

*

Twenty minutes later he was frustrated. It was some low-end pay-per-view site. Apart from the one line on the redacted file, there was no connection to Nicole at all.

Her words reverberated in his head. She'd accused *him* of putting pictures of her online to make money. How could she think so little of him? Maybe that was what being unfaithful did to a marriage. Perhaps one kiss could shatter trust overnight. No: he had to admit he and Nicole had been in trouble long before that.

*

The next morning, Wolf sat again at the table with his laptop. He went back to the router settings. The porn access had been enabled from inside the house, so he redirected his search. He brought up the global internet search history for the entire family, thousands of results, and ran a search on PeekaBoo.

Hundreds of entries popped up.

"What the hell?"

"What is it?" Nicole appeared at his shoulder, immaculate as always in running gear. Her hair was in a tight bun and she smelled of toothpaste and deodorant and a light spritz of something delicious, and her lips and cheeks were dressed in baby pink. Nobody would ever know from Nicole's appearance that her marriage was on the rocks and her dream job had just been pulled from under her feet. Had he been so self-absorbed he'd never looked below the surface?

"Someone's been on this website from inside our house," he said, turning back to his laptop. "Hundreds of times."

"Is it some kind of virus?" she said. "What's it called, malware?"

"I can see when it was accessed. Look, sometimes it's first thing in the morning."

Nicole brought the family diary over, cross-referenced the dates. "That's a Tuesday! Who looks at porn on a Tuesday morning!" She eyed him angrily.

"Nicole, this was not me," he said. Christ, their marriage really was a shambles. She thought he was some kind of pervert. He looked from diary to laptop, over and over. "Honey, it's Lauren."

Lauren

Lauren woke on Wednesday morning and she did not want to go to school. She didn't want to be at home either, but her parents hadn't spoken to each other since their shouting match on Monday night and she needed to know what was going on.

She switched on her phone. For the first time ever, she'd switched it off in the evening and gone to bed with *Anne of Green Gables*, her favourite book from when she was ten years old. She wanted to escape the real world and immerse herself in the naive optimism of a freckled, red-haired girl who literally had nothing. It was self-sabotage, torturing herself for turning her own life into the absolute shitshow that it had become. Now her phone pinged and pinged, over four hundred notifications. God. She opened Snapchat first.

Ella was missing. She'd been gone for eighteen hours.

There were messages from Theo and all her friends, photographs of Ella in a cute crop top and jeans outfit that Lauren had immediately gone out and bought the first time she'd seen Ella wear it. She swished through Instagram, Snapchat, TikTok, WhatsApp. Ella's picture was everywhere. Apparently, she'd gone for lunch and never come back.

Lauren knew that was true. She'd bumped into Ella leaving the little jewellery shop next to The Hungry Giraffe. They'd laughed at the fact that they were wearing the same outfit, despite Lauren being secretly mortified; Ella would have realised that Lauren had copied her. But she'd been too lovely even to suggest it. Just like she'd never mentioned that Lauren's hairstyle now matched hers. They had walked a few metres together until Lauren ducked into a shop on the pretext of needing to buy a birthday card for Mum. Mum's birthday wasn't until Christmas, but she'd been too embarrassed to walk any further dressed like twins.

She pulled on a hoodie and joggers and texted Theo.

What's going on? Do you want me to come over?

She got an immediate reply.

The police are searching for Ella. Have you seen her?

Share it, keep posting it.

Lauren typed back.

Has she run away?

She felt stupid even typing it. Theo didn't answer. Lauren felt the shape of the rape alarm in her pocket. She carried it everywhere with her now. There were too many freaks out there. Had one of them taken Ella?

I'll come over.

She dressed, found her trainers under the bed and was tying her laces when there was a knock on her bedroom door.

Dad was the only one who ever knocked properly. As in, he actually waited for her to say *come in*. But not today, apparently. Here he was, followed by Mum, who was holding her laptop out in front of her with two hands, as if it were a bomb. It was only half seven in the morning.

Oh. This was it. They knew. Fuck.

Lauren twisted the rings on her fingers furiously. She thought she was in the clear. There was no evidence online. The money was tucked away safely and the pictures deleted. She lifted her chin an inch.

"Honey, can we talk to you for a minute?" Dad said.

At least they were speaking to each other again. It had been ridiculous the last couple of days, everyone tiptoeing around each other in the kitchen. Mum had regained her self-control, which was both reassuring and disappointing. She'd hoped Mum would have had more to say about being able to eat what you wanted and not trying to impress everyone else. But instead she'd eaten the rest of her takeaway in silence and gone straight to bed, leaving Lauren alone with the mess on the kitchen table. Yesterday she'd been back in her running kit, drinking her protein smoothies and lifting one of Lauren's slices of bread out of the toaster. As if the night before had never happened.

"Sure," she said brightly, moving over to let them sit on the bed. Dad sat, but Mum hovered. "What's up?"

"I've, um, I've been updating our security settings, you know, on the wifi. And we've found a website that seems to have been used by you, love, that we feel isn't all that appropriate."

How quickly he moved from *I* to *we*. There he was, looking at Mum for approval. Mum's lips were sewn together, taking in every inch of Lauren's room, fingering Lauren's laptop on her desk. She was livid.

"What website?" Lauren started playing with the strings of her hoodie, to hide the flush of shame she knew was creeping up from inside it.

"It's called PeekaBoo," Dad said. "It appears to be a pay-per-view sort of site." He coughed. "Pornography."

Lauren almost got sick into her mouth. Porn? Surely that wasn't what she'd been doing. Was it?

"This particular site seems to have been only accessed from your computer."

How the hell did they know that?

"Have you been snooping through my search history?" It came out as a screech. She was losing her cool. Shit. "How did you get into my laptop?"

"The router provides a master search history," Dad said, as if it should have been obvious. "We've never had to use it before, but ..." he glanced at Mum, "we had concerns."

Lauren thought fast. She needed to come at this from a new angle.

"Well, so, maybe I had a look a couple of times," she said, picking up a nail file. "I'm hardly the only one, am I?" She stared at him meaningfully, saw his jaw clench. She'd pushed it too far. She back-tracked. "I mean, if I were a boy, you wouldn't even be surprised, would you? Isn't that a bit sexist?"

"So you admit you've been ..."

"These websites are for over-eighteens," Mum snapped. "And for good reason. Only *prostitutes* put themselves on sites like that! Why on earth would you want to see that? How did you provide proof of age? And how did you pay?" She tapped her toe, a gunfire staccato.

"My debit card," Lauren said quietly. This wasn't going how she'd planned at all. But they still didn't know the worst of it. That was all she had to keep from them now.

"Hand it over," Mum said. Her foot jiggled like crazy.

Silently, Lauren took her purse from her bag, handed over her debit card. "You can't take it, I need it for the bus!"

But Mum opened up her own laptop and she and Dad peered at it, Dad looking first through, and then under, his glasses.

"This is *not* the card you used!" Mum shouted and Dad put a hand on her arm.

"Lauren," he said gently. "This is really important. We think you set up an account in Mum's name to access the website. We need the truth now, honey."

"Why the hell would I do that?" Lauren was crying now, trying to appear furious, but they knew more than they were saying and she was trapped. "I'm not desperate, if that's what you think! I was curious. The girls in school were talking about it and I wanted to see ..." Shit, she was hysterical now.

"Mum got turned down for a job she really wanted because the company did an online background check that linked her to this website."

"What?" Lauren wiped her nose on her sleeve. "Are you going back to work?"

Mum was too quick for her. "Don't change the subject," she snapped.

"There was a data leak," Dad explained. "Lots of people's details were shared online."

"You mean, like, hackers? Then there's no proof that any of it's real!" Relief flowed through Lauren. "Hackers are hardly reliable, are they? And you said yourself, it's not even my card."

Mum and Dad looked at each other in a way that said they needed to talk.

"Maybe, honey. I'll check it out." Dad got off the bed, turned towards the door. But Mum was hunched over Lauren's laptop typing in random passwords furiously. Lauren wanted to snatch it away from her.

"But you've admitted to using the site," Mum said. "And your card is a debit card. The website only accepts credit cards."

"We need to take your laptop," Dad said. His voice was grim. He didn't believe her, but he wasn't prepared to call her out unless he had some proof. "*And* your phone." Mum stood over Lauren, her hand outstretched.

Lauren picked up her phone in panic. It lit up with incoming notifications.

"You can't take my phone," she said suddenly. This would buy her some time. "Ella is missing."

Kai

ELLA WAS MISSING. KAI stood in the hallway, empty cereal bowl in one hand, the other frozen on the kitchen door handle, listening to Mum talk on the phone. She was crying. He heard her say *strange man* and *park* and *search party*.

Theo had met a strange man in the park, who had upset him. Now Ella was missing.

Kai could help. He could finally be useful. It would put all the bad feeling between him and Theo behind them. Theo would be happy with him again. He had that photograph, the one from the park. It *must* be that guy, it *had* to be. Who the hell else could it be?

He reached for his phone, switched it on for the first time in days. He'd all but stopped using it. The last text he'd received was from Oliver, with the photograph of Lauren in the handcuffs. How petty that all seemed now in comparison to this. His phone bleeped, over and over. More than a hundred messages across every app and social media platform he used. Photos of Ella smiling. Ella holding the twins by the hand. Ella with her hockey team, her face circled in red pen. Ella, with her arm hanging loosely around Theo's shoulders.

Please share

Let's bring Ella home

Has anyone seen Ella?

Theo had texted him personally. Yesterday evening.

Hey. Have you seen Ella?

She went out for lunch hasn't come home for tea

That was over twelve hours ago. Kai hadn't replied. Theo would think he didn't care. He'd be so hurt that Kai hadn't even texted back. He'd go over there now. Join the search party. Do whatever he could.

He put his trainers on. With one hand on the flat door, a movement on the monitor caught his eye. There were two shapes outside, black and fluorescent yellow. Not down on the street, but right up on the fifth-floor landing. One of the neighbours must have let them into the block. Nobody would say no to the police. A sudden urge to tear the skin on his side tugged at him, to dig his nails into the flesh. The police had visited once before, on a Saturday morning, as he and Mum were eating breakfast in silence, pale and subdued, Dad's seat empty. That visit had changed their lives forever.

This was bad news too, he could feel it. One of the figures knocked. A terse rap. A demand.

Feeling ill, Kai opened the door.

"May we come in for a moment, please?"

For a split second, Kai wanted to turn and run back to his bedroom, hide in the wardrobe like a little kid.

But it wasn't about Dad this time. They were here for *him*.

Theo must have reported him, like he said he would. Told the police that Kai put those pictures of Lauren online. Shit.

But he hadn't actually done anything wrong. *Nothing*. He must remember that and not panic. The pain in his stomach made it hard to breathe.

"Is everything all right?" Mum asked, stepping into the hallway, the phone still in her hand. The two policemen looked very, very serious. Mum steadied herself against the wall and Kai knew she was thinking of last year too. They waited in silence.

"A local girl is missing," the taller one said, holding out a photograph of Ella, a close-up. "Since yesterday evening. We're asking door to door whether anyone has seen her or has any knowledge of where she might be?"

They weren't there for him. Relief almost made his knees buckle.

"It's Ella," he said quietly.

Mum put her hand to her mouth. "I've just heard," she said, waving her phone at the policemen. "Is there news?"

"Well, things have escalated quickly," the taller one said. "At first it seemed Ella might have simply lost track of time ..."

"But now?" The pressure of Mum's fingers on Kai's arm intensified.

"It seems there might be a man involved. Do you know of an older person Ella might have been spending time with lately?"

They all turned to stare at Kai. "No," he stammered. "Ella is older than me. I'm friends with her brother, Theo."

"Has Theo mentioned a new friend, perhaps? In their early twenties, maybe?"

"Think hard, Kai," Mum said, her fingers knotted together now, as if in prayer.

Kai's stomach churned. "There was a guy," he said. "Theo met him in the park a while ago."

"Do you know who he is?"

"No," Kai said quietly. Was he doing the right thing? "But I have a photograph of him."

There was silence in the hallway. Kai heard the deafening accusation from them all. *You spy on your friend?* He stumbled on. "I asked Theo about him. Theo said it was his football coach." He didn't say he thought Theo was lying.

The two officers shared a look that Kai didn't understand. They didn't believe him. "His football coach, eh?" The smaller one said, raising an eyebrow sceptically at the tall one.

"That's great, son, thank you." The tall police officer shook his head, irritated, and scribbled more notes on his pad. "Can we see the photograph?"

How could he show the photo without them seeing the ones of Theo and Lauren kissing? He would look like a pervert. Like Theo had said. Oh God, what if Theo had already told them something?

"I'll get it for you," he said, turning to go to his room.

*

He found it in seconds. There he was, the strange man. Tall, skinny. Putting something (*maybe pills for Lauren?*) in Theo's hand. Would Theo get in trouble for this? Kai hoped not. He wanted to text him, see if it was okay to share the photo with the police. What if they wanted to see Kai's phone? But it was more important to get Ella back. Theo would do anything for Ella, he idolised her. So did half the boys at school.

He printed the photo and emailed a copy to himself, showed both to the police.

"Well done, mate!" said the shorter, younger officer, beaming at him. "This is a massive help."

The tremors in Kai's legs eased. "Shall I email you the original?" he asked the taller one, who had pulled his walkie-talkie from its perch on his shoulder.

The policeman handed him a little card with an email address on it. Kai sent the message and put away his phone with a sigh of relief.

Mum peered at the photograph.

"No, this is wrong," she said, pointing at the man in the picture.

"What's that now?" asked the taller officer.

"Theo's football coach is Bob Spencer," she said. "He lives on the first floor and is bald and middle-aged. This is not Bob."

"I see," said the policeman. "It seems Theo has a secret friend. Has he mentioned anything else to you? Anything at all?"

Tears mounted behind Kai's eyes. Now he'd got Theo in trouble for no reason.

"No," he said morosely. Mum put her arm around him.

"Never mind," said the younger officer. "This photograph is still a huge help. You've done a good job."

Mum closed the door gently behind the two men and pulled Kai into a hug. "I don't know what I'd do if you went missing," she whispered into his hair.

Nicole

Nicole sat on Lauren's bed and scanned her phone furiously. Trust Lauren to drop a grenade just as she was about to be discovered. Ella was probably off at some silly party. At that age, Nicole hadn't thought twice about not telling her parents where she was. They were all overreacting.

But there it was, all over Facebook. Hundreds of posts. Even on that God-awful page that was obsessed with the takeover. Where Nicole had actually posted – anonymously, obviously – complaining about Kerry. Only after she'd found out about the kiss, but still. She scrolled on. A search party was scheduled for two o'clock this afternoon.

Christ, Ella was really missing. Imagine if Lauren disappeared. Right off the street, in the middle of the day. She reached towards her daughter to pull her in for a hug and stopped.

Lauren was staring at them, belligerent, defensive. Arms crossed, eyes narrowed. Did her daughter even care? Or was she too concerned about saving her own skin over this ridiculous website fiasco?

"Jesus Christ, she's been missing since yesterday!" Wolf shouted, his face red. "When did you find this out?" He glared at Lauren so viciously Nicole almost had the urge to defend her daughter. Almost.

Lauren didn't answer. Nicole grabbed her phone, scrolled upwards through the messages, Wolf at her shoulder. Theo had first texted at seven o'clock last night.

"Jesus Christ," Wolf said again. "You got this last night, *last night,* and you never said anything!"

"I'm sorry!" Lauren said in a small voice. "I only saw it this morning!"

"I need to get over there," Wolf said, turning to leave the bedroom. He jogged downstairs, patting his pockets, grabbing his keys from the bowl.

Nicole panicked. Where did this leave her? Her husband was rushing off to be by Kerry's side in her hour of need. Typical. She ran down the stairs behind him.

"But Wolf, we need to get to the bottom of this!"

"Not while my best friend's daughter is missing." He gave her a scornful look and she flinched. "Later," he said, quietly and firmly.

"We need to ..."

"Nobody's hurt, Nicole," Wolf said as he tied his laces. "So our daughter got a little curious online. I know it backfired on you, but she's safe, isn't she? We haven't got much to complain about!"

He slammed the front door behind him, leaving Nicole to figure out this mess by herself. Nothing new there.

She marched to the kitchen, fired off a quick email to Glorious. She needed all her options open right now.

> ...appreciate your transparency ... can honestly see there's been some error ... aim to get it cleared up as soon as possible ...

Lauren peered around the kitchen door. "Can I have something to eat?"

"Make it yourself," Nicole snapped.

"I will! Mum, don't be like that, I've told you everything! I'm sorry you lost the job."

"Stop lying to me, you little bitch!" It was out before she knew it, large and angry, as if splattered all over the wall in red paint. She couldn't take it back now. And, deep down, she meant it.

"Mum!" Lauren burst into tears and ran out of the kitchen.

Nicole had been called a bitch enough times in her life to know how it felt when the word hit home, when it was accurate, when it was deadly. Lauren's response told her she was right. There was more to find.

Nicole flipped open Lauren's laptop, typed in the login password from the pink post-it she'd sulkily supplied. Maybe it was better she was doing this herself, anyway. Wolf's orderly mind would have sought out clearly marked folders, files, categories of photos in albums. Nicole knew first-hand that a woman who wanted to keep a secret did none of those things.

First, she checked the deleted items. Nothing there except bits of homework. Nothing older than a few days. That meant she was on the right path: Lauren was covering her tracks.

No point searching recent files. No point searching for porn sites, Wolf had done that. Whatever was on that damn website had been deleted. More secrecy and lies. What did she want first? The secret credit card. A bank account.

There were two web browsers on the desktop. Google Chrome and Firefox. One by one, she opened them, brought up the search history, keyed in the search term "bank". Nothing.

Nicole knew there were newer, better browsers than Firefox, and Lauren liked anything new. She ran a search. There it was, Microsoft Edge, hidden in a folder labelled *Geography*. You could find anything if you were smart enough. Nicole was smart. And she was sick of being underestimated by her family.

She navigated to the Edge browser history, searched the term "bank". Bingo. Hundreds of entries for Plutus Bank. A login page. A bogus email address, one of those diversion ones that was no doubt linked straight back to Lauren's Gmail account, was already filled in on the username box. Lauren wasn't stupid enough to autosave the password. It didn't matter; Nicole had enough to go on.

She took a photo of the screen on her phone and closed the browser.

Back in Finder, she ran a search for .jpeg. Lauren lived for selfies; hers was a world of photo-sharing, photo-editing, photo uploads. The list was endless. But Nicole had time.

She made herself a black coffee, arranged the results by icons and began to scroll.

Forty minutes later, she found a photograph of her own passport.

Twenty-five minutes after that, she found a selfie of Lauren peeking over her shoulder at the camera, blowing a kiss, and wearing a purple lace bralette and denim shorts so short the round apples of her bum cheeks spilled out below them. A love heart had been added to the picture with the words *Hello, boys!* inscribed inside it.

Theo

THEO LIFTED A SPOONFUL of Weetabix to his mouth and put it down again, nauseous. The policewoman at the kitchen table looked up from her paperwork and gave him one of those head-tilt smiles full of patronising sympathy that made him want to throw the bowl against the wall and tell her to stop staring at him and find Ella already.

He went back to the lounge, where Dad paced by the window and Mum sat on the sofa, wrapped in a duvet. They were all still in yesterday's clothes. Audrey and Pete had arrived early this morning and were now running the house, making tea and stilted conversation and doling out hugs and snacks.

Theo felt awful. How could he have been so stupid? He should have told Dad about Mitch at the very beginning. Dad would have been cool about it. The fact that nobody was actually blaming him made Theo feel even worse.

He texted Lauren again. She knew Ella was gone; he'd seen the two blue ticks by the messages, but she still hadn't replied. That was messed-up. He'd been wrong to trust her. To keep her secrets. Lauren didn't play fair.

Kai hadn't replied either. That hurt more.

Mum dragged herself off the sofa, mumbling something about checking on Granny.

Theo touched Dad's shoulder. "Dad, I'm really sorry."

Dad pushed Theo's hair out of his eyes. "This isn't your fault, son. You were manipulated by a con man."

"What if Mitch *is* your son?"

"If he's taken Ella, he'll never be my son."

"Shall we try and find out?" Theo asked. He had an idea.

"What are you talking about?"

"You told the police you had a Brazilian girlfriend, who could be Mitch's mum?"

Dad sighed, as if Ella's disappearance was all his fault for having a fling more than twenty years ago. "Yes."

"Then let's look her up."

*

They found her quickly. Diana Santiago was on LinkedIn, marketing manager for a chain of hotels in São Paulo, and was still thin and beautiful with small white teeth and chocolate eyes. Dad typed in the number.

"I'll get Mum," Theo said, but Dad put a hand on his arm.

"Not yet," he said, putting the call on speaker. "Let's not get her hopes up."

*

Diana had a nice accent and a soft voice. "I'm sorry," she said after a long pause. "If I'd known I was pregnant before I left England, I would have told you."

Dad closed his eyes, looking even more sad if that was possible. Imagine Dad and Diana had gotten married. Theo would never have existed and Mitch might have turned out to be normal. Maybe not having a dad was worse than Theo could imagine. Kai's dad wasn't around, and Kai'd been acting super weird. Theo felt a pang of shame. Of responsibility.

"My mother convinced me to stay," Diana said, "but I know a boy needs his father. I took him back to England to begin school, but by then it was too late."

"Too late for what?" Dad said.

"For you," she said quietly, and Theo sensed Dad's heart break for a second. "You were already married," she went on, "and you had a beautiful daughter. A family."

At the mention of Ella, Dad's face hardened. "What's Mitch like?"

Mitch, it seemed to Theo, was a problem. Suspended from school over and over. Taking drugs. Crashing cars. Never kept a job.

"I was unhappy," Diana said, enunciating every syllable. Theo couldn't tell if she was to be pitied or whether she'd been a shit mum. But she sounded nice. "As soon as Miguel left school, I gave him an ultimatum. He can come to Brazil with me and be a good boy, or stay behind and fend for himself. He disappeared for days."

"So you left." It was a bald fact, and Theo couldn't tell if Dad also put Diana in the shit mum category. Despite what she'd said, Theo couldn't see how a mother could go to the other side of the world and leave her teenage son alone. He'd finish school in three years. He couldn't imagine life without Mum and Dad. And now, did he have to contemplate life without Ella? All because of Mitch and his lazy, selfish mother?

Diana started crying.

"You called him Miguel."

"He was teased for his name. In high school he started calling himself Mitchell." She put heavy emphasis on both of the syllables of *Mitchell* so it rhymed with Miguel.

"Diana," Dad pinched the bridge of his nose, as if he were in physical pain. "There's more. Mitch has contacted my son Theo." He put a heavy hand on Theo's shoulder. "But my daughter has disappeared. We think Mitch may have taken her."

"*Meu Deus*," Diana said and began to cry. It was the worst possible reaction Theo could imagine. Like she one-hundred-percent believed Mitch did this, that he could actually do something terrible to Ella.

"Does he have a criminal record?" Dad said. His voice sounded calm but his fingers dug hard into Theo's skin.

Diana blew her nose and exhaled loudly into the receiver. "No," she said, in control again. "He has not been violent. His full name is Miguel Santiago. There cannot be many people with this name."

She read out his phone number, a different one to the number Theo had.

Theo dialled. It was dead.

*

As Theo tossed the phone back onto the coffee table, Mum came in, hunched and lined and looking scarily like Granny.

"We've tracked down Mitch's mother," Dad said.

Mum froze, hand to her mouth. "And?"

"He's a delinquent. Possibly on drugs. No criminal record. But he's never hurt anyone."

The *yet* hung in the air.

Kerry

DS Gates was back. Kerry jumped up from the sofa, from the messages that had begun to flood in, wanting to skip over the ones that simply offered sympathy and prayers, afraid she might miss a morsel of information if she did. Ella's face smiled back at her from all the socials. Long, long threads of conversations to pore over, to pick apart, to glean non-existent meaning from, to disappoint. Edward Cousins had been true to his word – if not literally. He hadn't actually taken down the Bash Kerry Langley page, but he had changed the conversation. And now, almost four thousand extra people knew about Ella's disappearance. And for that, Kerry was grateful.

*

Gates wore a slick of peachy lipstick and a fresh blouse, apple-green, the kind of spring colour you chose when you wanted nobody staring at the dark circles beneath your eyes. Kerry was reassured by those dark patches. Gates had a daughter. She understood. She'd been up all night too.

"Andrew!" she called. But he was already there, assembled beside her wordlessly, instantly.

Wolf said he'd make more coffee. He'd arrived early with bear hugs, bringing an air of quiet fortitude and remaining glued to Andrew's side, their rift and the kiss forgotten.

Audrey appeared from Mum's room. "I'll take the twins," she said, leading Poppy and Alby to the den. Kerry heard the rustle of sweet wrappers and led everyone to the kitchen, where Pete, wonderful, dependable Pete, was unpacking a sandwich tray and chocolate cake.

"Neighbours," he whispered, pointing at the food.

They perched wordlessly at the table and waited for Gates to speak. Kerry could barely form full sentences anymore.

"Is this Mitch?" Gates asked, holding up a photo, speaking directly to Theo.

It was a photograph of Theo with a young man, standing in the park by The Bench near the trees. The man had brown hair, and he was tall and thin. But the photographer was too far away to capture the contours of his face, his eye colour. There was nothing from this distance to tell Kerry if he could be Andrew's son. If he was a good man. Whether he could harm her daughter.

Kerry examined Theo in the picture, his posture, his body language. Had he felt threatened? Afraid? The man had a hand on Theo's shoulder but Kerry could see the tension in her son's lithe body, how he leaned away from the touch. Theo wasn't happy. The man pressed something small into his hand.

Theo started crying. "Has he taken Ella?"

Kerry put her arm around him. "Let's take things one step at a time," she said. "First things first, is this him? Is this Mitch?"

Theo nodded and wiped his eyes on his sleeve.

"We've shared the photograph with our colleagues," Gates said. "We're sure to hear something soon. What's he giving you, Theo?"

"The photograph," Theo said miserably. "Of Dad and Diana."

"Let me see." Andrew reached for the picture and his face contorted in pain. Did he recognise himself in this young man?

Kerry reached out and took his hand in hers. "I'm sorry," she whispered.

Gates' phone pinged and she flipped open the screen. "Oh, good," she said. "The tech team have cleaned it up. You can see his face more clearly in this one." She held out her phone. Kerry and Andrew closed in on it, vultures circling prey. Up close, he was thinner. Sharp cheekbones, gaunt. An uncared-for look about him. Dirty clothes. A familiar lopsidedness to his smile. Kerry heard Andrew's sharp intake of breath, felt his body go rigid.

"Have you ever seen him anywhere else besides the park?" Gates asked Theo. "Can you think of anything else he might have told you about himself?"

"He used to leave the park that way," Theo said, pointing at the trees in the background. "Ella thought he was squatting at the old cabin. He did look a bit homeless sometimes. His clothes were dirty. He said he worked in London, but we didn't really believe him. He wouldn't give Ella his email address."

Something jolted inside of Kerry, a frisson of recognition, a peculiar déjà-vu feeling.

"I've seen him, too." She turned to Andrew. "Sitting on the wall outside your office. I thought he'd been stood up for a date. I actually laughed. There was something familiar about him …" She snapped her fingers. "The way he walked, that was it. God, that's weeks ago!"

Andrew grabbed the phone and zoomed in. Kerry watched him trace the outline of Mitch's face with his finger. Imagine finding out you had a son this way. She pulled Theo closer. This man was a stranger. It was no time to be getting attached.

"I've seen him too," Andrew said finally. "He's the man your mum was worried about. He was hanging around, pretending he wanted to buy a house." He ran a hand over a bristle of stubble. "Christ, I even spoke to him about the bus timetables."

"Sounds like this guy's been following you around for some time," Gates said.

"Do you think," Theo said, blushing as all eyes swivelled to face him, "that he could be the one who knocked Dad off his bike? The hit-and-run."

"I remember," Gates said. "A black Nissan. We'll need to consider the two events are linked."

"You think Mitch knocked his own father off his bicycle?" Kerry was shocked.

"We called that company on the business card he gave Theo – Linkwell. He did work there but was let go three months ago for persistent absence. They provided his address at the time and we spoke to his flatmates, who said he was often drunk or high and rarely paid his rent. They kicked him out around the same time. No history of violence but, given that he might have been hanging around Saltreach for the past three months watching you guys, we have to assume he might be a lot more dangerous than we first thought."

For a split-second, Kerry wanted to slap her. Slap her into consciousness that there was a young boy in the room who was blaming himself for his sister's disappearance. A father who'd discovered he had a son who was at worst a kidnapper and at best a manipulative bastard. There was no need to state the bloody obvious.

Gates took back the phone and punched in a number. Theo started crying again. Kerry and Andrew looked at each other in despair.

*

Kerry went upstairs and called Ella again, knowing it would go straight to voicemail. Where was her beautiful girl? It was nearly lunchtime. They knew now that Ella had met Jennifer Collins at The Hungry Giraffe for lunch yesterday. Jennifer told the police they each had a tuna salad and shared a chocolate mousse for pudding. What a lovely thing for her lovely daughter to do. So grown up. She'd been studying hard for her exams. The girls had split the bill and Jennifer waited at the café to be picked up by her mother. Ella had left to buy a pair of earrings in the quirky little boutique next door. She hadn't mentioned anything to Jen about a guy.

Kerry sat on the edge of her bed, locked her arms round her body, and rocked.

*

"Kerry?" Izzy, of all people, was in her bedroom. She hadn't heard the doorbell. She didn't want to deal with Izzy right now. God. Work. It was Wednesday. The takeover meeting was today. She'd forgotten about all of it. "I heard about Ella. I'm so sorry."

"She's missing." It sounded normal, her voice. Robotic, even. What the hell was wrong with her, sounding normal at a time like this? Maybe they'd had the meeting without her. Maybe it was too late to do anything and a hundred people would be fired. She didn't have the energy to care right now. "We think she's been kidnapped. Some guy's been trying to get inside our family. He befriended Theo, told him they were half-brothers. Christ, he might even have run Andrew off his bike! And yesterday, he took Ella. Jesus Christ, Izzy, how the hell do I get her back?"

She slammed her fist onto her bedside table, over and over. Izzy pulled her to her feet, wrapped her in a hug. “Oh my God,” she said. “Oh my fucking God.”

Kerry

IZZY HELD HER UPRIGHT. She felt strong and capable and powerful in her smart work suit, her razor-cut hairstyle. Kerry used to feel like that, but already it was a lifetime ago. She needed to pull herself together if she was going to find her baby girl. She pulled out of Izzy's embrace and went downstairs, Izzy two paces behind her.

If only she could go back in time for one day, she would take Ella out for lunch herself. What the hell had she been doing, leaving Ella and Theo to fend for themselves? They were even taking care of her mother for her! Christ, when all of this was over and Ella was home, and she *would* be home again, Kerry would be there for her kids, every step of the way.

Theo and Andrew huddled in the den, where Mum slept.

"Audrey's taken the twins to the park," Andrew said.

She put a hand on his shoulder and he patted hers. If she thought she'd aged overnight, Andrew looked ill. Pale, sagging, skeletal. He'd put his sling back on – his arm must be hurting. Not surprising. If someone offered to wrap Kerry up in cotton wool she'd gladly accept. Her body wasn't functioning any more. Her stomach growled yet the thought of food made her retch. Her joints ached, as though begging for rest, yet when she sat, her nerves forced her back to her feet. Her hair felt greasy and her t-shirt was on inside out but she hadn't the energy or inclination to change it.

"Any news?"

He shook his head sadly.

*

Izzy brought in a plate of sandwiches and a pot of tea and took a seat in the den with them. Andrew took one and thanked her, not even seeming to recognise her. Kerry took a bite and forced herself to chew, even though it tasted like clay.

"So what now?" Kerry asked. She was so tired. So very tired.

He reached over and gripped her hand. "We'll have her home soon, love."

His mobile rang.

*

"They have him," Andrew whispered, putting his phone on speaker. "Listen. They have Mitch."

DS Gates spoke, confident and assured. "We have indeed, following your son's description and that photograph, been able to arrest Miguel Santiago, aka Mitch, in the past half-hour. He is here at the station, about to be questioned."

"Do you have Ella? Was she with him? Is she okay?"

"Ella was not with him, I'm afraid." Gates sounded serious on the other end of the line and Kerry imagined her standing, tall and commanding, in a glass-panelled office, *Line of Duty* style. "We located him at Hatchurst Woods and our officers are conducting a thorough search of the area as we speak."

"We need to get down there," Kerry said. "Where the hell is Hatchurst Woods?"

"Ella was right," Theo said. "It's where the cabin is, in the woods behind the park."

"That's right," Gates said. "We went there last night and found signs of a squatter. We didn't want to get your hopes up as there was no sign of Mitch. However, he showed up this morning, very much the worse for wear. I'd urge you not to come down yet, Mr and Mrs Langley. It seems Mitch has been sleeping there for quite some time. We found his car, too. A black Nissan, by the way, with a broken front light."

"He ran me over," Andrew said to nobody in particular.

"What the hell are we supposed to do?" Kerry demanded. "You've kept us at home all this time! I need to *look* for her."

"With Mitch at the station, we're hoping Ella might be able to make her way home to you," said the detective. "If not, and depending on the statement Mitch gives, we may need you to make a public appeal."

"You're saying, if Mitch won't say where she is, or doesn't know where she is, this becomes a full-scale search. Missing person. TV, the whole thing?"

There was a brief pause. "Correct."

Kerry

IT WAS THREE O'CLOCK. They'd passed the crucial twenty-four-hour mark and a search party was underway. Kerry couldn't believe it. After months of fractious bickering and resentment, the people of Saltreach had put their differences aside to find her baby girl.

Pete and Andrew's beach protestors had repurposed their march. Edward Cousins had posted online, urging his Facebook followers to put aside their differences and show up at the ice cream kiosk at two thirty to join the search party. Izzy had closed the factory so that the combined staff of Bullfinch and Stonebridge could help. Andrew had texted to say the whole town was out looking, literally hundreds of people.

Izzy had offered to stay with her, but Kerry had needed them all to go, couldn't cope any more with the hushed silences, the offers of tea, the whispers. She'd sent Kai upstairs to keep Theo company and dispatched the twins to a friend. Now she sat downstairs, by her mother's bed, and prayed for her daughter to come home.

Mitch's statement threatened to tip her over the edge. He claimed to know nothing. Said he hadn't seen either Theo or Ella since Monday. But Mitch was not to be trusted. He had no alibi. They could keep him overnight without charging him. If he wouldn't talk soon, they would bring Andrew down to speak to him. Kerry wanted to torture him, to hang him up by the balls and beat the information out of him with a mallet.

"Where is she, Mum?" she whispered. "Is she lying in a ditch? Did he take her somewhere in his car?" The police said that was unlikely. The car had two flat tyres and a flat battery. That was good news, they said. It meant she was local.

Her mother patted her arm. "Don't worry, *alanna*," she said. "When Dad gets home from work, he'll tell us what to do."

Kerry groaned and buried her face in the blankets. It wasn't Mum's fault. Nobody could say the right thing, not even Andrew. There was nothing good to say until Ella was home safe, and this nightmare was over.

Her phone pinged. A photo from Andrew of a long line of people heading into the woods, shoulder to shoulder, heads down. Wolf was by his side.

It was all so, so wrong. They should be down on the promenade, chanting and holding up placards demanding the council simply allocate funds to clear the seaweed off the beach. Not staring at the ground in silent concentration. She'd rather they were slating her on Facebook, whispering in the office canteen. Anything but this. She'd seen pictures like this on the news and they rarely ended well. She stared at the photograph of Mitch. If that bastard was lying …

"What do you think, Mum?" She showed her mother the photograph. She wasn't sure how much her mother was aware of. Audrey had kept her occupied, put a little something extra in her meds to keep her from getting anxious. She'd offered Kerry one, too. Kerry had shaken her head and Audrey had pointed to where she was putting them up high for safe keeping, in case Kerry needed a little help sleeping. But Kerry knew she wouldn't sleep as long as Ella wasn't home.

Mum stroked Kerry's hair like she had when she was a little girl. "It'll be okay, sweetheart," she said over and over. Kerry lay her head in her mother's lap. "That man," Mum said then, in a different voice. Her lucid voice. Kerry looked up. Mum held the photograph up close to her nose. "You said it was Mrs King's son."

"That's right," Kerry said. Her heartbeat took on a new rhythm, faster, as though she'd swum right across the bay. "You knew it wasn't him, Mum. Who was it?" How long would her mother remain like this? She squeezed Mum's hand, urging her to remember.

"He used to come on Tuesdays," Mum said calmly. "When Andrew would come for tea. He'd hang around outside for hours."

Kerry jumped up, felt her brain explode, connections firing in all directions. She paced, pulling her thoughts apart to see if she was being logical or inventing new facts in her sleep-deprived state.

Ella went missing yesterday.

Yesterday was Tuesday.

Mitch went to Mum's house on Tuesdays.

"He said he wanted to buy a house in the road," she said, pinching her forehead, forcing herself to slow down, to sit.

Her mother snorted. "He was more interested in my house."

"Your house!" Kerry grabbed her hand. "Why didn't I think of that? Ella has a key! Oh, Mum, you're a genius!"

She jumped up, knocking over her chair, and shouted upstairs. "Theo, come down!"

Theo and Kai were in the room in seconds.

"Have they found her?" Theo's eyes were huge.

"I know where she is," Kerry said. "She's at Granny's house. I *know* she is. She would have been near there on her way home from town. I bet something happened with that bastard Mitch and she ran in to hide. She'll be out of battery, hiding out, wondering why we haven't come to get her." She was *certain* she was right. She would bring Ella home.

She thought of the dent on Mitch's car. He was dangerous. She shouldn't get ahead of herself. Shouldn't presume. But Mitch was currently in custody, lying to the police.

Theo grabbed her arm. "I'm coming with you," he said.

"No, sweetheart," Kerry said. She wasn't letting another child walk into danger. "I'll get a police officer to come. You stay here with Granny. In case I'm wrong. In case Ella comes back."

Sod's law, it was the first time since yesterday afternoon there wasn't a patrol car outside, but she couldn't tell Theo that. They were all out searching. The extra-large crowd must have required all hands on deck from the police.

"Please, Mum, I can't stay here." Theo grabbed her by the elbow. "You *have* to let me go."

"I'll stay with your granny," Kai said with the quiet, calm maturity that had always separated him from the other kids. "I'll make her tea, whatever. Keep her company. My mum is out searching anyway. If anyone comes, I'll call you straight away."

"No, darling," Kerry said to Theo. "Stay with Kai. I need you here. In case she comes home."

Lauren

LAUREN STAYED IN HER room, ostensibly listening to music, in reality, stressing about it all. Mum had called her a bitch. But Lauren *was* a bitch. She knew she was. She couldn't help it. She was missing that nice, Ella-type happy vibe. The kind of good energy that comes from feeling grounded, secure.

It wasn't like she didn't know she was pretty and clever and didn't *have* to be a model. Her science teacher had suggested pharmacy as a career option. A pharmacist wouldn't actually be a bad Plan B. As long as she didn't have to, like, touch the sick people.

But she'd never intended for all of this to go wrong. For that guy to show up at school. For Oliver fucking Nowell to blackmail her. If he even *looked* at her ever again, she would report him to student welfare.

And she'd definitely not intended to make Mum lose out on a job. She could never have foreseen that happening. It wasn't fair that they were blaming her. If Mum hadn't been so secretive, so *weird* lately. It wasn't just the job. She was angry at Dad. She'd been angry for months. Maybe even years. Lauren couldn't remember the last time she and Mum had had a day out together, or even the last time Mum had laughed out loud.

She felt bad about Ella, but Ella was sixteen. Maybe she'd finally given up on being perfect all the time and had actually gone off with some random guy after a party. Literally everyone in Ella's year had gone out last night, all bored of studying and stressing about their GCSEs. There had been a party at Dan Moseley's, down near the beach. There would have been plenty of pills passed round; K, Molly, whatever. Ella might just be sleeping it off somewhere.

God. It actually made what Lauren had been doing online seem trivial by comparison. *She* wouldn't get raped, or pregnant, or all those things Mum warned her about. At least not now, since she'd stopped dating older guys. And why was everyone making such a fuss over a couple of photographs of her? Because she was a girl? So typical! She lay on her bed and thought of the money she'd saved. One year left to get her GCSEs and she would be gone from Saltreach for good.

*

She'd almost convinced herself it was all about to blow over when Mum threw her bedroom door open. It bounced off the wall and the Longchamp purse fell out of the fake Chanel bag hanging on the hook on the back. Lauren screamed in fright.

"You little liar!" Mum screamed.

And suddenly, immediately, Lauren was primed, pumped, full of adrenalin. Really, she'd known this was coming. There was no way out now. She squared her shoulders, stood up, and eyed her mother levelly.

"I know *exactly* what you've been up to," Mum said, brandishing her phone screen like a weapon. There she was in her purple bralette and Daisy Dukes. Shit. How the hell had she missed a picture? She'd been so sure she'd deleted everything.

Lauren folded her arms and said nothing. Her heart beat faster.

"So you thought you'd set up a fake bank account in *my* name," Mum said, spit flying from her mouth, "and take a few lurid photographs and sell yourself like a cheap slut to the highest bidder?"

"Like mother, like daughter, eh?" Lauren said coolly, proud of the way her voice held steady. A cheap slut? Who the hell did Mum think she was? "I've seen your box in the attic."

That shut Mum up for a minute. Lauren could see her scrambling to come up with some kind of defence. She threw her phone on the dressing table, her jaw clenched with pent-up fury, and wrapped her arms around herself. Her fingertips pressed into her upper arms so hard Lauren knew they'd leave bruises.

"I was an adult when those were taken," she said levelly, flint in her eyes. "Not a child. They were taken by a professional photographer and I was chaperoned by my agent, a well-respected businesswoman. I got a few modelling contracts out of that and it put me on my way to a career in fashion. Those photographs were *not* designed to titillate sleazy men looking for a cheap wank."

Lauren flinched.

"Are the photographs still online?" Mum bent down and picked up the purse, stroked it lovingly.

Lauren shook her head.

"Is the bank account closed?"

Lauren nodded.

"How much money did you make?"

"Nearly three grand." She whispered it. The heat had evaporated from Mum's voice, the fury dissolved from her face. She looked heartbroken. Lauren closed her eyes.

"Why did you do it, honey? Just to buy pretty things like this?" She threw the purse on the bed and Lauren stared at it, the backs of her eyes burning. They stood opposite each other as strangers. Lauren felt shame singe her body from the inside out.

Mum reached out first. She tugged on Lauren's elbow, pulling her in. Lauren's body stayed taut in defence, her arms still strapped across her chest. Still, she said nothing.

"We don't need the money," Mum said softly. "You're a beautiful, intelligent girl. You get top marks at school. In a world where you can be anything you want, why would you want to be that?"

Lauren tried to find some fight left inside her, tried to untangle the mess of rationale that had driven her to set this up in the first place. She'd wanted to get out of here, earn some cash, and unpick her mother's claws from her skin. She'd wanted to escape this fucked-up, white-painted, white-carpeted, minimalistic freak of a magazine house where her parents either shouted or ignored each other and slept in separate bedrooms and kept secrets and seemed to hate each other. But maybe, just maybe, she was the most fucked-up of them all.

"Mum. I saw Ella yesterday."

Kai

Kai and Theo sat on either side of Theo's granny's bed in silence. They'd been playing cards, but she'd fallen asleep in the middle of the game. Kai didn't know what to say to make Theo feel better. He wasn't sure Theo could hear him anyway. He was in a world of his own, and every now and then, he would start crying.

"Where's Lauren?" Kai asked eventually.

Theo shrugged. "I haven't heard from her."

"Seriously?"

Theo said nothing. He'd gone back into himself. He was flicking on his phone, but Kai could see he wasn't actually reading any of the messages.

"Maybe she's with the search party," he said.

"I doubt it," Theo said. "I've been so stupid, thinking she actually liked me. Lauren only loves herself."

"Did she break up with you?"

"I don't think she wanted to be my girlfriend in the first place," Theo said bitterly. "She only wanted me to keep her secret."

"You mean the photos?" Kai felt nervous. He didn't want to row with Theo. Not today of all days. "Did she actually admit it?"

But Theo was too distracted to care. "I never saw the website."

"Did she tell you what they were for?" Kai said carefully.

"She said a modelling agency hired her." Theo finally stopped scrolling on his phone and clicked off the screen. "She wants to be a model. Or maybe an influencer. Isn't that why she's always being sent those parcels? Stuff to advertise?"

Kai didn't answer. Didn't mention that Lauren didn't promote products on social media.

"Why?" Theo said. "What were they really for?"

Kai was super aware of the fact he knew far too much about what Lauren had been up to. He wished he'd never opened that very first text from Oliver. But Theo was waiting for him to say something.

"She put pictures of herself in her underwear online," he said to the floor. "She wore handcuffs in one. It's a website where you pay to view photos."

Theo jumped up from his chair. "Kai, did you actually pay to see my girlfriend in handcuffs?"

"Oliver sent me a picture of her, that's all. I looked it up to see where it came from."

"Did you pay?" Theo's eyes were full of tears.

"Just to see how bad it was." No matter what way this came out, he looked bad. It *was* bad. "Anyway, you're the one who said you were keeping secrets for her. If that wasn't the secret, what was it?"

Theo shifted uncomfortably. He sat back down. "I promised her I wouldn't say."

"Well, I guess you two are over now, so I don't know why you're still protecting her. I'm here and she's not. Even after you ignored my texts for weeks. Doesn't that tell you something about friendship?"

There was a pause. Kai was about to apologise for being petty when Theo said, "Someone was stalking her. Remember that black eye I got? This guy showed up at school. She said he was an ex, but he was, like, *way* older. Lauren sent me out to tell him to piss off. He hit me, but he left."

Kai remembered. He'd seen it from the science lab window. Where he'd been eating his lunch alone because Theo wouldn't speak to him. But, if he was being honest with himself, he had really been alone because he was miserable about Dad and was too ashamed to tell anyone about it.

"I wanted to tell the police." Theo threw up his hands. "But Lauren wouldn't let me. Even though she was afraid he would show up again. I think he has something to do with the selfies."

"Are you kidding?" Kai said. "There's someone after Lauren too?"

*

It was worse than Kai thought. Lauren hadn't just posted a few photos online. She had an actual real-life stalker. A man who had shown up at their school, for God's sake, and punched a fourteen-year-old kid. It was well over a month since Theo had been hit in the face and he'd hardly spoken to Kai since then. Kai had put it down to that stupid kiss, that mortifying, shameful moment when he'd misread the situation. But now, it seemed like Lauren had been manipulating Theo all along, making him her bodyguard, demanding he keep her secrets. No wonder Theo had been acting weird.

Theo's phone rang and he snatched it up, breaking the tension. Kai prayed there was news of Ella. He couldn't hear the other side of the conversation, but Theo started pacing the room. It was his dad.

"No, Mum's not here."

"She thinks Ella might be hiding at Granny's house."

"To get away from Mitch."

"Because Granny's house is near the park and Ella has a key."

"No, she's not gone by herself. She was going to ask the police to go with her."

"What? Are you sure?"

"Oh."

He hung up the phone. "Mitch didn't do anything. They've arrested him but he has an alibi, apparently. Dad's on his way back here."

Immediately, his phone rang again. Kai could see Lauren's face light up the screen, her name highlighted in pink. They both stared at it.

"You'd better get it," Kai said. "In case."

Theo put it on loudspeaker for Kai to hear.

"I met Ella yesterday," Lauren said, without even saying hi. Her voice was snotty, like she'd been crying for a long time. "In town. At that cute bougie place on the high street that sells jewellery. About two o'clock."

Kai watched Theo's face screw up in disbelief and gently took the phone from him.

"Lauren, it's Kai," he said, surprised at how grown-up he sounded. His voice was finally consistently deep and he liked how it gave him an air of authority now. He wanted to shake Lauren. "The police have already pieced together Ella's whereabouts in town yesterday. Why the hell didn't you tell Theo this before?"

Theo leaned in. "Did she say anything? Was she meeting someone? We know she was in the park yesterday afternoon. Where was she going?"

"She didn't say," Lauren said. "But Theo, that's not the important part."

"What *is* the important part?" Kai snapped.

"We were wearing the exact same clothes," Lauren said, crying again, and Kai could hear someone in the background making soothing noises. "Jeans, crop top, black cardi. We even had the same hairstyle."

"So?" Kai was impatient. Girls all seemed to wear the same kind of clothes.

"Theo?" Lauren ignored him. "Theo, remember that guy? He said he would come back. I … I didn't want to worry you. But …"

Theo was pressing his fists into his eye sockets now, as if blocking out the realisation that something awful was happening. Kai hoped Theo's dad was nearly home.

"But WHAT?" he shouted

"Theo. He threatened to come back for me. What if … what if he got us mixed up?"

*

"What was Ella wearing yesterday?" Kai asked Theo after he'd hung up on Lauren.

Theo dug out the missing person's photo the police were using. "Mum picked this photo to use, because that's what she was wearing yesterday," he said. Ella was wearing a long black cardigan, white crop top, ripped jeans and trainers.

"What about Lauren?" Kai said. "Is she, like, *obsessed* with Ella or something?"

"She liked her hair," Theo said quietly.

*

Theo's granny sighed softly in her sleep, distracting them for a second.

"We have to tell the police," Kai said.

"Dad'll be here in a minute," Theo said. "Look outside, see if there's a police car. We can ask them."

Kai went to the window to check, but the street was empty. "What the hell are we supposed to do? Your mum is on her way over there now! She thinks Ella is alone!"

Theo dropped the phone twice before he managed to dial. It went to voicemail. "Don't go in, Mum. It's not Mitch. There's an internet stalker who's been after Lauren. We think he's got Ella by mistake." He rang back again and again. He sent it in a text. All caps and exclamation marks. No answer.

"Oh my God," Theo said. "We need to find out who this stalker is. What if he's like some sexual deviant who got off on Lauren's pictures?"

Kai said nothing. That was *exactly* what this guy sounded like. "Let's find out everything we can about the company," he said. "PeekaBoo. P-E-E-K-A-B-O-O."

Theo rang his dad. Kai could hear him, giving him an update. "Hurry back, Dad, will you? And Dad? There's another man. We have to stop Mum going into Granny's house. Can you tell the police?"

Kai ran searches on PeekaBoo from every angle he could think of. The information literally fell into his lap.

PeekaBoo is owned and operated by Grant International Limited. John Burrows is the CEO. The global HQ for Grant International is in Saltreach, Kent.

"Look at this." Kai said. "The company is literally local."

Theo

THEO AND KAI WERE still googling PeekaBoo when the front door burst open and Dad flew in with three police officers, Wolf, Pete and Audrey, and the detective, all behind him.

Dad hugged him hard, as if Theo was the one who'd been missing. He wanted to stay in the hug, to let the police figure out the rest. He wanted Mum to come home, and the twins to come back. But most of all, he wanted Ella.

But Dad pulled back. "What on earth do you mean, there's another man?"

Theo's head swirled. He couldn't remember everything. They'd talked too much about Lauren and the photos and who had taken them and who had looked at them. About Ella and Lauren and their hair and their clothes. He didn't know where to start. Dad's thumb was pushing into his shoulder. He knew Dad didn't mean it, but it hurt.

Then Kai spoke in his new, deep, grown-up voice. Kai was more like one of the adults tonight, calm and cool and organised. He explained everything step-by-step to the police. Dad let go of Theo's shoulder and everyone listened in silence. Theo saw Wolf look horrified when Kai told them about Lauren's stalker, but he said nothing. Lauren was safe at home, after all. Kai showed the police the company address on the laptop.

"We've called Mum to tell her not to go into the house," Theo said at the end of it all. "But it went to voicemail."

"Good work," said Gates. "Very good detective work indeed." She clapped Kai on the back and took a snapshot of the address from Kai's screen, nodded at her colleagues and said, "Let's get going."

But Dad hugged them both, told them they were amazing. "You've been terrific," he said, hugging Kai again. "Let's go," he said to Theo. "The police can take us to Granny's house. If Mum's right and Ella is there, I want to be there too."

"What about Granny?" Theo said.

"I'll mind her," Audrey said. "I'll feed her and clean her up." Pete put a hand on Kai's shoulder. "We'll feed this helpful young man too."

Dad nodded.

A tall police officer came back into the room and spoke to Dad over Theo's head. "I'm afraid your wife refused to wait for a police car," he said. "She's gone alone."

Kerry

KERRY PARKED THREE DOORS down from Mum's house and switched off the ignition. The light was fading and the street was empty. No one walked home from work. No kids ran in for dinner. Ennis Road had always belonged to the elderly, people who had tea at five and didn't venture out in the evening. Front rooms up and down the road were dimly lit and televisions flickered. Kerry knew that in house after house she'd see white-haired men and women, all hard of hearing, with the TV volume on max. They wouldn't hear someone coming in or out of Mum's house. They wouldn't hear if Ella was in trouble. If she screamed.

Mum's house was dark. A broken beer bottle stood on the front windowsill, and someone had vomited against the wall below, leaving a sticky beige mess on the pavement. Mum would be horrified. She'd been gone less than a week.

If Ella wasn't here, Kerry had no idea where she could be. Everything came back to Mitch. Sure, he'd been brought in for questioning, but he didn't have an alibi. For all anyone knew, he'd followed Ella here yesterday and … and what? Kerry clutched the steering wheel with both hands, fear curling around her heart like a snake.

There was a landline in the kitchen and an extension in the bedroom, but Ella hadn't called. Right now, she could be lying on the floor, hurt, unable to get help. No. Kerry shouldn't think like this. Ella had been smart to come here. She'd locked herself inside to wait this out, whatever *this* was.

*

The front room light was off, the net curtains stiff and still. Kerry climbed out of the car, and crept to the front door, silent as a fox. Gently, she tested the handle. It was locked. She wiped her hands, slick with sweat, on the front of her jeans.

A sliver of light sliced into the front room. Kerry froze, pressed hard to the wall, as the jagged shape spread across the lounge, seeping in from the kitchen at the back of the house.

Ducking under the front window, she stole along the pavement, past next door and round the back. Mum's gate was never locked. Kerry pulled it far enough to slip through the gap, not so far it creaked. The kitchen light was still on. There was no movement inside, nobody standing by the sink. Keeping her head down, Kerry tiptoed to the window, adrenalin surging through her body, sweat soaking her t-shirt, a chill on her bare skin. A rake, prongs outward, leaned against the fence. She grabbed it.

Slowly she raised her head, put one eye at the corner of the window. There was someone at the kitchen table, their back to the window, wearing a black hoodie. The hood was up, but it wasn't Ella. It was a man, broad arms leaning heavily on the scrubbed pine. White skin, hairy hands. He was eating. At Mum's kitchen table. As if he fucking owned the place. Heat surged through Kerry, sharp and blinding, every nerve sparking with fury.

Mitch. He must have already been released. Here he was, inveigling his way even further into their family. Maybe he'd been squatting here since Mum's accident. He would have known the house was empty, he'd been watching all along. Fucking hell, what if he'd *caused* her accident? He could have snuck in, left something lying around for her to trip over, pushed her even.

Kerry wished Andrew was there. She needed to see him, pastel and pristine with his neat hair and rolled-up sleeves, the epitome of calm, telling her that she was overreacting, to back away, to wait and let Gates handle it. To remind her that Mum had tripped on the step down into the kitchen because she was holding the iPad in one hand and an empty mug in the other. She'd told them.

The table was strewn with debris. Ella was nowhere to be seen. She could be lying, hurt, somewhere in the house. She could be … no, not even a monster would hurt a child and then sit and eat fucking chips. She scanned the table again. There were *two* cans of Coke, *two* parcels of food, one spread out on the table, one still neatly wrapped. If he'd brought food for her, she was alive. She was safe.

Only the bathroom at the top of the stairs had a key. Surely Ella hadn't been locked in that tiny room since yesterday. No wonder she hadn't been able to call. She must be utterly terrified.

Kerry crouched under the kitchen window. Her entire body burned with the need to find her daughter, her brain screamed that to go any further would be a fucking stupid thing to do. She should wait for the police. She pulled her phone from her pocket and saw a message from Theo.

Don't go in, Mum. It's not Mitch.

Oh God. She'd nearly gone in. She nearly, nearly had. She'd thought she could talk Mitch round with fake promises of introductions to Andrew and being welcomed into their family. But this was an actual kidnapper. A *criminal*. She'd been so, so stupid. Ella seemed suddenly very far away.

Kerry slithered down the wall and crouched in the shadows. She could have been hurt. Worse, she could have gotten Ella hurt. Just as she dialled Gates' number, the gate at the back of the garden opened and a row of uniformed police officers crept in, keeping low along the fence. Relief washed over her. The police would rescue Ella. Their leader knelt next to her.

"He's in the kitchen," she whispered. "Alone and eating chips. He's got his back to the window."

The man nodded, peered in, and grabbed his walkie-talkie. "Suspect sighted. Rear entrance." He grabbed Kerry's arm and pointed to the bottom of the garden where Gates beckoned to her. "Go."

But Kerry had come this far. She crouched further into the shadows and watched as he tested the handle. It turned. He gave a signal to the police officers next to him and burst open the door. "Police!"

Kerry watched through the kitchen window as the figure in black sprang up from the table as if electrified, upending the mess onto the floor. He stared at the police, frantic, his mouth open. He backed up against the kitchen cupboards, his hands rummaging around, desperate for something to grab. She couldn't see a weapon, but Kerry knew that if he opened the drawer by his hip, the first thing he would find would be the scissors. Right before he was handcuffed, she met pale, insipid, blue-grey eyes.

Police spread out from the kitchen into the rest of the house. Gates swept inside, issuing instructions. A police officer took Kerry by the elbow, tried to guide her away. But she needed to find her daughter. She held tight to the window ledge, ignoring his attempts to coax her down the garden. After a minute, Gates came out and beckoned her inside. "She'll only unlock the door for you."

She locked the door. She's safe. I knew it. My brave, clever girl.

Kerry pushed past the police officers shielding her from the man spread on the floor and took the stairs two at a time.

"Ella? Sweetheart, it's me. You can come out now. It's over."

Theo

Theo stood next to Dad in Granny's tiny back garden, held back by a policeman with a neck so thick it bulged over the top of his collar, like marshmallow oozing from a s'more. Dad gripped his arm so tight he was sure there would be fingerprints there by morning. They watched in silence as a short, stocky man in a black tracksuit was led out of the back door in handcuffs. It was Beardface – Lauren's stalker.

A new layer of guilt twisted Theo's insides. Another secret he should never have kept. The memory of his fist connecting with Theo's cheekbone, of skin splitting open, the fear that his skull had been smashed to pieces, made Theo rub his jaw reflexively. If this man could do that to Theo in broad daylight, at *school*, who knew what he could have done to Ella. This was all his fault.

"Fucking pigs," the man shouted at the two policemen who half-dragged, half-carried him past. "I only wanted to talk to her. I bought her dinner, for fuck's sake. I *love* her."

"Does he mean Ella?" Theo whispered.

"I don't know," Dad whispered back.

The man caught sight of Theo. "You!" he roared, eyes bulging, face red. "You little prick!"

Dad pulled Theo behind him. Once the man had been loaded into the police car in the lane, he turned and bent down and stared intently into Theo's eyes with those good-cop, tell-me-anything, I'm-on-your-side vibes. The best version of Dad, the one Theo loathed to disappoint. Theo held his breath.

"Is that Mitch?"

Theo shook his head. "No."

So many emotions scudded across Dad's face, layer upon layer, like waves unfolding on sand. Relief that his son wasn't a kidnapper. Fear that someone else had taken his daughter. Determination to be strong for Theo.

Each emotion punched Theo between the eyes. "No," he said. "It's Lauren's stalker."

But Dad didn't hear. He'd seen something over Theo's shoulder and was running. And there, by the back door, standing next to Mum, was Ella. She looked *normal.* Not hurt, not bleeding, but smaller, thinner, red-faced and blotchy-eyed, her hair in a mess and her clothes grubby, reaching out to hug Dad. Over his shoulder, she spotted Theo at the bottom of the garden and gave him a little wave. *Look, I'm okay,* it said. He ran to her.

Kerry

Kerry stared at her magnificent daughter, pale and tiny on the sofa, and stroked her hand. Life would never be the same for her again. For any of them, but especially for her. She, Andrew, and Theo needed to understand what had happened. Gates wanted a statement. But for just five minutes, Kerry wished everyone would disappear and leave her alone with her baby girl. She wanted to absorb Ella's pain and carry it with her own.

"I was walking home from The Hungry Giraffe," Ella said from the depths of the sofa. "After lunch with Jen. I popped into that new shop on the High Street for earrings and met Lauren. We had a laugh about being dressed like twins. But I just couldn't stop thinking about Mitch. I wanted to see him again, but I didn't have his number. So I went round to the park and sat on The Bench for a while, in case he was there, but he wasn't. So I went to the cabin and saw the black car with the dent in it." She looked at Andrew. "I knew then that he was dangerous, that he had hit you."

"Apparently he's quite remorseful over that," Andrew said dryly. "What happened next, honey?"

"I felt like I was being watched, that he might be hiding in the woods. I decided to come home. I was coming out of the park when I felt him behind me. He called me El and asked me to stop and wait for him to catch up, but I ran. Of course, I know now that it wasn't him. But I was sure it was."

"Of course you were, sweetheart." Kerry said. "Who else could you have possibly thought it could be?"

"Well," Ella said, her eyes lowered. "Someone followed me before. About a week ago."

"What?" Andrew jumped out of his chair. "Who followed you?"

Ella flinched, flattened herself even further into the cushions. Dismay coursed through Kerry, echoed on Andrew's face as he sat back down, folding himself small.

"Sorry, sweetheart."

"I didn't see who it was that time," Ella said. "I hid in Granny's house and when I came out, he was gone. Because Granny's house is so near the park," she said to DS Gates, "I ran there again. But I dropped my phone. And," she started crying, "he ran after me. I didn't have time to lock the door behind me. He got in."

"So you hid in the bathroom," Kerry said, nodding, stroking Ella's hand, kissing her hair. She could see it now, Ella terrified, locking the bathroom door, the flimsy lock, the key that must have felt as useless as a pencil in the face of a strange man on the other side of it.

"At first, I thought he'd made some kind of mistake. He kept calling me El and told me he'd enjoyed messaging me and loved my photos online. He hoped I'd bought something pretty with the money he'd sent me. I don't know what he was on about."

"We'll fill you in on all that later," Andrew said. "He got you mixed up with someone else."

Ella looked confused, but Gates was scribbling, flipping the pages of her notebook. Pete brought in a fresh tray of tea and cake. A PC by the lounge door spoke into a walkie talkie. Kerry desperately wanted them all to leave. But they needed to get to the end of the story first. Apparently the first statement was crucial.

"He told me not to be afraid, that he didn't mean me any harm. That he *loved* me. Then he'd get angry and beat on the door for hours and hours. He tried to open it from the outside. I could see the key turning."

The horror of the situation silenced the room. Theo's fingers scrabbled on the edge of his chair, as though he was mentally trying to turn the key back for her. Even Gates looked like she might lose her composure. She put down her pen and flexed her fingers, as if even she needed a break. But Ella kept talking. Kerry knew she was reliving it, her skin erupting in red splotches, her hands trembling.

"I screamed at him to stop. I cried and cried. And then he left. I could hear him downstairs, banging around, so I couldn't come out. And then this morning he started again at the door, begging me to come out. He said he loved me, that he'd been disappointed to see that I had a boyfriend. Apparently he'd seen us at the park? I didn't know what he was talking about. He said he knew where I lived and that he'd seen Dad coming home from the pub. I was so scared."

"Of course you were, love." Fucking hell. What was this all about? Was this guy in cahoots with Mitch? Theo had implied it was some ex-boyfriend of Lauren's who'd followed her online. The black-eye guy. The one he'd kept secret for Lauren's sake. Maybe he and Mitch were working as a team in some kind of elaborate scam. Thank God they were both in police custody right now.

"And later he left?" Gates said. "For fish and chips?"

"So he said," Ella said. "He said he bought me dinner. But I didn't hear him leave. I couldn't take the risk. I thought I was safer staying in there." She took Kerry's hand. Hers was cold, despite thirty-five-degree weather, despite the blankets and the hot chocolate. "I knew you'd find me."

A strangled noise came from Theo and Kerry took his hand in her free one. This wasn't just about Ella. Her two eldest children would have to live with this. Knowing a stranger could slip into their lives and and take them, as easily as a toddler swiping a sweetie at the pick and mix stand. Tomorrow she'd find a simple explanation for the twins. And a therapist for them all.

If Ella seemed to have shrunk from her ordeal, Theo looked like he'd grown taller. He'd taken on a grave, hollow dimension. A young man, suddenly, like Kai. Young men the world had already been hard on. *It wasn't your fault, Theo.*

Kerry

"Ready?"

Kerry led Pete, the two other directors, and their solicitor, Morgan, into the boardroom. She hadn't slept, her eyes were puffy, and she had a splitting headache. It was the first time she'd left Ella's side in twelve days. Twelve days of watching her daughter sleep and eat and breathe. Waiting outside the unlocked bathroom door in case she was secretly crying. Then locking the bathroom door so she could cry in secret herself. Ella had moved into her bed, Andrew and Theo had taken the twins' bunks, and Alby and Poppy cuddled up in Ella's double bed. Nobody was left alone. They went through boxes of tissues, wore oversized hoodies despite the May sunshine, drained by long sessions with the trauma therapist.

This morning Ella was starting her GCSEs, despite Kerry pleading with her to stay home. Exams no longer mattered to Kerry. She didn't want Ella to leave the house. She'd briefed the school, of course, and every possible care was being taken. Andrew was going with her, to sit in the hallway. Just in case. If anyone said *anything*, if any stupid little kid made a joke, a silly comment, or frightened her, they would have him to deal with. Or worse, Theo. Theo was taking the whole thing on his skinny little shoulders and walking around like he was Ella's personal bodyguard. Sometimes Kerry wondered if the whole ordeal had taken more out of him.

Right now, the adrenaline cocktail in her body made her feel like she was plugged into an electrical circuit and dialled up to the max. If Ella could go back to school, Kerry could face Stonebridge. Finally. She'd overheard Wolf tell Andrew that tension had been building at work and yesterday, a row had broken out on the ops floor. People needed to know where they stood.

She took the middle seat on the long side of the table, Pete on her right. Directly opposite was Izzy, in a well-cut, pale yellow blazer, gleaming white top, and discreet gold jewellery. The picture of innocence. Kerry felt conflicted. She'd seen glimpses of the old Izzy lately. She'd brought Lego for the twins, a football for Theo, and a beautiful bracelet for Ella. She'd arranged an enormous delivery from COOK so that Kerry didn't have to think about making dinner or venturing to the supermarket, and a giant goodie basket from all the staff.

But today she was Corporate Izzy, flanked by sleek, coiffed, and highly polished men in suits, and Kerry had no idea what to expect.

"As you know, we have rejected your redundancy offer," Kerry said bluntly. Cortisol peaked inside her and she fought to keep her voice calm. "It is simply nowhere near acceptable and I will not ask anyone to consider it. We have countered with a more competitive offer. However, this still puts one hundred families in the dole queue and, quite frankly, the other three hundred at risk.

"Furthermore, there has already been a substantial negative impact from Stonebridge's involvement in the business – both in terms of staff wellbeing, motivation, and performance – and in the wider community. Online, there have been hostile chats and Facebook pages fuelled by trolls, making accusations against Bullfinch and specifically threats towards me and my family.

Thankfully, in light of Ella's disappearance, those have now stopped and I pray they will not resume, depending on the outcome of this meeting."

She let the silence lie a moment, save for Pete's sharp intake of breath. Everyone had seen the public threads, but she'd kept the poisonous DMs to herself.

"A local, family-owned company like Bullfinch simply cannot function if operations are moved overseas. Our client base buys from us precisely because we're local. We have written testimonials from our ten largest clients – clients who between them have completed almost every single building development in the county over the past fifteen years – that they will withdraw their business *immediately* if this deal goes ahead in the way you suggest."

There was silence in the room. Kerry's cheeks burned but from the corner of her eye she'd seen Pete silently nod along with every word she'd said. It gave her faith.

Izzy's expression gave nothing away. She didn't make notes, she didn't even blink. Kerry wanted to reach out and touch her hand, to discover if she was the same woman who, only twelve days ago, had combed the woods for her daughter. To see if she was still human. Eventually Izzy steepled her fingers in front of her and leaned forward. "Is that everything?"

"Well," Kerry said, feeling desperate now. She'd hoped for some sort of instinctive feeling about how this would pan out. But Izzy was the ultimate ice queen. "Our legal team have found significant loopholes in your proposal. If we take this to court, and our people are more than willing to go down this route," Kerry mentally crossed her fingers, "it would look very bad for Stonebridge indeed. Given the many, many companies they have exploited in the past." She pushed an enormous stack of paperwork to the middle of the table. "We also have a list of people and companies who are prepared to testify in court against Stonebridge's history of bullying and intimidation."

There was silence in the room. One of the suits coughed and shuffled in his chair. The other one leaned forward as if about to speak.

"I cannot comment on the latter part of your speech," said Izzy in a loud, clear voice. "But, in fact, I quite agree with the first part of your argument."

The suit sat back in his chair and glanced over Izzy's head at his counterpart.

"I've conducted a thorough assessment of the business," Izzy continued. "Combined with the reports I've had from each division of the company lately, I believe you're entirely correct, Kerry. Without a solid network of local clients, Bullfinch simply doesn't have a strong enough sales function to cope once its operations are relocated overseas. I have already spoken to HQ on this matter."

Kerry's blood froze in her veins, like a lorry jack-knifed on the motorway. Her headache descended over her eyes and the figures in the room blurred. She'd failed them all. She'd pushed it too far. She should have found a compromise. A way to win for some. To save what jobs she could.

Silence echoed around the room.

Eventually, Pete spoke into the void. "Are you saying," he faltered and glanced at Kerry, "that if we do not accept your offer, you'll close the business entirely?"

Chaos broke out on their side of the table. Kim, the Sales Director, jumped to her feet and shouted obscenities at Izzy. Morgan, the solicitor, stood to restrain her. Alan put his head in his hands. He'd barely spoken since the first day Izzy had shown up, apart from a long apologetic email to Kerry. As Finance Director, he felt responsible for the whole sorry mess. She'd assured him that this wasn't his fault. Henry had deceived him, too.

The suits fidgeted. Kerry and Izzy eyeballed each other over the centre of the table.

"Is that what you're saying?" Kerry whispered. "Are you shutting us down?"

Kerry

"Are you shutting the company down?" Kerry said again, louder this time. Pete, Alan, Kim, and Morgan sat back down.

"No," Izzy said. "Stonebridge bought Bullfinch as an investment, not to turn into a car park. Your boss, Henry, gave us some rather rudimentary paperwork."

"He never told Alan what the reports were for," Pete snapped.

"Well, we've had a chance to deep-dive into the figures," Izzy said, ignoring him. "While Bullfinch operates very much at a local level, given the rate of development in the area it would be unwise of us to do anything to jeopardise that, such as moving operations abroad. The ops team will be kept as it is."

Kerry felt Pete's hand reach for hers under the table. She held it, never taking her eyes off Izzy. This conversation was nowhere near over.

"And the redundancy offer?"

"We will seek a much smaller number of redundancies," Izzy said. "All of them voluntary."

Kerry grabbed Morgan's hand on her other side. "And the size of the offer?"

"We agree to your proposal on that," Izzy said confidently.

One of the suits leaned over and whispered in her ear. "I'll deal with them later," she said calmly.

There was silence in the room.

"It's the least I can do. All things considered."

Kerry

AT FIVE THIRTY, KERRY sank into her office chair with a whoosh. Ella's exam had gone well. Andrew had texted her all day with updates, a photo of them in the kitchen eating carrot cake. Ella's favourite. She couldn't wait to get home.

She picked up Dad's photo from her desk. Lively blue eyes under thick brows, a small, upturned nose, laugh lines sketched around his mouth. Just as she remembered him.

She'd done it. Protected his legacy. Saved the jobs. Put the people first. Just as he would have done. She felt proud of herself, relieved it was over, and strangely empty inside.

There was a tap at the door. Izzy stood in the frame, a bottle of champagne in one hand, two glasses in the other. "You left the party."

"It's your party now, Izzy."

"It could be *our* party?" She set the bottle on the desk and held out one glass. An olive branch. But it was too soon for that.

"Why didn't you come to the funeral? I needed you and you just … vanished."

Izzy set the glasses down and took a seat, one leg crossed neatly over the other, her hands folded in her lap. Regretful, like a doctor delivering bad news. Whatever came next, Kerry knew she wasn't going to like it.

"I was having an abortion."

The revelation hung between them, tangible, like a burst balloon hissing air and taking with it every ounce of hurt and resentment Kerry had harboured for the past six weeks. For the past twenty-four years.

"I'm sorry," she said, reaching out to cover Izzy's hands with her own. "I'm so sorry you had to go through that."

But Izzy's face hardened and her fists clenched. "Easy for you to say now."

"What?" Kerry leaned back, the chasm between them cracking open again, afraid she might fall into it. "I *am* sorry! I would have said it then, but you never told me. Because of Dad …"

"Because of *you*. You might understand now, but you wouldn't have then. Not an abortion, not Saint Kerry!"

Kerry reeled. Good, Catholic, Kerry. Naive and judgemental. The Martyr. It all made sense now. If she'd been the one to get pregnant, Mum would have been mortified, prayed for God's forgiveness, for the daughter who'd sinned. She would have said rosaries and avoided the neighbours. And then, she would have helped Kerry raise her child.

But for Izzy, becoming a mother meant becoming *her* mother and for Izzy, that was unthinkable.

"Even so, I would have been on your side! I was always on your side." She folded her arms. "But fine. It was your decision. You didn't let an unplanned pregnancy hold you back from going after your dreams. Why on earth did you hold that against *me*?"

"Because of your mother." Izzy spat out the words. "Ever since the day of the fish finger accident, your mother hated mine. When I couldn't tell you about the abortion, knowing you'd judge me like she judged my mother, I knew we couldn't be friends any longer."

"Mum took care of you!" This was utterly ridiculous. "Yours didn't even come to the hospital!"

"That's what she told you, isn't it?" Izzy sneered. "Did you know she never even rang Mum to tell her about my accident? What kind of mother does that?"

Kerry's office spun. *That woman*. That was how Mum always referred to Barbara Holt, an edge of disgust to her voice. Kerry thought of Mum's vitriol towards Izzy, her vehemently taking Kerry's side against her when Izzy had failed to come to the funeral. Urging Kerry to move on and forget her best friend. Could it be true? Could it possibly be true that Mum would so harshly judge a single mother from the safety net of her middle-class semi and decide that Barbara didn't deserve to know her daughter was hurt? That would be unforgivable.

After the accident, she and Izzy had been watching *Dirty Dancing* for the millionth time over a shared bowl of popcorn. In the kitchen, Mum and Dad were arguing, words like *irresponsible* and *social services* and *tart* spiking over the sound of the movie. Izzy, pale and quiet, had turned the volume up, and Kerry knew she was desperate for her mother to come pick her up. They never spoke about it afterwards.

Now Izzy touched the scar on her hand. "You got the world," she said quietly. "You got everything we dreamed of back then. A career where you're admired and respected. And a family who adore you. I've had a lifetime of trying to prove I'm not just Izzy from the flats. What do I have? A career? Hah. I'm the most hated woman in Saltreach. The woman you told the entire town was here to fuck everything up. I was just doing my job."

Shame scorched Kerry's skin. How many times had she said that? How many times had she sneaked into Izzy's LinkedIn profile and ogled photos of her, her arms around influential businesspeople, wearing designer dresses, giving presentations and winning awards? Even Andrew knew it, knew she mourned the life she had never led. What had he said – *will I always feel like second best*?

Oh God. She'd got it all so very wrong.

Four Months Later

Nicole

NICOLE EDGED PAST THE too-big dresser in her too-small apartment, trying not to snag her blazer on the corner.

"Lauren? Are you *nearly* ready?"

"Stop nagging," Lauren appeared from her room bristling with resentment, shouldering her school bag like an assault rifle. "Fine. I'm ready. Happy?"

The red uniform suited her daughter better than the old blue one, made her blonde hair shine. Nicole stood back to let her pass through the door, secured both locks, and they waited silently for the lift to collect them from the third floor.

A fresh September breeze blew around their legs. Nicole's stilettos bit into her heels, despite the plasters. The distant London skyline was shrouded in fog and anyway, it was too far away to rouse any real excitement. Once the Saltreach house sold, she'd use her half to get something in a much nicer area.

Thankfully, the bus wasn't late today. They scanned their passes and found seats together. Lauren turned towards the window and doodled in the condensation, anything to avoid talking to Nicole. But she stopped short of putting in the AirPods she'd worn yesterday.

"At least the first few days are over," Nicole said. "You might make a friend today. Feel free to bring someone back to the flat for tea if you want."

Lauren scoffed. Nicole got it. Girls like Lauren didn't make girlfriends easily. They could attract boys with a toss of their hair, but those real, solid, loyal, sisterly friendships? Even Nicole had never had one of those.

But Lauren wasn't Nicole. She had to keep reminding herself of that. Lauren was young, and far smarter than her mother.

Nicole's stop was next. "Best of luck, darling," she said, patting Lauren's knee. "See you tonight."

*

Outside, Nicole battled against crowds of commuters, reached her office building, and swiped her lanyard at the turnstile. As the lift rose to the seventh floor and the doors slid noiselessly open, the glass walls of the reception area finally gave her the view she craved. The London Eye, the majestic buildings of Westminster, the thrum and fizz of city living. She straightened her shoulders, refreshed her lipstick. Her lawyer might have had to convince Glorious they should still offer her the job, but Nicole *knew* that she belonged here. These were her people. Saltreach had been a mistake. If only Wolf understood that too. Once the house was sold, and he was faced with a choice between a fabulous apartment in London or a drab two-bed in a dreary seaside town, he'd come to his senses. She knew he would. But today, she had a fashion show to plan and she was excited.

Lauren

A BURLY MAN IN huge brown boots and army surplus jacket sat in Mum's vacated seat and spread his legs wide, his knee knocking against Lauren's. He stank of BO and alcohol. Lauren stood and squeezed past him, facing away, feeling him block her exit for a second, then laugh softly under his breath, letting his fingers stroke the back of her thigh. She stepped on his toes as she passed and heard him swear. "Bitch".

A horde of red-blazered girls descended the stairs. Lauren watched enviously. They chatted and gossiped, blatantly staring at Lauren as they pushed to the front of the bus. She let them get off first and adjusted the shoulder straps of her black leather bag, identical to everyone else's.

*

She followed a group of long-legged, short-skirted, shiny-haired girls to the biology lab, burrowed straight for the back row.

"Lauren Bauer?" The teacher's voice stopped Lauren in her tracks. She reluctantly turned around. "Could you come and sit at the front, please, Lauren?"

There were titters from the other students as Lauren made her way, red-faced, back to the front of the lab.

"I know you've been here a few days already," the teacher said. "But since it's your first science class, you can sit here and let me know if there's anything we're discussing that you don't follow?"

She directed Lauren to an empty seat beside an ordinary-looking girl with brown hair tied back in a ponytail. No Russian eyelashes, no acrylics, no micro-bladed eyebrows, not even mascara. Probably exactly the kind of girl she should make friends with now.

"Hi," she said. "I'm Lauren."

"I know who you are," said the girl. She edged the tiniest fraction over on her seat, away from Lauren, as if she were afraid of catching nits. "Everyone knows."

Nobody was supposed to know who Lauren was. That was why she'd come to London instead of staying with Dad. She couldn't stand the shame of it at home, the wolf whistles from the boys as she passed through the school corridors, girls sniggering behind their hands, the photo of her wearing the handcuffs someone had taped to her locker.

"You must be mistaken," Lauren said frostily. "I don't know anyone here yet."

The girl smirked, slid her phone out of her pocket, keeping it discreetly below the lab bench. She tilted it away from Lauren, scrolled and tapped.

Lauren felt a panic attack coming on. She'd nearly mastered them, but no way was she taking out a brown paper bag here. She closed her eyes, started counting backwards from ten.

"Lauren's iPhone, I presume?" said the girl, with whom Lauren was quickly realising she would never be friends.

There was a low whoosh, and Lauren's phone vibrated in her pocket. She slid it into her lap.

AirDrop from Imogen's iPhone. Accept?

Of course she accepted. She couldn't help herself.

It was a link to a *Daily Mail* article about a girl being kidnapped in a case of mistaken identity. Lauren closed her eyes. She practically knew the article by heart. It had come out a couple of days after the *incident,* as she now thought of it.

> The attacker had originally been following the victim's friend, Lauren Bauer, who had been posing on an adult-content website and attracted the attention of Isaac Williams, local administrator for the company and nephew of infamous media mogul John Burrows. Both Williams and Burrows were taken into custody for questioning and Burrows has been remanded on bail, while Williams remains in custody.

Lauren knew the article went on to detail the charges brought against the two men and, more damning than anything, included a multitude of photographs of both Ella and Lauren, including pictures of them in their matching outfits, the black cardigans and white crop tops, looking like twins, best friends. For God's sake, it was like a uniform for girls their age. The mannequin in the local Zara had been dressed like that for all of April.

But it was the headline and cover photo that had ruined Lauren's life. Not just in Saltreach, but apparently in London now too.

Teen stripper responsible for best friend's kidnapping.

And the picture that would never, ever go away. Lauren, in her red vest and knickers, handcuffed to her own bed.

*

The teacher was talking about photosynthesis. The girl with the ponytail, Imogen, had shifted her chair even further away from Lauren and was studiously ignoring her. Most of the class were writing. Two girls sniggered behind their hands when they saw her looking. One reached her hand up over her head, mimicking the pose in the photograph, and pouted at Lauren. Then she raised her phone above the lip of the lab bench and took a photograph of her. They laughed louder.

The teacher stopped talking, walked past the front two rows of students to speak to them. The classroom door was still open and Lauren hadn't even opened her schoolbag yet.

But she would not leave. Would not let these bitches win. She was finally out of Saltreach and living in London. Despite the cosmic irony of the situation, Lauren would take the win in that. Next September she'd be in college. The world would be hers.

Lauren had been the ultimate bitch. She knew how to play the game. She would spend nine months here and ace her GCSEs. Move to a different sixth form. Start again. Go to uni. Become a pharmacist. Go abroad.

Somewhere along the journey, this would fade. It would stop being who she was.

Wolf

Wolf took a seat in Izzy's office. It had been completely redecorated in pale grey and orange, per the Stonebridge branding, and felt large and spacious now the company was finally paperless. The effect was professional, crisp, and not in the least inviting.

"You wanted to see me?" he said.

"I did." Izzy swivelled to face him. "I wanted to give you this in person."

She handed him an envelope. "It's your first payslip as our new IT Director," she said, reaching out her other hand to shake his. "Welcome to the board."

Wolf drew out a slip of paper with a pleasing number of zeros on it. He tucked it into his shirt pocket, trying to hide his delight. He shook Izzy's hand and held onto it for a fraction longer than was necessary. Unlike her office, her skin was warm and soft.

"Thank you." She was beautiful. Those pale blue eyes, the translucent skin. Stunning figure. "Now everything is in order, will you stay? Or do you just do the hard part and move on?"

He hadn't a clue about Izzy's life outside of her reputation as Kerry's ex-nemesis and Stonebridge slave-driver. He also didn't understand why she'd changed her mind about the redundancies. At first, he'd assumed it was some sort of favour to Kerry. Later, down at the pub with his new colleagues, he discovered that the news of what Bullfinch had managed to wrangle out of Stonebridge had spread. As a result, two other companies Stonebridge had snapped up in recent years were now taking them to court over unlawful redundancies. Wolf liked Izzy more for that.

"I've decided to stay," she said. "I like it here. It feels like home."

Wolf smiled.

Kai

It was PE. Swimming this term. Kai walked between Oliver and Theo to the changing rooms, no longer a knot of dread in his stomach. He didn't rush to a cubicle like he used to. He wasn't as fit or muscular as Theo, but he could no longer lift that fold of skin on his side, and his stomach didn't jiggle the way it used to. At first, he'd worn a rash vest to hide the scars. But everything was healed now.

The sessions with the counsellor, Mum's idea, had been revelatory. One to one at first, then a Zoom call with a couple of other kids like him. A support group for prisoner families. And next week, he would visit Dad for the first time.

"Miss your girlfriend, do you?" Oliver said across him to Theo. Theo ignored him. "Don't be like that," Oliver went on. "Just because she was selling to the highest bidder …"

"Piss off, Oliver," Kai said.

"I enjoyed a little strip tease myself," Oliver boasted, throwing his gym bag onto the bench, pulling out his swim shorts. "A *private* performance."

"You did *not*!"

"Yeah. I did. Took a little persuasion, but she saw the value in doing it. I knew what she was up to."

Kai felt Theo's pain, saw him redden and pull his shirt over his head to hide his tears. The girls in their year hated Oliver. Called him a perv.

He took a step closer, and Oliver backed up against the lockers. Oliver might be the fittest of them all, the school swim champion, but Kai was a full head taller and twice the width.

"You mean you blackmailed her?"

"Nah, mate. Not at all. She was happy to oblige." Oliver grinned, but there was less confidence in his voice, and he looked left and right, trying to decide which side of Kai to escape.

"You piece of shit," Kai said, but Theo pulled on his arm.

"Leave it," he said quietly. But when Kai came back to the bench, Theo muttered a *thanks* under his breath.

Kai took off his trainers, socks. He had his swimming shorts on under his trousers. He wasn't *that* brave yet.

They rinsed off under the showers, put on their goggles, walked to the deep end, toes over the edge. This was the part Kai found hardest, sure that everyone in the pool was staring at him, wondering who the fat boy was. Thinking he was disgusting.

But like the counsellor had suggested, he tried to concentrate on what they were really doing. A couple of girls, hands crossed protectively over their breasts, were obviously just as self-conscious as him. Two more sat on the sidelines, having handed over fake sick notes. A bunch of boys pretended to throw each other into the deep end. Nobody was looking at him.

Oliver barged past him to the centre lane. Kai couldn't help himself. He stuck out a foot.

Oliver's kneecap cracked loudly on the tiled floor and he howled. A teacher came running over and a circle formed around them. Kai quickly took a step backwards into the throng of pupils and found Theo staring at him, wide-eyed.

"There's enough perverts out there already," he said grimly, and turned towards the pool.

"Thank you," Theo whispered.

The middle lane was clear. "Race?"

Theo raised one eyebrow and nodded, flipped his goggles into place.

"Ready, go!"

*

Theo won, of course. But not by as much as he would have a month ago. Maybe even a week ago. Kai felt his arms cut through the clean, cool water and he felt powerful. Strong. In control of his own life.

Theo

DAD WAS SWEEPING THE kitchen floor. Again. He'd snapped at Poppy for spilling water and sent her and Alby out to the garden to play. The kitchen table was laid with the good cups, a homemade cake, and he'd boiled the kettle twice.

"Mitch's letter was nice," Theo said. He wished Mitch would hurry up and get here already. "He did say sorry." Dad nodded and disinfected the worktop, the lemon scent overriding the delicious smell of cake.

Theo kicked himself – surely that was the least Mitch could do for putting his own father in hospital. Given the circumstances, Dad hadn't pressed charges. But Theo supposed that didn't mean he'd forgiven Mitch.

He racked his brain for something sympathetic to say. "I think he was going through a hard time back then. You know, he lost his job and his flat …" He tailed off. Why was he trying to make Mitch sound good? He put his arms around Dad. "I'm sorry you're having to deal with this. On top of everything. You're the best."

Dad pulled Theo into the kind of bear hug that only Dad could give. Big and strong and warm and safe and solid. "*You're* the best," he said and Theo felt the vibration of his deep voice in his chest, the rise and fall of Dad's breathing, and wished for the millionth time that Mitch had never come to live in England.

*

The doorbell rang. The twins skipped inside as if on command, Alby leaving a trail of mud on the kitchen floor. Theo thought Dad might actually cry.

"I'll clean it up," he said, pushing Dad gently towards the hallway, but Dad caught his wrist.

"It doesn't matter," he said. "Come on. Let's do this together."

Theo opened the front door. Mitch was holding a bunch of purple flowers and a box of Celebrations. He looked a lot better than before. He wore a clean white t-shirt and nice jeans, and he'd shaved. He looked even more nervous than Dad.

"Hi," he said, holding out a hand. "I'm Mitch."

Dad took his hand and shook it slowly, as if trying to learn something about Mitch from the feel of his skin. The handshake lingered as Dad put his other hand on Mitch's elbow, and it became a sort of embrace, with a huge space between them in the middle. It was completely awkward, but from this angle, Theo could see more similarities than he'd noticed before. They were the same height, had the same pattern of freckles across their noses, the same hairy fingers.

Poppy and Alby came to the door eating ice creams they hadn't asked for. Alby was still wearing the muddy shoes. Theo knelt silently and took them off.

"Who are you?" Poppy asked from under an ice cream moustache.

"He's the new brother," Alby told her confidently. "Nice to meet you," he said and copied Dad by stretching out a hand to Mitch.

Theo started laughing.

"What?" Alby said. "Dad told us to be on our best behaviour."

*

Thankfully, Mum came downstairs and took charge, shooing them into the kitchen. Dad seemed to be struggling to know what to say, so Mum brewed tea and made chitchat with Mitch about Saltreach. Nothing real. Theo guessed that was Dad's job. Alby offered Mitch an ice cream and Poppy gave him a picture of their family that she'd drawn, Mitch included.

Only Ella held back, watching the conversation. But that was what Ella was like now. Theo had done that to her.

Not directly, obviously. But by keeping secrets. Specifically, Lauren Bauer's secrets. He couldn't imagine a future where he wouldn't be angry with Lauren. Her endless lies, her manipulation, the way she'd behaved when Ella went missing. But he would always be angry with himself, too. The therapist said he should forgive himself, that he'd shown great loyalty. That he'd done what he'd believed was right at the time.

But he'd been loyal to the wrong people. He'd protected Lauren, even though he knew he'd nearly driven Mum mad with worry over the black eye, and ultimately put his own sister's life in danger. He'd protected Mitch instead of being honest with Dad. And his best friend Kai – he'd let that stupid kiss almost ruin his friendship with the kindest person he'd ever known. Kai knew how to be loyal in the right way.

Theo's family was awesome. How on earth had he thought he should keep secrets from them? Now, he was an open book. He left his phone unlocked overnight in the kitchen. He checked on Ella consistently, monitored the search history on Alby and Poppy's iPads, told Mum and Dad he loved them every night.

He'd also put right one more wrong. He'd told Mum and Dad that Oliver Nowell had blackmailed Lauren and yesterday, even though Lauren had left Saltreach, he'd reported Oliver to the head teacher. He didn't know if Oliver would be at school tomorrow, but he wasn't afraid.

He watched Mitch carefully. He knew, of course, that Isaac was the real kidnapper and was currently awaiting a trial that probably wouldn't happen for at least a year. Two other local girls had since made allegations about him following them home. He'd flashed one of them.

Isaac had admitted the kidnapping. And to using his position as company administrator at PeekaBoo to steal personal data from the website database to find Lauren's address and follow her to school. He admitted deleting the complaints she'd made about him, and creating multiple accounts which he'd used to bombard her with messages. He'd said he was in love with her.

He'd also admitted to punching Theo. Mum and Dad *had* pressed charges for that.

But still, Theo couldn't shake off the memory that they'd suspected Mitch of this. He had behaved suspiciously enough to make them wonder if he'd kidnapped his own half-sister. Now that the blood test had proven paternity, they had to learn to trust him.

But even Ella was joining in now, cutting Mitch a slice of lemon drizzle cake and asking him if he'd had his car fixed. *She* wasn't treating Mitch like a felon.

"I'm sorry for knocking you off your bike," Mitch blurted out. "It really was an accident." Everyone fell silent. Would Dad forgive him?

"What I don't understand," Dad said, "is why you didn't stop?"

Mitch scratched his neck, leaving a pink mark. "I wanted to," he said. "I really did. I'd been following you for weeks. That sounds creepy now, I know. Especially given everything that happened …" He glanced at Ella, then back at Dad. "I knew where you worked, where the kids went to school. I watched you visit your mum …"

"She's actually *my* mother," Mum said.

"Oh." Mitch's face fell. "I thought I had a gran. I miss my Gran in Brazil." He cleared his throat. "I asked you about bus routes, remember? I wanted to see what your life was like *before* I decided whether I should … get involved."

Dad's face didn't change. He didn't even blink. Theo knew that face. He'd been on the receiving end of it many times. Dad wasn't a pushover – he just needed to understand. Theo knew it would take more reasoning, a better explanation. Mitch would have to be entirely honest.

"I was afraid, okay?" Mitch's temples began beading with sweat, reminding Theo of the antsy, fidgety Mitch he used to meet in the park. Always moving, easily irritated. "If you knew I'd knocked you off your bike, you'd never have wanted anything to do with me!"

"But I do know, and yet here we all are," Andrew said quietly, gesturing at everyone around the table. Even the twins were being quiet for once. Theo felt better, less gullible, when he realised not one of them really knew what to make of Mitch. Everyone wanted to believe he was good. But Theo wasn't sure anyone actually did.

"Well, you're a better man than I am," Mitch said, a note of bitterness in his voice. "I wish I'd had you growing up."

There was silence again and Theo felt the enormity of what Mitch was saying. Mitch didn't have a dad. And Dad was the best dad ever. How could he not feel compassion for a brother who had missed out on everything that had ever made Theo feel like himself?

"It's clearing up outside," Mum said gently. "Why don't the two of you," she nodded at Dad and Mitch, "go for a walk?"

Kerry

KERRY TIDIED AWAY THE lemon drizzle cake, relieved Mitch and Andrew were gone. That had been intense. This weird, skinny guy, who looked a bit like her husband and sons but felt like he came from an alternate universe.

She wondered what would happen on their walk. Obviously, Andrew had carte blanche to make whatever decisions he saw fit. She might never see Mitch again. Or she might find him installed in her family forever.

From what little she'd seen this afternoon, Mitch was carrying a chip on his shoulder the weight of an ocean. He'd lived a childhood with a dad-shaped hole in it and if Andrew wanted to fill that gap now, she would support him.

Losing her own father at the same age as Mitch was now had been the major turning point in her life, had set her on the trajectory which had propelled her right until this summer. Living in the shadow of imagined pride and disappointment, leaning endlessly into the past, forgetting that the present and the future were hers to create.

But now she *would* create. She found Ella and called her into her study. She was bursting to show someone. She opened a small blue box and pulled out a business card. "What do you think?"

"Oh my God, Mum," Ella said. "These are gorgeous!"

"You really like them?" Kerry felt shy. The logo was beautiful. The designer had taken the letters KLHR, *Kerry Langley HR*, and somehow made them look like waves, splashes of white against the backdrop of a navy sea that was definitely Saltreach Bay. In one corner was a small splash of red where the ice cream kiosk sat on the promenade. At the bottom of the image was a beach and her contact details printed in a deep blue against the golden sand, not a strand of seaweed in sight.

"They look amazing, Mum."

"Do you think I'm mad?"

Ella laughed. "For finally leaving The Firm? Or for setting up your own HR consulting practice with the nicest business card ever? No, you are definitely not mad, Mother. This might be the best decision you've ever made. After finding me, of course."

They were silent for a minute and then both reached for a hug. Kerry felt the pain in her heart she'd become accustomed to since that awful night and knew it had nothing to do with hereditary heart disease.

"You okay, honey?"

Ella shuddered. "Yeah. Sorry. That came out of the blue."

They both pretended it wasn't still at the forefront of their minds most of the time, that it was something they only remembered occasionally, triggered by something external, a door slamming, a stranger brushing too close to them as he passed. A man in a black hoodie.

"Glad you like it. Now, let's visit Granny."

*

Kerry parked in front of the little yellow house on Ennis Road.

"Let the others go ahead," she said to Theo, switching off the ignition and waiting while Ella led the twins inside Mum's house.

"I see you, Theo," she said quietly. "Always bending over backwards to be helpful. You still feel responsible, don't you?"

Theo nodded. Tears glistened in his eyes.

"Sweetheart, don't forget that by keeping Mitch a secret, you were trying to protect mine and Dad's feelings. By keeping Lauren's secrets, you were trying to protect her. You're a super kid, Theo. The absolute best. But the deal is, you can't be responsible for anyone else when you're still a kid yourself. That's my job, okay? And if I was doing it properly in the first place, you would never have been in that position."

He nodded, unconvinced.

"Sweetheart, you saved my life. Literally. That text you sent, telling me it wasn't Mitch in that house – that changed everything. I was out of my mind with worry. Desperate to get your sister back. If you hadn't sent that message, I might have actually gone inside, thinking I could handle Mitch."

"I'm glad you didn't," Theo said and this time, Kerry knew he heard her properly.

"I love you, honey. No matter what happens this afternoon between Dad and Mitch, you, Ella, and the twins will *always* come first."

*

Kerry pushed open Mum's front door. Marta looked up from where she was curled up on the sofa in the front room, reading a book.

"Hi, Mrs L."

"Hi, Marta. How's it going?" Kerry gave a nod towards the kitchen where she could already hear the whistle of the kettle. Mum was a new woman. They'd run every test imaginable on her. The dementia was still early stages, her fractured pelvis was healed, and she seemed to have a new lease of life. It wouldn't last forever but for now, the dilemma over her future was on pause.

"Wonderful," Marta replied, in her thick Lithuanian accent. "I am so glad to be out of that awful flat share. I can do my studies in peace. I am grateful."

"It's *me* who's grateful to *you*, Marta," Kerry said. "I couldn't face putting her in a home. She'd have become a shadow of herself in no time."

She put her head around the kitchen door. Mum had a plate of biscuits ready on the table, her walking stick hooked over the back of a chair.

"Clare?" she said, hopefully.

"Just me, Mum." She poured the tea and sat beside her mother. "Clare's coming for Christmas, remember?"

Mum patted her hand. She could still be in a home in a year or two. But having Marta living with her had made an enormous difference. She was eating well, the house was sparkling, and she and Marta watched *Coronation Street* together in the evenings. Clare might not have been there when Kerry needed her, but her monthly bank transfers were a life saver. Literally.

*

Andrew's coat was back on its peg by the time they arrived home. Kerry found him in the kitchen.

"Where's Mitch?" she said quietly.

"Gone," Andrew said. He was sitting at the kitchen table with a cup of coffee. His eyes were red.

Kerry shooed the children upstairs and sat next to him.

"What happened?"

"He doesn't really want to know us," Andrew said sadly. "It's all too little, too late."

"I'm sorry, love." She reached for his hand. "Imagine Diana *had* approached you all those years ago," she said. "Mitch coming and going on weekends, another mouth to feed. That would have been full on. But we would have coped. We're a pretty good team."

"We are," Andrew agreed, kissing her cheek. "Being married to you is much more interesting than being a professional cyclist or hiking the Inca Trail."

"You sure Mitch doesn't want to be part of it?"

"I think not, unfortunately."

"After all that? What did he want, then?"

Andrew made a face as if to say, *can't you guess?*

Kerry's heart broke for him. "How much?" she asked.

Andrew took a sip of his coffee. "Enough to cover a deposit on a flat and a few months' rent," he said quietly. "A bit extra to buy a few decent clothes and some furniture. Or a car. I offered to take him shopping, but …"

"Sweetheart, I'm so sorry," Kerry said. Imagine. After all that. If Mitch had simply reached out to Andrew directly in the first place, they might have had a real relationship. "Maybe when all this has settled, you two can try again. Start with a coffee. Build from there."

Not that she would ever admit it, but a small, secret part of her would always be glad Diana had done what she had. Andrew had been hers, hers and the children's. Remarkably and unfailingly there for them.

"Do you mind?" Andrew said, and his forehead crinkled up in concern. "It's a lot, but if I'd raised that boy …"

"Not in the least," Kerry said. "You did the right thing. You always do. And hey, my redundancy came through this morning. Even after putting aside the money for my brand new HR consultancy – which, by the way, already has its first customer, one Izzy Holt of Bullfinch Glazing, a Stonebridge company – we still have enough left over to fund an *incredibly* posh safari holiday to Botswana." She kissed him. "And maybe even a weekend for two in Paris."

Kerry

THE BEACH WAS EMPTY. The worst summer she would ever endure, finally over. The tourists were gone and the children had returned to school in box-fresh crisp, white shirts, battle scars hidden beneath the surface.

Kerry left her flip flops on golden sand, took a long breath of salty air, and strode into the sea. When the ice-cold water was deep enough, she felt her feet lift off the sea floor and let the water take the weight of her body.

After a moment, she flipped onto her back and stared at an azure sky, feeling the water seep through her hair and freeze her scalp. It was the best feeling in the world. All the worries that had swirled in her head for months and months and months simply froze.

Acknowledgements

WRITING A BOOK IS mostly a solitary passion project. I sit in my tiny study, surrounded by empty coffee cups, with my dog curled in her bed beside me. But the reality is that there's a pretty big team of people without whom this book would never exist.

My mum and dad, Anne and Padraig, my forever supporters, who taught me to aim high and believe in myself.

My husband, Nick, who lets me be 100% me and doesn't mind when I disappear for days on writing retreats. You are the best.

My lovely boys, Finn, Charlie, and James, who make everyday fun. I love you guys.

My sister, Deirdre, my best friend and always one of my first readers.

Dream team Andrew and Rebecca Brown from Author Elevator, who have made me an author and this book a reality. Their professionalism, creativity, and passion have elevated this project higher than anything I could have imagined for myself.

Suzannah Dunn, my fabulous tutor.

Benedicta Norell, my first editor, who taught me so much.

Many thanks to photographer extraordinaire John Knight of John Knight Photography for the fun photoshoot for my author pic, and all the pictures from my website and book launch.

Thank you to artist Katharine Jennings for a wonderful launch party.

So many wonderful family and friends who have read multiple drafts, brainstormed, helped me keep motivated and accountable: my brother Dave, Mawgan, Sarah, Dee, Lara, Judy, Elena, Jeremy, Ali, Natalia, Debra, Sharon, Mary, Laura, Natalie, Sally, and Susannah.

About the Author

I'M AN IRISH WRITER, from Gorey, in Co Wexford, recently named by Ed Sheeran as his favourite town in Ireland. I happen to agree with him and go home every chance I get.

When I was working in recruitment in Dublin in my late twenties, I met my now-husband through work, *Gavin-and-Stacey* style. After a year and a half of flying back and forth, I took a ferry to Holyhead and drove my little moped all the way down to East Sussex.

Since then, I consider myself lucky to have two homes. Sussex is a beautiful part of the country, and while I don't have the beach on my doorstop like I did growing up, I do have the Ashdown Forest, home to Winnie the Pooh and sometimes to me, either on horseback or with my dog, Pickle.

I grew up reading pony stories and *Malory Towers*. These days, I read widely, with a particular love of thrillers that centre around twisted families. I find families endlessly fascinating. There isn't one without secrets, conflict, black sheep, love, and so much that goes unsaid.

Maeve Binchy once said about herself, “I had a very happy childhood, which is unsuitable if you’re going to be an Irish writer.” I’m very lucky to be in the same boat; however, that doesn’t stop my imagination taking me to dark places, thinking of all the things that can go wrong, the dangers, online and in real life, that lurk, ready to slither into the gaps between best-intention-parenting, and children being naturally curious and adventurous and taking risks. So that’s what I write about.

* 9 7 8 1 9 1 9 3 4 8 4 0 7 *

BV - #0102 - 290126 - C0 - 203/133/21 - PB - 9781919348407 - Matt Lamination